STONE HEART

SUSAN K. HAMILTON

Copyright © 2022 by Susan K. Hamilton

All rights reserved.

No part of this book may be reproduced in any form or by any electronic or mechanical means, including information storage and retrieval systems, without written permission from the author, except for the use of brief quotations in a book review.

ISBN: 978-1-7373536-8-3

Created with Vellum

ALSO BY SUSAN K. HAMILTON

Novels

Darkstar Rising

Shadow King

The Devil Inside

Short Stories

"Chrysalis"

(ESCAPE! Anthology)

"Girl"

(DECEPTION! Anthology)

"Mira's Bridge"

A Shadow King Tale

(Passageways: Nine Tales, Nine Unique Literary Worlds anthology)

"Pearls and Swine"

(FAMILY Anthology)

For everyone who has ever made a foolish decision in the name of love.

CHAPTER ONE

Lauren Stone owned a big-ass, beachfront Spanish Colonial Revival in Santa Monica, California. With six bedrooms, five baths, and a pool that overlooked the sand, it was far too big for her, and when she bought it, people had clucked at her excess. Lauren, however, didn't give a rat's backside what they thought. She knew the adage was true: money couldn't buy happiness. It could, however, buy some very awesome toys.

Years ago, she'd promised herself that if her band, The Kingmakers, ever made it big, she was buying herself a big house with a view of the ocean. And Lauren Stone kept her promises.

She was sitting in the spacious, airy sunroom, where an overstuffed sofa and several chairs formed a rough semi-circle around a long coffee table and faced the bank of windows—and the arched glass doors—that led out to the pool. Exposed, dark mahogany beams ran the length of the stucco ceiling. Two ceiling fans provided a soothing breeze. Aside from the ocean view, this room was one of the things that had sold her on this house.

She got out of the plush chair and leaned in the arched doorway that opened to her patio and pool. Taking a deep drink of beer, she contemplated the expanse of sand beyond the fence, stretching from the edge of her backyard to the cerulean water. She liked how the color changed depending on the day and the weather.

At the sound of footsteps, she looked back into the room. "Hey, Augie!"

"Hey!" Her cousin's dimples deepened when he smiled.

Lauren grew up with three sisters, and Augustus "Augie" Stone was the brother she never had. A year younger than her, he was The Kingmakers' drummer.

"Connie let you in?" She'd let her housekeeper know she was expecting company.

"Yeah. Said you'd be out here." Augie leaned his athletic, six-foot frame on the other side of the curved doorway.

Putting her beer bottle down, Lauren pulled her hair back and tugged the scrunchie off her wrist to capture it all in a messy ponytail. It would have been the same dark brown as Augie's if she didn't get it highlighted regularly, but they both shared a soft natural wave that ran in the Stone family. For Lauren that meant minimal time trying to curl it—for Augie it just meant some unruly cowlicks.

"C'mon. Too nice to be inside," she said. "Let's sit by the pool. There's more beer in the cooler. I've got that new Elk Stone Amber I was telling you about."

"Lead on, my captain!"

Sheltered by a large red umbrella, the teak table was surrounded by four chairs. A few feet away, two padded lounge chairs waited. Augie flopped down on one, Lauren in the other.

As soon as she got comfortable, her phone buzzed. She glanced at it and started to laugh.

"Gonna share?"

"Just DJ being DJ." Lauren snickered again.

"What is it, fifty-two poop emojis in a row?"

"Close. He threw in a few eggplants for good measure." She tucked the phone into a shady spot under her chair, and they fell into an amiable silence. Lauren took a deep breath and let it out slowly, trying to let her anxiety exit with it.

"DJ's worried about you, you know."

"I've been through breakups before." Lauren forced her voice to be light. She *had* been through breakups over the years, more than she cared to admit. And there were times she wondered if she was capable of a long-term relationship with anyone. Rob had been fun, but the charm hadn't lasted. Her ex, however, hadn't taken the breakup well.

"Well, if you want to—"

"—Talk? I don't." She took another drink of beer. "Needy, manipulative little bastard." She thought about the salvo of nasty tweets Rob had flung at her like a monkey throwing its own excrement. It wasn't like she'd expected him to be happy about being shown the door, but the juvenile level of his response had been astonishing.

"I thought you didn't want to talk about it."

"I don't want to talk about *him*. I do want to talk about the new album."

"And?"

"The last one was good, not great. This one needs to be a home run." Worry painted her voice and she hated it. She drummed her fingers on the armrest. "I'm not ready to fade into the sunset."

"We're not fading into anything," Augie said. "Seriously, dude. You need to stop listening to the critics' podcasts."

Lauren chewed her lip. Augie wasn't entirely wrong. The band had taken a well-earned break after the last tour, but it was time to get back to work. Restless, she got up and walked to the fence surrounding the pool. Leaning on it, she stared out toward the Pacific. Wispy clouds streaked the sky, slashes of rose and gold in the setting sun.

A squeak told her Augie had gotten out of his chair. He leaned on the rail next to her and gave her a gentle hip bump.

"What's up?"

She shrugged. "Nothing."

"Liar, liar, pants on fire." He flashed her a grin, dimples appearing in his cheeks again.

"You're a child," she said with an affectionate laugh.

"Like that surprises you? But seriously, c'mon. You've got that pensive look. What gives?"

She tried to equivocate. "Usual brooding creative-type personality issues."

The noise—not quite a snort, but not a coughed "bullshit" either—that her cousin made told her he didn't believe her. But he didn't ask any more questions. They stood in silence, admiring the sun as it sank towards the horizon.

"I haven't gotten as much writing done as I wanted," Lauren said, tired of the quiet. She hoped that would satisfy Augie and he wouldn't press for more. Truth be told, she was struggling with her songwriting, and the last thing she wanted to do was 'fess up to that.

"So? You'll hit your stride. Don't get hung up on it."

"I guess." She watched a bird soar and bank in the sky. It was too far away to tell what kind it was, but she admired its freewheeling flight.

"You know I'm right. And getting the chance to work with Fitz is going to be epic," Augie said.

"I know! I've wanted him to produce one of our albums for a long time." The mention of Fitz perked her up. Fitz McCallum was one of the most sought-after producers in the industry, and the band had jumped at the opportunity to work with him. He had a reputation for turning everything he worked on into gold—even better, platinum.

"I'm glad we're going to New York for this," Augie said. "Haven't seen the seasons change in a long time."

Lauren cocked an eyebrow. "Fifty bucks say the first chilly day, you'll turn into a whiny little—"

"Don't hate me because I'm sensitive." Augie started to laugh.

Lauren joined him, but the laugh faded to a sigh.

"You sure that's all that's bugging you?" he asked.

"Nothing's bugging me." Lauren shifted her weight away as if that would let her avoid the question. She put her hand up to shield her eyes from the sun—and so she didn't have to make eye contact with Augie. Her thoughts churned. *What if I've got no songs? What if the trades are right? What if I've lost my mojo?* She felt the worry tighten around her chest, making it hard to take a breath.

She changed the subject; the last thing she wanted to do was keep talking about her writing.

"I'm not telling my mom I'm coming back to New York until I'm getting on the plane," she said. She and Augie had grown up in the Bay Ridge area of Brooklyn.

Augie turned toward her, a sly smile on his face. "And you want me to not call *my* mom."

"If you do, your mom will call my mom and all hell will break loose if she hears through the grapevine that I'm back." Lauren watched her cousin weigh his options.

"What's in it for me?"

"You blackmailing me?"

"That's an ugly word, but call it what you want, sistah." Augie leaned one elbow on the fence and watched her with a self-satisfied smile. Lauren considered giving him a kick in the shin, the same way she had when they were six.

"I'll owe you—big time. I love my family..." She left the rest of her thought unfinished.

"No quality time with Jackie?"

Lauren gave Augie another look. Jackie was her older sister, and they were about as different as two siblings could be—more fire and gasoline than oil and water. Her younger sisters, Carolyn and Stephanie, were a different story. They adored Lauren and Lauren adored them back.

"I love Jackie, but she makes me mental," Lauren said. "I want our plans set, and I want to have a place to stay *before* they know I'm coming."

"Deal," Augie said. "When we're home, I might look a few people up. Indulge in some good, old-fashioned reminiscing about our misspent youth."

"You're still in the middle of living your misspent youth. Couple years it's going to be your misspent middle age."

"You first." Augie never skipped an opportunity to remind Lauren that she was a year older than he was.

Out on the beach, people were wrapping up for the day, a stream of humanity leaving the white-gold sand for the asphalt and concrete of LA. A young man in bright red trunks, maybe twenty years old, walked toward the distant parking lot giving his girlfriend a piggyback ride. The wistful longing that bubbled up in Lauren's heart caught her off-guard, bringing her back to a time when she was the one getting the piggyback.

Danny.

Her heart stuttered.

She'd never been able to stop thinking about Danny Padovano, her ex from high school. She'd struggled with their breakup for years as she tried every conceivable trick to get over him, including a cocaine addiction that nearly ruined her. Finally, Lauren buried her broken heart so deep that it was easy for her to pretend those feelings didn't exist. She'd had other lovers over the years, but none of them had ever made her forget Danny.

He was the one person who loved her for *who* she really was, not *what* she was.

Unlike Rob and all the other exes.

She could feel Augie staring at her.

"Maybe I'll look Danny up while we're home."

"Pandora's Box," he said.

"It would be fine." Lauren set her jaw, refusing to meet his eyes or acknowledge the warning in his voice. She didn't want to argue, and she was well aware her cousin had never completely forgiven her ex for breaking her heart all those years ago.

They turned their attention to other topics related to the band's temporary relocation to the East Coast to record. Augie said he'd spoken to Fitz briefly, and the producer would be waiting for Lauren to call him.

After about twenty minutes, Augie glanced at his watch. "I gotta bolt. You'll call Fitz to confirm details?"

"I will," she said. "Catch you later."

He sauntered away, and Lauren went back to watching the final moments of the sun's descent until it vanished, leaving the sky a blue-violet with the barest hint of maroon on the horizon. But the gorgeous color couldn't keep her thoughts from straying to her writing difficulties and then to what Augie had said about looking up old friends. He'd stayed in touch with a few people over the years, but she hadn't. Not really. She'd had plenty of friends growing up, but none of them shared her passion for music—her obsession, as they called it. And once The Kingmakers took off—well, Lauren didn't have that much in common with them anymore.

After nearly twenty years, Danny was the only person she was interested in seeing. The tangled prick of anger and longing in her heart annoyed her. Their breakup had been devastating. And although it had been years since she'd seen him, she thought of him often. More often than she probably should. Her sisters occasionally shared news about what he was up to. When Carolyn told her several years ago that Danny had gotten married, Lauren pretended it didn't bother her.

But it did.

She chewed her bottom lip and wondered if going back to New York might be a mistake.

A week later, travel bag over one shoulder, Lauren walked toward the private jet scheduled to whisk her and Augie to New York. She tried to keep her laughter to a minimum as she listened to her sister on the other end of her cell. Up ahead, she saw Augie at the stairs to the plane. She waved, got his attention, and pointed at her phone. He gave her the thumbs-up, understanding her unspoken message.

"Yes, Carolyn. Mom knows I'm coming. Or she will when she checks her messages. I called her right before you."

"I'm so happy you'll be home!" Carolyn's voice was gleeful.

"I'm going to be working—"

"—But you'll be in the same state! We haven't been in the same state for ages! We have to go out when you get here. Can you get us into Blue Ruby? It's a new club in Manhattan? I've seen pictures. It looks amazing!"

Now that Carolyn was married with a set of twins, her clubbing days were a thing of the past—except when Lauren was in town. Then the two sisters always had one bang-up night out together.

"I'm not trotting around town like some show pony, Carolyn. This is a working trip, not a vacation."

"Lauren..."

"You sound like you're twelve."

"Is it working?"

Lauren couldn't hold in her laughter any longer. "Yes, it's working. I'll get us into Blue Ruby."

Carolyn's excited cheer forced Lauren to pull the phone away from her ear. She rolled her eyes—she'd gotten the whole clubs-until-four-in-the-morning thing out of her system years ago, but she couldn't say no to her sister.

"Promise?"

"I promise."

"Pinky-swear?"

"Oh, for God's sake, Carolyn... I'm hanging up now." Lauren wasn't sure if her sister could hear her over her own laughter.

"But we just got on the phone."

"Well, I just got in the cabin and the plane can't take off if I'm on my phone." Lauren pushed her sunglasses up on her head. "And the longer the plane's on the ground, the longer it takes to get home."

"Fine..." She sounded huffy, but Lauren could hear the exaggerated humor in her voice. "But I can't wait to see you! I love you."

"Love you, too." Lauren hit the red end-call button and flopped down in a seat across from Augie. They fist-bumped over the small table between them.

"Carolyn excited?"

"Understatement of the century."

Augie pulled out a set of noise-canceling headphones and was asleep by the time the jet reached cruising altitude. Lauren grabbed her journal and started to write. After an hour, she had several pages full of drivel. She rolled her shoulders and neck before she turned the page and started doodling. It wasn't long before the page was covered with geometric shapes, flowers, cartoon birds, and myriad other little sketches.

But no lyrics worth a damn.

She closed her eyes as she pinched the bridge of her nose. She hadn't had this much trouble writing since she'd wrestled her cocaine demons to the ground just before and during rehab.

A little snow can fix that, whispered a silky voice in the back of her head. A voice she'd muffled for many years.

Her eyes snapped open.

CHAPTER TWO

Danny's knuckles were white as he gripped the Jeep's steering wheel. If there was a graceful exit from this fight, he sure as hell didn't see it. Out of the corner of his eye, his wife's profile was granite. Set jaw, shoulders stiff, Heather stared straight ahead. He smothered a sigh. He was so tired of fighting with her over what seemed like every little thing. This time it was about him picking up extra shifts at work.

He wasn't sure what Heather expected. They had a mortgage to pay, plus tuition at St. Catherine's Catholic school for their three sons. Not to mention all the other bills that came with their middle-class existence. His salary as a detective—and hers as a kindergarten teacher—didn't stretch as far as it used to, and they needed those overtime dollars.

On the radio, the DJ nattered on, his deep baritone at odds with the inconsequential advertising dross until he queued up the next song. He said it was a deep track from the archive: "Bombshell," from The Kingmakers' very first album. Danny clicked the radio off and glanced in the rearview. All three boys were pretending not to hear their parents argue. The sigh he'd stifled moments ago escaped.

"What was that for?" His wife's voice lashed him.

"Just sick of fighting."

"Fine." Heather looked back out the window.

The reluctant détente in their skirmish opened the door for the boys to start squabbling with each other. After five minutes, Danny was fed up.

"Enough!"

"Matty started it," Lucas said.

"I don't care who started it. I'm finishing it." They pulled over in front of the white Dutch Colonial where he'd grown up. Tires crunched in the semi-frozen slush along the curb. Another day and the snow from the late March storm would be gone. Wouldn't be soon enough for him—after the thirty-plus inches of snow that had fallen this year, he was done with winter. He stared in the rearview mirror. In the back seat, Lucas looked sullen, but a grin crept across Matty's face. The ten-year-old knew how to push all his older brother's buttons.

"Matthew." There was no mistaking the warning in Danny's voice.

"Mom! I'm not *doing* anything."

"You're in trouble," Tommy—the youngest—said in a singsong voice.

"Shut up!" Matty glared at his younger brother.

"Your father said *enough*." Heather opened the door and grabbed the bag holding her casserole dish. "Come on, Nanny and Grampy are in the house. Danny, bring the bag of books in the back. They're for your mother."

Her steps were brisk, her heels clicking on the wide brick walkway. The boys followed. Danny stayed in the car for a second and relished the silence. He and Heather had been married for thirteen years. They'd had trouble on and off, but the past year or so had been rough. If he was being honest, rough was an understatement. They seemed to exist in a constant state of low-level antagonism that had become the norm as they lived increasingly parallel lives.

But Danny wasn't about to bring his marriage troubles to the table for Sunday dinner. Grabbing the books, he paused and looked at his childhood home. Green shutters popped against the white clapboards, and defiant crocuses peeked through the rapidly retreating snow. Three generations of the Padovano family had lived in this Brooklyn house.

When he was kid, Sunday dinners with the family were an annoyance. His mother had insisted on them, and God help you if you missed one. Now? Anyone who missed one was still in hot water, but Danny was glad that his own sons had the opportunity to have that kind of larger family gathering as part of their childhood. He hoped when they were grown, they'd appreciate the tradition the way he did now. Maybe start it with their own families. A pang of guilt touched him. He had grown up in a very happy home, and he understood they weren't growing up in the same.

Inside, he dropped the bag behind the door and went into the kitchen, where his mother was holding court.

"Danny!" Deb Padovano greeted her son with the enthusiasm of someone who hadn't seen him in a month, even though she'd seen him at church not an hour before. Danny kissed her proffered cheek.

Across the kitchen, his sister, Maggie, chopped vegetables as if it was a punishment. And for her, it was. She hated cooking and every Sunday got roped into becoming their mother's sous chef. Heather swept in, moved the casserole from the counter to the microwave, and started to clean the dishes in the sink. Danny managed two steps towards the door before his sister spoke up.

"Ma, aren't you going to make Danny help?"

"Oh no," Deb answered. "I have all the help I need with you girls."

Before long, the whole family was settled at the big oak dining room table. Danny's father, Richie, sat at the head while his mother sat to her husband's right. Next to her, Maggie and her daughter, Cole. Danny's family rounded out the group of guests. They said grace, adding a special prayer for Danny's younger brother, Joey, who was in the Army, and tucked into a huge meal and some lively debate and conversation. After, they retreated to the family room. A cardboard box rested next to one of the chairs.

Cole's curiosity was piqued. "What's in the box, Grampy?"

"Eh, old photos and books," Richie said.

"Cool. Can I look?" After an affirmative nod from her grandfather, Cole pounced on the box. Lucas joined her.

While the youngest generation of Padovanos rooted through the box like it was buried treasure, the adult conversation settled on the topic of college. Maggie said Cole was looking, and her top choice was Stanford. But, Maggie told them, she'd also tossed around Boston University and USC. Danny cringed, the ringing *ka-ching* of dollar signs echoing in his head. At least Maggie only had to figure out tuition for one.

Danny watched his niece. Petite, her hair was shoulder length, and she absently brushed her bangs out of her eyes. Although she was smiling, her expression still looked studious. In a few months she'd be seventeen, and she looked like a young woman now—not a little girl. It made him feel old. It seemed like just yesterday he was playing hide-and-seek with her in the backyard.

Tommy gave a handful of photos to his parents. "Look at Daddy in these pictures. And Aunt Maggie!"

Deb beamed at her grandson. "You look just like your father when he was your age."

"Check this out!" Cole said. "It's your high school yearbook, Uncle Danny." She flipped through the pages. "I bet there's some great pictures of you in here. Whoa... You really did go out with a rock star. Man, you have wicked street cred." Cole's dark eyes were huge, her smile giddy.

Danny's meal turned to mud in his stomach as Heather lanced him with a glare.

"It's nothing," he said.

Cole rolled her eyes. "Your high school ex is the lead singer of The

Kingmakers. Yeah, no big deal or nothing. I mean, look at that photo!" She held out the yearbook.

Splashed across one page was a picture of Danny and a pretty girl with dark hair. The background was the high school football field. He was standing behind her, arms around her waist, and they were both smiling. On the opposite page, there was a picture of them dancing at the prom. Her arms were around his neck, his hands resting on the small of her back while they gazed at each other—deliriously, stupidly in love.

Danny felt his heart constrict.

"That was a long time ago," he said, defensiveness souring his voice as he felt the weight of Heather's stare.

Cole, oblivious to his discomfort, continued blithely on. "This is the coolest thing ever. I mean, she's *famous.* And the two of you had a thing in high school. You know, this would be perfect for my paper—"

"—Your what?" The mud in Danny's stomach turned to concrete.

"My paper. For school. I gotta write a research paper on someone famous from New York. Doing it on Lauren Stone never crossed my mind. But I could interview you about what she was like back then. That would for sure get me an A!" Cole was beaming.

"Don't waste your time." Deb looked like she'd smelled bad cheese.

"Waste my time? Nanny, she's, like, a star!" Cole's voice was one octave below a squeal.

"Like I said, it was a long time ago." Danny grabbed a handful of peanuts from the dish on the coffee table and stuffed them into his mouth, giving himself a few moments to collect his thoughts.

Lauren had been a huge part of his life, a part that had ended painfully. The last thing he needed to do was open old wounds—especially ones that would pressure his already strained marriage. Even when he and Heather were dating, Lauren's ghost had weighed on their relationship. Heather hated being reminded that his ex was famous.

To his displeasure, the room erupted into a roundtable of editorial comments about Lauren and their relationship. They ranged from Cole's insistence it was the coolest thing ever to his mother's sharp retort that Lauren was a hussy and never good enough for Danny. Another sub-current in the conversation was whether Cole should even write the paper, a suggestion she rejected out of hand.

Finally, Danny had had enough. "Can we just drop it, please? Cole, I'll think about it."

Cole started to plead her case, but a sharp look from her mother ended that. The room settled and Danny thought he was in the clear, but then his thirteen-year-old looked up, his expression serious and thoughtful. "Dad? If she was your girlfriend, did you love her?"

"Girls have cooties!" Matty said.

"Nuh-uh. Mom doesn't have cooties and she's a girl!" Tommy folded his arms and nodded his head firmly, secure in his assessment of the cootie situation.

"Did you, Dad?" Lucas repeated the question, despite Danny's hopes that the cooties conversation would distract him.

Pressing his lips together, Danny resisted the urge to say it was none of anyone's business, but he felt every eye in the room settle on him. "Back then, yes, I did."

"Do you still?"

The question pierced Danny like a lance. "Now? Not the way I love your mom. But I hope Lauren's happy and found someone who loves her."

Lucas nodded, seemingly satisfied with the answer. "Cool."

Danny scooped up another handful of peanuts and stared towards the television but didn't see what was on the screen. He'd teetered on the edge of lying to his son—to his entire family. He thought about Lauren a lot. Every time he heard The Kingmakers on the radio, it brought up memories of when they were together. Memories of how things ended and unanswered questions about what might have been.

Did he love her still? An hour ago, he would have said no. But it became excruciatingly clear to him in that moment just how strong his feelings still were for Lauren Stone.

For the entire drive home, Danny waited for the other shoe to drop. Heather talked to the boys but didn't say a word to him. Once they were back at their house, his wife bustled around cleaning and getting things ready for the start of the school week. Danny eventually retreated to the living room to watch the Mets' spring training highlights. Lucas, who loved baseball, joined him.

But once the boys all went to bed, the chilly silence became oppressive. Danny finished his beer and walked into the kitchen. Heather was scrubbing a stain on the stovetop as if her life depended on it. Danny rinsed out the bottle and left it on the counter.

"What's eating you?"

"Nothing."

Danny knew very well it was *something*. And he was pretty sure he knew what. "Doesn't seem like nothing."

She dropped her scrubby sponge on the counter and turned, one hand planted on her hip. "You looked pretty cozy in your prom picture with your famous ex."

"Jesus, Heather. It was a high school prom. You can't be serious." He threw his arms out to the side, and her scowl deepened in response.

"You never talk about her."

"Why would I talk about her?" he said. "Yes, my ex-girlfriend from high school is a singer in a rock band. So what? Maybe I don't like dredging up a painful part of my past. Maybe I don't think it's cool to talk about my ex to my *wife*. Can we drop it?" Danny leaned his hands on the back of a chair, aware he was trying to crush the wood. Lauren had always been a sore spot for Heather.

"I just never liked that you hid her from me." Heather picked up a stray dishtowel and gave it a quick fold before jamming it over the oven door handle.

"I never 'hid' her from you, and you know it."

"I had to find out about her from one of your friends." Heather's retort was fast and biting.

Danny vividly remembered the night he'd brought Heather to his fifth-year high school reunion to meet his friends. One had immediately asked if Lauren was coming to the reunion, and another wanted to know what Danny thought of her new song. After that, the cat was out of the bag.

He snapped back at his wife. "Did I ever—*have* I ever—asked you about your exes? No. Because I don't care about them—they're in the past, just like Lauren. And if you'd actually asked me, I would have told you."

Heather's cheeks flushed dull red. "You slept with her."

"Why does that matter?" Danny stared at his wife. Heather had always had a bit of a jealous streak, but he never understood why she felt so compelled to compare herself to Lauren. Was whether or not he'd slept with a girl almost two decades ago really that important?

"So, you did."

He cursed under his breath. "Fine. Yes, we slept together. You want the full truth? She was my first."

"I see." Heather wouldn't meet his eyes.

"Why do you care?"

"I don't know—I just do."

"She's ancient history, Heather."

As they stared at each other in silence, Danny wondered how the gulf between them had gotten so wide. Over the years, he'd tried to be a good husband and father. He wasn't perfect, but he took his responsibilities seriously. Sometimes it didn't seem like that counted for much.

Heather grabbed the scrubby sponge and turned her attention to the stovetop. Danny watched her for a moment, then rummaged in the refrigerator for another bottle of amber lager. He wandered back into the living room. Whatever random show came on the television faded into the background as he mulled over the conversation.

She's ancient history, Heather.

He took a long drink out of his beer and tried to ignore the fact that he'd just lied to his wife.

CHAPTER THREE

Parked outside his parents' house, Danny sat in the Jeep for a long time. He'd relented and agreed to let Cole interview him about Lauren after his niece pleaded with him, saying how much it would mean and what a good grade she'd get. She'd followed that up with how important grades were if she wanted to go to Stanford. After that one-two punch, a please, and some sad doe eyes, he couldn't say no—he loved Cole like she was his own daughter.

He didn't want to dredge up the past. There was a lot of unresolved shit there. But he couldn't back out now. He'd made Cole a promise, and he wasn't going to disappoint her. She was family, and you didn't let family down.

Inside, he gave his mother a kiss on the cheek and dropped his coat on the back of a chair. Cole was curled up in the living room, ensconced in a worn leather recliner with a handmade afghan draped over the back. In the other chair, Richie was peering over the top of his glasses, reading some papers. Early evening sun streamed through the bay window, creating a puddle of warm light on the floor. It gave the room a cozy feel.

"Bringing your work home with you, Dad?"

"Ideas for a new set of ads," his father said. "Those June weddings will be here before you know it. People will start shopping for wedding rings soon."

Danny rubbed his thumb against his own ring.

"This is so totally cool." Cole was beaming with anticipation. "Thanks for doing this, Uncle Danny. And Mom won't be by for at least an hour, so we have plenty of time."

"Great." Danny forced a shred of enthusiasm into his voice.

Once they were settled in the den with its floor-to-ceiling bookshelves, Cole sat up straighter in her chair and got all serious as she put her phone on the table. "You're the best, Uncle Danny. I'll take notes, but I'm going to record, too. Okay?"

Danny smiled, her zeal working its way under his reluctance. "Sure. Where do you want to start?"

Cole tapped her phone screen a couple of times to start the recording. "Interview with Danny Padovano for Lauren Stone research paper. Interview date: April 1."

April Fool's Day. The irony of the date was the cherry on the sundae.

Cole laced her fingers in front of her. "Okay, well, first things first: when did you meet Lauren?"

"A few weeks into freshman year," Danny said. "She and her sisters transferred to St. Catherine's from a different school."

Even after all these years, Danny remembered the first time he saw Lauren like it was yesterday. She was dressed like all the other girls in their uniforms: plaid skirt, dark blazer, and white button-down blouse. What caught his eye was her hair: long, shiny, and dark brown, it had a hint of curl to it—and a streak of ruby red mixed in with the brown.

She had been talking to another girl and then stopped. She turned and looked right at him, as if she'd known he was staring. She smiled and then looked away. He would never, ever forget that smile.

"What did you notice about her first?"

"Her smile. And the big streak of red in her hair. The Sisters didn't like that at all. I mean, I thought she was pretty right away, but she had a great smile."

"What was she like?"

Danny rubbed his chin. "Smart. I mean *really* smart. But she didn't always let people see it. Definitely independent. Didn't mince words either. Lauren never had a problem letting the Sisters know when she disagreed with them, that's for sure. Especially when they had something to say about the evils of rock music. I think she got sent to the principal's office the first week."

He chuckled at the memory of Lauren proudly exiting the classroom, leaving a flustered Sister in her wake.

"Obviously she excelled in music class," Cole said. "You said she was smart—what was her best subject?"

"She was great in English. And she kicked my butt in chemistry."

"Really? That's cool. So, you noticed her right away, but when did you first go out?"

"First go out? Man..." Danny thought for a minute. "I wanted to ask her out that first day, but I was too chicken. Finally, I asked her to the Christmas dance that the school always has. What do they call it...?"

"The Christmas Cotillion?"

"That's it. Anyway, after that, I asked her out again. Rest is history." He offered a non-committal wave of his hand as if the rest of that history was no big deal.

"What was she like as a musician back then?" Cole adjusted the position of the recorder by a few inches, pushing it with the end of her pen.

"Driven," Danny said without hesitation. "Lauren pushed herself hard, almost like she was afraid she was already behind. But you could tell she was something special when you heard her play or sing."

"What's your fondest memory of Lauren?"

Danny blew his breath out and thought for a long time. "I don't think there's just one, but I guess I'd have to say how beautiful she looked when I picked her up for prom." He was a little uncomfortable with the raw honesty he heard in his own voice.

Cole grinned at him and raised an eyebrow. "So, after prom..."

"Next question." He knew she wanted the rest of the story, but Cole didn't need to know about the things that happened after his prom.

Their silent, fifteen-second game of chicken felt like an eternity. Cole gave in first.

"Okay, fine," she said. "What did you guys fight about? I mean, no couple ever goes without fighting."

Danny pushed the sleeves of his shirt up as a montage of arguments with his wife raced through his mind. His relationship with Lauren hadn't been like that at all.

"Me and Lauren? We didn't fight much. At least not until the end." Danny's voice dropped away, and he looked at a spot off in the distance. It took two tries for him to find his voice. "For a long time, the future felt so far away. Once we got to spring senior year, things started to change."

"What do you mean?"

"Everything gets more concrete. You start to understand that there are a lot of people you might never see again. For me, suddenly, all the time Lauren talked about leaving for Los Angeles... I realized she wasn't kidding."

"Why didn't you believe her before?"

"I did believe her. I mean, I knew she wanted to front a band. But... I don't know. I guess I thought she'd try to put a band together here in New York. Or she'd change her mind about moving across the country, away from her family..."

Away from me. It wasn't that Danny didn't understand pursuing a dream, but Lauren leaving had gutted him. "I couldn't understand why she wanted a life that, to me, felt so uprooted. It just felt like suddenly, we were on two different paths. That's what we fought about."

"That must have been hard." Cole must have seen something in his face because she didn't press him about what he said.

Danny nodded absently. "It was sobering for both of us to realize we were going separate ways. I got angry. I thought she loved her music more than me. Maybe she did. She probably thought I didn't love her enough to go with her." The sense that Lauren's music meant more to her than he did still hurt.

"Did you? Not love her enough?"

He looked at Cole sharply, the question cutting close. "I think I was afraid of the uncertainty back then. The life she was chasing? No guarantees. I couldn't wrap my head around living like that. Always on the go, no roots." He gestured around the room. "No Sunday dinners. But she could. So, she packed her car and drove away."

The memory he'd been holding at bay finally broke through. He'd gone to Lauren's house that last day. All her worldly belongings were stuffed into her used Chevy S10 Blazer. Her family and a few of her friends had gathered on the sidewalk to see her off, along with her cousin Augie. For a minute, Danny lost himself in the memory...

Hanging back, silent, Danny watched as Lauren shared a tearful hug with her sisters and her parents and listened to her mother lecture her about being safe. He waited by the truck and was glad when everyone else melted away, giving them some privacy. She threw her backpack in the passenger seat, ignoring him for a moment.

"Lauren."

She looked at him, anger and tears brimming in her eyes. Danny resisted the urge to reach out to her and put his hands in his own pockets. He didn't know what to say. She shook her head, a look of disgust on her face making him feel like a complete shit.

"Whatever," she said as she started to open the SUV door.

"Wait," he said. "Please."

"Say whatever it is you need to say."

"I wanted to see you before you left. This isn't how... I said some things..."

"Don't." She held up a hand.

He looked away and blinked back tears. He was a Padovano, and Padovanos didn't cry. He didn't want Lauren to see how raw and ragged his heart was. He took his hand out of his pocket and reached for hers. It felt small and warm inside his, and they moved a little closer.

"You can still come with me." A lonely note of hope drifted through her voice.

"I can't, Lauren. I can't go, and you won't stay."

A wall, thick with resentment and disappointment, slammed up between them.

"Guess we don't have much to talk about then." She pulled her hand away.

"When we broke up... You know... You know I didn't mean what I said? Right?"

"Doesn't matter." She brushed tears from her cheeks with the back of her hand.

"It does..."

The door slammed shut and the engine leaped to life as she turned the key in the ignition. She rolled the window down, and when she looked up into his eyes, they were full of pain. What little was left of Danny's heart shattered.

"Bye, Danny. You'll always be here." She tapped two fingers over her heart.

He didn't trust himself to say it back. It was too final. Too permanent. He stepped back and banged his hand on the top of the truck to send her on her way. He watched her drive until she reached the end of the street and took a left. As she disappeared, he whispered, "I'll always love you, too."

"Uncle Danny?"

He flinched, his regrets taking the wind out of him. "Sorry, Cole. Just remembering."

"I didn't mean to upset you."

"Upset me? You didn't—don't apologize. Not your fault I got lost in old memories. What else do you want to know?" He forced his voice to be brighter.

Cole went with a lighter question. "Which one of her songs is your favorite?"

"That's a hard question. My favorite can depend on my mood, but I do like 'Down to the Ground.'"

Danny rubbed his chin. He did like that song, but in truth, he didn't know much of Lauren's work. He couldn't help but know some of them—The Kingmakers had topped the charts plenty of times. But any kind of ballad? If it came on the radio, he'd skip to another station. The last thing he wanted was to hear Lauren singing about her broken heart. The heart he'd broken. Avoidance was easier.

"I'm not quite sure how to ask this next question," Cole said.

Oh, boy, here it comes, thought Danny, trying to hide his unease. He was positive the question would be about sex: whether he and Lauren had done it, how old they were, or any number of other uncomfortable inquiries. But there was no way in hell he was discussing any part of his sex life with his teenage niece under *any* circumstances.

"When I talked to Nanny, she said Lauren started using drugs in high school. Did she?"

Danny's shoulders dropped two inches, but his relief quickly turned to anger. "Your grandmother said *what*? Oh, for the love of... Unbelievable." He shook his head, remembering a few family dinners that Lauren had come to. His mother had barely spoken to her.

Cole didn't have to ask another question. Her puzzled expression was enough.

"Your grandmother never liked Lauren. Thought she was a bad influence. You know—" He made air quotes with his fingers. "—Sex, drugs, and rock and roll."

A mirthful giggle escaped Cole, but she didn't give up on the question. "*Did* she do cocaine in high school?"

"We drank at some parties. Mostly beer—and do *not* tell your mother I told you that. But as far as I know, she never touched cocaine until she got to LA." Danny neglected to mention the few times he'd scored them some pot.

Cole gave him a level look as if she wanted to press the issue, but she elected to move on. "How did you find out about her drug problem? And what did you think?"

"People around here would tell me when they heard things about her. And I'd see things on the news now and then. Made me sad to see it." He shifted in his chair. "I'd go to church and just pray that I didn't see any awful headline about her OD-ing."

He sighed heavily. Cole's questions were bringing up a lot of old feelings he'd locked away a long time ago. He shifted in the chair again, unable to find a comfortable position, and the chair groaned in protest.

"Any more questions?" He hated that his voice sounded tight and irritated. He did want to help Cole with her paper, but he was ready to wrap the conversation up. He hadn't anticipated how raw talking about Lauren would make him feel.

"Why did the two of you break up?"

Danny felt the color drain out of his face. "Like I said, we fought about going to Los Angeles or staying here. I got mad, and I said some things. Mean things I regret. And don't ask me what."

"I won't. Just one more question. Please? If you were going to tell Lauren one thing today—if she were right here in front of you, right now—what would you say to her?"

A few hundred answers flew through his mind, and he discarded all of them. They were all way too personal, too intimate. "I'd tell her I'm happy for her, for her success. She chased the dream and she caught it. Not everyone can say that."

Cole turned the recorder off. She came around the table and gave Danny a big hug. "This was awesome, Uncle Danny. Thank you so much. My project is going to turn out *amazing* thanks to you."

Danny stayed in the den long after Cole left, lost in his own thoughts.

CHAPTER

FOUR

Lauren rapped the brass door knocker. Carolyn's husband, Greg, answered, but couldn't even get a hello out or invite her in before the twins came careening down the hall dressed in their dinosaur pajamas, screaming for their Auntie Lauren. She dropped to her knees and wrapped the boys up in a bear hug.

"What are you guys still doing up?"

The twins, who were five, started talking over each other. Lauren managed to gather that their mother said it was okay for them to stay up late to see her, and that they'd been playing dinosaurs. Then they both roared at her like T-Rexes.

After she disentangled herself from the boys, she gave Greg a hug.

"I'm liking the beard on you," she said.

He rubbed his furry chin. "Thanks. Jury's still out. Carolyn should be ready in a second."

On cue, Carolyn sashayed down the stairs in a short, sassy navy dress with thin straps and matching heels with a smattering of gold glitter on them. She gave a little spin. "What do you think?"

"You look totally hot." Greg gave her a gentle swat on the behind as she walked by. Carolyn laughed and blushed.

Lauren elbowed her brother-in-law and tossed out a conspiratorial wink. "I promise I'll bring her home drunk and silly for you."

Carolyn said goodbye to Greg, kissed the twins and told them to behave, and hurried out to Lauren's car. She gave the deep red Lexus an admiring look. "Yours? And do I want to know how much?"

"Leasing. And no, you probably don't."

"This is nice," Carolyn said as she got cozy in the plush leather seat. "So, where are we going?"

"Where are we— Seriously? Where do you think?"

"You got us into Blue Ruby! You're the best!"

With traffic, it took them nearly an hour to arrive at their destination. But with Carolyn's happy chatter filling the car, Lauren hardly noticed the time go by. She guided the Lexus up to the curb, and a valet in a snappy uniform rushed over. He recognized Lauren immediately and assured her that he'd personally take care of her car.

Carolyn looked a little daunted at the line, which stretched down the block, but Lauren gestured for her to follow. As they walked to the front, people started to grumble until they saw who it was. The hushed *that's Lauren Stone* followed them up the line.

Blue Ruby's main doors were azure glass and next to them, a mountain of a human was squeezed into the security chair. By his side, a man skinny enough to fit inside one of the bouncer's pant legs surveyed the crowd. In one hand he had a tablet and the other brandished a stylus like a wand.

Just as they approached, a reporter pounced on the chance to get a few words with Lauren, who gave her five minutes. Finally, they reached the faux-gem-encrusted velvet rope, and the slender man greeted them.

"Miss Stone. We're delighted you could join us tonight," he said, checking something on the tablet screen. "Please, come in and enjoy your time at Blue Ruby. Just show this card at the bar—you're comped for the evening. If you need anything, I'm Sergio."

Lauren was sure to pass both men a generous tip.

Inside, the décor included shades of blue with brushed steel accents. The massive dance floor was packed, and a DJ on a raised platform churned out a mix of dance, rap, and techno music. They threaded their way through the crowd and managed to slip into a spot at the bar. Lauren eyed the glass shelves of high-end liquor. She tried to be cautious when she drank, given her history. But she never had the same issues with alcohol that she did with cocaine.

"First round's on me!" Carolyn laughed as she snatched the comp card from Lauren's fingers. She leaned across the bar and spoke to the bartender, but Lauren couldn't make out what she said over the music. A minute later, her sister handed her a glass with a translucent pink drink in it.

"What the hell's that?" Lauren eyed the rosy liquid.

"It's a White Gummy Bear."

Lauren tilted her head back and downed the drink, which wasn't much more than a shot, in a swallow. It tasted like a fruity dessert.

Carolyn looked proud of herself. "Good, aren't they? They go down easy but they'll knock you on your ass if you're not careful!"

The sisters traded their spot at the bar for the dance floor and threw themselves into the music with abandon. Lauren relished losing herself in the beat. It gave her the chance to not think, to be in the moment. Four songs later, they took a break to have another drink. Watching the milling crowd, Carolyn entertained them both with her running commentary on the so-called fashions being flaunted.

Carolyn pointed at one woman whose dress had such a deep vee in the front you could almost see her navel. "I mean, come on," Carolyn said. "You may as well just go naked. Seriously, is the cloth stuck on her with industrial tape? Imagine how much that hurts coming off! Like getting a Brazilian for your boobs."

Lauren's sides ached from laughing, and when she caught her breath, she excused herself to go to the restroom. It was bigger and more lavish than the first apartment she had shared with the band, and it even smelled better. She'd take cloying lavender over rotten food any day.

On her way back to Carolyn, she tried to navigate a cluster of people blocking the aisle. As she threaded through the crowd, she caught sight of a woman with straight, jet-black hair as she inhaled a line of white powder from the back of a man's hand.

The glimmering remembered sensation of how a hit of coke felt stopped Lauren in her tracks. The ghost of the euphoria, the feeling she was bigger than—faster than—any of the problems dogging her coursed through her. She'd been clean for ten years, but sometimes the memories were so visceral they terrified her.

Her hear raced as she stared, hypnotized, while the woman inhaled another line and rubbed her finger on her gum. That sly little voice in her head whispered, *They'll share with you. You know they will.* Lauren blinked and forced herself to step away. That voice was the last thing she needed in her life. She started to push past them.

A hand grabbed her arm. It was the man with the coke. She glanced down at his hand, at the hint of residual snow, and hated herself for it.

"Hey! You're that singer—Lauren Stone!" he said. "I saw you looking. You want a taste, baby?" He held up a little glass vial and waved it. "I'll give you a bump. I know you like it."

Sudden sweat made her skin cold, clammy. Lauren pressed her lips together and shook her head. Pulling her arm out of his grasp, she headed back to where Carolyn was waiting. But her new "friend" wouldn't give up. He followed her through the throng.

"Where you, going? C'mon, you can party with us. I know you like snow."

"Back off." Lauren pointed a warning finger at him as she tried to slow her breathing.

"Why you gotta get all bitchy? I'm just looking for a good time." He grabbed at her arm again. Lauren jerked it away as she recoiled from the chaotic look in his eye. She knew that look far too well.

Carolyn appeared at her elbow. "Everything okay?"

The stranger leered. "Hey, gorgeous. Just want to party with you ladies..."

"I said *no*!" This time, Lauren's voice was louder, more forceful. She felt Carolyn tense, reacting to her agitation.

"You don't mean that." His smile was silky, cunning. "We can have a great time together, all three of us." His tongue skimmed over his lower lip as he looked at Carolyn from head to toe and back again, his gaze lingering in all the wrong places.

"We absolutely do mean it. And stop looking at my sister like she's a piece of meat." Lauren put a protective arm out in front of Carolyn, trying to move her sister back. A few people around them started to tune in to the drama.

Their suitor took an aggressive step forward, and Lauren balled her hands into fists. If he put his hands on her, they were going to have a problem. The bouncer who'd been working the door earlier seemed to materialize out of nowhere. Quite a feat for a man his size.

"The lady said no. Time for you to leave." He grabbed the smarmy man's elbow in a crushing grip. Squawking protests erupted as he was escorted to the door. The crowd around them returned to their own business as if nothing unusual had happened.

"Jerk. Good riddance," Carolyn said. "You okay, Lauren? What did he want?"

"Overly starstruck. That's all." Lauren didn't mention that he'd offered her coke, or that the proposition had practically made her mouth water.

CHAPTER FIVE

Lounging on the sofa with her leg casually thrown over the arm, Cole scrolled through some videos on her tablet. One caught her eye. She watched it, her smile lighting up, and then she watched it again.

"Mom! Did you hear that?"

"Hear what?"

"Lauren's here in New York!"

"Who?" Cole's mother asked, only half listening as she sorted bills on the counter.

Cole rolled her eyes. "Seriously, Mom? Lauren? *Lauren Stone?* Look!" She brought the tablet over and plunked it down. The video was dated the night before. On the screen, a bottle-blond reporter was standing on the city sidewalk in front of a club.

"Hello, everyone! I'm Sherry Fordham, and we're outside Blue Ruby, one of the city's hottest new clubs. Joining me is Lauren Stone, lead singer of The Kingmakers. Lauren, I hear there's exciting news about your new album?"

"We're starting work on our latest project. The band's had a nice, refreshing break, and we're eager to get back to the studio. Fitz McCallum will be producing it. We're very happy to work with him."

"Does that mean you'll be staying in New York for a while?"

"It does. The band's temporarily relocating here while we record."

In the background, someone's voice rang out: "Kingmakers rule!"

"Well, that is great news for your fans! We are all eager to hear what The Kingmakers come up with!" The camera zoomed in on Sherry, all spray-tan and teeth. "You heard it here first! The Kingmakers are back in town and have a new album coming out. Back to you, Derek."

Cole couldn't stop grinning. "That is so cool! I mean, how fabulous would it be if she came to visit her family and I ran into her at the store or something?"

"That would be something," her mother said.

"This is so awesome!" Cole grabbed her notebook, scribbled a few notes, and then tossed it to the side and went back to daydreaming.

Everyone else had started eating when Danny and Lucas arrived late for Sunday dinner. They washed up in the kitchen, their jeans and t-shirts in stark contrast to everyone else, who were still in their church clothes. When he slipped into the seat next to her, Heather gave her oldest a look and then glanced at Danny, who nodded.

"Where did you run off to after church?" Cole asked.

"We were at Mr. Fiorino's house," Danny said when his son remained silent. "There was a mishap with a baseball. Instead of paying to repair the dent in his car, Mr. Fiorino said Lucas could work it off."

"It was an accident," Lucas said, his voice ever-so-slightly sullen.

"And?" asked Danny.

Lucas sighed. "We take responsibility when we make a mistake... and we make it right."

"That's right." Danny nodded and looked at his other two sons. He figured he'd have to do the same thing with them someday, but he hoped they'd learn a little bit from what Lucas was doing.

Once they both had full plates and started to eat, conversation around the table kicked into high gear. It wasn't long before the adults were wrapped in a heated debate over the response—or distinct lack of one—to the explosion on the Deepwater Horizon oil platform. Once that was done, they promptly moved on to the pros and cons of the Affordable Care Act. Danny smiled as Cole threw herself into it and held her own. The Padovano family was nothing if not opinionated.

When the discussion reached a lull, Richie asked, "What's going on for you at school this week, Cole? Other than taking over the debate club?"

Cole's cheeks turned pink at her grandfather's gentle tease. "I'm turning in my project on Lauren Stone tomorrow. It came out awesome! And I saw online that Lauren is here in New York to record her new album. How cool is that?"

Danny just grunted something like, "oh," and kept eating, eyes fixed on his own plate.

Cole continued merrily on. "You know what would be really amazing? If you had a chance to catch up with her, Uncle Danny. I mean, you haven't seen each other in years. And, well, if I happened to be around, you could totally introduce me to her!"

As soon as the suggestion came out of Cole's mouth, Danny felt his back stiffen. His marriage was foundering, and while the issues he and Heather were having ran much deeper than Lauren Stone, the suddenly resurrected ghost of his relationship with her had turned into a pebble that constantly irritated Heather.

"That's not really fair to put your uncle in that position," Maggie said to her daughter.

"Oh, don't be a downer, Mom."

"I don't think it is a very good idea at all." Deb's voice was terse.

Cole heaved an epic sigh and looked at her uncle, hoping for an ally.

He shook his head. "I'm sure she'll be way too busy to make time for me."

It hurt him to say it, because right then he would have given nearly anything to see Lauren again. To have a second chance to change how things ended. There were so many things he wished he had said back then—and so many things he wished he could take back.

CHAPTER SIX

Lauren's suite at the Somerset Hotel on 57th Street was hopping. She'd booked the penthouse for the duration of her stay in New York and always held a get-together for the band and their significant others before they kicked off a new project. She paused and watched Augie, along with the other three members of the band—DJ, Ox, and Stevie—in the living room laughing and joking as they swapped stories of their escapades over the years. The band was a second family. Seeing them together and hearing the stories, no matter how often they were told, made her nostalgic.

Years ago, after her cross-country drive from Brooklyn to Los Angeles, it hadn't taken Lauren long to ferret out the clubs where the truly talented musicians congregated. And once she found them, she played at a few open mic nights, putting the word out that she was putting a band together. She'd very quickly formed—and disbanded—two separate groups. Both mistakenly assumed that, although she wrote and played hard rock, she couldn't front the band because she was a girl. Lauren had quickly disabused them of that foolish notion—right before firing them.

"Lauren, I was at my *abuela's* house before I flew out and she asked me to tell her the story—*again*—about the night I met you," Ox said as if he'd read her mind. "Do you remember? The night you fired that *culero*, Donnie?" His thunderous laugh filled the room.

"How could I forget? I hired him for *my* band, and he had the balls to tell me all I needed to do was strum the guitar and look pretty."

That night was still vivid in Lauren's memory: She'd fired Donnie on the spot, and when he tried to sweet-talk her, Lauren offered up a verbal shredding that literally made him cry. A few minutes after that, Ox had come over and introduced himself.

"You bought me a shot of tequila and asked if I was in the market for a new bass player." She had to admit, approaching her in that moment had taken a big pair of brass ones, and she admired Ox for it.

"Kinda knew there was an opening."

As it turned out, Ox—whose given name was Antonio Ochoa—was one of the best bass players she'd ever heard. Short, stocky, and as stubborn as his nickname implied, he'd quickly proven he was as determined as she was to be a success—and that he was a straight shooter who didn't put up with a lot of bullshit. When Ox introduced her to his old friend, DJ Scott, Lauren quickly agreed to add the gifted keyboardist to the nascent band.

From there, they burned through six guitarists in quick succession. Just as Lauren started to wonder if they'd ever find the right one, she heard Stevie Adebeyo play. He hadn't even finished his set when Lauren called Ox to tell him she'd found their man.

She pointed at Stevie. "But you," she said. "You played hard to get."

"Well, I thought you were a bit dodgy, mate." He tapped the side of his head. "You'd torched all the guitarists before me." His Nigerian grandparents had immigrated to England, and his own parents moved to America when he was sixteen. He'd picked up a lot of American mannerisms but never fully lost his accent.

"I was discerning," she said.

He laughed. "You just scared the shite out of everyone else."

"*Zorra*," Ox coughed the word into his hand.

"Watch it," Lauren said. "That means a couple of different things —and I know both of them."

"Then you know which one I mean." Ox let out another belly laugh.

Lauren playfully waved him off and gave Stevie a fond look. His reluctance had worked in her favor. It had given Augie just enough time to bolt to California after graduating. As soon as Augie and Stevie joined the band, everything fell into place. It all just clicked. Thinking about it sent a chill down Lauren's back.

Her burst of nostalgia morphed to anxiety as the specter of her writing block reared its ugly head. It wasn't that she hadn't written *anything*—it was more that inspiration was sporadic at best—and the results? They were piss-poor as far as she was concerned. She had much higher standards for herself.

"... *Checkmate* was decent," Ox said, referring to their last album and pulling Lauren out of her introspective reverie. She realized she'd lost track of the conversation.

Lauren rolled her eyes. "By whose standards? Certainly not mine."

None of the singles from *Checkmate* had cracked the top ten. The best single had hovered around number fourteen for a few weeks before a one-night stand with the twelve slot. Then it got kicked to the curb.

"She's still pissed that they called us over-the-hill on the Rock-Talk podcast," Augie said to the others.

Stevie's long-time girlfriend, Gabby, came in from the other room and settled in next to him while Ox cracked open another beer.

"Those two morons suck. Who the fuck cares what they say?" Ox said.

"Preach on, brothah. Preach on." Sitting in a comfortable chair, DJ raised a fist in the air before he leaned forward and tapped his beer against Ox's. He was all California surfer boy—highlighted shaggy blond hair, blue eyes, and a two-day scruff.

"And the way we shut them up is with an amazing album," said Augie.

Lauren pressed her lips together and looked at the floor. An amazing album needed amazing songs. And she hadn't written a single fucking one that would remotely qualify as "amazing."

"Ah, we'll be fine. We'll adapt." Everyone stared at Ox. A creature of habit, being flexible was not one of his strengths.

"Bollocks." Stevie called him out.

"Hey, you know me, Mr. Flexible."

DJ gave a disbelieving snort. "Flexible? No one needs to hear you brag about your sex life."

"Jealous bitch," Ox said.

The familiar banter continued, easing Lauren's anxiety and giving her a sense of family and shared history. In the coming weeks there would be days they'd spend sixteen, eighteen hours at the studio, and other days when they'd gather at someone's place to collaborate. And there would be a few days in there where they'd all want nothing to do with each other.

They had learned over the years that they were better off living close to each other, but not together, while they recorded. It gave them room to separate when tensions flared and enormous opportunity to be close when it counted.

But for now, they ate, they drank, and they laughed. DJ and Stevie embroiled themselves in an earnest debate over which Van Halen video back in the '80s was the best. Lauren's eclectic playlist switched and the notes of Thin Lizzy's "The Boys Are Back in Town" came on, but the song was drowned out by Ox and Augie playing the latest version of *Call of Duty*. They shouted at each other and the screen. Lauren stood behind them offering color commentary about their ability—or distinct lack of it—to shoot the enemy. Augie let out an anguished cry as his avatar was hit by a ridiculous number of bullets.

"You suck at this," Lauren said to her cousin. "I'm glad you're not really in the Army. You can't hit shit!"

Ox, after jumping off the sofa and doing a victory dance around the living room, pulled out his cell phone and started tapping away at a text. Then he took a picture of Augie's forlorn face and typed a little more. He hit send and laughed.

"Who'd you send that to?" DJ popped a handful of M&Ms into his mouth.

"Cam and Jake. I told them I just crushed Augie on Xbox." He gave an exaggerated, cackling laugh like an evil genius and rubbed his hands together. Cam and Jake were his two oldest sons. They were fifteen and fourteen, the product of a two-year marriage to his first ex-wife and lived in California with their mother. His second ex lived in Texas with his other two children, Michelle and Robbie. Wife number three had lasted six months before he got that error in judgment annulled, and not soon enough as far as Lauren was concerned.

It was just past midnight when Stevie emerged from the guest bedroom carrying his daughter, Maya. She was still sound asleep, her head on his shoulder. He kept his voice at a whisper. "Time for us to go. Got to get my little luv into her real bed."

The others took Stevie and Gabby starting to pack up as a sign they should all call it a night. Everyone said their goodbyes and headed out. DJ gave Lauren a hug, picking her up off the floor and spinning her around.

"This is going to be awesome, and I can't wait to get out on tour with you."

"You say that now. After a year on the road, you'll be sick of me."

"Never! Sick of Augie? Yeah. Stevie and Ox? Totally. But never you." He winked.

"Dude, move your ass! We ain't getting any younger over here," Augie said from the door.

Lauren was still laughing even as the elevator swallowed up the rest of the band. She liked starting off a production session with a party like this. It put everyone in a good mood and reminded them they were all friends. At some point during the project, when the forced togetherness started to chafe, they'd need the fun memories.

Lauren yawned into the quiet of the penthouse. As she brushed her teeth, she studied herself in the mirror and wondered what fans would think about the relatively early night. Would they be disappointed to learn that The Kingmakers didn't always keep the party going until the sun came up anymore?

Later that night, she woke up, breathless and covered in sweat, the ghostly dream-feel of Danny's hands on her body visceral. She fumbled with the clock on her nightstand. The neon blue numbers told her it was 2:00 a.m. Crawling out of bed, she stripped off her sweat-soaked tank top and tossed it aside. She rummaged through her bureau drawers until she found a new one.

Out in the kitchen, the glow from a night-light limned the room. She splashed a little water on her face and leaned in to get a drink from the faucet.

I need something stronger than this, she thought, eyeing the bottle of whiskey on the counter. Instead, she grabbed the orange juice out of the refrigerator and drank straight from the bottle. It was one of the perks of living alone: no one complained about late-night eating habits.

She thumped down on the stool at the kitchen island and replayed the dream in her head. It had been a long time since she'd had one that intense. She swore she could still feel Danny's hands on her body, the scrape of the unshaved stubble on his chin rough on her shoulder as he kissed her neck. Years ago, after she'd moved to the West Coast, she'd had dreams like this all the time—vivid, passionate, downright carnal. Augie had told her more than once on tour that she'd woken him and the others on the tour bus by calling out Danny's name in her sleep. Over the years, the dreams decreased in frequency, but they never went away.

But this one? This one had an intensity, a level of desire she hadn't felt in years. Lauren rubbed the bridge of her nose. She reached for one of the notepads and the pen she kept handy. She wanted to capture the dream's details before they faded; there was probably a song buried in this one somewhere.

She closed her eyes and tried to remember. There had been swings, little kid swings like she used to play on in elementary school. And a pine tree. There had definitely been a pine tree, but those details were ephemeral, intangible. What burned through all of them was *him*. In the dream, she'd heard Danny behind her. He'd called out, laughing, but before she could turn, he had her in his arms. She'd relaxed, feeling safe and sheltered. The warmth of his skin made her realize they were naked. As he'd tangled his fingers in her hair, she'd leaned her head back, a soft moan escaping her lips as he kissed her harder and his hands slid along her body until he grazed—

Her eyes snapped open. "Jesus!"

Cheeks on fire, Lauren hurried out of the kitchen to take a cold shower.

CHAPTER SEVEN

The blaring horn from a taxi jarred Lauren out of her aimless daydream as her SUV pulled up to the curb. She glanced out the window and got her first real look at the exterior of Velocity Studios. The building was older with a brick façade and tall arched windows. Around the glass doors, insets of brushed steel gave the brick a sleeker, more modern look. She unbuckled her seatbelt and was about tell her driver that he didn't have to get the door. He was, however, already around the car with his fingers on the handle.

"Really, you don't need to—"

"Part of the job, Miss Stone."

If she was being honest, Lauren would have preferred to drive herself, but taking the car service afforded her an opportunity to return some calls and attempt to scribble out a few songs. Not that she'd actually done any of that during the ride. She chewed her bottom lip. Maybe once they were all in the studio, the ideas would flow. If not, she was screwed.

Velocity's waiting room was small but an interesting mix of contemporary and luxurious style. The reception desk, chairs, tables, and shelves all had clean, fashionable lines, but anywhere you could sit was all sumptuous padding and soft leather. Awards, framed news articles, and photos of Fitz and the myriad stars he'd worked with in the past lined the walls.

At the front desk, Tisha Marion looked up and greeted her warmly. As Fitz's right-hand woman, she kept him organized, worked the schedule, and solved any issue that came up. When they'd first spoken on the phone, Fitz had told Lauren that if she needed anything, Tisha was the person who could get it.

"Fitz will be ready in just a second—morning call's running a little late. Get you anything?" Tisha pushed a few willful two-strand twists back over her shoulder as she stood up.

Lauren thanked her but declined. Tisha let her know that Ox and Stevie had arrived and that they were in Studio A. She held out a large manila envelope that was addressed to Lauren, care of the studio.

"For me?" Lauren wasn't expecting anything, and the return address wasn't familiar. She took the envelope, slid a finger under the flap, and tore it open. Inside was a stack of paper, neatly stapled in one corner, with a note clipped to the top sheet.

Dear Lauren,

You don't know me, but I feel like I know you! My name is Nicole Padovano-Shea (my friends call me Cole). I'm a student at St. Catherine's and I think you know my family: you dated my Uncle Danny in high school (I'm Maggie's daughter).

I'm a huge fan, and I had to do a research paper on a famous person from New York and decided to do my assignment on you. I did a bunch of research about you and your career, but I also did interviews with my uncle and some other people from my family. I thought you might be interested in reading it—at least, I hope you will be—so I have enclosed a copy for you.

Fingers crossed you like it!

Good luck with your new album.

Sincerely,

Cole Padovano-Shea

Lauren's breath caught in her throat as she flipped the note up. The cover of the paper displayed the title in a bold chunky font: From St. Catherine's to Sunset Boulevard – A Profile of Lauren Stone. *She interviewed Danny? About me? Oh, Christ on a raft.*

In high school the only thing Lauren had been passionate about —aside from her music—was Danny. And when they broke up, part of her world crumbled. People tried to tell her that first loves always seemed that way. Like the world was ending. But she would get over him. They told her that someday Danny would be a distant, dusty memory. Barely worth thinking about. There would be others to take his place.

As far as Lauren was concerned, they were all full of shit.

Had there been others? Yes. Had any of them taken Danny's place? Hell, no. Everyone else had wanted something from her. Danny had loved her before she was famous. He knew the real her. Loved the *real* her.

"Lauren?"

"Sorry. Back in high school I dated this guy, Danny. We had a real thing, you know? Apparently, his niece is a fan, and she wrote a research paper on me. She sent a copy." Lauren waved the papers a little.

Tisha laughed, her twists shaking. "That's a new one. Here, I'll hold onto that until you wrap up. I'll put it in with the packet and you can take it all home together."

"Great. Thank you." Lauren paused. "Studio A?"

"Down the hall. Last door on the left."

Lauren had barely made it halfway down the hall when Fitz's office door popped open and he darted out. A small, slight man with wiry gray hair that was thinning in the back, he bustled with energy and enthusiasm. He gave Lauren a big hug.

"Lauren, darlin'," he said with his Irish lilt. "I'm sorry ta be late.

Bloody wankers just would na get off the phone. How many times do you need to reconfirm what you just bloody talked about? Now, come along. Let's go join the lads and have a chat 'bout this project you're wanting to do."

Six hours later, The Kingmakers and their new producer had discussed the schedule, how the band liked to schedule their time, access to the studio during off hours, and other logistical items that needed to be handled. Then Fitz wanted to just hear them play—to tune his ear, as he said. During the different conversations, Lauren artfully dodged Fitz's questions about how many songs they had in the pipeline.

When they finished, she went to the front and gathered her stuff from Tisha, who let her know that Roberta, The Kingmakers' primary publicist, had dropped by and left a few things. Lauren was glad she didn't have to talk with Roberta. She found the woman abrasive and her tactics occasionally questionable. She knew Augie felt the same, and she'd been meaning to talk to the management team about finding someone new.

As her driver navigated the New York streets, Lauren settled in and looked through a few of the documents Tisha had sent with her. One was a copy of the contract. She and Augie would go through that later. They'd both—at the insistence of their fathers—taken summer business courses at a local college while they were still in high school. That foundation, plus the experience they gained over the years, had made both competent at reviewing contracts despite not being lawyers. So, in addition to the band's legal team, they always made sure to go through the paperwork themselves.

Then she picked up Cole's paper and flipped through. Cole had started with a summary of Lauren's professional career but then went back to the beginning, her life before becoming famous, and then brought the timeline up to the present day. She even provided her own assessments of the band's albums, citing reasons she agreed or disagreed with industry pundits. Lauren put the paper down in her lap as she started wandering through memories.

Leaving Danny behind was the hardest thing she'd ever done. Even as angry as she'd been over their breakup, she'd watched him in her rearview mirror all the way down the street that day—and cried half the way to California. Each morning she'd wonder if she could do it without him, swinging back and forth between hating herself for leaving and being furious with him for not coming with her.

Unbidden, a memory surfaced about the first Christmas dance he'd asked her to. It had been an awkward, hesitant question, and her answer had been just as uncomfortable. They'd been what, fourteen years old? They'd danced together, that awful, wonderful first slow dance where no one knew exactly what to do. But they'd gotten more comfortable and closer until Sister Agnes reminded them to leave space enough between them for God. They'd been mortified.

Lauren chuckled. That dance was just one of many firsts she shared with Danny Padovano.

First dance.

First kiss.

First relationship.

First time.

First love.

Lost in her thoughts, Lauren didn't realize the SUV had stopped and she jumped when the driver opened the door. She gathered up her papers and got out of the Escalade.

First love? she thought. *Try only love.*

CHAPTER EIGHT

The phone on the faux-marble kitchen counter rang.

"Cole. Get that, please, my hands are full." In the kitchen, Maggie angled a pot lid to let a bit of steam escape.

"Why do we even have a landline anymore?" Cole reached across the counter.

"Because."

Cole pushed the answer button. "Hello?"

"Good evening. May I speak with Cole Padovano-Shea, please?" The woman on the other end of the phone sounded very businesslike.

"This is Cole."

"Hello, Cole. My name is Roberta Thompson-Traeger. I'm a publicist with Red Ridge Entertainment and represent Lauren Stone and The Kingmakers."

"What? No way!"

On the other side of the room, her mom looked up. "Who is it?"

Cole covered the receiver. "Mom! You won't believe this! Lauren Stone's publicist is on the phone!"

"I'm delighted you're so excited to hear from me," Roberta said, clearly having heard Cole despite the muffled microphone. "Ms. Stone received the paper you wrote, and she was quite impressed. In fact, on her behalf, I'd like to invite you and the rest of the Padovano family to be in the audience for her interview with Martin Sandoval on *Backstage*."

"No way! In the live audience?"

"I'll need to know how many tickets—"

"Mom! Get this! We're going to be in the audience for Lauren's interview with Martin Sandoval! The whole family is invited. We'd need, what? Seven, eight tickets?"

"Cole, give me the phone."

"Mom!"

"The phone, Cole. *Now*."

Cole heaved a larger-than-life, sixteen-year-old sigh and handed the phone to her mother.

"Hello? This is Maggie Padovano, Cole's mother. Who is this?"

Cole leaned forward, straining to hear any piece of what Roberta was saying. Her mother raised a warning finger at her.

"I see. And when is all of this supposed to happen?"

Cole folded her hands in prayer and mouthed the words, "Please, Mom? *Please?*"

"Uh huh. Where?"

Cole wanted to scream and clapped her hands over her own mouth as she caught her mother's eye.

"Well, Cole and I can be there—"

Cole leaped up, ecstatic.

"—I'll extend the offer to the rest of the family, but I can't guarantee how many will come. Is that a problem? No? Okay, we'll see you next Saturday."

Maggie barely had time to hang up the phone before Cole threw her arms around her. "Ohmygod! Mom! We're going to be in the studio audience! That is the coolest thing ever! Do you think we'll get to meet her? I can't believe she read my paper! I can't wait to tell *everyone*!"

At the next Sunday dinner, Cole was beaming, and Danny didn't have to wait long to find out why.

"Guess what!" she gushed. "I sent a copy of my paper to Lauren, and—*get this!* — her publicist called me Friday night. We've all been invited to be part of the studio audience when Lauren does her interview on *Backstage with Martin Sandoval* on Saturday! Isn't that awesome?"

The sudden chill that radiated off Heather washed over Danny in concussive waves. He loved Cole but, in that moment, he wished she'd just shut up and stop going on and on about Lauren.

"You'll come, right, Uncle Danny? And you too, Aunt Heather? This will be so cool!"

"I don't know," Danny said around a mouthful of broccoli. Before he could say anything else, Lucas chimed in.

"That would be cool. We can go, right, Dad?"

Danny passed the buck. "It's up to your mother."

"C'mon, Aunt Heather." Cole turned on her best charming smile. "How many chances do you get to be in a studio audience?"

"Mom?" Lucas asked at the same time.

"Yeah, can we, Mom?" Matty asked.

Heather put her knife and fork down and her hands in her lap. Danny could see they were curled into fists. A tremor flitted across her lower lip before she plastered on a smile. "I suppose we can go."

"Awesome!" Cole high-fived Lucas.

After dinner and dessert, everyone lingered for a little while so Tommy could play a game of Trash Pandas against his older cousin. He lost. Danny tried not to laugh as his youngest bemoaned his fate and demanded the chance to "reclaim his manhood." With a glance at the other boys, Danny knew they'd taught their little brother that phrase since neither would make eye contact with him.

Back at their house, Heather snapped into Monday-morning-prep mode: making lunches, vacuuming, doing yet another load of wash. She couldn't believe three boys could produce *that* much dirty laundry. All the while, she waited for her husband to bring up the whole Sandoval thing.

Finally, she wearied of waiting. "What were you thinking?"

"I know," Danny said, his expression chagrined.

Heather, however, didn't want contrite—she wanted an apology. "You put me in an awful position. 'It's up to your mom?'" She flung the shirts in her hand into the laundry basket. "Come on, Danny. I had to say yes regardless of how I felt. I tell them no and I'm the bad guy."

"I wasn't sure if you'd want to go—I didn't want to make the decision for you."

"That's a cop-out and you know it," she said. "All you had to do was say *I'll talk about it with your mother.* But no, you just put the whole decision on me. You *know* I don't want to go sit and watch your ex sing a bunch of songs about how much she cares about you." Disgusted, she pushed past him.

"Then don't go."

Heather couldn't believe those words came out of her husband's mouth. "Don't go? You think I'm really going to let you go without me?"

"Let me go?" Danny said. "You say it like I need supervision. Not like I'd be alone. Maggie and Cole will be there. My dad. *Our children.* What do you think's going to happen? She's going to conk me over the head and carry me off?"

Heather didn't answer. She turned back to her work in the kitchen. She could feel Danny fuming behind her, but she didn't want to talk about it anymore. A minute later, he went back to the living room to watch TV. She knew, logically, there was no reason to be jealous of Danny's ex. They hadn't seen each other in years.

But Lauren was a glamorous, famous rock star. And Heather?

Well, she was just Heather. And rightly or wrongly, the rock star trumped the soccer mom each and every time.

By the time they were ready for bed, Heather had been stewing about things long enough to have something to prove to herself. In the bathroom she fluffed her hair and slipped on one of Danny's work shirts, making sure the top few buttons were undone. Danny was getting into bed when she came in.

The floor squeaked, and he looked towards her, his face still shuttered from their argument. But she saw his eyes run up and down, lingering on where her legs disappeared under the cotton material.

"I don't like fighting with you," she said.

"I don't either."

She slid under the covers and reached for him. Lately it seemed the only sex they had was make-up sex, but she needed to know that her husband still wanted her. Danny put an arm around her waist and pulled her closer, and she could feel him pressed up against her.

As he kissed her, Danny undid the remaining buttons, kissing her throat. His hands felt cool as they massaged her breasts, and she pulled her knees up a little as he moved to cover her, settling between her thighs. A small sigh escaped her as he pushed inside. Heather tightened her fingers on his arms as he paused. Then Danny's hips moved harder, more deliberately. A louder moan gathered in the back of his throat.

"Shhh! Quiet! You'll wake the boys."

Her rebuke made him pause. But he started again, driving in and out until he buried his face in her neck to muffle the sounds he made when he finally came. He rolled off her and they lay side by side.

"Good night." She turned on her side, away from her husband. It had been fast, faster than Heather had wanted, and she felt dissatisfied. *At least snuggle with me,* she thought, hoping Danny would slide in behind her and hold her against him.

"Night." Danny turned the other way.

Wrapped in the covers, Heather found she wasn't ready to sleep.

She'd wanted more—needed more—from their lovemaking. To feel sexy. Desired. He'd obviously been happy to oblige, but there hadn't been much foreplay—and she certainly hadn't had an orgasm. But that was par for the course: sex between them was rarely spontaneous anymore, and it was more tepid than hot. Danny seemed to just close his eyes and take care of business.

Half the time she didn't even look up at him, not wanting to see him with his eyes closed and wonder what he was thinking about. Because she was pretty sure it wasn't her. She wanted to be angry about that, but she couldn't. If she was being honest with herself, she occasionally fantasized about her favorite movie star—but it wasn't the same. There was no way on earth she was ever getting the chance to be with George Clooney.

But when do we have time to fix it? We barely have time for sex anyway. Is this as good as it gets?

It hadn't always been like this. When they were dating, and first married—even after Lucas was born—Danny could hardly keep his hands off her, and Heather was the same. They'd been late for dinner with friends more than once because one of them had gotten frisky. She wondered if her husband ever thought about how they used to be, in the early days, until a darker thought crossed her mind.

Does he even think about me at all? Or does he think about... about... her?

Heather told herself to stop, that she was being ridiculous. But once the idea wormed its way into her head, it sat there and festered. Her eyes burned with unwelcome and unshed tears. Her jaw ached from being clenched, but she was not going to explain why she was crying in the middle of the night—she'd sound like a damn fool.

On his side of the bed, Danny also lay awake. In the dark, he felt his wife shift under the sheets. Heather initiating sex had been a nice surprise. They didn't have sex much anymore, and most of the time, he was the one who dropped the obvious hints—and over the past year, even that was rare. And while he was physically sated, his mind was restless. Something seemed missing, and this wasn't the first time he'd felt this way.

I should be happy my wife wants to have sex. But even when it's spontaneous, it seems rehearsed. Just another checkbox on the to-do list. Hell, I worry more about being quiet than enjoying it. They hadn't always been so boring. He and Heather had been in love once, or at least he thought so.

He wasn't so sure anymore.

CHAPTER NINE

The day of the Sandoval show, Lauren lounged in one of the chairs in her suite at the Somerset, staring out the window. She'd become quite fond of this particular chair and its soft, buttery gray leather. Her cell phone chimed.

"Hey, Augie. What's up? What's that noise?" She could hear an odd crinkling noise in the background.

"Groceries. I'm at my parents'."

"Mamma's boy."

"Whatever. I wanted to see if you were set for Sandoval tonight."

"Ready as I'll ever be," she said. "Gotta be at the studio in a couple hours. You know, if you need an excuse to bail on your chores, you could come do the interview with me."

"Hell no. Paid my dues last time."

Lauren couldn't argue with that: The last time the band had done a press tour, Lauren, Ox, and DJ had all come down with a wretched head cold, leaving Stevie and Augie to do all the heavy lifting. She jumped out of the chair and paced as they talked. Solo interviews always made her anxious.

"You'll watch, won't you? I'll need to get talked off the ledge after, once I decide how horrible I was." She bit a thumbnail, hating that she sounded so insecure.

"Dude, you'll be fine. You're an old pro at these."

After Augie reassured her, he said he'd text after to let her know where to meet him and DJ if she was interested in going out. More grocery bags crinkled in the background.

"Be right there," Augie said to someone else.

"Mamma's boy," she repeated.

After they hung up, Lauren tossed her phone onto the table and flopped back into the chair. She leaned back into the leather's embrace, mulling over her reluctance to do the interview. It wasn't that she minded the interview itself—she had no problem talking about songwriting, the band, or anything related to music. But the press always seemed to want to know about her stint in rehab, something she never liked discussing. And she'd walked out on interviews before when people got too pushy.

The worst years of her addiction and rehab had been a dark, lonely, awful chapter in her life. She never quite understood why people wanted access to that part of her. Maybe some wanted to understand. To Lauren, though, the inquiries always had a voyeuristic quality, as if the asker wanted to pull some perverse sense of joy out of her pain. Those people could go screw.

Maybe tonight I'll shock everyone and not hold back, she thought. *Let out all the sordid details for them to wallow in.* That sudden sense of recklessness sent an adrenaline-soaked thrill through her. She checked herself, the sensation setting off warning bells. After a few deep breaths, she looked at the clock. There was no more time for procrastination.

Lauren chose an outfit with enough flash to look like a rocker but reserved enough to not earn a what-was-she-thinking award. It did get tiring, being judged for what she was wearing and what she was doing, but it was the life she'd signed up for. She'd always had a penchant for denim and leather but loved a splash of something shiny or metallic. And then there were the boots—her signature item. She picked out one of her favorite pairs.

While Lauren endured the hair and makeup guru's ministrations at the studio, Danny pulled into a parking lot down the street. Over the course of the week, he'd become more and more conflicted about tonight's show. It seemed somehow unfair to be excited about seeing Lauren, but at the same time, he hadn't seen her for nearly twenty years. Heather didn't want to be there, and the fact that Lucas had downloaded two Kingmakers albums and had been chattering all week about them hadn't helped.

On the sidewalk they met up with Cole, Maggie, and Richie, then made their way to the ticket window, where Maggie asked for Roberta. The clerk directed them to the side so other audience members could get in. Danny could hear her on the phone letting someone know they were waiting up front.

Roberta—a painfully thin woman dressed in a severe, serious suit, her hair pulled into a tight French twist—came bustling out of a side door to greet them. Her eyes darted back and forth, scanning the crowd, and she held her hands close to her body, rubbing them constantly. She practically crackled with nervous energy. Danny's cop instincts went on high alert.

Roberta shook Cole's hand. "So, you're the young lady who wrote the paper? Lovely to meet you. I'm Roberta, Miss Stone's PR representative. If you could all follow me, I'll show you to your seats. Once the show's done, an usher will bring you backstage."

Cole's smile doubled. "We're going to meet Lauren?"

Danny blanched as his heart started to race.

"Of course! I know she's very curious about the young lady who wrote that paper!"

The enthusiasm in Roberta's voice sounded forced to Danny. He didn't like her, and he liked her even less when she glanced at him and said, "I'm sure you'll all find the show to be quite exciting."

With wide eyes, Cole took in all the details of the studio. When she realized their seats were right in front, she pressed her fingers to her lips, smothering a delighted squeal. "These are stellar seats! I can't believe we're actually here."

"Totally. This is awesome," Lucas said, using his cousin's favorite word.

Despite his own misgivings, seeing his niece this excited made Danny happy. Maggie caught his attention, glanced at her only child, and rolled her eyes good-naturedly. He let Maggie and Cole take the first seats, and Lucas squeezed by to sit next to his cousin. Danny sat, and Heather took the next seat, with Matty and Tommy ending up between her and Richie.

The stage crew zig-zagged across the set as a big clock counted down to the start of the show. At first Danny tried to follow the activity, discern a pattern, but soon he let his mind wander. He'd seen photos of Lauren over the years, but those didn't tell him anything. Had success changed her? Had she achieved what she wanted? Did she ever think about him? His stomach twisted into a knot, and it was hard to tell if he was feeling trepidation or anticipation.

An eager buzz filled the room as the show's host, Martin Sandoval, walked onto the set. His black hair was sprinkled with gray, and he sported a thin, very well-trimmed beard along his jaw. An assistant adjusted his microphone and touched up his hair. After, he took a moment to chat with the audience until the director gave him a thumbs-up. Then he took his seat, adjusted his jacket, and on cue, Martin sat up a little straighter and smiled toward the camera. The audience was shushed as the countdown started.

"Three... Two..." The "LIVE" sign illuminated. They were officially on live television.

"Hello, everyone! Welcome to *Backstage*. I'm your host, Martin Sandoval. Tonight, we have a terrific guest, and I'm so excited that she's here. She's a rock and roll legend with a career that spans close to twenty years, eight albums, multiple Grammy awards, and collaborations with some of the biggest names in the business. Please give a warm welcome to Lauren Stone of The Kingmakers!"

Applause and whoops greeted Lauren as she walked out on the stage. She stopped partway to her chair and waved both hands. Someone in the back whistled, and she blew a kiss to the audience with a laugh. They bellowed their enthusiasm back at her.

Danny stared, his eyes roaming from her head all the way down to her feet and back again. She looked every inch the rock star: faded blue jeans that fit her perfectly, a cropped leather jacket over a shirt made of a slinky material with silver threads that glinted when she moved, and funky black boots with silver chains around the ankles.

Heather's hand closed over the top of his, her fingers stiff and claw-like. Her smile was thin and looked forced, and he knew she'd seen him staring at Lauren. He flushed, the knot in his stomach winding tighter.

On stage, Martin shook Lauren's hand and gave her a kiss on the cheek before inviting her to sit down on the small loveseat opposite his host's chair.

"Lauren, thank you so much for spending time with us tonight."

"My pleasure, Martin." She settled in, crossing one leg over the other.

Danny leaned forward slightly, drawn in by her warm, inviting voice—it had a natural, sexy quality that didn't stray into a breathy stereotype. It made him feel the tiniest bit drunk.

Lauren pushed a little of her hair over her shoulder as she waited for Martin to get to the questions. Despite bitching to Augie about doing the interview alone, she was eager for the chance to start talking about the new project. And she could still feel that reckless sensation swirling around, tempting her to do something unexpected.

"So, I'll get the first question out of the way. When can we expect to hear the first single from your new album?"

"Whoa!" Lauren said. "Slow your roll, Martin! We're just getting started. We have a very iterative way of working. You never quite know where a great spark will come from. Or how long it takes to get there." She winced internally as the thought of her mostly empty notebook jabbed her, a tiny knife in the ribs.

"Fair enough. Let me ask you this, then. Many bands live together while they're recording, but The Kingmakers don't. Why is that?" He leaned back in his chair and smiled again, an unspoken invitation for Lauren to join the conversation.

"Oh, we've done that—the live-together-while-you-work thing. In the beginning we had to—was a matter of money. There were times the five of us crammed into a single bedroom apartment. But we've learned over the years that we need a central space to be together, be creative, put in those long hours that you need—and that we all need a little space to call our own."

She paused and chuckled. "What I'm trying to politely say is that sometimes we get on each other's nerves. We've learned that what works for us is living close, but not together."

"Fascinating," Martin said. "The Kingmakers have been around for a long time, and you've got a devoted fan base. But there's a whole new generation that's starting to learn about you and your music. Let's do a little bit of history so they can get to know you better. When did you know you wanted to be a rock star?" He laced his fingers together and hooked them over his knee.

Lauren pursed her lips and thought about her answer for a moment. "I don't know if I started out wanting to be a star. Well, okay, maybe a little. I did want to be Heart's Ann and Nancy Wilson all rolled into one. But fame or no fame, I wanted to make a living performing. I always loved singing. Our family joke is that I started to repeat lyrics before I said 'mommy' or 'daddy.' But even when I was very little, really all I wanted to do was sing and play music."

"So, part of your DNA." Martin steepled his fingers and nodded, encouraging Lauren to continue.

"I guess. Everyone has their own dream. Be a doctor, cop, astronaut, hairdresser, TV show host..." She gestured at Martin and was rewarded by a ripple of laughter from the audience. "Honestly, there's nothing else I could have done in this life that would have made me as happy as music does."

Martin went on to ask her about who influenced her career. Lauren said not only Heart, but also named Stevie Nicks, Aerosmith, and a few others. He quizzed her on her first impressions of the other band members, and what her biggest revelations were about life on the road during the band's early years—and how those had changed as they gained experience.

"Thank you so much for sharing all that, Lauren." Martin changed his focus from her to the camera. "We're going to take a quick break, but we'll be right back with more from Lauren Stone. Don't go away!"

A sign over the set blinked to life, the word "commercial" lit up in big yellow letters. An army of assistants swarmed the stage, fussing with both Lauren and Martin. She shifted restlessly under their attention, and they disappeared as quickly as they'd materialized. The lights flashed, signaling the show was going back on the air, and the murmur from the audience faded. Martin beamed at the camera again.

"Welcome back. We're here tonight with Lauren Stone of The Kingmakers. So, Lauren, tell me, do you have any regrets? Things you'd do over, do differently, if you had a second chance?"

The smile on Lauren's face faded as she gave Martin a measured look. He was dancing around the question, but she knew what he wanted. No matter how much time went by, her cocaine problem always came up. It pissed her off. She raised her chin defiantly.

"Of all the things to discuss, you want to beat that dead horse again?" Her voice held a bullwhip sting.

"That whole time in your life is quite important—"

She heard the wariness in his tone.

"—No, the music's important. Our charitable work is important. Our future as a band is important. Dredging up the past cloaked in discussing 'regrets' is just a backhanded way for you to ask—"

"—About the cocaine?" Martin pressed the issue.

Her anger flared, and she felt her whole expression harden. She leaned forward as if she was going to get up and leave. Fear darted through Martin's eyes.

She didn't like talking about her addiction. She never had.

And he knew it.

Some artists who'd struggled with the same demons shared their whole story. A way to process what had happened to them, what they'd gone through. A way to maybe—*maybe*—prevent others from making the same mistakes. But for Lauren, sharing those stories dredged up painful reminders of her own failures.

Just like how she was failing now, letting the band down with her lack of creativity. Letting every single person in the studio audience down. She glanced away. *I don't deserve their admiration. They have no idea how screwed up I am,* she thought.

"Yes, the cocaine," she said. Then the simmering recklessness boiled over, the idea of just sharing all of it sending a thrill coursing through her. It was the same kind of rush she'd get when she got high, and she grabbed onto it without thinking twice. Lauren locked eyes with Martin.

"After our first album debuted at number one and then went platinum, everything exploded for us. Everyone knew who we were, wanted to be around the band. Whatever we asked for, we got. No one batted an eye—it didn't matter how outrageous the request was."

In a flash of memory, she remembered one time Stevie had asked for a llama, and one was waiting in his hotel room. It had ruined the room and spit on Stevie. The hotel had politely told them to never come back.

"I thought I was a grown-up—a responsible adult," she said.

"But really, I was barely twenty-one years old. A kid in a grown-up suit with no supervision, a seemingly endless supply of money, and a wild lifestyle."

She turned her head slightly to the side, angled away from the audience, and gazed past Martin's shoulder to hide the pain. It gave her a moment to collect herself, reassert some control before she said *too* much.

"And emotionally, I wasn't in a good place," she said. "I'd been through a rough couple of years—lots of ups and downs that started when I left home. It's hard. Leaving everything you know—*everyone you love*. You don't realize what a big hole it can leave in you, how empty you can *really* be inside. And I tried filling it with all the wrong people and all the wrong things." She bumped her fist against her chest. That kind of pain was all too familiar.

"You certainly generated your share of headlines," Martin said.

Lauren's retort was quick. "Hopefully I still do—but for different reasons."

"Of course—" He tried to backpedal but Lauren cut him off.

"—But you're right. I acted out. A lot. There are a couple hotels that still have me blacklisted, even after all these years. Everyone jokes about that, but frankly, it's embarrassing. I went to too many wild parties, closed down too many clubs. I put way too much snow up my nose. I was destroying myself—and the band—and it took a long time for me to realize that."

"What changed? What brought you to that realization?"

Lauren could hear the eagerness in Martin's voice, the hope he was going to get some sort of bombshell revelation. She narrowed her eyes. It wasn't enough for the TV audience to notice, but it sent a clear message to Martin—a warning that her willingness to be that exposed was running short.

"We busted our asses those first few years," she said. "We did four albums in three years and supporting tours for *all* of them. By the time we did *Dog & Pony Show,* I was in trouble. Honestly, *Dog & Pony* isn't a very good album. There are decent songs on it, but compared to the previous ones? It was so far below what the band was capable of—what I was capable of. When it tanked, I blamed everyone else. It was all their fault but never mine."

Lauren took in a deep breath and pressed her lips together. She could feel Martin—and the audience—holding their collective breath along with her. She'd always been cagey about the moment she knew she needed help. But they wanted the truth? Fine, she'd give them the goddamn truth. Maybe then, people would stop asking her the same fucking question.

"The guys, they really laid it out for me—what I was doing to myself, what I was doing to the band," Lauren said, her voice catching ever so slightly. "It was a come-to-Jesus meeting, and I was horrible to them. *Horrible.* I said things. Awful things. Things I'll regret until the day I die. And then..." She stopped as she felt the larger tremble in her voice. Lauren took another deep breath and lifted her chin again—there was no way in hell Martin Sandoval was going to make her cry on live television.

"Then?" Martin's voice was deceptively gentle.

"Then Augie played me a song he'd written. He said it was something he wrote to play at my memorial service. And he wanted to make sure I heard it before I died."

Even acknowledging that song existed ripped open an old wound in her heart, leaving it raw and exposed. Hearing Augie sing that day had broken through all her denial. It had been excruciating. But it had also thrown her the lifeline she needed as she realized that someone still cared if she lived or died, even if she didn't.

At the mention of this mystery song no one had ever heard, she saw the idea form in Martin's head. She put an immediate stop to it: "And no, *you* don't get to hear it. *No one's* ever going to hear it. I made Augie promise me that."

Lauren's sigh was morose, and her shoulders dropped. "I can't pinpoint exactly what about that moment made everything change. But I knew then, right then, that if I didn't fix things—if I didn't get *right*—" She tapped her head. "—I was going to lose everything. I was destroying my talent. Ruining the band. Demolishing my career practically before it even got started. I checked into rehab two days later. When I was finally off the blow and the worst of my withdrawal symptoms were over, I listened to all the albums we had out at the time. One after the other. *Concrete Beach* and *Sunset Highway* are amazing. The third one, *One for the Road*, is good but you can hear the decline—my decline. You can *hear* what the drugs are starting to do to me. And then I listened to *Dog & Pony Show*."

She looked at the floor. "The only real difference between the first one and the last was me on coke. And I promised myself I wasn't going to be one of those singers you see ruined and desolate by the side of the road, sitting all alone in the wreckage of their careers."

Lauren shifted in her seat, straightened her spine, and pulled her shoulders back. She was supposed to be invincible. Perfect. She offered Martin a level stare, daring him to ask another question about her addiction. He got the message.

"I know that's a very personal subject, and I truly appreciate your willingness to be so candid with our audience tonight." Martin looked at the camera. "Right now, we're going to take a quick break to hear from our sponsors, and then we'll be right back with more from Lauren Stone on *Backstage*."

Lauren had never talked—in any interview—about the song Augie wrote. She spent the commercial break with her eyes closed, trying to find an inner place of peace and quiet amid the raging turbulence. It was impossible, not while one person fluffed her hair, another dabbed foundation on her cheek, and a third yelled something about the lighting. The studio audience hushed and she knew the director must have signaled they were going live again.

"Welcome back! Before the break, we were talking with Lauren Stone about the more difficult days during her early career," Martin said. "Lauren, I appreciate you being so forthright. We've discussed some heavy stuff. What do you say we do a quick lightning round of fun questions?"

"Delightful." She hoped the cool tone of her voice made it clear that delight was not the emotion she was feeling.

"Very good, then. Favorite food?"

Lauren didn't hesitate. "Italian and pizza, no question. Best pizza I ever had was from Dom's Pizzeria Supremo near where I grew up. Never found anything else that comes close."

"Pets?"

"I wish. I'd love to have a dog, but it just isn't practical with how unpredictable my schedule is. But that's one reason I support animal shelters that adopt out dogs and cats... If I can't give one a forever home myself, maybe I can help them find one with other people who will love them."

"Tattoos?"

Lauren cracked a smile. "Three at the moment. One on each arm and one on my ankle."

"Secret vice?"

For a split second, Lauren considered saying "meth" just to see the expression on Martin's face, but that would have been all over the gossip sites in an instant. Instead, she said, "Cat videos. Especially cat versus Christmas tree."

"Now, tell me, what is the hardest part of what you do for a living?" He folded his hands in his lap and waited for an answer.

Lauren bit her lip before she responded. "The hardest part? Guess I'd have to say it's hard to have friends. Once you reach a certain point in your career—if you're successful—then you don't know if people want to be your friend because they like you or because they want something from you. Makes it hard to trust people. I miss the friends I had here when I was growing up. They liked me for who I really am, not who they thought I ought to be."

Her words hit Danny like a punch, and the wash of sadness that skimmed Lauren's face made it worse. *What a hard way to live,* he thought as he compared her words to his life. He was surrounded by family and friends. People he trusted. People he loved. He sank deeper into his seat, a frown folding the corners of his mouth.

"Would you consider yourself lonely?" Martin asked Lauren.

"Lonely? Some days, sure." Lauren tilted her head, considering the rest of her answer. "Everyone probably does now and then. But I spend a lot of time with the band, and their families. Especially Augie. I mean, we're cousins and all, but he's more like a brother to me."

"Do you fight like siblings?"

"Oh, yes."

The laugh that underscored Lauren's answer rolled through Danny. He'd missed that sound. Restless, he shifted in his seat again. Out of the corner of his eye, he saw Heather pull her arms in closer against her body.

"What about the rest of the band? Ever any romantic entanglements?"

Once again, Lauren set her jaw. Danny recognized the expression. She had always valued candor, and he could tell she didn't appreciate Martin's efforts to be coy.

"Entanglements? Let's speak plainly here. What you want to know is if I'm sleeping with anyone in the band." She crossed one leg over the other and tapped a finger on the armrest of the chair.

"It isn't uncommon for band members to have relationships with each other," Martin said. "Fleetwood Mac is a classic example of that: there were marriages, divorces, multiple affairs. Those undercurrents had a profound effect on their music and their success. Has that same type of dynamic shaped The Kingmakers?"

Next to Danny, Heather's whisper was sharp. "I bet she's slept with every single one of them."

"Jesus, Heather. She's *related* to one of them."

"Whatever."

Up on the stage, Lauren said, "Not an issue for us."

"Never?"

When Lauren's pause lingered, Martin leaned forward slightly. Danny didn't like it. It was sensationalistic, intrusive. He also, quite frankly, didn't want to know if Lauren had slept with one of her bandmates.

"You're fishing in the wrong pond, Martin," Lauren said. "Maybe for some other bands, the drama fuels them. I don't think it would work that way for us. Wrecking what we have is too big a risk." She shook her head as she spoke.

Lauren kept her last answer short. It wasn't the first time she'd been asked about relationships within the band, and she knew it wouldn't be the last. Whatever may or may not have gone on between her and another Kingmaker, it was her business—not anyone else's.

After she was silent for a few beats, Martin moved on. "Could we persuade you to sing us a song, Lauren?"

Lauren replied that she'd love to when really, she just wanted to say it was about damn time they got to the music. The showrunner had staged a guitar for Lauren. Discreetly tucked next to the loveseat she occupied, it was hidden from the audience. She lifted the instrument, felt its weight and balance, and picked at a couple strings. As she made a small adjustment to the tuning, Martin asked another question.

"What inspires you to write a song?"

Nothing. The thought flashed through Lauren's mind before she answered. "Inspiration's everywhere. Experiences. Observations. Relationships. What matters is the emotion. That's the soul of your song. Doesn't matter if it's joy, despair, love, or hate. Without the emotion, you don't have anything for a listener to connect with."

"That is so very true. The very best songs tell a story with that emotional resonance. The listener can relate because they've felt those same feelings. What are you going to perform for us tonight?"

"Tonight, I'm going to do "Without You," a song from our very first album."

She started to sing. A critic had once described her voice as warm and golden, with a husky quality that never went so far as to be raspy. Lauren had never cared how people described it. Her voice was her voice, and all she really wanted to do was share it with the audience.

"Another cheap motel room, another night on the road. And all I want is someone to hold. In an ocean of strange faces, I'm an army of one. I'm alone without you...."

Through "Without You," Lauren sang a story of being alone and thinking of someone she loved, someone who—no matter the distance—occupied her thoughts and dreams. She painted images of lonely nights in sad hotels, surrounded by strangers. when the only thing that mattered was being with the person she loved. As the notes drifted away, the audience erupted in enthusiastic applause. Lauren looked out at the crowd, but she could only see shapes—the stage lights prevented her from making out any actual faces. Nonetheless, she acknowledged them with a big smile and generous wave.

Martin touched his hand to his heart. "Gorgeous. Just gorgeous."

Lauren inclined her head at the compliment.

"And so evocative. We talked a moment ago about how critical an emotional connection is, and you clearly have one to whoever that song is about."

"I do... well, I did, I guess." Lauren's voice caught on the words. "He's always been very important to me."

From his comfortable chair, Martin beamed as if she'd given the perfect response. Unease settled in Lauren's gut.

"I asked my staff to do a little research, to uncover the inspiration for "Without You." And that's your former high school sweetheart, Danny."

Lauren couldn't see the screen over the stage but could see the small confidence monitor at the front. On it was a picture of her and

Danny from their high school yearbook. She was sitting in front of Danny, and he had his arms wrapped around her, his chin on her shoulder, while she held onto his arms. They were smiling and looked happy—and so very young.

Her heart jumped into her throat.

"That's a picture I haven't seen in a long time." Her voice was soft, filled with the fondness of timeworn memories.

"Well, then I'm very excited to be able to facilitate a bit of a reunion." Martin lit up. "Tonight, I'd like to welcome a special guest in our audience..." Martin turned in his chair to look out at the audience, and as he did, a secondary set of lights flared to life.

Lauren couldn't breathe.

Danny was sitting in the front. He looked a little older, but she'd recognize him anywhere with his square jaw and dark hair. What she didn't see was his easy smile—instead Danny looked stunned, and next to him was a blond woman who looked apoplectic. On his other side was a young girl, around sixteen years old, and a boy who was Danny's spitting image. Lauren realized Maggie was there, and Richie, too. They all looked utterly surprised at the light and the applause, and then—just as suddenly—the light dimmed.

Lauren twisted in her chair to impale Martin with an enraged glare.

CHAPTER
TEN

Outraged didn't even begin to describe how Lauren felt. But they were on live television and making a scene would make the situation worse. She wrestled her fury down, but it continued churning below the surface. Martin asked her several more innocuous questions in a in a clear effort to mollify her anger. Her answers were cordial, but she barely remembered what she said. The only thing she wanted was for the show to end.

Finally, Martin adjusted to face the main camera. "That's going to do it for this edition of *Backstage*. Lauren, thank you so much for spending the evening with us and sharing a little of yourself and your music."

"My pleasure, Martin." She managed to sound sincere.

"That does it for tonight. Join us next time when we sit down with rap sensation Deion D."

The house lights came up and the "live" sign went dark. The producer yelled from the back that the show was a wrap. Lauren scanned the audience—hoping for a fleeting glimpse of Danny before he left—but she couldn't pick him out of the crowd. Martin's proffered hand went ignored as she stalked to the edge of the set, seeking a modicum of privacy. Her heart hammered in her chest like it was trying to shatter her ribs and escape.

An intern scrambled to remove Lauren's lapel mic. His hands trembled, and he bobbled the transmitter. She heard Martin approaching from behind, the flat soles of his dress shoes tapping on the hard floor. She rounded on him, seething.

"What the actual fuck, Martin? How *dare* you—"

The intern skittered away like he was avoiding sniper fire.

"—Lauren—"

"—Don't interrupt me! Bad enough you bring up shit you *know* I don't like talking about. But this little stunt?" Lauren got right in Martin's face. "I've got a really long memory for people who screw me over."

Martin held up his hands in surrender, a plea for mercy. "Lauren. Lauren, I am so sorry. It was my understanding you knew about this. That you'd asked for it."

Her eyebrows shot up. Asked for this? Anyone who knew her at all would know she hated surprises. "The Padovanos were clearly in the dark, too! Why would I do something like that to people I care about? Did you *see* their faces? They were horrified!"

"I had no idea I'd be surprising them. Or you. I would have never..."

In the face of Martin's clear chagrin and regret, Lauren's indignation cooled an iota. He was obviously mortified, and while he was known to be a tough interviewer, he didn't have the reputation of being an ambush artist.

"Then what grade-A genius came up with this?" Lauren asked. Before Martin could respond, she came up with the answer herself. "Goddamn it. It was Roberta, wasn't it?"

"She told me and my producer that everyone was aware, but you wanted to have it look like a surprise," Martin said. "I am beyond embarrassed this happened, and just as livid as you—" The way he wrung his hands reminded Lauren of a little old lady.

"—I *highly* doubt that." Frustrated, Lauren ran her hands through her hair.

"I thought since she was your rep... I shouldn't have assumed. I should have verified with you. This is not how I run my show, Lauren. I apologize—"

"Fine." Lauren offered a single word response to Martin's apology before she stormed through the studio shouting Roberta's name. Martin and three security guards followed hot on her heels. It didn't take long to spot Roberta off to the side of the stage. She was waving her arms as if she was hurrying someone along.

"What kind of stunt was that, Roberta?" Lauren asked as she got closer. "You ambushed me, you ambushed Martin—and you certainly ambushed the Padovanos!" Lauren didn't care that she was shouting or that several people stopped and stared.

Roberta made a dismissive *pish* noise. "You're overreacting. The press will eat this up with a spoon. Now, say hello to—"

"Do *not* change the subject! I've warned you before about stunts like this." Lauren wasn't having any part of Roberta's bullshit, and she didn't even look at whoever it was she was about to be introduced to. Right now, she didn't really care.

"This was an *opportunity*, Lauren." Roberta's voice took on a scolding tone that did nothing but enrage Lauren further. "I'm your publicist and that means getting you in front of the press. Remember, there is no such thing—"

"Don't finish that sentence! Just. Don't." Lauren held up her palm. "There *is* such a thing as bad publicity, and when you waylay an unsuspecting family like it was my idea? That makes *me* look like an ass."

"Lauren, really. You're being a bit of a diva."

Lauren's eyes doubled in size. "Excuse me?"

Roberta's demeanor was bored tolerance as she started to turn away, as if she was ignoring a demanding toddler. It was the last straw for Lauren.

"A diva? *Are you fucking kidding me?* That's it, Roberta—you're fired!"

The word "fired" got Roberta's attention, and her face contorted in shocked disbelief.

"What?"

"I said you're *fired*. Now get *out*! And enjoy explaining to Tony why he's lost one of his biggest clients." Lauren pointed imperiously toward the exit sign even though she really didn't have the authority to throw Roberta out.

For a moment, the publicist glared and stood her ground. Then a security guard stepped forward. Lauren was the guest—and the star—and Martin was gesticulating wildly that the guard should do whatever Lauren wanted. He squared his shoulders and gestured to Roberta.

"Ma'am. If you'll come with me?"

"Don't you 'ma'am' me!" Roberta's shrill voice grated.

The guard put his hands on his hips. Roberta blustered, her face scarlet, and stomped to the door. Lauren stared daggers at her back until she vanished from sight. After, a sigh escaped her and she looked down, shaking her head. This interview had turned into a complete disaster—and she was sure it, and the incident just now, would be all over the media in short order.

In her peripheral vision, Lauren noticed a group of people. She'd been so focused on dealing with Roberta, she hadn't really noticed them. It must have been who Roberta was about to introduce before. A flush of embarrassment crawled up her neck. She took one more deep breath to calm herself and turned towards them. Then everything stopped, her words of apology melting into nothing, as she found herself looking right at Danny.

Lauren froze. A knot of people surrounded him, but they faded into the background—his face was the only face she saw.

"Danny..."

"Hi, Lauren."

"I'm so sorry about all this—I had no idea you were here

tonight," she said. "Or that Roberta was planning that stunt. I would have never—*never*—agreed to it if I'd known."

"S'okay. I had a feeling you were as surprised as we were. Your eyes were the size of baseballs."

At the sound of his voice, Lauren's face softened, and her eyes grew shiny. After all these years, he was right in front of her. He looked great. There were more laugh lines around his eyes, and the barest hint of silver was scattered through his dark hair. But there was no mistaking that it was her Danny, with his broad shoulders and that wide, easy smile she remembered so well.

She cleared her throat, unsure of what to do, and it seemed Danny didn't know either. Shaking his hand seemed awkward. What she really wanted was to throw her arms around him and hug him, but she hesitated, uncertain how he'd react.

Danny solved that problem for her. "How about a hug? For old time's sake." He opened his arms just enough to invite her in, and Lauren walked into them without hesitation.

She closed her eyes, savoring the feeling of being wrapped in his arms again. She felt solid, grounded, safe. It was like a piece of her life that had been off kilter was finally back in the right place. When she opened her eyes again, a blond woman was staring at them, completely stone-faced, and Lauren realized she was probably Danny's wife. Lauren stepped back but knew their hug had been closer, and lasted longer, than it should have.

"It's really good to see you," Lauren said to him. "How have you been?"

"I'm good. You sounded great tonight."

"Thank you, I can't believe— "

The blond woman pushed forward. "I'm Heather. Danny's *wife.*"

Lauren didn't flinch at Heather's tartness; she'd dealt with jealous girlfriends her whole career. What did pique her curiosity, however, was how confounded Danny looked.

"It is very nice to meet you," Lauren said, the sweetness of her voice a counterpoint to Heather's vinegar. Heather muttered something Lauren couldn't quite make out and offered a perfunctory handshake. After, she slid a possessive arm through Danny's, claiming her territory, and tossed Lauren a look that was nothing short of hostile.

Jesus, if she was any more territorial, she'd pee on him, Lauren thought. She offered Heather one more smile and refocused on Danny.

"And these must be your boys," Lauren said. She still couldn't believe how much the oldest two resembled their father, and she still felt chagrined that they'd seen her argument with—no, her lambasting of—Roberta. And that she'd dropped an f-bomb in front of them.

"This is Lucas, Matty, and Tommy."

Lucas and Matty shook her hand while Tommy waved shyly. Next to Lucas, a girl with short dark hair looked like she was about to explode with energy.

"I'm guessing you're Cole?" Lauren said. "You did a great job on your paper."

"I am! You read it? Really? And you *liked* it? Oh, it is *so* great to meet you! This is just, wow, I don't even know."

Cole's excitement and enthusiasm were infectious, and Lauren felt the tension in her shoulders drop away. "Of course I read it. It has a nice balance of highlights and lowlights from my career without making it a gossip tale. I hope the Sisters gave you a good grade."

"An A+." Cole's smile was a touch smug.

"She's her mother's daughter, I see," Lauren said to Maggie.

"In more ways than one," Maggie said.

"Me and Lucas were talking earlier," Cole said. "It's so cool you're going to record in New York. You're going to do all of it here and not in LA?"

"We are. I'm sure you know we're working with Fitz McCallum. He likes having all the artists in the same place to record, and his studio's here. So we're here, too. I've got a little more writing to do, and then we'll start doing serious work in the studio."

"How long will you be here?" Cole asked.

"Probably at least a few months," Lauren said, ignoring the specter of her writing block as it hovered in the back of her mind, taunting her. "You know, you should come to the studio one day and watch a session."

Cole's whole face lit up like she'd just been handed a million dollars. She clasped her hands in front of her. "Oh, Mom, can we? Please? That would be so awesome."

"We'll see. Depends on school and when things are happening." Maggie's smile was affectionate.

"There will be vacations coming up."

"Don't push your luck, young lady."

Cole surrendered. "Shutting up now!"

As the group laughed, Lauren locked eyes with Richie. He'd been so kind to her when she was a teen, and the sentimental memory made her well up a little. His hair was silver and his middle portlier than she remembered, but he still had a sparkle in his eye and the charming smile that his son had inherited. He didn't even ask, he just pulled her in for a tight bear hug.

The pleasant chatter continued, and Lauren asked after the rest of the family. Richie said that when Joey, his youngest son, got out of the Army, he was going to join the family business, helping to run Richie's small string of jewelry stores. Lauren also learned Maggie was divorced and about her job at Bayard College. Cole shared what colleges she was considering applying for—none of which included Bayard, much to her mother's clear dismay. Lauren made sure to ask how Danny's mother was doing. He said she was doing well and offered some vague excuse for why she hadn't come to the show. Lauren knew Deb was perfectly fine and was just as happy she hadn't come. Enduring Deb's disapproval would have made the night's debacle so much worse.

Before Lauren could ask any more questions, Heather's fingers tightened, talon-like, on Danny's arm. "We should get going," she said. "The boys need to get their sleep."

"Mom!" Lucas sounded mortified.

"Heather!" Danny's tone was a rebuke as they exchanged acrimonious glares. Their dynamic made Lauren wonder what was really going on with them.

"I understand," she said to Danny. "I'm sorry we didn't have longer to catch up. Hard to cover almost twenty years in twenty minutes. But it really was so good to see you." She almost asked Danny if he could stay so they could talk more, but she refrained.

Without even thinking, she and Danny hugged again. As he pulled her close, Danny whispered in her ear. "I've missed you. More than you know."

She closed her eyes and let her cheek press against his. "I've missed you, too," she whispered back.

After a final round of goodbyes, Lauren watched one of Martin's security officers usher the Padovanos to the exit. Another guard caught her eye with a subtle wave. He told her that her car was there. She nodded to acknowledge she'd heard him but lingered backstage for a long time.

CHAPTER ELEVEN

Just before 8:30 in the morning the next day, the wind and rain chased Augie into Velocity Studios. He shook the water from his shoulders and muttered to himself about better weather in California. He was surprised to find Tisha ensconced behind the reception desk on a Sunday, but before he could even say hello, the sound of a muffled f-bomb drifted down the hall.

"What time did she get here?"

"About six-thirty, I think," Tisha said. "She grunted a hello when I saw her. Other than that, it's just been, well, *that*."

"And you're here on a Sunday... why?" Augie selected one of the coat hooks—some trendy and modern triangle-shaped pieces of walnut along the wall—and hung his coat.

"Favor for Fitz. In case you all need anything."

"You see Sandoval last night?"

"I did. Great interview until, well... they both looked like they'd seen a ghost." Tisha dropped a folder into the file cabinet and closed the drawer.

"I have half a mind to rip Sandoval a new one myself, but I'm sure Lauren took care of that." Augie knew his cousin wasn't just going to forgive and forget something like this. But Lauren's ability to hold onto a grudge with terrier-like tenacity wasn't the real reason Augie was concerned. That worry was one hundred percent centered on Danny.

He remembered how much Lauren had loved Danny, how many regrets she had. He also knew how much the end of their relationship had fueled Lauren's descent into addiction—trying to put Danny behind her was the main reason she'd careened through a spate of failed relationships and spun out of control. She'd been looking for a way to forget him, to fill the empty part of her where Danny used to be. And as she'd so aptly remarked the night before, she'd filled it with all the wrong people and all the wrong things. And Augie'd had a ringside seat to the whole debacle.

Tisha got up from her desk and brushed some invisible lint off her artfully ripped jeans. "I'm making coffee. You want a cup?"

"Love some."

"Like hers?"

Augie scrunched up his face. "Hell, no, dude. Black with one sugar. None of that extra light extra sweet BS."

"You got it, hon."

As he appeared in the door of the conference room, Lauren flung her pen down in disgust. He didn't even get the chance to say good morning.

"It was Roberta. She set the whole fiasco up, and I fired her ass last night."

It was a statement, a challenge, as Lauren dared him to disagree with her. But Augie didn't take the bait. He'd always had a good sense of how to handle his cousin. His level head and mellow attitude often softened her drive and sharpness. Instead, he answered her in funny, cartoonish voices, playing both parts of the conversation.

"Good morning, Augie. How are you? ... I'm good, Lauren. My mom said to say hello to you. ... That's nice. How's she doing?"

"Point taken," Lauren said, humbled. "Let's start over: Hi, Augie. How are you?"

"Not bad. How are *you*?" Augie ignored all the chairs and hopped up to sit on the edge of the table.

"I can't write a goddamn song to save my life."

It wasn't the answer he expected, but he was glad she'd said it. Lauren had been evasive about her songs, and he'd wondered if something was wrong. But that was a discussion for later.

"You sounded great singing 'Without You.'"

Lauren didn't respond.

"You also told Sandoval about the song I wrote you," Augie said. "You've *never* talked about it before. You never even told *Carolyn* about it." He slid back on the table a little so he could let his feet swing.

"I know." Working her jaw, Lauren looked anywhere but at him.

"Why now?"

"I don't know." She pursed her lips. "Guess I was just tired of the game. Everyone always wants to know. Now they do."

"They're not going to stop asking about it." His fingers tapped out a beat on the table.

"I can pretend for at least a little while," she answered.

Her response didn't make him feel better, but he pressed on. "So, how are you doing with the rest of it? You didn't answer any of my texts last night."

She covered her face with her hands for a moment, then abruptly jumped up and stalked over to the tall window. Lauren pressed her palms on the glass and looked out.

Augie waited, noticing that her reflection in the glass looked worn out.

"I'm angry," she said. "Confused. Embarrassed. You should have seen the looks on their faces, Aug—they all thought I'd set them up. Even Danny."

She turned to face him and for a moment, she looked sad and lost, but then her temper flared again. "I let Roberta have it right there in the studio and threw her out. You should have seen her when I fired her. Tony's been calling but I *don't* want to talk to him."

Augie nodded. Tony Vaughn owned Red Ridge Entertainment, the firm that ostensibly managed and represented the band. Augie didn't think they should leave Red Ridge, but he wasn't sorry to be rid of Roberta. But like Lauren's songwriting issues, keeping Red Ridge Entertainment on the payroll was a conversation that could wait.

"I'll take care of Tony," he said. "Did you talk to Danny or anyone after? I saw Maggie in the audience."

"I did. I didn't realize they'd been brought backstage. They got front-row seats to me ripping Roberta new one." A satisfied smile flashed across her face before it morphed to embarrassed. "Even Danny's kids."

"I'm sure it's not the first time they've heard someone curse. How are they all?"

"Good. Maggie's daughter seems like a nice kid. Definitely a straight-A-overachiever type. Anyway, Cole wrote the paper I told you about. I invited them to come by the studio to see us record." Lauren came and sat on the table next to Augie.

"How was it seeing Danny?" Augie asked, finally getting to the question he'd wanted to ask all along.

Everything about Lauren brightened. "It was great! He hardly looks any different. It took all of, like, two minutes for it to feel just like old times. I could have talked to him all night."

"Good. Glad it wasn't awkward, considering the circumstances." It was a lie. Augie very much wished it had been awkward and uncomfortable.

"You going to see him again?" He hoped she'd say no.

"We didn't talk about that, but I'd love to."

Augie didn't want to go any further down the rabbit hole they were circling, so he changed the subject. "Stevie's grandparents are arriving from London today, so he's getting them settled. DJ and Ox went to Atlantic City. They'll be back later tonight. But I had a feeling you might be here today..."

"So, you wanted to check in on me."

"No-yes." Augie blended the two words. "Since it's just you and me today, anything you want to work on?"

"Nothing specific. I've had a couple ideas rattling around, but I can't get them into any kind of form I like. Not even rough ones." Lauren's knuckles whitened as she tightened her fist. Tension rolled off her in waves.

"Seriously, dude. Everything okay?"

"Fine."

Her answer was too fast, too sharp.

"Was there something *you* wanted to do?" she asked.

"Not really." Augie shook his head. "I'm going to experiment a little." He slid off the table just as Tisha appeared in the doorway with his coffee. "Ah! Caffeine! You are a goddess, Tisha."

"Sweet talker. Can I get you anything, Lauren?"

"I'm not really singing today, so another coffee would be great if you don't mind. Extra—"

"—Extra light, extra sweet. I got you, girl."

Lauren smiled. "And Tisha? I'm sorry I was such a bitch this morning."

"Don't you even think twice about it, hon. Everyone's a bitch until the third cup." Tisha winked and sauntered out of the room.

CHAPTER TWELVE

Danny was still half-stunned by everything that unfolded at the Sandoval show, and Sunday passed in a blur. The whole family typically attended the mid-day Mass at St. Catherine's, followed by the traditional late-afternoon family dinner after church. This meal was one step short of a brawl—with Danny's mother vocally insisting the entire stunt must have been Lauren's idea and Danny vehemently defending her.

After dessert, Danny and Heather packed the boys into the car and—by some miracle—managed to get most of the way home before they started to argue. It started with chores that hadn't been done, then took a radical turn sideways into the month's budget. After the boys went to bed, it escalated and was about everything except for the elephant in the room. Danny was relegated to sleeping on the sofa that night, and when the sun came up, he left the house as soon as he could after he saw the boys.

The moment he walked into the squad room, the comments started. He was bombarded from all sides, fellow detectives and cops calling him a TV star and lobbing questions about his famous ex-girlfriend. He walked the gauntlet with gritted teeth.

"Give it a rest already!" he said to the room in general. "Christ, don't you guys have anything better to do? Like solving a crime or something?" He dropped into his chair, muttering an obscenity under his breath.

His longtime partner, Jason Matsui, leaned back in his own chair and put his hands behind his head. "Did you really think no one would bring it up?"

"How the hell does *everyone* know?" Danny's voice was one step short of a snarl. His personal life was his business, not something he wanted on display for the world to see.

"You really don't get it, do you? You do know the reaming Lauren gave that woman is all over social media? You can see you and Heather and Maggie in the background."

"Friggin' wonderful."

"How'd Heather take it?"

Danny scowled. "How do you think? She's pissed. She says she's not, but she is. I spent the night on the sofa." Even this morning Heather had been on a slow boil, but she'd insisted that nothing was wrong, even though they'd fought like cats and dogs the night before.

"You seem to be taking this whole stunt pretty well." Jason pulled his chair closer to his desk and adjusted his computer screen to account for the morning sun glare.

"*Lauren didn't do this.*" Danny heard the anger in his own voice. He knew Lauren and that wasn't her style. He opened the top drawer of his desk and popped the top off a bottle of ibuprofen, then downed three of them.

Jason was about to ask another question when their captain came out of his office.

"Hey, rock-n-roll Romeo, get in here. You too, Matsui. Got a case for you."

"I'm never going to hear the end of this," Danny muttered under his breath.

CHAPTER THIRTEEN

Lauren sat on her balcony nibbling at a bagel while she drifted in an ocean of memories. Danny factored into a lot of them. She couldn't help thinking about him, but she also wandered through memories of growing up and things she'd promised herself over the years. She'd kept most of them, but it drew her thoughts to the end of the Sandoval show.

While she hadn't used the word "promise" when she invited Cole to visit the studio, it felt like she'd made one. But she wasn't sure if Cole thought the invitation was sincere, and that bothered her. She glanced over at the autographed CD case on the table. It would be easy enough to mail it, along with a note, to Cole, but it really wasn't Cole she wanted to talk with.

She spent a little time strumming on her guitar, just listening for the notes. They had a day off from studio work today. An accident had taken out the power in the area around Velocity and, according to Tisha, it wouldn't be restored until at least dinnertime.

Just before lunch, Lauren walked down the hallway in Bayard College's admissions office. She was dressed in jeans and a NY Rangers t-shirt, sporting a ponytail pulled through the back of a tattered old baseball hat with a faded sunrise logo on the front. A small bag dangled from her fingers. She adjusted the hat, letting her finger run over the frayed edge. It was overdue to be thrown out, but Lauren loved it for some odd reason and refused to part with it. She kept the brim pulled down and her sunglasses on, and the few people she met in the hall didn't pay her much attention.

Stopping outside Maggie's office, Lauren paused. She scolded herself for her cold feet and rapped softly on the doorframe.

Maggie glanced up. "May I help you?"

Lauren pushed her hat up and took off her glasses.

"Lauren!"

Maggie's surprised tone was flavored with concern, and Lauren hesitated again, wondering if she'd misstepped. "I'm sorry to just drop in. Am I interrupting?"

"No, no. Please, have a seat. I do have an appointment—" She peeked at the clock. "—in about fifteen minutes, but I'm free until then. What's up?"

"First, Augie asked me to say hello," Lauren said as she sat in the guest chair. "But I really wanted to stop by about my invitation to have Cole come see us record. We didn't really get into details, but I wanted to make sure you both knew the invitation was serious. And it totally extends to you as well. The rest of the family, too, if they're interested." Lauren knew she was talking too quickly.

"That's a very generous offer. I'll give it some thought," Maggie said.

Lauren offered Maggie a business card. "This is the number at Velocity. Tisha will help set everything up if you decide to come."

"Seems like an awful lot of effort just to give me a phone number," Maggie said. "You could have just called the college for my number." She rummaged in a file drawer to find her wallet and tucked the card inside.

"When have I ever done anything the easy way?" Lauren asked as she felt the heat rise in her cheeks and neck at the gentle rebuke. "But it also gave me an excuse to hand deliver this."

She handed the bag to Maggie. Inside was a CD of The Kingmakers' first album, *Concrete Beach*. Autographs from the band were scrawled across the cover art in silver ink.

Maggie turned it over in her hands. "Signed by the band? She'll be over the moon."

"So many people download these days, but you can't autograph a digital file." While Lauren appreciated the innovation of digital music files, she preferred physical CDs and albums. Being able to hold it, to look at the cover art, read the lyrics and jacket notes always gave her a deeper sense of connection with the bands she loved. She wanted The Kingmakers fans to feel the same.

"And it is totally up to you," Lauren continued. "But like I said, the invitation to the studio is for real. I just didn't want Cole to think I forgot."

Maggie laughed. "Trust me. You might forget, but Cole will *not*."

Lauren stood up from the chair. She'd taken up enough of Maggie's time and she was due at Augie's soon.

"Can I ask you a question?" Maggie asked.

"Sure."

"The other day, you said the hardest thing about your job was not being able to make friends. That you always wondered if you could trust people. Do you regret choosing this life?"

Lauren faltered. Her career took a higher toll sometimes than she cared to admit. There were exceptions, but she'd learned the hard way that most people had ulterior motives.

"Regret choosing music? Never," Lauren said. "I love what I do. I can't imagine doing anything else. Other regrets? I have a few. Everyone probably does. One of my biggest is losing your brother. Sometimes I think letting go of Danny was the biggest mistake I ever made."

Lauren hadn't planned to be so bluntly honest, and Maggie's mouth formed a small "O" of surprise. Lauren reached out and picked up a photo from the collection on Maggie's desk. In it was Danny, Heather, and their sons. A happy, domestic scene.

"How is he, Maggie? Really?" Lauren looked away, knowing it was unfair to put Danny's sister in that position.

Maggie paused longer than she should have, and Lauren knew she wasn't going to get the whole story. "He's good. But I think Cole's paper brought up a lot of memories he hasn't thought about in a long time."

"It did for me, too." It was a half-truth. She'd thought about those memories over the years, more than she should have, but the past few weeks had brought them back in high-definition color.

"But he really is good," Maggie said. "He loves being a cop. He loves being a dad—those boys are his whole world."

Lauren gazed down at the photo. "I don't think I could've given him this life. And my world? It would have been hard for him. Maybe too hard. But... I wish... I wish I had tried. That *we'd* tried harder. Not just assumed the things we wanted were too different."

"You were both kids back then," Maggie said.

"Maybe. Doesn't really matter now, I guess. But I'm glad he's happy."

A flash of trepidation danced across Maggie's face when Lauren said that, but she didn't elaborate. Lauren looked at the photo for another moment before she put it back on the desk.

"I've taken enough of your time. Good to see you, Maggie." Lauren stood up. When she got to the door, she stopped and looked back. "I really am glad Danny's happy... but I wish we'd fought harder for each other back then. Things might have been different if we did."

CHAPTER FOURTEEN

After leaving Maggie's, Lauren's mood turned melancholy. What she'd told Maggie was true—she couldn't have given Danny the life he had now. But could they have made a life together in her world? She'd been plagued by doubts, regrets, and what-ifs about their relationship for years.

Back at her posh apartment, she sat on the balcony overlooking the park and soaked up some sun. She scribbled ideas in her notebook. A few of the lyrics had promise, but none had the soul she was looking for—that still eluded her.

Finally, Lauren decided that if she was feeling so damn nostalgic, a trip to the old neighborhood was in order. Maybe she could ferret out some inspiration there. She spent the afternoon driving around. She cruised past St. Catherine's, stores where she used to shop, the mall and movie theater where she had hung out with friends. She sat in the parking lot for a long time, remembering all the times she'd gone there with Danny. And all the time they spent making out in his car.

Her growling stomach interrupted her reminiscing. With a glance at her watch, Lauren realized it was later than she thought.

She knew, however, exactly what she was going to have for dinner. A fifteen-minute drive later, she pulled into an open parking spot across the street from Dom's Pizzeria Supremo.

The front of the shop was unassuming: a simple clear glass door sandwiched between two large windows. The window on the left had *Dom's Pizzeria Supremo* in bold red letters, and the one on the right sported a neon "open" sign and a few posters stuck on the glass. Framing all of it were two sections of brick that separated Dom's from the stores on either side.

A little brass bell chimed when Lauren opened the door. It was like stepping back in time—nothing had really changed. The tables and chairs were the exact same ones she remembered. The counter and the menu hanging above it were the same, as were the pizza ovens lining the back wall. Behind her sunglasses, Lauren welled up for a second before she brushed away the sentimentality.

Big Dom Bonati was at the register. "Ready to order, young lady?"

"My usual," Lauren said. "A slice of pepperoni and a slice of the *bianca*."

Dom scribbled the order down. As he ripped the piece of paper off the pad, he really looked at Lauren. Her smile grew wider as he paused.

"I don't believe my eyes!"

"Been a long time, Big Dom."

He hustled out from behind the counter and kissed Lauren on both cheeks before dragging her to a wall, where he proudly showed her a picture. It was Lauren when she was about sixteen, playing her guitar on his sidewalk. She'd autographed it back then, telling Dom that someday it would be worth a lot of money.

"You kept it," she said. Seeing that old photo, so full of hope and promise, gave her a warm feeling.

"Kept it? I treasure it!"

"Hey, give me one of your menus," she said.

Dom didn't question her. Lauren took the menu and plucked a

Sharpie marker out of his pocket. She wrote, *I came all the way from LA for a slice of Dom's!* across the menu and then signed her name with a flourish. Dom beamed and promised to add that to the wall as soon as he bought a proper frame. Lauren tried to pay for her slices, but Dom was having none of it. She found a booth to sit in and devoured the food when it arrived—and then Dom brought her two more slices.

Danny pulled into the parking lot behind Dom's. Three generations of the Bonati family had run this place. It had been, and still was, the one and only place to have pizza as far as Danny was concerned. At sixty-five, Big Dom still ran the business, which he'd taken over from his own father years before.

The Mets and Yankees were playing, and Danny was on his way to watch them with his father—it was a tradition for the Padovano boys to enjoy the first game of a Subway Series together. He looked forward to the day when Joey would be out of the Army and back in New York so he could join them again. Until then, it was Danny and his father, and tonight, he had offered to stop for the pizza on his way over. Normally, he'd bring all three boys with him. But they'd gotten into hot water for playing a video game that he and Heather had declared off-limits and were grounded.

A pimply-faced teen loitered behind the register. He eyed the badge looped around Danny's neck and stuttered a little as he took the order. Danny guessed he had a baggie of weed stashed on him somewhere, but he didn't feel like busting the kid's balls. In the back, he could hear Dom's deep bassoon of a voice as he lectured one of the workers about the art of pizza sauce—*You don't wipe it like you're painting a wall! Per l'amor di Dio! You swirl it. Swirl it!*

Then another voice grabbed his attention. "Detective, I have an alibi, I swear! Don't put the cuffs on me!" Even though she sat at a booth in the back, he could see the mischief sparkling in Lauren's eyes. Then she smiled. That warm, beautiful smile. Danny felt it all the way down in his toes. He walked over to the booth.

"What are you doing here?" he asked, leaning an elbow on the booth corner.

"Like I could resist getting a slice at Dom's," she said. "Join me?" She gestured to the open half of the booth.

They chatted for a few more minutes, smiling and joking. Without even realizing it, both leaned forward, elbows on the table, heads closer together, so their conversation could be quieter, more intimate. Danny couldn't believe how easily they slipped back into their comfortable cadence. Later, he wouldn't remember exactly what they said, only how amazing it had felt to be with her again.

"Oh ho! Look at the two of you. Inseparable, just the way it used to be." Big Dom's booming voice filled the room.

As his boisterous laugh enveloped them, Danny realized how close they were to each other. He drew back, an abrupt gesture that startled Lauren. His cheeks warmed, and Danny could only assume his face was as scarlet as hers. How many times had they sat there, eating pizza, holding hands? Sat there talking about things they'd do together?

"Meeting here to reminisce? Ah." Dom tapped his heart with his hand.

"No, this was total chance." Danny regretted how defensive he sounded.

Big Dom just nodded and smiled. "Well, the next time you want to catch up over some pizza, you come here—just like old times—and the pizza will be on me."

After Dom went back to the ovens, Lauren finished the last few bites of her pizza as they called Danny's order number. Disappointment and guilt buffeted him. He wanted to stay. For the first time in a long time, he'd lost himself in the moment. Forgotten, just for a few minutes, about his responsibilities and worries.

Yes, he and Lauren had been lovers, but they'd also been friends. Right now, he felt like he was talking to an old friend again. And there was a lot more he wanted to talk about. More than he might have suspected a few weeks ago.

"Looks like your order's ready."

"Yeah..."

He saw the discontent flash across her face. Then she brightened. "Gimme your phone."

"What?"

"You know, the thing people use to take selfies?" She grinned and purloined the phone from his hand. Going right to the contacts, she added her name and cell number. She handed the phone back and pulled her own out. With a few taps, she added an entry for him.

"Here, give me your number," she said. "I'm sure I'll have some breaks from the studio. Maybe we can catch up a little more?"

"That'd be great."

Danny punched his cell in and handed the phone back to Lauren. The kid from the cash register called his name again. He was reluctant to leave but couldn't bring cold pizza to the game.

"I gotta run. Subway series tonight."

"Padovano family tradition," she said.

"But I would like to catch up more," he said. "Like for real, not just a five-minute chat."

"I'd like that."

Danny grabbed both pizzas and left the shop. As his feet hit the sidewalk, he looked back over his shoulder once and then walked to his car, his emotions even more conflicted than before.

CHAPTER FIFTEEN

The old dishtowel was stained, and it just got worse as Danny wiped his hands on it. He gave the washer hose a critical look. He was glad Heather had noticed the connection was corroded—a flooded bathroom wasn't a headache he needed to deal with.

"It should be all set now." He tossed the rag into the laundry pile.

"Okay."

Heather started sorting the laundry into three different piles. The silence following her one-word answer lingered long enough that Danny gave up and walked into the kitchen. He wasn't expecting a tickertape parade for a simple plumbing fix, but something beyond the chilly reception he'd gotten from the moment he woke up would have been nice. Filling a glass at the faucet, he gulped the water down. His wife followed and grabbed the dirty dish towels from the oven handle.

"How was last night?" she asked.

"Fine." The one-word response was petty, and he knew it.

"Have your usual?"

"Yeah, couple pies from Dom's."

"Nothing exciting?"

"Game was a little dull actually."

Heather turned from the stove and put a hand on her hip. "Were you even going to bother telling me you had dinner with your ex?"

"I had dinner with my dad."

"Don't lie to me!" Heather's cheeks and neck reddened. She pulled out her phone and thrust it in Danny's face. "Rachel saw the two of you."

On the screen was a text message that said, *<Hey, H! Was just passing Dom's. Saw Danny chatting with THE Lauren Stone. It must be so cool having a famous friend!>* followed by four starstruck emojis. Underneath it was a photo. Taken from outside the pizzeria, the glass distorted the image a little, but it was clearly Danny and Lauren. They were smiling and undoubtedly having a good time.

"Oh, for Christ's sake." Danny flung his arms up in the air. "She was there having a slice when I came in. We sat and talked for twenty minutes while my pizzas cooked. Then I went to my father's."

"You should have told me!"

"When was I supposed to tell you? You were asleep when I got home, and this is practically the first time you've talked to me today!" Danny's shoulders and neck ached from the tension. No matter what he did, he was always wrong.

"And I didn't know I had to report all my comings and goings to you," he continued. "Then I guess I should tell you I talked to Rachel at the grocery store last week. Oh, and Mrs. Mulroney? I helped her take her groceries from the car to her door, too."

Mrs. Mulroney was their 82-year-old neighbor across the street.

Heather started to speak and then paused. She held up a finger at him, and once she gathered herself, said, "I shouldn't be finding out from my best friend—over a text—that you're hanging out with another woman."

"I wasn't 'hanging out with another woman,'" Danny said, air quoting the last few words. "I was having a conversation with a friend. Maybe Rachel needs to mind her own fucking business."

"And maybe you need to be honest with me about sleeping with your ex!"

"What the— Sleeping with—?" Danny's mouth dropped open. Was Heather out of her mind? "What are you talking about?"

"You're sleeping with her, aren't you?"

"*No!*" Danny was offended. He wasn't perfect—he had his own issues and demons, just like everyone did. But he was married, and that meant something to him regardless of any regrets he might have. Did she really think so little of him?

"I saw the way you looked at her the other day. And the photo Rachel took? You look pretty cozy." Heather's face was blotchy, her eyes shiny.

"The Sandoval show was the first time I've been in the same room as Lauren since high school." Danny didn't care that he was shouting. "When exactly was I supposed to be sleeping with her?"

"You're always working late—"

"—Stop! Just stop! How can you even say that? I work late because we have private school tuition for three kids, a mortgage. Jesus, Heather, we're *married*!" Danny was furious at the accusation. He stormed away before he could say anything he truly regretted.

Heather was so angry she could barely think. The rational, reasonable part of her mind tried to interrupt, to remind her that Danny—despite the troubles they were having—wasn't a bad husband. Remind her that she was basing her thoughts on fear and not on facts. Then she thought of the song Lauren sang during the Sandoval show and the way Danny watched her on stage.

The sharp stab of jealousy gave way to anger, but she wasn't sure whom she was mad at. Lauren for having such a strong emotional connection to Danny after all these years? Danny for still having feelings for his ex—and hiding them? Cole for writing the stupid paper to begin with? Or herself, for playing the part of the fool so artfully?

CHAPTER SIXTEEN

The Kingmakers made decent progress the next time they were in the studio together. Lauren ignored the fact that they were working on a song Stevie had been developing and not something she'd come up with. At least she tried to. Although most of their songs were written and performed by Lauren, there were always two or three that came from other band members. Still, it needled her to no end.

A lunch of steamed chicken and mixed vegetables with a small side of rice took the hangry edge off for Lauren, and she finished it with a banana from the platter of fresh fruit Fitz always had available. Leaning back on the sofa, Lauren put her feet up on the coffee table and closed her eyes. Before long, her mind was wandering through the replay of her unexpected meetup with Danny.

"What are you smiling about?" Augie asked.

Lauren opened one eye. "Thanks for messing with my Zen."

"You're about as Zen as a cat in a room full of rocking chairs."

Lauren laughed. Sometimes Augie knew her far too well. "Actually, I went and got pizza at Dom's the other day—"

"—And you didn't call me?" Augie looked like she'd kicked him. "*Dude.*"

"And I ran into Danny while I was there."

"Oh." Augie's voice was painfully neutral.

"Don't start with me," Lauren said. Couldn't he just be happy that she'd had a good time catching up with an old friend? She decided not to share that she'd exchanged numbers with Danny.

"What? I didn't say anything." Augie grabbed an apple from the platter.

"Exactly the point. I know what you're thinking—"

"—Like, Danny-your-ex-from-the-Sandoval-show Danny?" DJ asked. "He kinda looked like a jackass to me."

Ox interrupted before Lauren could react to DJ's comment. "I'm guessing his wife wasn't there. Or she would have tried to beat you with a pizza pan. I mean, that's one *esposa enojada*—I saw the way she looked at you when she was in the audience. She ain't a fan."

"I don't know why. I've never even met her." Her conscience poked her with a sharp nail. While she might not know for certain, Lauren had a pretty good idea why Heather didn't like her.

"Well, you're not paying attention then, luv. The way he looked at you? He's still got feelings for you, girl. That's why the missus is so pissed off," Stevie said as he messed around with his Gibson.

"Whatever." Lauren waved him off.

There was no more time for conversation once Fitz bustled into the room. He announced that lunch was over and they'd best get cracking. They worked through another song, but Lauren could tell that the producer wasn't pleased with what the band was doing.

Later that night, she found herself thinking about what Stevie had said. She roamed through her apartment, restless, feeling caged. Did Danny still have feelings for her? She knew how she felt. Well, she thought she did. The old attraction was still there, and that remarkable level of comfort and trust.

Are these feelings just ghosts? she wondered. *Echoes of what was?*

She grabbed her notebook, the spark of a song flaring. But after about three scribbled lines, the ephemeral idea vanished into the night. Disgusted, Lauren threw the notebook down. It bounced off the sofa and sprawled on the floor. The pen followed. Lauren curled into a corner of the sofa and pressed her fingers to her temples.

If I don't come up with anything soon, I'm done.

CHAPTER SEVENTEEN

Danny stared down as the coroner's assistant finished draping white sheets over the bodies at his crime scene. Under one of them, a man's body. A fan of his blood spread out on the otherwise pristine hardwood floor. Beneath the other, a woman, the red marks around her throat a stark contrast to her pale skin. But what twisted in Danny's gut were the two smaller sheets on the second floor of the townhouse. It was bad enough when kids died, but a full family murder-suicide? It left a raw, gaping hole inside him.

He was quiet and withdrawn on the ride back to the precinct and while he typed up his notes. It was an open and shut case—the husband had lost control. A neighbor told Danny that the wife had served her husband with divorce papers the day before. The townhouse had a security camera, and it had shown exactly what happened in gruesome, graphic detail.

The husband had stormed in, shouting, waving some papers in his hand. The wife screamed back. In a flash, the papers scattered, and the husband's hands were around her throat. She'd scratched and struggled but sank to her knees as the pressure became too much. Once the wife was dead, he'd pulled her limp form into his arms as he cried.

Then he got up and paced, pulling at his hair and sobbing. Twice he went to the bottom of the stairs, and twice he stopped himself until, the third time, he disappeared upstairs. When he came down again, he was stone-faced. He went to his office, where he unlocked his gun safe and pulled out his Glock. Back in the living room he'd stared at his wife, her rag-doll body a heap on the floor, until he put the muzzle under his chin and pulled the trigger.

Rolling back in his chair, Danny rubbed his eyes. He tried not to think about the kids. They'd been suffocated. He struggled to master the sadness and fury in his heart. How could someone do that? How could a father put pillows over his children's faces and press down? The oldest of the two had been about Tommy's age, and all Danny wanted to do was hug his sons. Feel them in his arms, hear them laugh and tease him, saying Daddy was getting all huggy.

Despite his very primal need to touch his sons, assure himself they were fine, Danny was reluctant to go to dinner. The case had already made him late, and the very last thing he wanted to do tonight was go to a potluck at his parents' house. They already ate there nearly every Sunday, but his mother seemed convinced that a few extra family dinners would fix the problems between him and Heather. And to add to the drama, Heather had accused him a second time of sleeping with Lauren—an accusation he vehemently denied once again. He was getting tired of being falsely accused.

By the time Danny arrived, dinner was being cleared off the table. The boys, along with Cole, were in the TV room with their grandmother.

"Sorry I'm late." His jacket landed on the back of a kitchen chair. He leaned to give Heather a kiss on the cheek but only grazed her as she turned her head away without a word. Danny sighed and saw Maggie and his father glance at each other.

"Heather..."

"Late again." Frost coated her voice.

"Don't start. We caught a case—" He watched as she dumped a plate full of pasta—what he assumed was supposed to be his dinner—into the garbage.

"I'm not starting anything, Danny. You started it. Clearly, you're not ready to finish it." She wiped her hands on a towel and stalked out of the room, brushing past Richie on her way. Maggie gracefully slipped out as well.

"Un-fucking-believable," Danny muttered under his breath.

Danny stood and fumed as Richie went to the refrigerator. He grabbed cold cuts, cheese, tomato slices and a leftover dinner roll. A minute later, he handed the makeshift sandwich to his son. Danny just blinked at it.

"Gotta have something for supper," his father said.

"I suppose."

"Want to talk about it?"

Danny offered a non-committal grunt. "I had a crappy day at work, and I'm so tired of fighting when I'm home. I'm tired of getting accused of something I haven't done."

"And what's that?"

"Having an affair with Lauren."

"Beg pardon?"

"Heather's convinced that I've been running around ever since that stupid TV disaster." Danny adjusted the sandwich bread to prevent a tomato slice from making a run for it. "She thinks everything I do is because of Lauren."

"Have you seen Lauren at all?"

"Once—and only by coincidence," Danny said. "She was at Dom's the night of the baseball game, so we talked while I waited for the pizzas. One of Heather's friends saw us talking and texted a picture to Heather, and because I didn't instantly confess to a fifteen-minute chat, there's the proof. I'm a cheating lowlife."

"Hmmm." Richie's answer was little more than a rumble in his chest.

"And don't get me started on my overtime." Danny took another bite of sandwich and chewed like he was trying to punish it.

Out in the other room, Maggie gestured for her sister-in-law to join her in the foyer where they had a hint of privacy. Heather glanced over to make sure the kids were still occupied with their grandmother, then reluctantly joined her. She was feeling raw and didn't want to talk, but she couldn't keep avoiding Maggie.

"I don't mean to pry, Heather, but what's going on with you and Danny? I've never seen you guys like this."

Heather sighed. "I don't know. Ever since that whole scene at the TV studio, everything feels out of control."

"What do you mean?"

"When we met Lauren after, and he hugged her? I just... I hated it," Heather said. "I got jealous. But since then, I can't stop thinking about it. When she's singing, it sure seems like she still has a lot of feelings for him." Heather frowned harder. "I know what I saw, Maggie."

Maggie was quiet for a moment, and Heather could tell that she was wrestling with what to say. Her stomach twisted into an anxious knot.

"I'm not discounting what you're feeling, Heather. And I'm not trying to be unsympathetic, but like it or not, she and Danny have history."

"I know, but Danny's been so distant. He's been late a lot. And sometimes I see him lost in thought, and he has this look on his face. I know, right in my gut, he's thinking about her..." Her voice trailed away for a second. "I think he's still in love with her. I think they're having an affair."

Maggie flinched. "What? You think Danny's cheating on you? He wouldn't."

"No...yes. I don't know. I know he's seen her." Heather folded her arms in front of herself, feeling miserable. "Before, I would have never thought it, but now it's all I think about."

Heather told her sister-in-law about the photo Rachel had sent. And that Danny hadn't told her about it. Maggie tried to persuade her that maybe Danny had just forgotten. Heather wasn't buying it.

"Seriously, Maggie? Would you forget?" Heather shifted her weight from foot to foot.

"Point taken. But I know my brother. He wouldn't step out on you. Maybe there's a reason he didn't say anything? He wouldn't..." This time, it was Maggie's voice that faded.

Heather gave her sister-in-law a hard stare. "Maggie? What aren't you saying?" she asked, even though she dreaded the answer.

"It's nothing."

"Tell me!"

Maggie hemmed and hawed for a moment. "Well, Lauren stopped by my office the other day. She brought an autographed CD for Cole and mentioned the invitation to visit the recording studio again. We spent about ten, fifteen minutes visiting, but she did talk about Danny and some of her regrets."

"Regrets about what?"

"About letting him go."

Heather felt dizzy. Her voice was barely a whisper. "Oh my God."

"Don't jump to conclusions. Danny isn't the type to sleep around. He wouldn't cheat on you with Lauren—or anyone."

Heather turned away, not wanting Maggie to see that she didn't believe her. She found herself staring at Cole, who'd come in from the TV room. Based on Cole's shocked expression and huge eyes, she'd heard at least part of the conversation.

Heather, her eyes filled with anger and tears, fled upstairs.

Behind her, she heard the remnants of their conversation.

"Mom?"

"We'll talk about it later, honey."

Out in the kitchen, Danny took another angry chomp out of the sandwich. "Every time I've been late it's been legit, but she doesn't seem to care. As far as she's concerned, I'm guilty as charged."

"Have you been thinking about Lauren much?" As usual, Richie's question was thoughtful and reserved, but it still brought Danny up short. He considered his answer, his brow creased with uncertainty.

"Thinking isn't a crime." Danny regretted his gruff tone as soon as the words were out of his mouth. "Sorry, Dad. Do I think about her? Sure, I do. I can't help it now—Heather brings her up every chance she gets."

"Hmm." The corners of Richie's mouth turned down.

"That's the second time you've 'hmm'-ed me."

"Back then, you were so in love with Lauren, your mother and I worried the two of you would just elope and run away. Made your mother crazy. When the two of you broke up, I knew how much it hurt you. But you never talked about it. Ever."

"I was eighteen, Dad. My first broken heart. I don't do that touchy-feely stuff now. I sure didn't do it back then." Danny polished off the last of the sandwich.

"I know. It's never been easy for you to talk about things like that. But just because you don't *talk* about something doesn't mean you don't *feel* it. Maybe this whole thing is bringing back all the stuff that ate you up inside while you pretended it didn't." While he talked, Richie took some plates out of the drying rack, wiped them with a towel, and put them in the cabinet.

Leave it to his dad to hit the bullseye. Danny stared down at the counter.

"You had nowhere to put it. You didn't have an outlet like Lauren did with her music."

Danny grunted, a formidable—and unintentional—imitation of his father's 'hmm' rumble. "Yeah. She poured all her anger at me into her music. The jerk who broke her heart."

"Not every song she wrote is about you, you know."

Danny felt his neck redden as he realized how self-indulgent he sounded.

"She broke your heart, too," his father said as he dried a glass and put it away. "But maybe you should listen to a little more of her music. You might be surprised what you hear. Might give you some perspective, maybe even a little closure."

It will take more than a few songs to get that kind of closure. He leaned against the counter, morose.

"And maybe talking about it a little more might help, too. Keeping it bottled up isn't going to help anyone." Richie folded the dishtowel and hung it on the hook by the stove.

Inside, Danny conceded his father had a point, but before he could continue that thought, the door to the kitchen squeaked open. Heather came in. Her eyes were shiny.

"Am I interrupting?" she asked.

"Not at all," Richie said. He got up and brought a random dish from the counter to the sink and rinsed it off. Danny was pretty sure it had already been washed.

"I'm sorry I lost my temper," Heather said. "It's just been a really stressful week."

"It's okay." Danny didn't mean it. It really wasn't okay. He was embarrassed she'd behaved like that in front of his parents, but holding a grudge wasn't going to fix it. "Why don't we get the boys and head home?"

"Okay." Heather looked over at Richie, her face contrite. "Richie, I'm sorry. I shouldn't have..."

Richie held up a hand to forestall the rest of her sentence. "Don't you worry about it. Everyone has a bad day once in a while."

After stronger hugs than the boys wanted from their father, especially Lucas, and a heated discussion culminating in a best two-out-of-three Rock, Paper, Scissors match the boys decided that Matty would ride home with his father and Lucas and Tommy would go with Heather. On the drive home, Matty chattered away for a little bit but then put his headphones on to listen to music.

Left to his thoughts, Danny went back over the fight, how he'd been feeling, and what his father said. He finally decided his father had a point about clearing the air with Lauren. If he opened up a little about how he was feeling, that might make all the difference in the world. Trying to deliberately avoid his ex, and some of the emotions that were bubbling up, was just making everything worse. He needed to address this head-on. They had to talk. Clear the air for real.

By the time he got home, Danny was comfortable with his decision. He got into bed and mumbled a good night to his wife. Then he fell into a deep sleep and didn't wake up until the alarm went off in the morning.

CHAPTER EIGHTEEN

On Wednesday, Danny left work at the end of his shift and drove across the city to the Somerset Hotel. A smartly dressed security guard and a concierge waited at the elegant marble desk. Both looked up and smiled as Danny approached.

"May I help you, sir?"

"I need a moment of Miss Stone's time."

"Is she expecting you?"

"No, but if you could tell her Detective Danny Padovano is here?" Danny flashed his badge.

"Of course, sir." The concierge picked up the phone and punched a few numbers. "Miss Stone? This is George at the front desk. There's a police detective here to see you. Your name again, sir?"

"Padovano," Danny repeated. "Detective Padovano."

"A Detective Padovano." George waited. "Yes, of course. I'll send him right up. You're very welcome, Miss Stone. My pleasure."

"If you'd follow me, Detective." George walked across the private lobby area to an elevator bank, and Danny wondered if he was going to be escorted the whole way. George got on the elevator with him, swiped a key card, and punched in a code. Then he pushed the button for the penthouse.

"Once you exit the elevator, go to the door straight ahead of you and knock. Miss Stone is expecting you."

"Thanks."

George slipped out, and the door slid shut. *The penthouse suite,* thought Danny. *Fancy.* He looked at himself in the gleaming interior of the elevator. There was certainly nothing fancy about him. His tie was askew, his shirt rumpled. It had been warm out that day, and at one point in the afternoon, he'd rolled his sleeves up. Now one was sagging halfway down his arm. He looked like he'd just fallen out of bed.

He leaned his head back against the wall. He was going to have to explain to Heather where he'd been, but he knew if he'd tried to talk to her about it ahead of time, she would have lost it. That made him doubt his decision to come talk to Lauren at all, and he almost changed his mind. But when the elevator door opened, he took a deep breath and stepped into the hall. He'd come this far, and he wasn't going to chicken out now. He knocked on the pristine white door. It opened immediately.

"Danny! This is a surprise. C'mon in," Lauren said as she pulled the door wider. Her hair was down and loose, the soft wave giving it a tousled look. Barefoot, she was dressed in comfortable jeans and a maroon tank top that hugged her curves. Everything inside Danny coiled tighter, a visceral, almost primal response. He stuck his hand in his pocket and rubbed his thumb along his wedding band.

"Sorry to drop in without calling. I'm not interrupting, am I?"

"No, not at all." Lauren stood back and held the door open.

Once he stepped over the threshold, Danny's mouth sagged a little. He was pretty sure her "suite" was bigger than his entire house. The gourmet kitchen opened to a large living room that had a full view of Central Park. There were a few other doors he could see, and he guessed there were at least three or four bedrooms along with a master suite. It boggled his mind to even consider what this place cost.

"Not that I mind, but why are you here?" Lauren asked.

"I was hoping we could catch up a little more. I should have called first..." Danny wasn't quite sure what to do next. What was he thinking to just show up here unannounced?

"No, it's fine. I'm glad you came by. Can I get you something to eat? Drink? I assume you're off duty?"

"Off duty. A beer would be great."

"Go get cozy." She gestured towards the living room, where a leather sectional sofa made an L shape, the longest side facing a wall with a large television mounted to it. There was small upright piano tucked in a corner and a couple guitars propped in stands. Some notebooks were scattered on the coffee table, but when Danny sat down, what he noticed was Lauren's copy of their high school yearbook. He unknotted his tie and pulled it out from his collar. He stuffed it in his pocket before flipping through a few yearbook pages.

"You brought your yearbook with you from LA?" He took the beer Lauren offered. She put a bowl of chips on the table.

"No. I grabbed it when I was over at my mom's." Lauren sat on the adjacent cushion. "Being here, seeing you. Decided to wander down Memory Lane." She pointed at one of the photos. "Do you remember Triple M?"

"Mary Margaret McLellan! I haven't thought of her in years."

"Man, she was the pride and joy of the nuns, wasn't she?"

Back in the day, Mary Margaret could always be counted on to rat out her fellow students if they even *looked* like they were going to do something wrong. The Sisters loved her—her fellow students, not so much. Their Triple M conversation turned to other familiar faces from the past.

"What ever happened to Brendan Chan?" she asked. "Always figured he was either going to find the cure for cancer or become a serial killer."

"He's a teacher—at St. Catherine's!" Danny was laughing so hard he was nearly crying.

"No shit?"

"My hand to God—Matty has him for social studies."

Soon their conversation turned from the past to more of the present. Lauren quizzed Danny about his work. He talked about what he loved—and what he hated—about being on the job. He told her about a few the more humorous arrests he'd made. His favorite was one of his first as a beat cop—a very drunk college student had stripped naked, climbed on top of a parked truck, and proceeded to serenade all passersby with his version of "You've Lost That Lovin' Feeling."

"I was the rookie. That meant I got stuck getting the naked guy off the truck."

"I'm sure that was fun." She rolled her eyes.

"Oh yeah." He took a swig of beer. "Photographer for the paper got a picture. A few days later, I came in to find my locker plastered with pictures of me with the idiot looking like he was trying to hump my leg."

Lauren wiped an amused tear away. "Oh, God. That's an image I'll never get out of my head!"

"You and me both." Danny's deadpan answer made her laugh even harder. As their mirth subsided, they lapsed into a silence. While it wasn't entirely uncomfortable, the ghosts of old decisions and regrets stalked them through the stillness.

Lauren finally broke the quiet, asking, "So, how are you, Danny? For real."

She looked at him with an earnest, thoughtful expression. God, he'd missed that. He remembered their conversation at Dom's and how he'd realized then how much he missed her friendship. But Lauren had been more than a friend or a girlfriend. Back then, she was his *best* friend. They'd shared everything when they were younger: hopes, dreams, secrets, lies. And they'd always had each other's backs. He bit his lip, wrestling with what he wanted to say, how to spin the insanity somehow.

Instead of spinning, he blurted out the truth.

CHAPTER NINETEEN

"I'm not sure anymore... everything seems like it's coming off the rails."

Taken aback by his statement, Lauren reached out and squeezed Danny's arm. "I'm sorry. God knows I'm the last person who should give out life advice, but I'll listen if you think it'll help."

"Maybe. I don't know." He leaned forward and rested his elbows on his knees, fiddling with the unbuttoned cuff of his sleeve Then he coughed out a bitter laugh. "My marriage is all fucked up."

"Your wife certainly didn't seem to like me."

"You don't know the half of it."

She waited while Danny pressed his fingers against his temples. He opened his mouth to speak and closed it again as if he was weighing whether or not to expand on his last statement. Instead, he went back to the beginning.

"Me and Heather, we'd only been together three months when we met up with Kev, Mario, and Paul for St. C's fifth-year class reunion. Of course, they all asked if I'd seen you, heard your new single, and if you were coming. Well, Heather wanted to know why someone like you would be at our reunion. Then she got the whole download on my famous rock-star ex."

"Ah. I'm guessing you'd never mentioned me—and that Kevin shot his mouth off?"

"Right. And she took it personally—like I'd been hiding you on purpose. Never let go of it either. She's always had a jealous streak, but something about this, about you ... I never understood it."

Lauren nodded. That explained a lot about Heather's behavior after the Sandoval show.

"But everything changed a few months later—when Heather got pregnant."

"And you were a stand-up guy and married her."

Danny put down his half-full beer, the bottle clinking when it hit the coffee table. "Yep. Did the right thing. At least I thought it was the right thing. We had Lucas, and life was pretty good. He was—he is—my pride and joy. All three are. But somewhere along the line, me and Heather? We started down different roads. We're only occasional lovers, and sometimes I think we've even stopped being friends. There have been a lot of days when I've wondered: if she'd never gotten pregnant, would we have ever gotten married?"

Danny ran a hand over his hair as he looked at some distant spot. Lauren wondered if he regretted telling her so much.

"What're you going to do?"

"I don't know. Shit, I'm sorry. I didn't come here to unload all my crap on you."

"You can unload your crap on me any time, Danny." She paused. "Do you remember how simple it was when we were kids? Well, maybe not simple from our perspective then, but looking back?"

"I know what you mean. Shit gets complicated when you grow up. Remember our first dance? Sister Agnes embarrassed us both? Do you remember what she said?"

Lauren nearly doubled over laughing. "Oh, God, that's right. She poked us both with a ruler and said we'd better leave enough room in between us for God! Guess she didn't want our naughty bits touching!"

"I didn't know what to do. I felt awkward enough just dancing with you. That made it so much worse." He grabbed a few chips out of the bowl.

Lauren shifted, angling her body towards him so she didn't have to crane her neck. She kicked a decorative pillow off the sofa, and her leg ended up resting against his. He didn't move away. Neither did she. She cocked an eyebrow as he looked at her and a smile formed on his lips.

"What are you grinning about?"

"Remember our first kiss?"

"Of course." Her answer was immediate. "We went to the movies, what was it—man, I don't even remember the movie. I do remember how nervous I was when you held my hand." She paused, smiling as she stared into space.

After the movie, they'd had about half an hour before Danny's father was due to pick them up. She and Danny had wandered to a spot by the food court, near the fountain, where a smattering of fake trees and bushes were supposed to make it feel like a garden. At that hour, all the food kiosks were closed. They'd found a little space near imitation birch trees that afforded a little privacy.

"I remember some awkward small talk."

Danny sighed. "I was so desperate to kiss you, but too chicken-shit."

"And I couldn't take the pressure."

Lauren remembered standing there, looking at Danny for what seemed to be forever. She'd looked down, screwing up her courage and when she looked up again, she rose up on her toes and kissed him on the lips. It was fast, barely a touch, and they both drew back slightly. His hand had felt very warm when she threaded her fingers through his and whispered, "We can do that again if you want."

The second kiss wasn't nearly as awkward.

"Lauren?" Danny tapped her knee. "You in there?"

She jumped. "Sorry," she said, flustered. She rubbed the back of her neck. "Got distracted."

CHAPTER TWENTY

Lauren wasn't unhappy that Danny had shown up. Unexpected company had never bothered her much. But she was surprised. When they exchanged numbers at Dom's, she'd thought they'd get together for coffee. Maybe a dinner. She had to admit, him coming over to hang out had crossed her mind, but she'd dismissed the idea, thinking it was too much to ask for. Now that he was here, she couldn't imagine a more perfect evening. It was almost like they'd never been apart, and all the memories and the laughter gave her a giddy high.

At one point she nearly asked Danny what he remembered about their first time together, but stopped, fearing that would cross an unspoken line. Instead, she leaned toward the table and flipped a few more pages in the yearbook. In front of them was a full color spread of prom pictures. Theirs was in the corner of the right-hand page. Danny was dressed in a classic black tux. Lauren's hair was done up. She wore a dark blue gown with a with a modest neckline and a skirt made of a shiny, iridescent material. Even back then she'd loved clothes with some sparkle, and she remembered how the skirt had swirled when they danced. She had a corsage on her wrist, and they stood in front of the traditional backdrop, smiling and happy.

"You know, we clean up pretty darn good," she said. "I loved that dress, and man, you were hot in that tux!"

"I don't know about that."

"Definitely hot."

Memories crowded around them: the anticipation of going, intimate slow dancing, the argument that almost ruined the night, the after-party ... and after the after-party. Prom wasn't the first time they'd had sex, but they'd made it an exceptional night. Lauren closed the yearbook.

"Did you really come here tonight to look at old pictures?" Lauren wasn't sure what she wanted him to say. Part of her hoped the answer was as simple as that, but another part of her knew it was much more complicated.

Danny leaned back on the sofa, his shoulders tight, a shadow across his face. "I've just been thinking about you a lot lately. First when Cole said she was doing that paper, and then after that TV thing..." He hesitated, then plunged ahead. "I realized that there was a lot of stuff I didn't face after we broke up. I guess I buried it all and just tried to forget—but now that you're back? It's all coming back, too." He chugged the last of his beer. "The things I said. I didn't mean—"

"—We both said some things, Danny."

"I called you reckless."

"And I called you a coward. We were dumb kids, Danny. Dumb kids who said stupid shit."

"If you get right down to it, I was afraid you hated me."

"Hated you?" The word startled Lauren.

"For not going with you. That I didn't fight harder for us..." His voice trailed away, and he turned his face towards the window.

"Jesus, Danny. No, I didn't hate you back then. I don't hate you now. Angry? Yeah, I was angry when we broke up. I was sad, too, but I didn't fight for it either. We both wanted different things—and you *know* what would've happened if one of us had given up what we wanted to be with the other."

"We *don't* know." His voice turned stubborn.

"Don't bullshit me," Lauren said. "Yes, we do. You wanted to be a cop—and not just any cop, you wanted to be NYPD like your uncle. You talked about being a cop like him the same way I talked about being in a band."

Lauren knew her point hit home when he dropped his eyes.

"I'll ask again: what would have happened if one of us had given up our own dream for the other?"

Danny deflated a little more. "We might have resented each other."

"*Might* have?" Lauren didn't push the point. Instead, she said, "You'd hate my life, Danny. Even when I'm not on stage, I'm in the public eye. Everything always changes, things are rarely the same. You'd either be in the spotlight or forced out of it. I know you, Danny, and it would mess you up."

He didn't like what she said, because the obstinate frown she remembered so well creased his face. When he finally spoke again, his voice held a melancholy note. "And if you'd stayed with me, you would have always wondered what might have been."

"I would have felt held back." *And,* she thought, *I would have hated you for it.*

"But shouldn't we have tried?"

It was Lauren's turn to look away, and she bit her lip. She'd wrestled with that question, that doubt, for years. "I honestly don't know. But after hearing my songs, how could you think I hated you? I can't always talk about how I feel, but I sure can sing about it. You know that."

Danny leaned forward, resting his arms on his knees again, and looked at the floor. His words were muffled, dusted with embarrassment. "I haven't listened to most of your music."

"What?"

His next words rushed out as he tried to explain himself. "I've listened to some of the big anthem songs, but the ballads?" He shook his head. "Too afraid I'd hear about how the boy you loved deserted you. Broke your heart. Longer I went without hearing them..." He let the rest of his sentence trail away.

"Danny!"

His head jerked up at the sharpness in her voice.

"You're an *idiot*."

He recoiled as if she'd slapped him.

"Stay right there." She got up and disappeared into the other room and returned carrying an acoustic six-string guitar. Her name was carefully scripted on the upper part of the body, near the neck. In the opposite corner were several hand-painted ivy leaves. Surprise washed over Danny's face.

"You still have that?"

"Still have—? Of *course,* I still have it." The guitar in her hand was special—Danny had given it to her for her sixteenth birthday—and Lauren was a little offended he thought she might get rid of it. "Just about every song I've ever written professionally has started with this guitar. Of all the ones I own, it's my favorite." She sat down and started to strum, an affectionate smile blooming on her face as she caressed the guitar.

"On *Concrete Beach*, our first album, yeah, there are a few broken-hearted songs. I poured my heart out in them. But if there's one album I'd want you to listen to, it's *Trajectory*, the one we did when I got out of rehab. For starters, I was focused again, and The King-makers were back on top of their game. Second, there's a song on there that I specifically dedicated to you."

"To me?"

"Yes, to you. Look at the CD jacket: right after the song's title it says, 'for DP.' It's called 'Rearview Mirror.'" She started to pick out some notes and sing.

"I wish time and distance didn't matter. I wish I'd known what the future would bring. When I left, I said no regrets but now I see it all so clearly laid out behind me, scars and skeletons, regrets and tears..."

With the lyrics, Lauren told the story of someone confronting their past, how they thought they knew everything, and grasping—too late—what they'd really left behind. There was sadness woven through the words, but the song was also about acceptance and moving on. It was soft and melancholic, reflective and touching. Lauren let her voice trail away at the end, and after a few seconds, she allowed her eyes to meet Danny's. His were as shiny as hers felt.

"If I had to choose one song of mine for you to listen to, it would be that one." She put the guitar down as the emotions rolling through her threatened to sweep away her tenuous control. "Excuse me again for a sec. I'll be right back."

In the bathroom, Lauren splashed cold water on her face and stared at herself in the mirror. Despite what her lyrics had just said, she hadn't moved on. The more time she spent with Danny, the more she realized she still cared for him—yes, loved him. She pinched the bridge of her nose. Part of her wanted to race back to the other room, throw her arms around him, and kiss Danny like it was her last night on Earth.

"Pull your shit together," she said to her reflection. "You and Danny were a long time ago."

When she came back to the living room, Danny was holding her guitar. With a light touch, he ran his fingers along its curves, tracing the painted vines. Lauren forced herself to focus on something—anything—other than his hands and what they'd feel like on her skin.

"I cried when you gave me that guitar."

"I knew how much you loved it. You admired it every time we went to the music store. But with your dad out of work, I knew your parents wouldn't be able to afford it."

She nodded, remembering that lean year. "They were so stressed about paying for Jackie's college tuition. Plus me, Carolyn, and Stef were all at Saint C's."

Danny and Lauren talked for a little while longer, sharing what they'd done in the intervening years. Lauren told him outrageous stories about The Kingmakers' very first tour that made him gasp and laugh. Finally, Danny glanced up at the big clock over the mantle. It was nearly ten o'clock. Lauren's eyes followed his.

"Have to go?" She swallowed her disappointment.

"Unfortunately, I do." He pushed himself up from the sofa.

"I'm so glad you came over," Lauren said as she walked him to the door. An awkward silence settled between them as they struggled with things they still wanted to say. Finally, Danny broke their reticence.

"Lauren. I... I can't stop thinking about you. After all these years, you'd think I'd be over you, but I'm not."

Lauren caught her breath. She wasn't sure what she expected Danny to say, but it certainly wasn't that. He reached out and touched her arm, and a bolt of energy coursed through her. An instant later, Danny's arms were around her, his lips on hers with a bruising, passionate intensity. Lauren's heart hammered in her chest as she let him in, matching his fire with her own. His arms tightened, the press of their bodies against each other intoxicating. She ran her fingers over his back, and a low sigh coiled in her throat as Danny tangled his fingers in her hair.

They pulled away from each other, stopping the kiss as quickly as it started. Lauren wrapped her arms around herself, confused and conflicted. Danny was married—what the hell were they thinking? Danny looked just as stunned, guilt and passion warring in his eyes.

Lauren's whole body was on fire. She would have given anything in that moment to kiss Danny again. But they were balancing on the head of a pin—the slightest shift and they would be past an ill-advised kiss and into a full-blown affair.

"I'm no saint, Danny. And I won't deny it: I want this to happen in ways I can't even describe. But this is insane! I can't be—*I won't be*—"

"—Lauren—"

"—Even if we did this, would it end differently than high school? When I'm done with this album, I'm leaving. Then what? I'd just be the woman who broke up your marriage."

"You wouldn't be breaking up my marriage." Danny stepped closer. She didn't step away.

"No?"

"Things have been strained between me and Heather for a long time."

"But you're still with her."

"Sometimes, now, it feels like we're just going through the motions. I love my family. I don't want to hurt any of them." He bent his head a little closer, his mouth only inches from hers. "But you, you're a force of nature."

"We can't." Every logical, rational part of Lauren said this was beyond a bad idea. It was a foolish, reckless, and downright dangerous idea—but the passionate part of her wanted nothing to do with common sense. She never wanted to lose the emotions surging through her at that moment. She felt vibrant and electric in a way she hadn't felt in years.

Danny's voice got low and husky. "We shouldn't... But I want you so much it hurts."

He was so close. Flushed and disoriented, she shifted, unsure if she should turn away—or even if she could—but Danny's arm slid around her waist again, bringing the two of them even nearer while his mouth hovered near hers.

"Please tell me you want me, too," His voice was little more than a murmur.

She did want him, even as she tried to convince herself otherwise. When she looked into Danny's eyes, her knees nearly buckled. There was so much there. Confusion, longing, pain, fear, love, lust, even hope... all the same things that were tangled in her heart.

She was lost.

"Danny—"

She didn't finish. His mouth closed over hers, pulling her into another kiss. For a moment, Lauren stiffened against him, a last, weak protest before desire overrode any sense she still had left. She embraced the kiss, welcoming him as she wrapped her arms around his neck and softened against him. She slid her hands down over his chest and started working the shirt buttons. Her fingers dug into him as Danny's hand slid under the hem of her tank, grazing the bare skin beneath, and started to move up her waist...

Oh, God—what are we doing? Lauren pushed away, her eyes wide as she gulped in air. "Danny, wait! You—no, *we* need to think about this. Do you get what's about to happen here? What this means? You're *married*, for Christ's sake!"

Danny's face twisted, his bliss crumbling before her eyes.

Lauren put a hand to his cheek. "What I said was true. I do want this—I've always wanted this. But this isn't just about us."

"Lauren—"

"Listen to me!" It was a demand. "We're not a couple of kids. There are repercussions—giant fucking repercussions. What happens to us—to you, your family —when I leave? Because I *will* leave."

"I... I don't know. I just don't know." Danny sounded lost.

"Neither do I." Lauren crossed her arms in front of her, suddenly cold.

"I have to go." Danny took a few steps back.

"I know."

"I'm not sorry. I'm not sorry I came here tonight. I'm not sorry I kissed you or that I said what I said."

Lauren nodded and kept her eyes averted, listening to the squeak of the doorknob.

"I'll call you," Danny said.

The door closed with a dull thud, and Lauren pressed her palms against it before she sank down on the floor. Leaning against the door with her face with her hands, she started to cry.

In the hall, Danny stood paralyzed. Coming to see Lauren wasn't the bright idea he'd thought it was. He thought they'd talk about old times, maybe he'd get a little resolution—realize his emotions were just faded old memories. But that wasn't what happened. Seeing Lauren at the Sandoval show had cracked the wall he'd built to hold back all those old memories and feelings.

Coming here tonight hadn't plugged the leak. It had blown a hole right through that dam. Now, everything was flooding back, raw and real, painful and wonderful.

Danny hadn't gotten over anything.

He was still very much in love with Lauren Stone.

CHAPTER TWENTY-ONE

The next morning, Lauren was late to the studio. Her mind brimmed with thoughts about Danny and their encounter the night before—and she'd been awake half the night thinking about him. Catching her lower lip in her teeth, she wrangled with the knowledge that the man she'd kissed, the man she quite honestly wanted to sleep with, was married to another woman.

She wasn't proud of that. She'd been raised to believe that marriage was sacrosanct, but she also knew many marriages didn't last. DJ was divorced. Ox had seen three marriages break up. Lauren didn't have an issue with divorce—sometimes it was the best option for a couple. But while people were married? You didn't mess with that.

But Danny was her rock. The only man who had ever loved her for who she really was, not for her fame or what she could do for him. *It isn't like I've blown up their fairy tale,* Lauren thought, attempting to mollify her discomfort. Danny said that he wasn't happy in his marriage, that his relationship was foundering.

Because she was late, she brought a box full of pastries to buy the band's forgiveness. Her gambit worked, and while she indulged in a dark-chocolate-cherry piece of heaven, she stole a few minutes to herself and pulled out her phone. After a hesitation, she found Danny's info in her contacts, tapped the "message" icon and wrote: *<Hi. Glad you stopped by last night.>* She hit send before her better judgment could make her delete the text.

And while the sugar-laden treats did give her a hall pass for being late, no amount of frosted cinnamon buns or cranberry-orange scones could hide the fact that the band didn't have their shit together. Lauren was secretly glad because it meant her own distracted mind didn't stand out as much as it might have—although once or twice Augie caught her eye, his expression asking if she was okay. She averted her face and gave a non-committal wave. They kept at it until early afternoon but had little to show for their efforts.

"Don't worry about it," DJ said to them as he picked up his jacket. "It's a slow start, but it's all good. We'll kick the rust off in no time."

Stevie fist-bumped him. "Just gotta find our groove. Back at it in the morning."

Lauren's phone pinged. It was from Danny: *<Me, too. I'll call soon.>* She tried not to smile but couldn't help herself.

"Who's the text from?" Augie asked. "You kept checking your phone today, and this is the first time you've smiled."

"Danny." Her answer was simple and matter of fact, like she was telling him it was raining out.

Augie's eyebrows went up.

"He stopped over last night. We had a couple beers, caught up on a lot of stuff. I even played him a few songs. Did you know he hasn't really listened to our music?" Lauren worried her voice sounded too forced and light.

"You're kidding."

"No, I was surprised, too." Lauren wasn't sure if Augie meant the songs, or that Danny had come over.

"What else did you guys talk about?"

"That's about it. Just a lot of reminiscing." Lauren kept herself busy tucking a few things into her messenger bag. She slung it over her shoulder.

"Did he apologize?"

"Did he what?"

"Apologize. For hurting you. Breaking your heart. Dude's been on my shit list for the past eighteen years." Augie spun one of his drumsticks through his fingers.

"Augie. Don't."

"I'm just sayin'."

Lauren could feel the frown pinching the corners of her mouth. Danny *had* broken her heart, and even though they'd talked around it the other night, she still remembered. And the memory still stung...

Lauren strolled out of St. Catherine's, uncowed by the detention she'd just served for asking Sister Angelica if she regretted never having sex. The class loved it; Sister Angelica had not. But in a matter of weeks, Lauren knew she'd be free—and headed for the West Coast.

She switched her backpack from one shoulder to the other. There were still plenty of students around, all finishing whatever after-school sport or club they were in. Augie waved to her, and not far from him, she saw Danny waiting for her. Her happiness dampened when she saw the pissed look on his face. He'd been like that all week, and she was sick of trying to guess why.

"Hey, D." She hooked two fingers into his belt.

"You're going to go, aren't you?" His voice was gruff and angry. She withdrew her hand and took a step back.

"You mean to LA?" His silence was the confirmation she needed. "You know I'm going, Danny."

"But what about us? You're okay just leaving us, leaving me here?"

Lauren felt her face heat. They'd gone over this, and rehashing it again wasn't going to change anything. "I don't want to leave you here." She hated the quiver in her voice. It made her feel weak. "Come with me, Danny. We'll go to LA together."

"Leave New York? My family? I can't."

"What's stopping you?"

She watched Danny struggle, trying—and failing—to find the right words. Her lips pressed together. Why was he acting so hurt? It wasn't like her plan to move to California was new. She'd been talking about this, planning this, since freshman year.

"You're taking a huge chance. Jesus, Lauren, you don't know what kind of trouble you'll find out there!"

"No, I don't. But I'll deal with it, whatever it is. You think if I stay here, behind your white picket fence, I'll be safe? What kind of macho bullshit is that?" Lauren ground her teeth. She couldn't understand why Danny had suddenly become so opposed to her going. He knew how important this was to her.

Danny started to wave his hands as he talked, and the volume of his voice teetered on the edge of shouting. "You think you're going to take off for LA and everything will just work out. That's reckless! And stupid. What happens when things turn into a shit-show? When everything falls apart?"

Lauren was stunned. How could he say that to her? She had never—ever—been that angry with someone, and she went back at him, ferocious. "When I fail? You think I'm going to be a failure? You're an asshole. How can you even say that to me? So, all the times you told me how great my singing was, my songwriting? Those were all lies? Just to make me feel better?"

"That's not what I meant—"

"You know, I wouldn't be alone in LA if you came with me. But you won't because you're too scared... gotta be a good little boy because Mommy doesn't want you to go. Coward."

Danny sputtered when she threw that back in his face. "You're so fucking selfish, Lauren. You don't care about anyone but yourself. You don't give a crap about me. About your friends. Your family."

"That's not tr—"

"—Never mind. Just forget it. Go live your life. Just don't think there's

going to be someone here to catch you when you come running back home. We're done." Danny grabbed his own backpack.

"Done? You're breaking up with me?"

"I guess I am. Why would I stay with someone who doesn't love me?"

Didn't love him? The tears burned as they sprang into Lauren's eyes. How could he say that to her? How could he even think that?

"Danny!"

He left her standing on the sidewalk.

The sting of the memory still sharp, Lauren moved the conversation along. "We caught up. I told him about life with the band, he told me about life as a cop. That's about it. It was a nice evening hanging out with an old friend."

Lauren ended her comments there. That kiss—the kiss she'd been thinking about all day—was nothing more than a fluke. A momentary lapse of judgment. At least that's what she kept telling herself. And she didn't feel like sharing any of that with her cousin. Augie worried too much, and she didn't want him asking a lot of questions. Especially when she didn't have any good answers.

CHAPTER TWENTY-TWO

Danny did call Lauren, and they met for coffee. She called him, and they met for lunch. Then for ice cream. Each meeting was in a public place, ostensibly removing the temptation they'd faced at Lauren's apartment. But each time, the attraction felt stronger, the emotional connection deeper. Their orbits drew them closer, and neither one seemed to be able to do anything about it—or even want to.

About three weeks after Danny dropped by her place, Lauren texted him to suggest grabbing another cup of coffee. The band had started working at some ungodly hour of the morning and decided to wrap early in the afternoon. Stevie and his girlfriend were bringing their daughter to Central Park to play, and Lauren was going to meet up with them. She was hoping for a little time with Danny before that.

They met not far from the Central Park carousel. Lauren was wearing old, comfy jeans, an AC/DC t-shirt, and sunglasses. Her hair was up in a loose knot. When she saw Danny, his jacket was slung over his shoulder and the sleeves of his button-down shirt were—as usual—rolled up to his elbows. Lauren offered her cheek for a kiss, and they started to walk. As they strolled, she told Danny about the progress—or lack of it—that the band was dealing with in the recording studio.

"Ohmygod!" The voice was girlish and high-pitched. "You're Lauren Stone!"

The knot of twenty-somethings only needed to hear their friend once before flocking around Lauren. Cell phone cameras materialized, and Danny was shouldered out of the way. Lauren graciously signed autographs and took a few pictures, all while being peppered with questions that ranged from the status of her album to whether Augie had a girlfriend to her latest breakup. At last, she extricated herself from the group.

"Everyone always that pushy?" Danny asked, his voice snappish.

"Sometimes." She didn't care for his tone.

They started walking again, and Lauren moved over to be right next to Danny. Her fingers brushed his, but this time he pulled his hand away.

"What?" she asked.

"It's like everyone's staring at us. And the cameras. All we need is one person to take the wrong picture of us and share it and all hell's gonna break loose."

Even though she knew he had a point, Lauren bit the inside of her cheek while she swallowed her anger and frustration, almost choking on the implied shame of being with Danny. Her arms rigid at her side, Lauren started to walk faster, and Danny had to hustle to keep up.

"Lauren."

"I'm not some dirty little secret."

"I *never* said that!"

"Well, that's how you're acting. And if that's how you feel, then we need to stop whatever this little dance is that we're doing."

Before they could say anything else, another voice called out: "Danny! Yo, bro!"

Two soldiers dressed in fatigues were coming towards them. One was waving and smiling. He had the same mischievous grin as Danny.

"Joey?" Danny blurted out his brother's name.

Their burgeoning quarrel forgotten, Lauren was delighted by Danny's flabbergasted expression. Joey wrapped him in a bear hug, pounding his big brother on the back as he laughed.

"But—you're supposed to be in Germany!"

"I was. But in a couple days, I'll be a civilian again."

"You're getting discharged? I had no idea! Have you told Ma and Dad?"

"No. Gonna come over Sunday and surprise everyone at dinner." A conspiratorial snicker escaped the youngest Padovano.

"Ma will lose her mind," Danny said. "Call me. We'll figure out how to sneak you into the house. That's so great you'll be home. The family's all going to the beach for a few days leading up to the Fourth—"

"—Wouldn't miss it."

Jealousy nipped at Lauren when Danny mentioned the holiday family event. She had no right to take issue with time he spent with his family, but she wished she could be part of it. As the brothers talked, Lauren took a step back and took off her sunglasses. She watched them, smiling. He might be the younger brother, but Joey was over six feet tall, whereas Danny only hit six foot if he stood up straight and held his breath.

She realized a moment later that Joey's companion was staring at her, and she knew she'd been made.

"Joey, you remember—"

"—Lauren? Is that really you?" Joey's eyes sparkled with mirth. "Shit. I haven't seen you in years. Well, not in-person anyway. Bunch of guys in my unit got plenty of pictures of you!"

Lauren laughed. Danny glowered.

She gave Joey a hug. "You were just a little pain-in-my-ass the last time I saw you."

"Ah, now I'm probably just a big pain-in-the-ass. And this slack-jawed fool here is my friend Vinny."

Vinny took off his hat, eyes round. "Vinny. Ah, Vincent. Vincent Novak. Sure is a pleasure to meet you, ma'am." Based on the drawl, Vin wasn't from New York. He turned scarlet as he talked. Lauren found it charming.

"I'm no ma'am, got that?"

"Of course. Yes, ma... Aww, shoot." Vinny turned even redder and rubbed his hand over his cropped hair.

While the brothers conspired about the best way to surprise their mother, Lauren chatted with Vinny and took a couple photos with him. He thanked her several times and only needed to be reminded once not to call her "ma'am." Some passersby noticed the commotion and stopped to admire her. It took another fifteen minutes to disentangle herself from the new knot of fans vying for an autograph or a picture, but once she did, she found Danny off to the side, his face pinched and frowning.

"You never get a moment to yourself, do you?" There was a shadow of discontent in his voice.

"Life I signed up for." Not wanting to reignite the argument about her very public private life, Lauren changed the subject. "Your mom's going to be thrilled to have Joey home."

"You're not kidding! I still can't believe my kid brother has been in the Army for six years."

They talked about Joey for a few minutes and then walked in silence, simply enjoying each other's closeness and watching other people who were in the park pass them by. No one else gave them a second look, and Lauren enjoyed the slow relaxed pace and the warm summer sunshine. Today's session in the studio had felt frantic and intense, and she relished the chance to slow down. Danny's hand brushed hers, and their fingers entwined loosely. She loved how it felt, but she pulled her hand away.

"What's wrong?" he asked, and she could hear the umbrage in his voice.

"I loved that," she said. "More than I should. But we can't walk around holding hands. What if Joey had seen us like that?"

Danny's sigh was dejected. "You're right."

Silent, they walked along the wide path that circled around and brought them back to the carousel. Lauren leaned on the rail and looked through the arched openings in the brick. Inside, the brightly painted horses galloped in a circle while children held the shiny brass poles and laughed. Danny leaned on the rail next to her, close enough for their arms to touch. But before long, he glanced at his watch.

"Go," she said. "You don't want to miss Lucas's game. He'll be looking for you."

"See you again soon?"

She nodded. Despite their discussion before, Danny gave her another kiss that left her nearly breathless, and she felt another brick in the wall she'd built between them crumble to dust. Lauren watched until the crowd swallowed him.

She put her fingers to her lips, imagining she could still feel his kiss. It was so easy to be distracted. Thinking of kissing Danny was a short distance to remembering the many times they'd been together. And from there, it didn't take much to imagine what it would be like to be with him now. The thrill of her daydream was quickly followed by shame as thoughts of Danny's sons, and his wife, pushed their way into her mind. She had no business thinking about him like that but couldn't stop herself.

What the hell are we even thinking?

After watching the carousel for a few more minutes, she meandered along until she reached a playground area reserved for small children. Stevie was lying on his back in the grass with his legs straight in the air. His daughter was shrieking with laughter as she balanced on top of his feet. Gabby waved Lauren over, and they both watched Stevie play and laugh with Maya.

"That's an odd look," Gabby said. "Don't tell me you've finally got a biological clock kicking in?"

"Bio-what? Oh, hell, no. I can barely take care of myself. I like being an auntie to my sisters' kids," Lauren said, a snort of laughter tinting her voice.

Over on the lawn, Stevie had moved on to spinning Maya around him like she was an airplane. Gabby called over a warning to not make their daughter too dizzy or he'd be the one cleaning up puke.

Have I ever wanted kids? Lauren wondered. *I guess I did a long time ago.* She didn't know if that was because she actually wanted children or because it was what she was supposed to want. That had been everyone's plan: grow up, get married, have babies, retire to Boca. That didn't sound like a plan to Lauren—it sounded like her version of hell.

But as she watched Stevie, who had finally put his daughter down and was watching her chase bubbles, Lauren found herself thinking about Danny again. He was the exception to every rule she'd ever had. But things wouldn't be different this time around. She was on a road to another broken heart if she didn't do anything about it. Problem was, she really didn't want to stop.

CHAPTER TWENTY-THREE

The Red Parrot Café was a favorite of Lauren's. She'd found it within two days of moving back to New York. A short walk from her place, it was open almost 24/7 and not only served top-notch coffee, but they made iced cinnamon rolls that were to die for. It was late enough in the evening that she relegated herself to decaf only. What she really wanted to do was drown her sorrows in some top shelf tequila but showing up hung over at the studio in the morning wasn't an option.

The more she pushed herself to come up with that hook, the brilliant idea that would turn into the single the band needed, the more mired she became. She was wading through a bog of creative quicksand that pulled her further under with every rejected idea. Pressing the heel of her palm against her forehead, she fought the urge to fling the coffee against the wall.

She hated admitting anything that made her look weak or incapable, and she hadn't told anyone—not even Augie—how much she was really struggling. She'd watched too many other artists circle the drain, cranking out mediocre music in a desperate attempt to keep their careers alive. The thought of that happening to her and The Kingmakers made her stomach heave.

But I'm not fooling anyone. The guys know something's up. They see the crappy material I'm bringing to the studio.

That very day, as they were wrapping up their session, Lauren overheard DJ saying to Stevie that he was worried about her. That something was obviously on her mind and throwing her off her game. She pinched her nose, the gesture old muscle memory from her abusive affair with cocaine. The action came wrapped in an almost wistful longing, and Lauren flinched. That wasn't going to solve her writing problem. She flagged down the waitress and ordered a cup of tea.

She fussed with her phone. Earlier she'd texted Danny to say that she hoped his day had gone better than hers, and that she was going to head over to Red Parrot. She didn't ask him to come, but she hoped he'd at least answer her message. The absence of alerts on the screen didn't make her feel any better.

"Hey, good-lookin'."

Lauren was halfway through her second cup of peppermint tea when Danny thumped down into the chair next to her.

"Hey!"

"Glad I caught you. I'm heading to meet Joey, so I can only stay for a minute."

"A few minutes is better than none. How are things?" She could see the waitress watching them, and Lauren made sure to keep both her hands firmly on the warm mug.

"Work's work," he answered. "Lucas is doing really well with baseball. Kid keeps it up, and I might not have to worry about paying for his college. Matty seems to prefer hoop. Tommy's more art and music."

"Hey, don't knock music," Lauren said. Danny laughed, and the deep notes warmed her.

"Speaking of music," she continued. "I invited Cole to come watch a session in the studio while we were recording. I haven't heard from her or Maggie, but I was thinking—you should stop by, too. Say hello to Augie, meet the rest of the band."

"I wouldn't want to be underfoot."

"Whatever, wise guy. You're never underfoot, and you know it. I'm serious."

"I know, and maybe."

The answer was evasive, and Lauren guessed it was because of Heather. "I don't mean to put you in an awkward position, I just thought—"

"Don't even... You didn't. I think it would be cool to see the studio. But between work and the boys, my schedule is, you know, crazy."

Lauren let it go. "I get it. But the offer stands."

"So how is the album going?"

It was Lauren's turn to equivocate. "Pretty good. Couple songs are fighting me, though. Can't quite get them where they need to be." The self-doubt in the back of her head screamed that she was full of shit, and that the songs weren't just fighting her, they'd abandoned her. But Lauren kept a smile plastered on her face. "Songwriting can be a thorny process."

"You'll be fine," he said casually. "You're Lauren Stone!"

Deep down Lauren wondered if "being Lauren Stone" was enough.

CHAPTER
TWENTY-FOUR

Despite the anxiety consuming Lauren, The Kingmakers were right on schedule for how they usually came together during album production. Each day, they started with a short jam session to warm up. They'd pull chairs into a semi-circle in front of Augie's drum kit, and someone would start. A few notes, a cadence, and everyone else would join in. They'd spend an hour doing that most days before Fitz had them get down to business.

Today had started the same, and they'd come away with some interplay between Augie and Ox that had a lot of promise. But looming later in the day was a production meeting, and Lauren wasn't looking forward to that conversation. There were three songs she needed to finish, and she hadn't. She berated herself for not stepping up, and she knew the guys had noticed her mood swings. But they didn't know the source.

Once the meeting started, after they got through schedule minutiae, the band dug into a problematic set of lyrics. A few ideas got moved around, and then Ox picked out some bass lines that caught everyone's attention. Twenty minutes later, a tap on the studio window interrupted them. Tisha was in the control room and she had company: Danny.

Augie and the rest of the band made no pretense of subtlety as they looked through the window. Ox craned his head to the side to get a better look at Danny. While they couldn't hear what Lauren and Danny were saying, the couple's body language spoke volumes. Augie's brow furrowed when he saw Danny run his hand down Lauren's arm.

"That's him, huh? The one she used to date? Shorter than I thought he'd be." DJ's squint was critical.

"Yep. That's him. *The* Danny Padovano." He wondered if this was the reason Lauren's moods had been all over the map. Without looking at it, Augie made a small adjustment to his ride cymbal and gave the bell a tap. Satisfied with the sharp ping that resulted, he quieted the bronze alloy disc.

"I don't like him," DJ said. "Looks like a jackass."

Stevie's observation that Lauren and Danny just looked like old chums distracted Augie from the odd note in DJ's voice.

"I don't know what's up," Augie said to Stevie. "But I don't like it."

"Don't really matter if you like it. Kinda her business." Ox fiddled with the string on his bass without looking at it.

Augie rolled his stool back and stared at the other three. "Any of you idiots remember what happened the last time Danny broke her heart? It almost *ended* her."

"Don't be such a drama queen, Augie. That was what? Almost twenty years ago? Shit, she'd been split from him for almost a year when I met her." Ox continued to watch the scene beyond the window.

Augie swiveled to stare at Ox. "Dude," he said, the single word an indictment of Ox's nonchalant attitude. "You didn't see the actual breakup, but every goddamn one of you saw the aftermath."

Ox set his jaw in a stubborn line. "*Mano*, she ain't made of glass. Plus, she left him behind, and it was—literally—years before her coke problem."

"She might have left, but he's the one who broke off their relationship." Augie pushed the words out through his scowl. "And it took years to *develop* her coke problem."

Ox was about to respond, but Stevie interrupted them. "You're right, mate. She's not made of glass, but I'm with Augie. We've got a shite-ton of work ahead of us on this album. Her lyrics are nowhere as good as they could be. I don't want some barmy affair taking her off the rails now—not when the critics are licking their chops and waiting for us to tank."

"Bunch of nervous-fucking-Nancys," Ox groused. "She's had other relationships bust up, and she never went south. Been a pain-in the-ass, yes. Let her handle her business."

Augie glanced out the window again. "Those other relationships weren't Danny." He wanted to be glad for Lauren but seeing her with Danny didn't make him happy. It filled him with dread.

"Plus, what do you think she's going to do if we all tell her it's a bad idea?" Stevie asked.

"She'll want it even more. They fooling around or not?" DJ pressed his mouth into a thin line.

Augie stood up. "We'll know soon enough. If they are, it isn't like she's going to be able to keep a secret."

"Going to chaperone?" DJ asked.

"Have to take a piss, if you need to know."

"Well, awesome. I'll alert the media."

Augie couldn't help but crack a smile. "You're an asshole."

"Yeah, but you love me."

Augie gave DJ the finger.

"You said to stop by sometime," Danny said. "I just thought it would be a nice surprise. I'll go if this is a bad time." He squeezed her hand and rubbed his thumb across the back of it.

"No, it's fine. I'm always happy to see you." Lauren's throat tightened, making it hard to swallow. They weren't sharing a bed, and they hadn't kissed since that one lapse in judgment at her apartment. But they weren't being honest either and that fact ate at Lauren.

"You don't seem happy," he said.

"I just—" She cut herself off. "What are we doing, Danny? We might not be sleeping together, but we're sneaking around—and like I said before, I won't be anyone's dirty little secret, not even yours."

"I'll figure things out, I promise."

They were so engrossed in their conversation that they didn't notice Augie until he was in the room with them. Both had the decency to look embarrassed. Her cousin gave Danny a grunt as he walked by.

"Augie hates my guts, doesn't he?"

"Hate's a strong word," Lauren said, even though she suspected it was true. "Come in for a minute, meet the rest of the guys."

She took Danny's hand and led him into the recording studio. "Danny, this is DJ, Stevie, and Ox. Guys, this is Danny."

"Good to meet you, mate," Stevie said.

"The man, the myth, the legend." Ox laughed.

After a short silence, DJ gave him a measured look, a nod, and a curt, "S'up?"

When he passed Lauren and Danny, Augie heard enough of the conversation to convince him that they were more than just friends. Rather than go back to the studio, he waited in one of the side offices for Danny to leave. Soon he was rewarded for his patience as Danny came down the hall.

"Danny, give me a minute." Augie jerked his head towards the empty room. Once they were inside, Augie shut the door, and the two men sized each other up.

"What do you want, Augie?" Danny raised his chin defiantly.

"I want to set you straight on something. I'm not going to ask what's going on between you and Lauren." Augie leaned back on the desk and drummed his fingers on the smooth wood top.

"Good. It's none of your business—"

"—For now." Augie gave Danny another once-over before locking eyes with him again. "If you do anything to screw her up—"

"Whoa, hold up there! What do you mean, 'screw her up'?" Danny stiffened, his posture defensive. Augie sprang up as well. He was pretty sure they wouldn't come to blows but couldn't guarantee it.

"You weren't there, Danny. You didn't go through the whole cocaine thing with her. I'm not blaming you, or saying it was your fault, but Lauren was lost for a *long* time after you broke up with her. She held it together for a while, but she went down a dark road back then. I *never* want to see her like that again. *Ever.*"

"You think I do? Jesus, Augie. I wasn't there, but I saw the headlines."

"You saw the headlines?" Augie's voice dripped sarcasm as he took a step closer to Danny. "You didn't see *shit*. You weren't the one holding her up when she was doubled-over sick, or when she had panic attacks. You didn't wake up every single fucking day and wonder if you were going to find her sprawled on the floor, dead. So don't you think for a single goddamn second that you know what she went through."

Danny opened his mouth, but Augie didn't let him get a word in.

"If the two of you want to relive your youth for a few nights, fine. That's your business. Whatever. But tell her that. And if you want to be with her—and not with your wife anymore—tell her that, too.

Just don't tell her one thing and then do another. Do *not* break her heart, Danny. I don't know if she could get over you a second time."

"Augie—"

Augie poked a finger into Danny's chest. "And if it comes to that, cop or no cop—I swear to God you'll answer to me."

CHAPTER TWENTY-FIVE

The heat of early July was no match for the glacial impasse between Heather and Danny. By the time the Fourth of July holiday arrived, they were barely speaking. They tried to pretend in front of the family, but there was no mistaking the tension. Heather was drained. While the many late nights at work for Danny had lessened, she felt he was further away from her than ever. She lost count of the times she'd seen him doing work around the yard or house with a small smile and a faraway expression on his face. He certainly didn't smile that way when he looked at her. In fact, he hardly looked at her at all anymore.

Finding time for sex had been next to impossible even when things were good. Like most married couples, their days were filled with work and kids and commitments, and they were exhausted by the time they went to bed. Romance was non-existent. Now the sex —if it happened at all—was perfunctory and, frankly, dull. They both just went through the motions. One more chore to be checked off the list.

For Danny, life was just as mundane. Get up in the morning; chase down the dregs of society; fix the house; mow the lawn; help the boys with their homework; and tumble into bed. When he did initiate sex with Heather, it felt like she was obliging him. Doing her wifely duty because she had to, not because she actually *wanted* him. Half the time she looked to the side as if she was bored and just wanted it to be done. Danny finally started closing his eyes so he didn't have to see her disinterest.

The times he could steal away to visit with Lauren were his refuge. The colder and more distant his marriage felt, the more he craved the closeness, warmth, and camaraderie he felt with Lauren. They might not be sleeping together, but at least it felt like she wanted to be around him.

Just ahead of the summer holiday crowds, all the Padovanos—minus Cole, who had been spending the last two weeks with her father in Michigan—took a Friday off and went to the beach. They packed the cars with coolers, chairs, umbrellas, and more. The sun dominated a clear blue sky, sending the temperature well into the 80s—exactly what everyone wanted for a day at the shore. Heather brought a book to read and was delighted watching her boys play with Joey. They were so excited he was home and couldn't get enough of their uncle. Watching them made her smile, and she hadn't smiled much lately.

As the sun slid towards the horizon, the family packed up. Heather tucked towels, her book, and a resealable bag full of suntan lotion and aloe ointment into a giant pink and green polka-dot beach bag. Joey and Danny were carrying the oversized cooler to the car. Nearby, Tommy was using his father's phone to take pictures. "Got some good ones, Mom!"

"That's good, honey. Let me have the phone and I'll put it in the bag."

Tommy half-walked, half-ran over, swiping through the pictures and stumbling in the deep sand. "Look at the seagull one!"

He handed the phone to his mother and was off like a rocket to find his brothers. Heather bobbled the phone and managed not to drop it. But when she picked it up, it wasn't a seagull she was looking at—it was a selfie of Danny and Lauren. And it was from last week.

That cheating bastard! She closed her eyes and took a deep breath. As much as she wanted to scream at him, to absolutely eviscerate him, the beach wasn't the place. But this was the last straw.

By the time Danny got up the next morning, Heather was already barreling her way through her Saturday morning: laundry, then cleaning the kitchen, bathroom, and bedrooms. He said good morning but got a standoffish response. He didn't question it, just went outside to start the yard work that had been piling up. He fixed the front railing and went out to get gas for the lawn mower. When he got back, the house was quiet.

He tried to remember if one of the boys had something going on today—a game, birthday party, or an overnight with friends—but nothing came to mind. He sighed. He'd get an earful from Heather if he'd forgotten he was expected to attend an event. He sent her a quick text. When he didn't hear back right away, he headed over to his father's place to borrow a couple tools he needed for his next project: shelves over Matty's desk. He ended up talking with his father for a while and by the time he finished, Danny was starting to wonder where Heather was. She hadn't returned his text yet, and she usually called if she was running late.

Danny said goodbye to his father and had just given his mother a kiss on the cheek when his cell phone rang. He glanced at the screen —it was Heather.

"Where are you?" he snapped, not bothering with a hello.

"I could ask you the same thing." Heather's voice was curt.

"What are you talking about? I'm at Dad's. You weren't at the house when I got home, so I came to borrow the drill for Matty's shelves." Danny put a finger in his free ear. The cell connection was terrible. "Where are you?"

"With my parents, in Connecticut. The boys are with me."

"What are you talking about? At your parents' cottage? Since when?" Danny slapped his palm against the island's tile top. Out of the corner of his eye, he saw his parents glance at each other. His mother crossed herself.

"I'm sick of it, Danny!" Heather shouted.

Anger and tears flooded her voice, and a lance of pain hit him because he knew he was the reason for both.

"Heather—"

"I'm not going to sit around and play the doting wife while you screw around with your old girlfriend. You never look at me anymore, you never touch me. I'm through, Danny."

"Heather. HEATHER! I am not fooling around with anyone!" His conscience prickled as he said it.

"Don't lie to me! I saw the selfie on your phone: you and Lauren in the park—"

Danny's jaw dropped. She'd gone through his phone? For a split second, Danny was speechless.

"—And I know you were having dinner with her at Dom's the night of that ball game. Rachel saw you and texted me. When I asked you about it when you got home, you lied to me. You said you had dinner with your father when you really had dinner with her."

"We've been over this a hundred times already! I *did* have dinner with my dad." He might not have lied about having dinner with his father, he had deliberately not mentioned seeing Lauren. That was a lie of omission, but it was a lie, nonetheless. Guilt gnawed at him, warring with the frustration and emptiness that had turned his marriage into a shell.

"How many other times have you been with her, Danny?"

"Stop!" he yelled. "I'm *not* sleeping with her—we're still married, in case you forgot." Again, in his peripheral vision, Danny saw his mother cross herself. He turned his back so he couldn't see her.

"In case I had forgotten? *Really?* I didn't think you'd noticed. You certainly haven't treated me like your wife in a long time."

"I don't want to do this on the phone," Danny said. "When will you be home? We'll talk about it then!"

"Now you want to talk? You've had plenty of chances up until now."

"When?" Danny demanded.

Heather ignored his last question. "We're not coming home. We're spending the rest of the summer here with my parents. Maybe being in different states will help you get this out of your system and then—*maybe*—we can figure out if there's anything left in this wreck of a marriage worth saving."

The floor seemed to drop away from under Danny's feet. Heather wasn't coming home? She wasn't bringing his boys home? The sour nausea that crawled up his throat and lingered for a split second was washed away by the wave of anger that crashed over him.

"What the fuck are you talking about? You're *leaving* me? No! You are not spending the rest of the summer with your parents. What about Lucas, Matty and Tommy? When am I supposed to see... Heather? *Heather?*" She'd hung up on him, Danny hit redial and got voice mail.

"Heather! Call me back!" Danny was furious. His wife's parents owned a small vacation home near Hammonasset Beach in Connecticut. It was more than a two-hour drive away—and if the highway was backed up, the trip could take closer to four. If Heather stayed there for the rest of the summer, it would be nearly impossible for him to see his sons.

Danny stared at the phone in his hand. "I can't believe this. She says she's going to spend the summer with the boys at her parents' beach cottage."

"We gathered that," Richie said.

"I haven't done anything," Danny said. "Nothing! And this is what I get?" He jammed his phone in his pocket.

"Nothing?" Deb said, her voice prim and heavy with disappointment. "When this one's around, there's always some kind of trouble going on."

She flipped open the newspaper to the entertainment page. There was a photo of Lauren relaxing on a bench, talking with Stevie. Danny recognized the AC/DC shirt and realized it must have been taken the same day he and Lauren ran into Joey, and suddenly all his worries about cameras being everywhere flooded back... plus there was the damning selfie on his own phone.

Danny ground his teeth. He couldn't claim total innocence—he hadn't done "nothing," as he'd so boldly exclaimed a moment before. Some people wouldn't have an issue with what he and Lauren were doing. But plenty would, and his mother was firmly in that camp. As far as she was concerned, even *thinking* about being with Lauren was tantamount to cheating. And if that was true, then Danny had been cheating for his whole marriage.

"I'm *not* sleeping with her," Danny said, his voice tight. He'd made mistakes—big ones. The time he'd spent with Lauren. The time he kissed her. As much as he wanted to deny it, it was indistinguishable from cheating. But he hadn't crossed that last line; he hadn't had sex with her despite how desperately he wanted to. He wanted that fact to matter somehow, but it didn't. In all the lies he'd told, it was the one truth—and, rational or not, being presumed guilty of the one thing he *hadn't* done infuriated him. He grabbed his keys.

"Danny?" The tone of Richie's voice made him pause at the door. "Where are you going?"

"I don't know," was all Danny said before he walked out of the house.

After he got into the car, Danny slammed his palm against the steering wheel. The string of expletives that poured out of him would have shamed a longshoreman. He scrubbed away some rogue tears with the back of his hand and then drove off. For the first ten minutes, he drove aimlessly and was lucky he didn't get in an accident or pulled over. Finally, he managed to settle down enough to focus and headed into the city. He found his way up Madison Avenue until he reached East 79th Street and took that into Central Park. There was a small area near Bank Rock Bay where there were a few parking spots reserved for NYPD vehicles. He pulled over and parked, flipping his NYPD car identification onto the dashboard. Then he sat, silent, staring out towards the water while his mind churned.

I'm not perfect, he thought. *I've made plenty of mistakes. But I've sure as hell been trying. I could have slept with Lauren that first time and I didn't. And now everyone thinks I'm guilty? And Heather just walks out and takes the boys?*

He sat in the car for two hours, playing recent events over and over in his brain. Things he'd done and not done, alternating between angry, devastated, guilty, sad, and too many other emotions to sort out. But one thing he realized was that he truly felt alone. Abandoned. Heather had left. And what would his family think? They'd be on Heather's side. There was only one person he could turn to.

He turned the key, and the engine roared awake. Putting it into drive, he headed down West Street until he reached the south side of the park. From there it was a short drive on 7th and then 57th until he reached the Somerset.

He gave his car to the valet and dialed Lauren's number.

It was midnight.

Lauren was waiting at the door when he came up. "Danny? What's going on? Are you okay?"

"Heather left," he said, walking past her and into the apartment. "She left and she *took my boys*. She's at her parents' place in Connecticut so I can get it out of my system."

Lauren was shocked. By herself, in the dark of night, she'd

wondered if Danny would ever leave Heather. But she hadn't considered that Heather might be the one to leave.

"Get what out of your system?"

"You."

"Jesus."

"Heather's convinced I'm sleeping with you. Doesn't matter if it isn't true: I'm guilty as charged." Danny paced as he talked.

Lauren's gut twisted. "Danny, I'm sorry, but... what we've been doing? Not exactly on the up and up."

"I know." Even though he looked down, Lauren could still see the anguish on his face. But it was the suffering in his voice that broke her heart. "She took my boys."

There was nothing Lauren could say to make him feel better. She knew how much Danny loved his sons and trying to make the situation seem less terrible would be little more than empty platitudes. She hated feeling helpless.

He caught her around the waist and pulled her closer.

"Danny!"

"I'm tired of fighting it," he said. "I don't know if this is a one-night stand or something else... I just know it's something I want." As he spoke, Danny closed the small distance still between them.

"We can't." Lauren's voice was barely a whisper. She put her hands up, as if to push him away, but they hovered a fraction of an inch above his chest. She didn't dare touch him.

"I know this is crazy," he said. "If you want out of this mess, tell me now. Tell me now and I'll go—and I won't come back. I won't ever bother you again."

"Don't say that." Even as confused and conflicted as she was, Lauren couldn't bear the thought of Danny leaving. Not now. Her life felt like a swirling mess, and he was the one solid piece of land in the middle of it. She looked up, meeting his eyes as they searched her face.

"Don't go," she said, her hands coming to rest on his chest. "Tonight's enough, at least for now."

CHAPTER TWENTY-SIX

Hanging over the city, the moon washed everything in Lauren's bedroom with a silvery light. Danny rolled onto his back and pulled the sheet up over his waist. With a languid stretch, Lauren curled up alongside him, resting her head on his shoulder and sliding an arm across his waist.

The past two hours had been a blur. From the moment she'd allowed him to stay, they'd been all over each other. A trail of clothes led from the living room to her bedroom, and the sheets on her bed were in complete disarray.

Since returning to New York, Lauren had daydreamed about being intimate with Danny again. Would it be awkward? Not as good as she remembered? Tonight had dispelled those worries. The sex was intense and gratifying and forgetting everything else had been easy. But now that the afterglow was dimming, reality loomed heavy over them both. Lauren heard a long, slow breath come out of Danny.

She studied his profile. "Are you sorry?"

"About this? No."

Lauren thought his answer was a little too fast, a little too firm, but she let it go as he rolled towards her and kissed her, sliding his hand along her side. The feel of his skin against hers gave Lauren chills, but she squirmed loose. She needed a moment, a modicum of distance. She swung her legs over the edge of the bed. The air was cool and goosebumps appeared on her arms.

"I'm getting some water," she said. "Want any?" She grabbed his shirt from the floor and pulled it on. She was almost at the bedroom door by the time Danny said yes.

Ice crackled in her glass as the water hit the cubes. Lauren took a deep drink, a droplet of water escaping and running down her chin. She pressed her head against the cool metal of the stainless-steel refrigerator, unsure what to think. Even after all these years, he remembered all the ways she liked to be touched. The awkwardness of youth and inexperience was gone, replaced by a maturity and worldliness.

She thought about the passion they'd shared, and the memory of him inside her made her tremble. It had been a long time since being with someone had brought her that much joy. But at what cost? His marriage? His sons? What was she thinking? Her throat tightened, making it hard to swallow.

Back in the bedroom, she found Danny sitting on the edge of the bed, staring out the window towards the city. Lauren settled behind him. She kissed his shoulder as she handed him the glass. After taking a drink, he put it on the nightstand. Lauren slid her arms around his chest and rested her chin on his shoulder, sharing the view of the park and cityscape.

She squeezed him a little tighter. Danny shifted and twisted around, gently pushing Lauren back down on the bed. Her worries dried up, forgotten again as she lost herself in the way he was looking at her. Everything she wanted, everything she missed, was in those eyes. Lauren moved her hands from Danny's back, down his arms, and back again as he kissed her throat and her shoulders with rough lips.

She arched beneath his hands and let out a sigh that transformed into a moan as Danny's mouth eased down her body, planting lingering kisses along the way to her hip and back up until he reached her throat. Digging her fingers into the sheets, she wondered if he could feel her heart pounding.

"You're even more beautiful now than you were back then," he said as he rubbed a thumb against her cheek.

Now.

The word, bright and sharp, hooked Lauren. All they had was now. This moment. And she didn't want to waste any of it.

She kissed him, ferocious, and leaned forward, pushing Danny down on the mattress. He offered a token resistance before he relented. Astride him, Lauren ran her fingernails from his waist to his chest. Letting her fingers graze back and forth over his nipples, she felt his entire body tighten. His fingertips felt rough as they trailed up her thighs and over her waist, along her ribs, until he cupped her breasts in his hands. A soft moan escaped her as she was consumed by her desires.

He twisted a little and she moved back, giving him the room to raise himself up. As he teased her with his fingers and tongue, Lauren ran her fingernails up his sides and down his chest. Raising up slightly, she leaned her weight forward and he resisted, tightening his arms to hold her close against him. He felt solid and strong.

"Lie back," she whispered, gently nipping at his earlobe.

He complied, letting her weight carry them both down to the mattress. The moment they did, she moved against him, surrounding him. She savored the feeling of him inside her, but even better was hearing him groan and call out her name.

"Say my name again," she said, rocking against him.

Instead, Danny grabbed her hips, stilling her. He looked lost and unsure. Lauren put her hands over his, working at his fingers until he laced them with hers. She waited while emotions she couldn't name played across his face.

"What's wrong?" she asked.

"You don't want to listen to me," he said.

Lauren could swear she saw a flash of tears in his eyes. She brought his hand up to her lips and kissed it. "What are you talking about? I love hearing your voice."

He worked his jaw but said nothing.

Lauren leaned down, her lips brushing his ear. She nipped his earlobe and whispered, "Talk to me, Danny. Tell me what you want."

Danny thought he might die. What *did* he want? Did he even really know? He couldn't remember the last time anyone had asked him that—or if they'd listened to his answer. But in that moment, he wanted Lauren. He wanted to give himself over to her. Let all his walls down and abandon any sense of restraint. Feel as free as he did when he was younger—before grown-up responsibilities anchored him down. He hesitated, and when he looked up, he saw Lauren mouth the word "anything."

Danny threw caution to the wind. "I want to shout your name when I finish."

He expected Lauren to laugh at his simple request. It wasn't particularly racy or unusual, but he'd been shushed for so long. Instead, she studied him, and he saw something in her eyes that said she understood. She knew there was a deeper meaning behind the request. Then a sensual smile spread across her face that thrilled Danny to his core.

As she moved along his length, controlling the tempo, Danny gave himself to her with abandon. He held on as long as he could, not wanting it to end, and when he finally came, he bellowed Lauren's name into the night before collapsing against the mattress, completely spent. By the time they curled up together, sleepy and sated, it was three in the morning.

When Danny opened his eyes again, the sun had taken the moon's place and bright light cascaded through the window. For a split second, he wondered, had last night had been a crazy fever dream. No. He was in a huge, king-sized bed, naked, with Lauren sleeping next to him, her hair a dark, wild mess splashed across the ivory pillowcase.

His heart leaped and then dropped into an abyss as ice washed through his veins, and the events of the past twenty-four hours crashed down around him.

What have I done?

He'd slept with Lauren—started the affair that his wife had been accusing him of for weeks. His stomach clenched, anger, guilt and uncertainty mingling into a sour ball that weighed him down. Heather had left him. Taken his sons and left. Even though he hadn't slept with Lauren until last night, he couldn't blame Heather—he was the reason she'd left.

Next to him, Lauren shifted under the sheet. She looked peaceful and content, and for a moment, the bitter knot inside him eased. When he moved again, she opened her eyes and stretched.

"Hey, good looking," she said. Her voice held the soft note of someone coming out of a deep, satisfying sleep.

Danny didn't say anything. He wanted to be happy. He *was* happy, but everything had changed. What was he going to do now? He threw his legs over the side of the bed and reached for his pants. He looked around, unsure where the rest of his clothes were.

"Danny?"

"I... yeah, I have to go." He reached down and grabbed a sock.

She responded with silence. He turned to offer an explanation that made sense, just in time to see her jamming an arm through her t-shirt as she left the room. He followed.

"Hang on," he said. "I didn't mean—"

"No, I get it," she said. She pulled a bowl of cut-up melon out of the refrigerator. Using her fingers, she popped a chunk into her mouth. Danny's stomach growled. If she heard it, she didn't offer him any.

"I just wasn't expecting you to bolt with barely a word," she said.

Like you're ashamed. The unspoken implication lingered, intertwined with her words like a choking bittersweet vine.

Danny came around the island to stand beside her. He cupped her face in his hands and kissed her. "I'm not sorry," he said. "Not about this. And not of you. I just..."

"A lot's happened," she said.

That was a royal understatement.

"I need to sort through some things," he said.

"I understand."

Danny hoped she was telling the truth. He tracked down the rest of his clothes, which were strewn about, and then found one shoe. It was hard to pay attention to finding the other when Lauren was in nothing more than a t-shirt and a pair of panties. She located the missing shoe and gave it to him. When he got to the door, he put his arms around her.

"What do we do now?" Lauren asked.

"I don't know," was all he could say.

After Danny left, Lauren went back to bed. She wasn't sleepy but cocooning herself in the blankets gave her a sense of comfort. Rather than fluff the pillow, she punched it, turned it over, and manhandled it again. The reality was, she was a little pissed Danny had left so abruptly. She hadn't expected him to stay all day, but she'd fallen asleep dreaming about a lazy morning in bed and breakfast together. Four chunks of melon eaten straight from the bowl was hardly a meal.

But she couldn't blame him. Danny's life had turned upside down in twenty-four hours. She pulled the blankets a little tighter. She'd had a hand in all this, and a feeling—guilt? remorse? shame? She wasn't sure what it was—buffeted her.

His wife left him, she told herself in a vain attempt at rationalization. But every walk in the park, shared coffee, time spent reminiscing had opened the door a little wider. And she'd let Danny walk right through it. Lauren turned onto her back and stared at the ceiling. It had been a wonderful, glorious night. She'd felt more loved and wanted in those few hours than she had in a very long time. And she knew they needed to stop before they went any further. They could still treasure whatever memories they'd made last night.

But the truth was, she'd quit Danny cold turkey when she first left for LA. Now, she'd fallen off the wagon, and fallen hard. And now that she'd had a taste of what she left behind, she wasn't sure she could stop.

CHAPTER TWENTY-SEVEN

As Danny drove home, his abrupt departure gnawed at him. The only thing worse would have been bolting before Lauren woke up. He considered turning around but couldn't. He wanted time to think.

Then another realization dawned on him: it was Sunday. And Sunday meant family dinner after church. Despite everything that happened, skipping Mass was too rebellious, not to mention what his mother might say about his absence. He was so concerned about what might be waiting for him at dinner, he barely remembered the drive home.

He showered and changed and hurried back to his Jeep. But at the end of the street, Danny stopped at the intersection. He sat there, frozen, until the driver behind him leaned on the horn and blasted him out of his reverie. He turned left instead of right. He couldn't bring himself to go to St. Catherine's and make the long walk down the nave to join his family.

St. C's was the same church where he and Heather had been married.

He wasn't ready for that.

Instead, he drove until he found another church, one dedicated to St. Jude. He hustled in just as the priest was beginning the sermon. Two old biddies clucked a reprimand as Danny slipped into a pew at the very back.

He didn't hear much of what the priest said. He simply stared at the front of the church, his mind churning. Even though this wasn't where he'd been married, the phrases "forsaking all others" and "death do us part" lashed him. Had he been lying when he took those vows? No, he told himself. He'd meant all of them. At least, back then he had.

The congregation knelt to pray. He'd never been particularly devout, going to church on Sunday mostly because it was expected—a duty—and not out of any deep, abiding sense of faith. However, now seemed like a smart time to start praying. The padding on the kneeler was non-existent, and the wood dug into his knees.

God? Danny P. here, got a sec for me? That was how he'd started all his prayers when he was a little boy. *I don't know what to do. I married Heather because she got pregnant. I mean, I loved her—I still do. But are we in love with each other anymore? You know what's going on with us. We're not happy. And I know... I'm not perfect. I've screwed up plenty.*

Danny shifted, moving his knees a little in a futile hope of comfort. He thought of Lucas, Matty, and Tommy, hundreds of miles away and out of reach. *How could she take them away from me?* He was about to make the usual excuse—that he hadn't cheated on her—but he checked himself. He might not have been physically unfaithful until last night, but in his mind, he'd been down that road a thousand times.

The congregation stood and again, Danny was a few seconds behind everyone else. *St. Jude, you're the patron saint of lost causes. No matter what I do, someone gets hurt. Please help me figure this out.*

Sunday dinner was halfway finished by the time he arrived. The empty chairs where his boys usually sat were a kick to the gut. He grunted a hello, and the conversation paused for a few seconds too long. Danny knew his mother had blabbed something about Heather to his siblings. But he didn't address the elephant in the room. He filled his plate and started eating, stubbornly staying silent while the others talked.

Once the table was cleared, Danny grabbed Maggie and Joey and asked them to step outside for a second. He wanted to make sure they had his version of the story, not just his mother's.

"What's going on, Danny?" Maggie asked. "Ma said Heather was out of town with the boys. She said to ask you what was going on—"

Joey interrupted. "—No, she said to ask what you'd *done*. Then she crossed herself about a dozen times, which means this isn't some fun weekend away. Seriously, bro. What's going on?"

There was no sense in trying to spin anything. "Heather left."

His sister did a double take. "What do you mean she left?"

"She walked out, Maggie. I got this crazy call on Saturday with her saying she was tired of everything going on and wasn't going to put up with it."

"What stuff going on?" Joey asked.

"You haven't been around for most of this," Danny said to Joey. "Heather's convinced I've been running around with Lauren."

"Well, you're not having an affair. Are you?" Never one to dissemble, Joey's question was pointed.

"I wasn't." Danny's answer was blunt and aggressive, inviting a confrontation.

"What do you mean by that?" Maggie's voice went up a little, and her eyes got huge.

"Wasn't?" Joey said at the same time.

"Heather walked out on *me*. I told her repeatedly that I wasn't sleeping with Lauren, and it was the goddamn truth. But after she left, I thought that if I'd already been tried and convicted, then I may as well do the crime." Danny folded his arms, stubborn and defensive.

"Shit—" was all Joey managed to say.

"—Danny! What are you thinking? You're *married.* How could Lauren—"

"—Don't put this on her, Mags. This was my decision. *Mine!* I went to Lauren." Danny's voice was quiet, but there was iron in it.

He turned to go back to the house. He didn't want to continue the conversation. In fact, he didn't really want to be around his family at all.

Joey surprised him by asking, "Are you and Heather getting divorced?"

Danny stopped walking. "I don't know. We haven't talked about it outright, but I admit, I've wondered if we wouldn't be better off taking a break and separating." He felt the bluster and fight drain out of him. "I just thought we'd talk about it before it happened."

Before they finished talking, Danny asked them both to give him a little space, and he asked Maggie if she'd tell Cole later. He wasn't ready for whatever questions his niece would have. They went back inside to have dessert and listen to Cole regale them with stories about her visit with her father, including several about the very cute lifeguard at the lake near her father's house.

But Danny stayed quiet, Deb was frosty, and an odd feeling of unease suffused the room.

Back at his own house, Danny grabbed Saturday's mail on his way in and tossed it on the kitchen table. There were dishes in the sink from the day before, but he didn't feel like dealing with those. Instead, he went upstairs for a shower. After washing his hair and scrubbing down, he stood under the spray, letting the water run over him.

Knowing he'd caused Heather so much anguish didn't feel good. It had never been his intent to hurt her. But he'd been in pain, too, trapped in a no man's land—and now perception and reality were the same. It gave him an odd sense of relief even though his marriage was foundering. He'd slept with another woman, a woman he'd loved for most of his life. It didn't make the future any easier or any clearer, but somehow, he felt like he knew where he stood.

What he didn't expect was how empty his house felt. With the three boys, there always seemed to be noise and activity, quiet only settling over the house when they were asleep. Now the silence was uncomfortable. Once he got out of the shower, he found himself looking at photos. That's when the guilt started to gnaw at him, tearing meat off his bones. This wasn't just affecting him and Heather, it was affecting his sons, and he knew they were confused, upset, and scared.

He pulled out his cell and called Heather's number.

"What?" Her voice was abrupt and cold, and Danny bit his tongue.

"I want to talk to the boys for a minute."

The next voice he heard was Matty's. "Dad? Hey, Dad!"

"Hey, kid. How are you? Get some good beach time in today?"

"We did," Matty said. "We were at the beach for the whole day today. I'm a little sunburned but we swam a lot, and there's some kids in the cottages next door so we played beach football."

In the background, Danny could hear Tommy demanding the phone. The boys bickered for a moment until he heard Heather tell Matty to pass the phone over.

"Daddy?"

"Hey, kiddo. Having fun at Gram and Gramp's?"

"Yeah!" Tommy's voice was pure childhood excitement. "At the beach today, I built a sandcastle and we used seashells for windows and then Grandpa was a sea dragon and attacked it and later this week, we're gonna go to a water park. You coming with us, Daddy?"

"That's sounds great, buddy. But I have to work." Tears threatened to drown Danny's voice. He pressed his hand over his eyes, a vain attempt to dam up his tears as a different part of his heart exploded.

"Don't be sad, Daddy. When you come up, you can play the dragon, okay? Lucas wants the phone now."

Tommy was gone before Danny could even respond. He wondered if his sons were missing as much as he thought they would.

"Dad?" His older son's voice came over the phone, and he sounded worried.

Danny took a breath before answering. "Hey, champ. How are you?" He didn't want Lucas to hear how upset he was.

"I'm okay."

"But?" Danny knew that tone from his son.

"We always come here for a family vacation, but you're not here," said Lucas. He dropped his voice to a whisper. "Mom's been crying. Are you getting divorced?"

The question broke Danny's heart, and he tried to be careful with his answer. "Me and your mom haven't said anything about a divorce. Your mom needs a little time out of the city, so she surprised you guys with a trip. I want you to have a good time and not worry, okay? Tommy said you're going to a water park?"

"Yeah, later in the week."

"That's great! You have a good time, but remember, you're the oldest and that's a big responsibility. Make sure you listen to your mother and keep an eye on your brothers, okay? And you guys can call me any time you want while you're there."

"Okay, Dad."

Danny wished his eldest's answer sounded more reassured. "I'm serious," he said. "You call whenever you want."

"I will. Oh, dinner's ready. Do you want to talk to Mom?"

"If she wants to talk to me." Danny wasn't sure what he and Heather had to say to each other at this point, but he wanted Lucas to feel better.

"Mom, do you want to talk to Dad before I hang up?" There was a pause. "Here's Mom."

"Heather?"

The only answer was a beep—and then silence.

Danny wasn't surprised, but he was a little pissed. For the sake of the boys, Heather could have at least said good night.

After, Danny listened to the stillness in the house again. Sometimes the boys were too boisterous, but he'd much prefer that to the silence. Danny thought about how sad Lucas sounded and fought back the tears again, wrestling them down and hiding them away. The emptiness echoing around him was too much.

He tapped the screen of his phone and sent a text to Lauren. *<Want company?>*

A moment later, her response came back: *<Of course. Leaving the studio in about fifteen minutes. I'll tell the desk to send you right up.>*

Danny made sure to bring a change of clothes for the morning.

CHAPTER TWENTY-EIGHT

Lauren arrived at the studio the next day with a guitar case over her shoulder and wearing a cat-that-ate-the-canary expression.

"Well, look at you," Tisha said. "Someone had a good night." She arched an eyebrow as she looked Lauren up and down.

"It was a very good night," Lauren said. She stopped and knelt, fussing unnecessarily with the lace on her boot. She hoped that would end the conversation.

"Good for you, hon," Tisha said. "I'm glad someone's getting some because I'm certainly not. They're in Studio C today. Fitz needs A for a review but he'll be with you shortly." Her voice followed Lauren down the hall. "And when you're ready to dish, I want to hear all about it."

Lauren demurred. Trish was fabulous and quickly becoming someone Lauren considered a friend, but her affair—she winced inwardly at the word—with Danny wasn't for casual coffee talk. Maybe someday, but not now.

DJ recognized the case containing Lauren's favorite six-string as soon as she came in the room. "Now we're getting serious," he said. "She's bringing out the big guns."

"One of these days, I'm taking that guitar away and proving you don't need a lucky charm. Freakin' superstition." Ox guffawed, amused at himself.

Lauren stopped where she was and locked onto Ox with military precision. "You ever put your hands on this guitar, Ox, I will personally key the crap out of your precious little vintage Porsche."

Ox gasped. "You wouldn't."

"Touch that guitar and you'll find out," DJ said. "And I'd bet good money she'd trash the engine, too. You do *not* mess with the mojo." For emphasis, he keyed out some dramatic notes on his keyboard.

Fitz hustled into the room, a five-foot, four inch ball of energy. "Ah, wonderful ta see everyone. Good, good. I want ta get started." He bombarded them with a list of tasks that included going through some tapes, laying down vocal tracks from Lauren on two songs, and deciding once and for all if Augie would do the vocals for a song called "Wolf" that they'd been toying around with.

When they broke for lunch several hours later, Lauren pulled out her phone and sent Danny a message. Based on how the day was going, she knew they'd be late tonight and probably the next. Likely she wouldn't be able to see him until at least the middle of the week.

He replied a minute later: *<Dinner Thurs?>*

<My place. I'll cook.> She could feel Augie watching her and kept her face averted, pretending to go through email. She tried using some of her hair to hide her expression, but it didn't work.

"So, what's going on with you?" Augie asked.

"I, uh... I guess I have a dinner date later this week."

"A date?"

Lauren swore she heard disapproval in his voice, but maybe it was her own guilt. She pivoted in her chair and cocked her head. "With Danny," she said, daring Augie to make a comment.

He called her bluff. "Not a good—"

"—Don't really care."

"Lauren..." Augie said.

"Don't. Just don't." She turned and walked away, knowing exactly what the concerned expression on Augie's face looked like. She didn't know what made her angrier: that he was judging her or that she deserved it.

The Kingmakers plowed through the afternoon and worked well into the evening. Lauren and Augie stayed even later to collaborate on some lyrics. By the time they were done, Lauren's nerves were frayed, and her writing difficulties showed no signs of abating. The next two days were the same: long hours at the studio with only a little progress and quite a lot of bickering. Listening to them once, Fitz told Tisha he was sick of the "bloody lot of knobheads" and that they "needed ta be sent off with a flea in their ear"—which he said loud enough for all of them to hear, before stomping off to have a shot of whiskey in his office.

By the time Thursday arrived, Lauren was counting the minutes until dinner. She wasn't even all that hungry. She just wanted some quiet time with Danny—time with no demands, no arguments, no debates, and no big decisions. They'd planned on meeting at her place at six o'clock. At 5:45 she was still at the studio, embroiled in a verbal brawl with Stevie and Augie about the direction of a song.

"I wrote the goddamned thing, and I know what it means." She waved her hands in frustration as she yelled.

"It doesn't make any sense." Augie slapped a hand on the table.

"Our fans can handle a little complexity." Lauren's jaw ached from grinding her teeth.

"Augie's right on this one, luv," Stevie said. "You might know what it means, but I don't think anyone else will. The lyrics are a bit obscure."

"We have to face it," Augie said. "You're having a tough time writing this time around, but we can't hide behind vague concepts. Fans aren't going to connect with this." He yanked the papers out of Lauren's hands. "They're going to hate it."

They're going to hate it. The words hit Lauren like a punch to the gut. She felt her face turn scarlet as she was put on the spot. Until then, no one had really addressed her writing struggles head-on.

"I'm not—"

"—Don't bullshit us," Augie said. "Yes. You are."

Lauren's eyes darted around the room, and all she saw was agreement and pity. It shredded her inside. Her face felt like it was on fire. "Screw you!" she shouted and stormed out, slamming the door in her wake.

Furious and self-conscious, Lauren went back to her apartment. Just after she arrived, a text from Danny told her that he was going to be late for dinner. It was almost a relief—she was still steamed, and this gave her a chance to calm down. It was nearly eight o'clock when Danny came through the door, looking haggard.

"I'm sorry I'm late. I hope you're not pissed."

"No. I had a shitty day at the studio. A little alone time was just what I needed. Hungry?" The aroma of meat sauce with basil, oregano, and garlic curled through the room, and she pulled salads out of the refrigerator.

"Starving. You make the sauce?"

She smiled. "I did. From scratch."

Lauren's maternal grandmother had been from Italy and had taught her granddaughters how to make sauce and handmade pasta. Lauren loved cooking her Nonna Sofia's recipes but didn't get the chance to do it nearly as often as she liked. She gave the pot a stir and adjusted the burner temperature. Then she grabbed a large saucepot, filled it with water, and put that on the stove, too.

Danny disappeared to change and wash up. While he was gone, Lauren put her iPod on shuffle mode and connected it to the wireless speaker. When Danny returned, Lauren was engrossed in her cooking. Aerosmith's "Walk This Way" came on, and without even thinking, Lauren started to move to the beat and sing along with the lyrics.

She felt Danny come up behind her. He planted a lingering kiss on her neck and shook his hips in time with hers.

"And what—exactly—are you doing?" She leaned back slightly and let out a sigh. This was the first time today she'd felt remotely relaxed.

"Helping?"

"Nice try," she said. "Go slice up the bread. Otherwise, I'm going to overcook the pasta."

He reluctantly let go and pulled the loaf of Italian bread out of its bag. He sliced about half the loaf before setting the table and uncorking a bottle of wine. While he poured two glasses, Lauren tested the pasta, deemed it sufficiently al dente, and dumped it in a colander.

"So, what was going on today that made you late? You looked like a wreck when you came in."

Danny hesitated, a shadow passing across his face. "Murder case," he finally said. "Not something I want to talk about. What about your day? Why so shitty?"

Her shoulders slumped. "Fight with Augie and Stevie. We made good progress to start, worked through some bass line ideas that Ox's been wrangling. Then me, Augie, and Stevie got into it over one of my songs. I mean, *really* got into it."

Lauren combined the pasta with her sauce and added it to two large bowls. She grated fresh Pecorino-Romano cheese over hers and raised her eyebrows at Danny. "Just a little for me," he answered.

There wasn't much conversation during dinner—Danny appeared famished and wolfed down his meal. He did, however, take a moment between mouthfuls to rave about the sauce. After he wiped up the last of the marinara with the bread, they cleared the table. Lauren put her half-finished bowl in the refrigerator while Danny poured them both a second glass of wine. They took the wine and sat on the sofa together.

"I liked watching you cook," said Danny as he rubbed his hand up and down her leg. "You were definitely in the zone."

"I was? Guess it's just second nature to get into the music. I sang with Aerosmith once—on the Billboard Music Awards about, oh, six, seven years ago? It was amazing."

"That must've been cool. I'm such an idiot for never seeing one of your concerts."

"Yeah, you are, but I love you anyway..." The words slipped out before Lauren could stop them. She held her breath, wondering how he'd react.

For a second, he sat like a statue, but then he moved a little closer.

"I love you, too. Always have." There was a gruff catch in his voice, and she searched his face, looking for any doubts, any regrets. She didn't find them.

The kiss was soft, intimate, lingering—an invitation that promised so much more. When they pulled away, Lauren ran her fingers along Danny's cheek. She smiled as he glanced toward the bedroom, tempted, but she shook her head no.

"Not yet." She picked up her notebook. "Duty calls."

Reluctant, Danny moved away as Lauren opened the notebook and started to nibble on the end of her pen. He leaned his head back and shut his eyes—they were tired and burning. Letting himself wander through his memories, he thought about watching Lauren perform when they were young. When she was seventeen, she played with a local band at some of the area bars. They weren't supposed to let her in because she was underage, but people liked the band and the bars liked the money, so they'd look the other way. Back then, he'd always been torn. He loved watching Lauren perform but the crowds made him wary.

A frustrated sigh interrupted his thoughts. He opened one eye to find Lauren frowning at the pages.

"Remember playing at O'Malley's Pub back in the day?" He

hoped his question would distract her from whatever was aggravating her.

"Oh, God. I haven't thought of that dive in a long time."

"I've never understood how you can feel so comfortable up on stage. All those people watching you."

"That never bothered me." She got a faraway look. "But, man, it's a real rush. People screaming at you, for you. Singing your songs back to you. I'm not sure I can really describe it—it's something you have to experience."

"And all of them wanting to be you... or be *with* you." Danny couldn't help but think of the more hard-core fans. His mouth went a little dry.

"Part of the life," she said. "That's why I learned self-defense and why we have security with us on tour. Most of the fans are cool, but there are some idiots out there. I'd be lying if I said there weren't."

Danny made an indistinct noise of disgust. Even back in the O'Malley's days, Lauren had a little cadre of groupies who would follow her around. Most were harmless teenage boys hoping maybe—just maybe—she'd notice them. But there were older ones, too. More than once, Danny had to explain to some over-enthusiastic fan boy that Lauren wasn't a chew toy.

Lauren stood and stretched, cat-like. She leaned close to him and said, "I don't make a habit of sleeping with groupies, but in your case, I might make an exception." Her tone implied there would be no sleeping, at least not immediately. She didn't have to ask him a second time.

Later, as Lauren lay dozing in his arms, Danny found himself thinking about O'Malley's again. Back then, there might have been a hundred people at the bar on any given night. But what would a Kingmakers show be like now? With *thousands* of men there—grown-ass men, not little boys. Each one singing along with Lauren. Each one watching her and imagining all the different things they'd do if they got her alone.

A bolt of insecurity coursed through Danny, and he tightened his arm around her without even thinking. She murmured in her sleep. He told himself that he was being an idiot, but the last thing he thought about before he fell asleep was a stadium full of screaming fans.

CHAPTER TWENTY-NINE

Lauren was rarely without a notebook. She'd filled thousands since she first started writing songs. The very first, which was now tattered but safely ensconced in a secure storage locker, had a Joe Cool Snoopy on the cover. In Lauren's lap now was a brand-new spiral-bound journal. She'd picked one with an abstract sun made of different-sized diamond shapes on the cover, hoping a fresh set of pages would open the door to some fresh ideas.

She didn't realize Danny had come in from the other room until he started massaging her shoulders. She sighed and closed her eyes, trying to relax, as his thumbs pressed into the muscles at the base of her neck and down between her shoulder blades. She kept her eyes closed and rolled her head from side to side, attempting to loosen her neck.

"Still no luck?" he asked.

"No." That morning, they'd made love—early, as the sun was coming up, before Danny had to leave for work. As she lay in his arms after, Lauren had dissolved into tears as she confessed her difficulties writing, the friction it was causing in the band, and how insecure she felt about her talent.

"I don't know what's wrong." Even she could hear the defeat in her voice. "We've got some songs. Most are average. Couple are marginally good, but when we work on them, I don't hear a hit. Not one that people will grab on to. Maybe the critics are right. Maybe we are old news..."

"Bull. It will come to you, but the more you worry about it, the harder you'll make it. Like Lucas playing baseball. He's so worried about hitting, he swings at anything—so we always work on being patient. And waiting."

"I suck at waiting," Lauren said with a rueful smile. "Hey, I've been meaning to ask you something. I know I mentioned it to you once before, but I still haven't heard about Cole coming to the studio."

When Danny's hands stilled, she knew what the answer was.

"I don't know about that," he said. "Cole brought it up the other day, and the conversation got a little testy. I think with what's going on right now—with us—her visiting might not be in the cards."

The answer didn't surprise Lauren, but it did disappoint her. She'd been looking forward to Cole's visit and her youthful exuberance. She changed the subject.

"I bet you're looking forward to the weekend?" Lauren closed the notebook and tucked her pen into the metal spiral. Tomorrow, Danny was leaving early in the morning to go spend the weekend with his sons. Lauren was glad he'd have the chance to see the boys. She'd overheard him on the phone with them a few times, knew how much he missed them. But visiting with the boys meant he was visiting with Heather, too. She worried about how hard the weekend might be for Danny.

Or maybe it won't be so difficult, she thought.

Every time she thought of Danny with Heather, Lauren could swear she saw the future. And it didn't include her. Who was she fooling? Danny wasn't going to give up his family and join the three-ring circus that was her life. She swallowed her fears—Danny didn't need all her drama on top of everything.

Danny went to the kitchen and got some water. He brought Lauren a peach. She nibbled at it, not really hungry even though she hadn't eaten much dinner. With a sigh, she opened the journal again. An hour later, she had cobbled together what might be the start of a halfway decent chorus. Hopefully, when the rest of the band heard it in the morning, they'd like the concept.

Morning, however, came far too early. Lauren woke up when Danny crept out of bed and into the shower. It was still dark but by leaving before rush hour, he could make it to Connecticut by the time the boys were having breakfast. Lauren listened to the hiss and patter of the water.

When Danny tried to slip from the room, she rolled over. "No sneaking out."

"I was trying not to wake you. You were restless last night." He sat on the edge of the bed and ran his hand over her hair.

"Have fun. See you when you get back?"

"It'll be really late. I'll probably go to my place."

Lauren used the dim morning light to hide her frown. "I'll miss you."

He leaned down and gave her a soft kiss. "I'll miss you, too. Now go back to sleep."

After he left, Lauren catnapped for a bit before she crawled out from under the sheets. The shower's hot spray made her skin tingle. Pouring a mound of pomegranate body wash on her loofah, she scrubbed every inch of her skin. As she toweled off after, she listened to the quiet, and an ache of loneliness settled over her. Danny hadn't moved in with her—not officially—but he was there enough that she missed his presence when he was gone.

She hoped he had a good weekend with his sons, but a sense of foreboding blanketed Lauren when she thought about Danny and Heather together for the weekend. *Heather's still his wife,* she thought. *Does he still love her?* That train of thought continued, picking up steam as she got dressed. She considered breakfast but decided she wasn't hungry, then headed for the studio.

More than a hundred miles away, Heather watched as Danny pulled into the cottage's driveway. He hadn't even shut the door to the Jeep when his sons ran out to meet him—even Lucas, who was already starting to show all the signs of becoming a full-blown teenager, attitude and all. He wrapped all three in a huge bear hug.

From the porch, a smile flitted across Heather's face. For all the problems they had, Danny had always been a great father. She never doubted how much he loved those boys. The three escorted their father up the driveway, telling him all the things they were going to do this weekend: go to the beach, play baseball, have a fire in the backyard, and much more.

Heather had asked her parents to be cordial for the sake of the boys. They offered Danny a cool but polite hello. She allowed Danny to give her a kiss on the cheek, which was more than she thought she'd be willing to do. Maybe the weekend wasn't going to be one constant battle.

Augie knew it was going to be a long day when the first thing out of Lauren's mouth at the studio was, "Don't start with me." That set the tone for the day. Depression and angst radiated off her and seeped into the corners of the room where they coiled up and waited, lashing out at inopportune times. There were high points, when the band did make some progress, but all in all, none of them considered the day a real success.

As the day wore on, tempers thinned. "Why don't you write a song about PMS," Ox said. "That should come naturally enough."

Augie shut his eyes and sighed. Ox was always blunt, sometimes to the point of thoughtlessness. Normally, Lauren was totally willing to get right back in Ox's face and call him out, but today she just looked unhappy. She sat for another second and then stalked out of the room without a word.

DJ smacked Ox in the back of the head. "You're as much of a jackass as Jackass," he said, using his personal pet name for Danny. "Just once, try keeping your mouth shut."

Augie listened to them bitch at each other until Ox said *jódete*—fuck you—to DJ, ending their quarrel and putting the final nail in the coffin for their studio work. Augie wasn't sure what to think. The band had gone through rough spots before, but nothing like this. Everyone was on edge, everything spinning out of control. And Lauren was right in the center of the storm. The only other time he'd ever had this feeling, Lauren ended up in rehab.

He went looking for his cousin and found her on the second floor, in one of the small offices. She was curled up on the extra-wide windowsill, looking down at the street.

"Lauren? You okay?"

She shrugged but didn't look at him.

"Want to talk about it?"

"I'm making myself crazy." She sounded stuffy—she'd been crying. "Danny's visiting his sons, but that means he's also spending the weekend with Heather." Lauren looked at the floor, and Augie couldn't tell if she was regretful or if she just didn't want him to see her cry. One tear escaped anyway.

"What are you doing, Lauren?" Augie's question was soft and completely rhetorical. He knew Danny's wife had walked out. He knew that Lauren and Danny were fully into their affair or whatever it was that was going on between them. He knew his cousin, who he loved like a sister, was up a creek. And he knew there wasn't a damn thing he could do about it.

Lauren leaned her head back until it thumped against the edge of the window trim. She shut her eyes. "I don't know, Augie. I'm an idiot? I make rash decisions? No news flash there... but I feel *so* much. Whenever I'm with him everything is brighter, crisper, newer. He's the only one who's ever loved me for *who* I am. And I love him, Augie. I've never stopped loving him..."

"Does he love you?" It was a risky question.

"Yes."

Augie didn't believe it. Not after Danny had been so callous before. For a second, he wondered if he should give Danny the benefit of the doubt, consider maybe he'd changed or regretted how things ended with Lauren. Augie decided he wasn't feeling that generous.

Her shoulders bent and when she looked up at him, Lauren's eyes were resigned and sad.

"But?"

"I can pretend while he's here," she said, "but I know I'm going to lose. This will end, and it will be a complete fucking car wreck. He's not going to divorce his wife or leave his boys to be with me." She bit her lip.

"Did you ask him to?" Augie leaned a shoulder against the wall. He didn't really want to have this conversation, but he'd already put it off too long.

"Ask him to...? What? To leave his family? For Chrissakes, Augie, *no*. I would never ask him to do that..." Her voice hardened, but Augie didn't let that deter him.

"Well, you're sleeping with him, aren't you? You're creating a relationship with him again. You might not have asked the question, but you've put him in that position." He knew she'd get pissed, but he couldn't give his cousin a complete free pass on this.

Her expression turned furious. "Screw you, Augie. *Screw. You.* Whatever he decides with Heather, he needs to decide on his own."

Augie stood his ground. "And you've got nothing to do with it? Nothing at all? She's his *wife*, Lauren, and you're sleeping with him. Doesn't matter if you ask the question. Eventually, he'll have to choose between the two of you."

"Exactly," Lauren said. "And he's not going to choose me. So, one way or another, I'm going to get burned." Lauren glanced out the window, and when she turned back, her cheeks were streaked with more tears.

Augie's voice softened. "And that's why I'm so worried about you, Lauren. The longer this goes, the worse it will be for you. Why are you doing this?"

Her bluster and ire vanished. "Why? What else have I ever known, Aug? Love is for fools, and I'm the biggest one out there."

Lauren got up, brushed by Augie, and disappeared out the door.

If she'd been home, back in California, Lauren would have driven to Red Rock Canyon or Lake Arrowhead to get some space and perspective. For a minute, she considered booking a flight back to Los Angeles but talked herself out of that. Instead, she went to The Pool in Central Park and sat near the bridge, watching the water cascade down and into the Loch.

Lauren thought a lot about what Augie had said about whether she should stop things with Danny before they went any further. She should. She knew it. She'd known it from the first night they slept together. And she knew exactly where the relationship was headed if they kept going. It was going to be an unmitigated disaster. An absolute dumpster fire.

But she couldn't bring herself to stop. The tantalizing, infinitesimal chance that things wouldn't go catastrophically wrong was too tempting to turn away.

The whole weekend was torture: wondering what Danny was doing and thinking. She hoped he was having fun with his sons, but what was happening with Heather? Were they fighting? Ending their marriage? Reconciling?

The chime on her phone sent a bolt of anxiety through her, but it was Carolyn's smiling picture on the screen. Lauren let it go to voice mail. Carolyn knew what was happening with Danny, but they hadn't talked about it. Lauren guessed pretty much everyone in both families knew. Something like this wasn't going to slip by unnoticed, and Deb wasn't going to waste the opportunity to paint her as a home-wrecking interloper.

But I'm not, Lauren told herself. *It isn't like I walked into a fairy-tale happy marriage and set a bomb off.* That knowledge assuaged some of her remorse—but not all of it. Alone in her apartment, Lauren sank deeper into her own personal darkness.

She knew she had to end things with Danny.

But knowing and doing were two very, very different things.

CHAPTER THIRTY

On Saturday, Danny spent the day at the beach with Heather and his in-laws, but most importantly, with his boys. They left the cottage just after sunrise and, for a short time, practically had the beach all to themselves. The day was filled with swimming, building sandcastles, and beach football. He reveled in the games and hearing them all shouting, "Dad! Dad!"

When he wasn't playing with his sons, Danny talked a little with Heather, trying to gauge how she was feeling. She didn't make any digs about Lauren, even when an old Kingmakers song came on the radio, and Danny was grateful for that. He wouldn't have known what to say anyway. As the sun started to set, they went to a local clam shack for dinner. Back at the cottage, Danny was nearly asleep on his feet at nine, but he forced himself to stay awake. If he went to bed, it would turn into Sunday, and he would have to go back to New York.

Sunday morning opened with a magnificent waffle breakfast. The entire cottage smelled like crispy bacon and maple syrup. After, Heather's parents took the boys with them to pick up the things they'd need to make s'mores that night. Her father, in an unsuccessful attempt to be subtle, mentioned that he had to pick up an antique doorknob from a dealer a few towns away and that they'd all be gone for at least two hours.

Danny waved to the boys as his in-laws' Volvo rolled down the dirt and gravel driveway. Wood creaked as he sat down on the cottage steps. He drained the last of his coffee and set the mug down next to a white and red polka-dot flowerpot. Heather stood nearby, half turned away from him, her arms folded tightly across her body and a frown pinching the corners of her mouth. The boys had been a buffer, but now it was just the two of them. Neither said anything for what felt an eternity.

"We're going to need to talk sometime." Danny laced his fingers and rested his elbows on his knees.

"Then talk." Heather's voice was tight, laden with tears. There was room next to Danny on the steps, but she remained where she was.

"Let's start with the fact you walked out on me," Danny said. "You walked out and took Lucas, Matty and Tommy with you." He looked at his wife, angry, and then looked away. He might have stayed in the house physically, but emotionally he'd walked out before Heather ever did. That slice of truth stung and just made him more defensive.

Heather matched his anger with her curt retort. "Well, I wasn't going to stick around and be made a fool of anymore."

"A fool? What are you talking about?"

Her look was incredulous. "Seriously? I wasn't going to sit there and play the good wife while you screwed your girlfriend. I mean, Goddammit, Danny, you lied to me." She turned to face him, arms still taut across her body like a shield. "You were meeting Lauren all the time. The night of that baseball game? Rachel's photo? You lied to me about seeing her that night."

"A lie of omission," Danny said. "But it wasn't because I was sneaking around. She was already there. We shot the shit while my pizzas cooked. I didn't tell you because I knew you'd flip out—same way you do every time Lauren gets mentioned—and then we'd fight. And I was sick-and-fucking-tired of being accused of something I hadn't done." It had been twenty minutes and two slices of pizza. Danny was tired of hearing her beat that dead horse.

"Whatever." Heather rolled her eyes.

"That's exactly my point!" Danny jumped up. "You didn't believe me when I was telling the truth, so why should I bother? Why should I even try to be a good husband?" He resisted the urge to kick the cheery-looking flowerpot and stomped down the stairs.

"That's right. You've been so good—"

He cut her off. "Don't you come at me like that. I'm a good father, and I've tried to be a good husband. We haven't been happy for a long time, Heather. And I stayed. I *stayed*! I wasn't the one who walked out and took the kids. I wasn't the one who quit on us. You used Lauren as an excuse to bail." He backed up a step as Heather's neck turned scarlet. He must have struck a nerve because that only happened when she was utterly furious.

"Quit on us? I didn't quit on us!" Heather shouted back. "I know you don't want me anymore. Maybe I'm too old, too ordinary. I'm clearly not enough. You never touch me anymore, Danny. And when you do, you shut your eyes. You can't even *look* at me! I'm that fat and ugly!"

Danny's mouth dropped. Their problems in the bedroom had never stemmed from how attractive he thought she was. He'd always thought Heather was beautiful with her blond hair and big eyes and all her soft curves. That was never the issue—their problems were a by-product of all the other frustrations, slights, and disappointments that had eaten away at an already insecure foundation to their marriage.

"I can't look at you? I'm not into you? Heather, I can't remember the last time we had sex when I didn't look down to find you looking to the side, off into space. Looking anywhere but at me. Shushing me like you're ashamed. Do you know how that made *me* feel? Do you even care? Do you even want *me* anymore?"

"Do I want you? I—"

Instead of finishing whatever she was going to say, Heather grabbed his shirt and kissed him. Hard. For a split second, Danny was confounded. But then an electric surge of emotions that he didn't have the capacity to decipher sparked, and he pulled his wife tight against his body. Overwhelmed by turmoil and the realization that they'd each made terribly false assumptions about the other, they fumbled their way into the house and into the guest bedroom. The sex was a sprint, and they were breathing heavily when they finished.

"Heather..." Danny said as he pulled his pants up.

"Let's not talk right now." She buttoned her shirt and ran her fingers through her hair to untangle it.

They finished dressing and returned to the porch. Danny sat down again on the steps while his wife made a show of inspecting her mother's rose bush. The silence was awkward, accentuated by a deliriously happy songbird. Out of the corner of his eye, Danny saw Heather glance at him, and then away. His heart clenched.

"Make-up sex isn't going to solve our problems," he said.

"I know." Heather pushed some stray hair behind her ear. "I have to ask you something, Danny. You said that you weren't sleeping with her before... Are you now?"

Danny wanted to spare her the pain the truth would bring, but he couldn't lie to her. Not about this. After a long silence, he said, "Yes."

"I see." The tears made her voice thick.

"You left, Heather. You left and took our kids."

"We left each other."

Danny hung his head. She was right. They'd both made mistakes, but he'd really fucked things up. He was surprised when Heather moved to sit on the step next to him. She looked spent.

"What do we do now?" his wife asked.

"What do you want?"

Heather wiped tears from her cheeks. "Crap. I... I... want us to be a family. I want it to be the way it used to be. But I know things can't ever be that way again. Too much has happened. We stopped trying. *She* happened. But despite everything, I still care about you. I shouldn't love you, but I do."

Danny rubbed his forehead. Did he even deserve that much generosity from his wife? Probably not.

"But you need to decide what you want, Danny. Do you want to be with me? Or do you want to be with her? Until you know that, there's nothing we can do." Heather picked up his dirty coffee cup and retreated to the cottage, leaving Danny sitting on the steps with his remorse and his shame.

For the rest of day, the two stayed in their neutral corners. The boys had a great time and tried to draw out the s'mores fire so Danny didn't have to leave. He assured them he'd be back before too long and made them promise to behave for their mother. He stayed long enough for all the boys, even Lucas, to go to bed. When he drove out of the driveway and into the night, Danny felt a weight settle back on his shoulders.

An hour into his drive, he yawned. He had at least another hour before he got back home. The highway stretched out ahead of him, the faded yellow lines hard to see in his headlights. His turn signal clicked as he changed lanes so he could pass an older couple in a little Prius.

He glanced at the clock. It was after midnight. He turned the radio on so there was more than silence in the car, but he didn't really listen to the music. He thought about the boys, about Heather and their spontaneous interlude... and about all the confused, conflicted feelings tumbling through him.

But despite everything, I still care about you, Danny. I shouldn't love you, but I do.

"I've made such a mess of everything," he said aloud. "I am so screwed."

CHAPTER THIRTY-ONE

Lauren did her best to give Danny space when he got back from Connecticut. She didn't have to be a rocket scientist to guess that he was wrestling with the situation—and she was keenly aware that their relationship was weighing on him. It tied her up in knots. Between her studio schedule and his caseload, they didn't see each other much. When they were together, she offered to listen if he wanted to talk, but didn't push him.

Beyond Danny, Lauren had her own issues to deal with. Conflict continued to churn in the studio. Tempers frayed as work on the album stalled. When an article appeared in *SpinDoctor* magazine that hinted at their studio problems, the writer asked: *Are The Kingmakers over the hill? Has their time come and gone?* Fitz cut it out and put it on the wall. If he thought it would light a fire under her ass, his strategy backfired. By the time the calendar turned to August, Lauren was mentally wrung out.

Lauren and Danny managed to carve out an evening together and spent a quiet night at her place. Just before lunch the next day, they went out for groceries. Using a delivery service would have been easy enough, but Lauren saw it as a chance to get out of the house—and away from her infernal notebook, which had become a symbol of everything that was screwed up.

She loved the little local grocery store she'd found near the Somerset. The store's footprint was small, but the owners packed a plethora of goods into the space, including a surprisingly robust produce section and small butcher shop. While Danny looked for things he needed, Lauren perused the produce section. It was the perfect season for berries, and she had plans for a fruit salad for supper. She was evaluating a dragon fruit when a stranger crowded into her personal space.

"Excuse me," she said, moving her basket between them. Out of the corner of her eye she could see him staring. He barely moved even when her basket banged into him.

"It really is you!" he said.

Lauren glanced just long enough to assess him. He was tall and heavyset with sagging jeans and a Yankees t-shirt. His hair looked uncombed, as if he'd just rolled out of bed, and the thinnest hint of a mustache shadowed his upper lip. She didn't really care what he looked like. What annoyed her was the way he was looking at her. She'd seen that look before: the die-hard fan with no sense of personal space.

"Excuse me," she said again.

"You're Lauren from The Kingmakers," he said, moving enough for her to reach the fruit display. "I'm Frank. I'm a huge fan. Like, your biggest fan!"

"That's very kind of you. I'm glad you like the band's music." She kept a subtle eye on him while she picked a pineapple. She tugged on the leaves to see if it was ripe and added it to her basket. Normally she tried to be accommodating for fans, like all the times she stopped for pictures, but every now and then—like today—she just wanted a little privacy.

"I've been to all your shows. I can't wait for the new album. Can you tell me about some of the songs? Just a hint? I won't tell anyone else."

Enthusiasm oozed out of him. Lauren demurred, stepping back and around him to continue her shopping. He pivoted to follow, continuing with his questions. The few answers she offered were polite but short. She knew his type. All questions and starstruck awe, but he wasn't radiating that creepy, obsessive energy that marked him as dangerous—this guy wasn't a threat, he was just clueless.

"Any tips for getting backstage passes for your next show?" His voice brimmed with zeal.

"Our manager handles that stuff. But it was nice to talk to you." She turned to head to the register when he reached out and caught her elbow.

"Don't go yet! Can I get a pic—"

"Hey!" She jerked her arm away, her voice sharp and scolding. Frank's face crumbled. She didn't like being snappish but putting his hands on her crossed a line. Before Lauren could say anything else, Danny barreled in, the force of his entrance knocking her to the side. Frank dropped his basket in surprise.

"Back off." He pushed Frank back a step and flashed his badge. "You know I can arrest you on battery charges, right? For putting your hands on her like that?"

Sweat broke out on Frank's forehead and upper lip. "B-battery? I just wanted—"

"Yeah, I know what you wanted—"

"—Danny—" Lauren started to say, but he talked over her.

"—I'm willing to let it go this time, but you need to step off. Pick up your basket and—"

"Danny! That's enough!"

Danny's head snapped to the side, his expression confused. Frank looked just as confounded.

"Lauren... ah, Miss Stone," Frank said, "I didn't mean... I just... I'm sorry." His face was awash with contrition and a little fear. He picked up his basket and started to shuffle away. Lauren felt terrible.

"Wait," Lauren said. "I'm sorry. This is a big misunderstanding. You said your name was Frank, right? Get your phone out." When he didn't move, she said it again. "Seriously, get your phone. You wanted a picture, right?"

He glanced at Danny, wary, but it was nothing compared to the glare she skewered Danny with.

"I don't want to be a bother," Frank mumbled as he looked at the floor.

"Really, it's no bother."

Lauren took a couple of quick selfies with him, picked up her basket, and walked to the register without a word to Danny. In the checkout line, she heard him say her name softly, but she didn't turn around. She chatted pleasantly with the clerk and left with her bags. Danny had to hurry to catch up to her on the sidewalk.

"Why are you pissed at me?"

She paused long enough to stare him in the eye. "I'm not having this conversation in public."

They walked in silence the rest of the way back to the Somerset, but the détente didn't last once they got to the apartment.

"Who do you think you are?" Lauren asked as she put her bags on the counter.

"Why are you mad at me?"

"Seriously? You barge in, physically assault a man—"

"He grabbed *you*! Who knows what else he might have done."

"I've been grabbed in worse places by scarier people than him." Lauren pointed at him using the carrots she'd just taken out of the bag. "I am not some damsel in distress you need to save. You barge in and take over—then talk over me like I'm not even there? That's bullshit."

She could see the conflict on Danny's face. Lauren understood why he did what he did, that he only wanted to keep her safe. But he was going to have to learn to handle situations like that differently.

"He could have hurt you." Danny's tone moderated an iota.

"Anyone could. I know your intent was good, but you need to trust my judgment. He was overzealous, not dangerous." She put the last container of raspberries on the counter and folded the bag.

"Overzealous can turn dangerous pretty goddamn fast," Danny said. "I've seen the results of that first-hand!"

Lauren conceded the point. "I know you have. I'm not trying to be dismissive, but I've dealt with this for a long time. My instincts are solid."

"So are mine." Danny folded his arms, his jaw set in a stubborn, angry line.

"Look, I appreciate that it spooked you," she said. "But asking if everything was okay would have worked just as well. Danny, I know being a cop makes you see trouble everywhere, but you can't swoop in like that every time a guy wants to talk to me."

"If I see them grabbing you—"

"You are *not* my bodyguard. If someone's behavior scares me, believe me, you'll know. And then you are free to handle it, but otherwise you need to keep a leash on it." She slammed a cabinet closed.

They stared at each other until Danny dropped his eyes away. "It won't happen again."

Lauren knew a lie when she heard it, but she chose to ignore it.

Her cell phone's buzz interrupted any more discussion on the subject. She picked it up. "Hi, Augie."

"Hey, up for a couple visitors? Me and Ox are in the lobby."

"Sure. C'mon up." She tossed the phone back on the counter before she opened the raspberry container, then picked out a couple berries.

"You should wash those," Danny said.

She very deliberately ate them both without so much as a drop of water.

By the time Ox and Augie got off the elevator, Lauren had two bottles of beer open and ready for them. After several stories about Lauren and Augie when they were teenagers that had Ox howling, and another round of beer, the conversation turned to the following weekend's event: Bruno Cardoso's launch party.

"Who is this Bruno guy?" Danny asked.

"Record exec. A little *loco*, but most of 'em are. Started a boutique label, and this party is to promote his two new bands," Ox said.

"Dude, I heard he invited every big name he could find," Augie said.

"Why do that? Won't that overshadow the new bands?" Danny asked.

"Because the more stars, the more press," Augie answered. "The more press, the more chances to promote his new bands."

"I'm so glad you're coming to the party," Lauren said to Danny. "It'll be a blast."

"Yeah, should be something." Danny didn't sound enthusiastic, but Lauren's phone rang again, distracting her. She excused herself to take the call. Ox took the opportunity to raid the pantry for beer-friendly snacks.

"Can I ask you something?" Augie said.

"Sure." Danny felt his guard go up. He and Augie had come to a quiet détente, but they were far from good friends.

"That was a pretty lukewarm response. Do you not want to go to Bruno's party?"

"What do you mean?" Danny glanced to see where Lauren was. Even though she was still on the phone, he dropped his voice. "I'm going to embarrass Lauren."

"What? How?"

He made a sour face at Augie. "Look at me. I'm blue-collar at best. You've seen my suits. They're fine for a cop, but most of the people who'll be at this party wouldn't even wipe their ass with my shirts."

Danny had a point. The press would be there, and while Lauren wouldn't care in the least what he wore, a lot of other people would. Augie understood how savage they could be; Danny really had no idea.

"I can help you out," Augie said. "Come to my place about four o'clock on Saturday."

"Seriously?"

Augie didn't appreciate the suspicion in Danny's voice. "C'mon, Danny. I might not be thrilled about what you've got going on with my cousin, but I'm not a complete asshole."

Ox came back out and flopped down again. "What are guys talking about?"

"Sports." Augie tossed the white lie out with aplomb. "And how much your beloved A's suck."

CHAPTER THIRTY-TWO

Danny lay in his own bed, staring up through the dark at the ceiling fan above him. Despite how much he loved being at Lauren's, he still had a house to maintain. He'd be with her tomorrow at the release party, so tonight he was at the cream-colored Art Deco bungalow his family called home.

Alone.

The emptiness and silence gave him ample opportunity to think about his sons. And his wife. He tossed in his and Heather's bed. Even with the fan blowing on him, the air felt sticky. Turning on his side, he punched the pillow. A glance toward the nightstand told him it was one o'clock in the morning, and he was no closer to sleep than an hour ago. Danny knew he should get up and do something rather than toss and turn in the dark.

Even with the tension, it had been nice to talk with Heather on the phone earlier—and he realized that he missed *that* Heather, the one he could actually have a conversation with, one without all the yelling.

"Ah, fuck me," he said aloud.

I do miss Heather, he thought. *I miss the boys. My whole life I've done everything I'm supposed to. Been a good son. A good cop. I thought I was a good husband... But being with Lauren? She's spontaneous, free. Everything I'm not.* He knew his thoughts sounded maudlin but couldn't stop them.

He wondered if this was how he'd feel if he stayed with Lauren. He couldn't go with her on tour—it would kill him to miss that much of his sons' lives. And his family? What would life be like without Sunday dinners or summer weekends at the beach? Never being home for Thanksgiving or Christmas? His stomach roiled.

Is this what my life would turn into? Alone in some random apartment, looking at the ceiling and listening to the silence while Lauren toured the world?

The unwelcome memory of Frank, the avid fan from the grocery store, shoved its way to the front of his mind, unlocking a whole new set of worries. Anxious and uncertain, Danny got up and went into the living room. He turned on the TV and flipped the channels until he found old reruns of a medical procedural. Eventually, he fell asleep in the recliner.

Once he woke up, a whole different set of worries lined up for him. Number one was the launch party that night. He forced himself to wash the pile of dishes in the sink and do a few other chores around the house he'd been neglecting. All the while, he wrestled with his conflicted feelings.

Later in the day, he went out to D'Agostino's and got an Italian sub for dinner. There would be food at the party, but that wasn't going to start until late—and if it was all was crazy frou-frou hors d'oeuvres he couldn't even pronounce, he'd be starving. After he ate, Danny showered, shaved, and did his best to put any doubts or worries he had about the future out of his head. He changed and headed out to Augie's place, and several hours later, they arrived at Lauren's.

As he opened the door, Augie yelled out, "We're here! Get a move on, Grandma."

"Unbunch your panties." Lauren's voice drifted out of the bedroom. "Limo should be here in about twenty minutes."

"Isn't the limo overkill?" Danny asked.

"Nah," Augie said. "Band usually does this for events. That way no one drives home loaded. Ox and DJ will arrive on their own, but they'll leave with us."

Lauren strolled out of the bedroom. Her tank-top style shirt was made from silky material, but it had an overlay of hexagonal metallic pieces reminiscent of chain mail. Her midnight black jeans seemed painted on, and she'd paired them with high black boots adorned with fancy silver buckles that went all the way up each side. On her left arm were several bracelets, and around her neck was a black leather necklace with a silver disk hanging from it.

She stopped, did a slow turn, and held her arms out to the side. "Well?"

"Dude, you're rocking it tonight."

"You look amazing," Danny said.

Lauren looked pleased by their comments. "Check you out," she said to Danny. Layered under a stylish leather jacket, his button-down shirt was a deep maroon. The outfit was simple but clearly high-end.

Lauren gave him a smack on the backside. "You look totally hot in that."

"Hey, hey, hey. I'm right here," Augie said.

"Well, then, you'd better not look." Lauren's reply was tart and sassy.

Inside the stretch Escalade, hidden by the deeply tinted windows, Lauren settled next to Danny on the pristine leather seats. Augie sprawled in the seat opposite them. They picked up Stevie and Gabby on the way, and once they were in the car, Augie popped the champagne. Lauren raised her glass as the limo pulled out into traffic.

"Here's to a rockin' night out," she said. They all echoed the sentiment and clinked glasses.

The vehicle rolled to a stop for a red light. A group of people on the sidewalk bobbed their heads and stared, trying to get a glimpse of who was inside. All those prying eyes made Danny edgy and uncomfortable.

"How do you get used to the people staring at you?" he asked.

"You learn to live with it," Stevie said. Danny didn't believe him.

The driver's voice drifted over the intercom. There were a few cars ahead of them, but he'd have them all to the main door in a few minutes.

"What are the Vegas odds on how late DJ is?" Augie asked.

Stevie's prediction of fifteen minutes elicited an unladylike snort from Gabby. "Fifteen? That'll be the day. Thirty at least. You all know he's the girl of the group. Takes him forever to get ready."

The limo erupted with laughter. It was a common joke among the band that only DJ could put so much effort into looking like he'd made no effort at all. Danny leaned over and glanced out the window again. There was a knot of about two dozen reporters and photographers standing to one side of the hotel entrance. His stomach turned over, churning the champagne. He wished he'd eaten more.

The driver came around to open the door for them. Stevie got out first and reached back to help Gabby. She was wearing a short dress that showed off her very long legs and some of the reporters shouted questions to Stevie. Augie followed and some random woman in the crowd screamed, "Augie, I love you!" He blew her a kiss and got, "I want to have your babies!" in response.

Danny was next and held his hand out for Lauren. Camera flashes exploded as soon as her first boot emerged. Danny's head spun—the evening was just getting started and it already felt out of control. Lauren smiled for the photographers. Cries of "Lauren, over here!" rang out and she turned back and forth for a moment, letting them get their fill. Then she slid her arm through Danny's—eliciting another volley of photographs—and they walked into the hotel.

"And that," Stevie said, clapping Danny on the shoulder, "was your first press walk. Well done, mate!"

Bruno was waiting for them. Dressed in an off-the-wall suit, including a lavender jacket with throwback Eighties shoulder pads and pants with a blue-violet and lime green paisley print, Bruno certainly stood out in a crowd—and that was a statement considering the unusual ensembles on some of his guests. He had sunglasses à la Elton John tucked on top of his slicked hair. When he saw Lauren and the others, he threw his arms open wide.

"Darlings! Look at you! You look fabulous!" He greeted and hugged his way through the group, and then stopped. "What? No DJ? No Ox?"

"On their way," Lauren said.

"Well, then I will see all of you later for a group photo op! Enjoy the party!" He turned and was swallowed up by the crowd. All Danny could do was stare and blink in Bruno's wake.

Inside the ballroom, there were two bars and a long buffet table smothered with food. He was happy to see that, in addition to the requisite cheese and fruit trays, there were at least a few appetizers—like cheeseburger sliders—that he recognized. There was also a separate table with a chocolate fountain surrounded by bowls of fruit, marshmallows, pretzels, and a dozen other things to be dipped and eaten.

"Something to drink?" Augie asked.

"Just a beer," Lauren said.

"Same for me," said Danny. "Thanks."

While Augie was getting the beer, there was some commotion across the room. Three young men with spiky bleached hair were laughing and joking, being a tad too loud and flamboyant.

"Who are they?" Danny asked.

"Those are the guys in Roughhouse," Lauren said. "They're one of Bruno's new bands. Their first single just came out. A little too punk for my taste, but they've got a lot of potential."

"I remember being young and stupid," Augie said as he rejoined them.

"Remember?" There was laughter in Lauren's voice. She took the beer he offered her.

"Dude," Augie said, feigning offense.

"They make me glad I don't have daughters." Danny watched them with a critical eye. Those three were pretty much every father's worst nightmare. His attention was pulled away when Augie saw Ox across the room.

"There's my wingman," Augie said. "You'll excuse me, but we have to go charm some of the single ladies at this bash."

The crowd swallowed Augie, and Danny was about to ask Lauren a question about Bruno's new band when a hand landed on her shoulder. She turned toward a man Danny recognized.

"Jon!" Lauren threw her arms around him and kissed both cheeks. "How are you? How long has it been?"

"Too long. You look amazing."

"Liar. But I'll take it. Jon, let me introduce you... Danny Padovano, this is Jon Bon Jovi." She moved back slightly so Danny could reach out and shake Jon's hand.

"Good to meet you," Danny said. He wondered if his face looked as reverential as he though it did, and then cringed inwardly, worried he'd embarrass Lauren by looking like some dumb, starstruck fan.

"Same."

Lauren and Jon chatted for a few minutes, sharing commentary on guitars, the party, and Bruno's new bands. They agreed that the youngsters would figure it out—or they'd crash and burn, joining the ranks of one-hit wonders. Someone waved from the crowd, and Jon excused himself. Danny stared after him.

Lauren nudged him. "You okay?"

Startled out of his reverie, Danny half-laughed. "This is just a little surreal—"

"—Laauurrrreennnn!" DJ bellowed her name as he cut through the crowd to reach her with Ox, Stevie, and Gabby in tow.

He shouldered between Lauren and Danny, bumping him out of the way to give her a big hug. Danny scowled. While DJ hadn't been openly hostile towards him, Danny suspected the band's keyboardist was not his biggest fan. Augie hated him, but at least he knew where he stood on that account. Ox and Stevie had been cordial. DJ, of all the band members, had been the least welcoming.

Augie joined them a minute later and the whole band clustered together, laughing and toasting. A photographer—the only one Bruno had allowed into the party—hurried over to get a picture.

"Yes, yes!" Bruno scurried up, materializing out of thin air. "Definitely a photo of The Kingmakers together. You all look tremendous!"

Bruno took charge trying to arrange the photo to his own liking, much to the photographer's obvious frustration, and shooed Danny and Gabby out of the way without a second glance. When Danny tensed up, Gabby laid a gentle hand on his arm.

"Gotta learn to go with the flow. If you're going to be with her, you've got to be okay with taking a back seat."

Danny's response was an even deeper frown.

As he gathered and posed The Kingmakers, Bruno chattered on. "I can't wait to hear what you come up with on the new project. I'm sure it will be tremendous. Dish a little for me, Lauren. How are things going?"

Lauren's stomach tightened. How was it going? It sucked. So far, the whole album was shaping up to be an utter disaster, but she couldn't admit that to Bruno. That would just get the rumor mill churning faster, and she couldn't bear another article talking about the band being "past their prime."

"Terrific," she said. "You'll be amazed when you hear it."

It was a bald-faced lie, and the rest of The Kingmakers froze, smiles plastered across their faces. Lauren knew they'd be pissed at her because now they were fully on the hook. Bruno would tell *everyone* that their new CD was going to be exactly that—tremendous. But she knew—as did the rest of the band—the project was shaping up to be a colossal disappointment.

CHAPTER THIRTY-THREE

Bruno's soirée was still going strong when The Kingmakers made their exit around two in the morning along with Big Mac Daddy's front man and several others. Augie, Ox, and DJ wanted to go clubbing. Stevie and Gabby were ready to head home. Lauren and Danny wanted some quiet time together. They spilled out of the hotel entrance along with several other guests, smiling and waving while the remaining knot of die-hard photographers snapped away.

Their limo pulled up, and the driver was out in an instant to open the door. With all of them inside the limo, things were a little crowded, but everyone was laughing and in a great mood—thanks, in part, to the large amount of alcohol they'd consumed. The guys gave Danny some good-natured ribbing about him being starstruck at the party. He took it in stride, knowing that what they were saying wasn't far from the truth.

Lauren's world was so different from his. One day, a party like this... the next, seemingly endless hours in a studio poring over lyrics and bass lines and guitar bridges. He didn't even want to think about what it must be like when they were on tour. But those thoughts flew out of his head when Lauren settled closer to him.

He watched as she laughed and joked with the others, completely at ease with her musical family. *She was remarkable tonight,* he thought. *Why on earth is she with someone like me when she's surrounded by all of them?* He couldn't think of a single good reason why Lauren would want to be with him.

"Hey," Lauren said, obviously noticing his expression. "You shouldn't be thinking about serious things tonight. Tonight's all about fun." She shifted up on her knees and to Danny's surprise, threw one leg over him and sat in his lap. Facing him, she looked down, wrapped her arms around his neck, and kissed him. Hard. Ox let out a catcall whistle.

"Were they like this in high school?" Stevie asked.

"Pretty much," Augie answered. "Except there are no Sisters now to keep them in check."

"You're just jealous." Lauren looked over her shoulder at her cousin. "'Cause skinny little you couldn't get any in high school."

There was more laughter in the car, but Danny didn't like the stinging glare he got from DJ. He locked eyes with the keyboardist for a split second before he decided getting mad wasn't worth the trouble. Instead, he slid his arms tightly around Lauren's middle and pulled her down towards him. He kissed her again, moving his hands up the sides of her waist. As far as he was concerned, this was much better than talking, and he'd wanted Lauren in his arms all night long. He was just drunk enough not to care that the others could see exactly what they were doing.

"Oh, for Chrissakes. Drop them off first, would you?" DJ said.

That was exactly what happened. When they reached her place and got out, Ox put the window down and shouted, "Behave yourselves, kids!"

Once they were in the elevator, Danny crowded Lauren and backed her up against the wall, hooking his thumbs into the waist of her jeans. She laughed as she worked at his shirt, a single button at a time, knowing it was making him crazy. She kissed along his collarbone. His skin felt warm under her fingers, and she dragged them down his chest. Tangled in each other's arms, they nearly fell out of the elevator when the doors opened.

After Lauren closed the apartment door behind them, she turned, and the way Danny was looking at her made her breath catch. That was how she always wanted to be looked at. Someone who saw the real her—the woman behind the rock star. She took hold of the hem of her silver shirt and inched it up over her head. With a careless toss, she dropped it onto the floor. It got the reaction she was hoping for. Danny ran his hands through his hair as he stared at Lauren in her jeans, boots, and a lacy little black bra.

"Jesus Christ, you are so sexy," he said, his voice hushed.

"Then take me to bed. All I've thought about tonight is being with you." She curved her fingers in the front of Danny's pants and unbuttoned them in one smooth motion. She didn't need to offer any more encouragement.

Later, Lauren ran her fingers across Danny's chest as they lay in her bed. Half the pillows were strewn about the floor and the sheets were askew. He caught her hand and brought it to his lips to kiss.

"I was thinking the other day," she said. "Remembering."

"Remembering what?"

"The very first time we had sex."

"Oh, God." Danny put a hand over his eyes as he laughed. "We were sixteen, right? I almost died of shock when you said you were ready. And then I had to go buy rubbers! I went halfway across the city to make sure no one saw me."

Lauren let her mind wander. It had been a warm, spring night.

They'd gone with friends to the Memorial Day parade. After, they made themselves scarce and drove to Pelham Bay Park. After a leisurely afternoon of walking the beach and making out whenever the chance arose, they got a couple of cheeseburgers for dinner and watched the sun go down. In the twilight, they searched for—and found—a secluded little area where they could still see the water.

"You were worried about getting naked," Lauren said.

"I was worried what would happen if the cops found us naked."

Lauren remembered how she'd pulled her shirt up, and Danny's dumbstruck expression when she'd let it, and her bra, drop to the ground. Danny must have been lost in the same memory because he said, "Well, when I saw you toss your shirt, I almost finished before we got started!"

Their awkwardness that far away spring day was soon overcome by flat-out enthusiasm as they threw the second blanket over themselves. The first time was fast and a bit slapdash as they fumbled their way, giggling, through the process. The second time, they didn't rush—and they'd started to understand what all the fuss was about.

"I almost gave you a black eye when we got tangled in the blanket." Lauren's voice was mirthful, and she pressed her fingers to her lips as she smiled. She let out a soft sigh. "I'm glad you were my first."

They kept talking, pressed up against each other in bed, and it was nearly dawn by the time they fell asleep. When they woke, Lauren called down to the hotel's kitchen and ordered an extravagant breakfast. As they lounged over brunch in bed, they rehashed the previous night's festivities.

Danny and Lauren weren't the only ones talking about Bruno's bash that morning. His posh event was big news in the Arts & Entertainment sections of the Sunday papers, with several photos clustered on one of the pages. Cole had been riveted to both the paper version that her mother insisted on getting as well as the paper's website. In the middle of the printed edition's page was a picture of Lauren and Danny leaving the party. Danny had an arm around her shoulder and Lauren's arm caught his waist. On Lauren's other side was Augie, and just behind Danny, with his hand on Danny's shoulder like an old friend, was Big Mac Daddy's front man, Dario D'Scala.

Cole was beside herself when she saw the photo. She knew Heather and her cousins wouldn't be at dinner, and she wasn't really surprised when her uncle wasn't there either. But when no one acknowledged either the photo or Danny's absence, her frustration mounted. By the time dessert rolled around, she was tired of the small talk.

"I'm sorry," she said to everyone around the table. "I know it's complicated, but the photo in the paper is so glamorous. I mean, Uncle Danny? Hanging out with all the stars like Dario? It's kinda awesome."

"I'm sure your Aunt Heather doesn't think it is quite so... awesome." Her grandmother's voice was tight.

Cole's chest constricted. She loved her aunt, and it hurt knowing Heather and Danny were having problems. But Cole couldn't resist the star-crossed lovers' story either. What if her uncle was meant to be with Lauren all along?

"I didn't mean it that way..."

"Cut Cole some slack, Ma. That's Lauren's world, and if they're going to be together, then I guess it will be Danny's world, too," Joey said.

"No." Deb's voice was firm. "There's nothing complicated about it, and they don't get a free pass, or get to be 'awesome.' Danny's married. End of story. And she's nothing more than the other woman. An interloper who's *ruined* Danny's marriage."

"Ma," Maggie said. "Danny and Heather were having trouble. It didn't start when—"

"—He's a *married* man! Do *not* make excuses for him." Deb

slammed a hand on the table as she jumped up and stormed into the kitchen.

The rest of dessert was eaten in virtual silence.

Cole remained quiet and withdrawn on the ride home. Her mother tried to draw her out, but Cole rebuffed her attempts and went straight to her room. An hour later, she reappeared. She waited in the doorway while her mother pulled the last few plates out of the dishwasher.

"Did I mess up Uncle Danny's marriage?"

Maggie bobbled the last dish. "Oh! Cole, I didn't know you were there."

"Sorry. I was thinking about what Nanny said. About everything." Her voice quavered. "This mess is my fault, isn't it?"

"Oh, sweetheart, no. Come here." Maggie gestured her over and hugged her. She kissed the top of Cole's head. "This is not your fault. Don't blame yourself for any of this. They've been star-crossed from the start."

Cole broke free of the hug and leaned on the kitchen island. "But if I hadn't written the paper, then that Roberta lady never would have called. And we never would have gone to the Sandoval show. That was where everything started, right? And it was all because of my stupid paper."

"Maybe that was the first time they saw each other, Cole, but your uncle and Lauren are both adults. Everything that happened after that came from decisions *they* made." Maggie leaned on the island across from her daughter. She reached out and put one of her hands over Cole's, giving it a gentle squeeze. "You didn't make them do anything."

Cole wanted to believe her mother, but it wasn't easy.

CHAPTER

THIRTY-FOUR

Danny was worried that lots of people would notice the photo, the same way everyone seemed to know about the Sandoval interview. But when he went to work on Monday, only two people brought it up. Unfortunately, both seemed to think they had every right to ask him very personal questions about the party and about his relationship with Lauren. It made him angry, and he was grateful when he and Matsui got sent out to investigate a case.

As he was driving them to interview a witness, Danny said, "Thanks, Jason."

"For what?"

"For not giving me shit today."

"About the picture?"

Danny slowed the car ahead of a stoplight to let another car into traffic. "Go on, go," he said, waving at the other driver before answering Jason's question. "Yeah. Some people seem to think they have the right to know all about my business."

"Kinda comes with the territory, doesn't it? Public figures don't always get the luxury of privacy."

“I’m not a public figure.”

“You’re in a relationship with one. Guilt by association.”

Danny frowned, Jason’s phrasing hitting him on a couple of levels. In the past, he’d dealt with the rich and famous in investigations, and he’d never had much sympathy when they complained about having no privacy. He’d reacted the same way Jason did: it was the life they signed up for. But now that he was in the hot seat, he had a new appreciation for how they felt.

And he didn’t like it at all.

“C’mon, go! Idiot. Step on the gas!” He yelled at the car ahead and didn’t bother answering Jason.

“But since you brought it up, what was the party like?” Jason asked.

“Pretty incredible. I had a great time, don’t get me wrong. But watching her and the guys? They’re so at ease. I mean, I know celebrities are just people, but I sorta felt like I was pretending to be one of them when I’m really not.”

“I guess you’d get used to it, but... do you even want to?”

After a pause, Danny offered a surprisingly candid answer: “I don’t know. When I’m with Lauren everything seems to work, but when I’m alone... I just think and think about her, about Heather. About the two different worlds.” He drummed his thumbs on the steering wheel.

Jason made a non-committal grunt. “Heather seen the picture?”

Danny tightened his knuckles. “Probably. I haven’t talked to her since Friday. They’ll be here this weekend for a visit—my niece’s birthday—so I’m sure I’ll find out.”

Truth be told, Danny was a little terrified of how Heather would react.

On Tuesday, Lauren stayed late at the studio. The Kingmakers had all come in early to try making up lost time. They’d made decent progress on one song, which was more than they could say happened the previous day. But Lauren was keenly aware that she was the main reason they were behind. She stayed after everyone left to noodle through some more lyrics. Finally, she'd also insisted that Tisha go home as well.

By the time seven o'clock rolled around, she'd had enough and was ready to head out. Maybe she could get a little more done after a relaxing bath. As she shut the lights out in Studio D, Lauren heard the little alert bell for the front door chime. She berated herself for being forgetful: she'd told Tisha that she'd take care of locking the door. She walked cautiously to the front lobby.

Standing there, with her back to the studio area, was an older woman with white hair. She was looking at the memorabilia Fitz had hung on the wall: awards, news clippings, photos of him with famous musicians ranging from Stevie Wonder to Tom Petty to U2 and many more. From her dress, she seemed ordinary enough, not like someone who was looking to rob the studio. Lauren relaxed a little.

"May I help you...?"

"You can start by staying away from my son!" Deb Padovano spun to face Lauren, her voice filled with enough righteous indignation and anger that it shocked Lauren into taking a step back. "You are ruining Danny's marriage! Thanks to you, Heather's moved out. She's so hurt, it breaks my heart—and those boys? Richie told me not to come, but you... This is *your* fault! Have you no respect? No decency? Do you even care how much pain you're causing?"

"I—"

Deb didn't let her finish. "Of course you don't! How could *you* ever have any respect for the sanctity of marriage? Have you had a single, serious, committed relationship? Do you have any idea how hard it is to make a marriage work? If you did, you'd be ashamed of yourself. You don't have any respect for yourself or for anyone else!"

Deb's harsh words sank in like a scorpion's sting and, when

Lauren was a teen, would have driven her to tears. But she wasn't a child anymore, and she wasn't about to let Deb bully her.

"Don't you dare speak to me like that!" Lauren was gratified to see a split-second of shock cross Deb's face. "I didn't come back here looking to hurt anyone, and certainly not to get in the middle of a breakup. Whatever was going off the rails in Danny's marriage started long before I came back."

She took a couple steps forward. Deb had never liked her, and that was fine. Lauren could live with that. "But you don't care about that," she continued. "You made your mind up about me a long time ago—I could have joined a convent and you'd still find a way to belittle me for it."

"You're nothing but a bad influence on everyone around you." It was a blanket indictment. Deb held her small purse in front of her like it was a shield.

"Give it a rest, Deb! You spent so much time worrying about what a bad influence I was going to be on Danny—did you ever stop to think what a good influence he might have been on me? You're so eager to point out what a terrible sinner I am—well, you're a sinner, too. We all are. Isn't that what the priests tell us? Don't you dare call me a sinner and hold a halo up over your own head. Or should I start calling you St. Deborah?"

Deb's eyes widened. "I'm *nothing* like you. Don't you imply otherwise. You? You're selfish. It's always been about you and your music, and never about what happens to other people—"

Selfish. The word cut her as much as it had all those years ago when Danny used it. Lauren pushed the pain down.

"—Well, you're sure making it my business—"

"—All you're going to do here is leave wreckage in your wake. Do you even care that you're breaking my grandsons' hearts? Or are they just an obstacle in your way?"

Lauren gasped at the accusation. She opened her mouth to respond, but Deb barreled ahead, cutting her off.

"Heather's devastated. You have everything you ever wanted: fame, money, cars, lovers… she can't understand why you have to have Danny, too."

"I love Danny. I—"

"—*Love?* This isn't love. You never loved my son." Deb threw her a withering, disdainful look. "This is greed and lust, plain and simple. You're taking what you want and throwing the rest away. Adding him to your collection." Deb went to the door and looked back over her shoulder as she opened it.

"And I'll tell you something," she said. "You can go back out on the road with your band and your groupies and your drugs, but you'll never be able to forget that Danny didn't love you enough to marry you. He waited and married a *good* woman. He's *still married* to a good woman, and the only thing you'll ever be is his *whore.* Live with that."

Deb slammed the door behind her.

Danny trudged down the precinct steps. Over the course of the day, he'd been on a pendulum. One moment reliving the highlights of his weekend with Lauren, then swinging back to thinking about his wife, his sons. Everything he had to lose. They were his heart, and all he was doing was hurting them. He couldn't keep doing that.

He was nearly to his Jeep when his phone vibrated. He pulled it out and held it up to his ear. Everything inside him clenched when Lauren barely managed to say his name before she broke into a sob.

"Lauren? Are you okay?"

"I'm sorry," she said, her sobs garbling her words. "I'm at the studio. Your mother was here…"

Danny blinked. *What?* His mother had gone to Lauren's studio? He got into the Jeep and shut the door. "My mother? At the studio? Holy Mother of God, what did she say to you?"

Lauren's tear-filled voice shook. "She told me to stay away from you... that I'm selfish and I'm a home wrecker. She said I've ruined your marriage and that I don't care what happens to your sons. And that's *not true*, you know that!"

"Jesus Christ—"

"—and she told me that no matter what, I'd always know you didn't love me enough to marry *me*. And the only thing I'll ever be is your *whore!*"

Danny saw red, but he collected himself before he spoke. "I don't think that. I would *never* think that. Are you okay?"

There was still a tremble in Lauren's voice. "Yeah. I just... She surprised me. And the things she said..."

"Don't listen to a goddamn word. Are you okay to get back to your place? I'll come over as soon as I can..."

"You don't have to come over—"

"—Yes, I do. Can you get home okay?"

"I have a car coming."

"Okay. I'll be there as soon as I can." He paused. "Lauren, I'm sorry."

"I know." Her voice was a sad, lost whisper.

Danny hung up the phone and immediately drove to his parents' house. He was going to deal with this right now. When he arrived, Danny walked in without knocking. He stormed through the kitchen and into the living room, startling his father.

"Where's Mom?"

"She went out. Said she had an errand to take care of. Why?"

With the most impeccable timing ever, the front door opened, and Deb waltzed in, looking smug. "I'm home, hon. I—oh, Danny. This is a nice surprise."

Her nonchalance stymied his anger but only for a fleeting moment before he exploded. "Are you insane? You had no right to ambush Lauren like that! And the things you said? Do you have any idea how upset she is?"

"Deb?" Richie asked.

She ignored him. "I don't care if she's upset. No one seems to care that Heather and your children are unhappy. Someone needs to put a stop to this. You certainly haven't. She's disrespecting our entire family!"

Danny completely lost it, his voice reaching a roar. "Are you fucking kidding me?"

"Danny!" Richie's voice was stern. "That's your mother you're talking to."

"You want to talk about disrespectful? You waylaid her. Told her she's a horrible person. You called her my *whore*!" Out of the corner of his eye, Danny saw his father's eyebrows shoot up.

"That's exactly what she is." Deb spat out her words. "You're a married man, Danny. Married! And she's sharing your bed. What else would you call her?" She dropped her purse on the side table.

Danny locked eyes with his mother. "A woman I care about deeply. This is none of your business. *None.* Don't go near Lauren again, do you understand me? Not again!"

"She should be staying away from you! Do you have any idea how that photo in the paper will make Heather feel? How it made me feel?"

Danny threw his arms in the air. "And there it is. How it made *you* feel. You don't give a shit about Heather. Or about my marriage. You only care about how this makes you look in front of the rest of your church friends."

Deb's face contorted and her voice went higher. "That's not true, the ladies and I—"

"Don't finish that sentence. Just don't," Danny said. He'd had spats with his mother over the years, but nothing like this. He couldn't remember ever being this angry with her.

"I raised you better than this."

Danny's mouth opened, but he stopped himself before he said something he could never take back. As angry as he was, she was still his mother. He muttered a curse under his breath and stormed out. The Jeep's tires squealed as he tore out of the driveway.

Inside the house, Richie poured himself a small glass of whiskey. Deb didn't say anything when she came back from the kitchen with a glass of water. She didn't look at him and went right to the stairs.

"Deb." Richie couldn't believe she was just going to walk away without a word.

"What?" She glowered at him, still spoiling for a fight.

"What do you think you're accomplishing? This is Danny's business. Not yours, not mine, and you're certainly not helping by attacking Lauren or by shutting him out. You hardly say two words to him during Sunday dinners now."

"Why should I? He's behaving abominably! I expect better from my own son!"

Richie shook his head, feeling a deep frown settle into his face. "Have you stopped to think that what you did made things a lot worse?"

"Worse? How?"

"Because now Danny feels like he needs to defend Lauren. This might have been a short-term thing. Danny may have come to the conclusion—all on his own—that he still loves Heather and wants to work things out with her. That's going to be hard for him to do when all he's thinking about is protecting her from you."

"That girl doesn't deserve to be defended or protected..." She took two steps up the stairs.

"Deb, that's enough."

"How do you know it will be a short term 'thing,' Richard?" From her vantage point on the stairs, she could look down at her husband. "Maybe it will be a long-term thing. Have you thought about that?"

"I have thought about it," Richie said. "And you know, if that happens, we're going to have a new family dynamic to deal with.

Even though I don't agree with what Danny's doing, I trust him. I trust that *my son* will make the right decision in the long run. He's the only one who can make it, Deb."

She made a disgusted noise and continued walking upstairs. Richie went to the base of the staircase and called after her, "I can't decide for him, and neither can you. And when he makes it, we'll have to live with it regardless of whether or not we like it."

CHAPTER THIRTY-FIVE

After the blow-out with his mother, Danny went straight to Lauren's, where he did his best to calm her down. It took a few hours, but he stayed until Lauren fell asleep. He watched her for a little bit to make sure she really was asleep, stewing the entire time. His mother had no right to interfere like that. Rubbing his face, he muffled a sigh—Lauren finally looked peaceful, and he didn't want to wake her. But he had to go home. He dropped a kiss on her forehead before slipping out of the apartment.

The next morning Danny was still furious, and his mood didn't improve as the week went on. He considered skipping Sunday dinner, but Heather was bringing the boys for Cole's birthday. He didn't want to miss his kids—or his niece's birthday—but he wasn't sure he'd be able to remain civil with his mother.

"I'm still so pissed at her. I don't want to go to dinner, but the boys..." Danny said to Lauren as he ran a hand through his hair. He leaned back in the patio chair and looked out over Central Park.

"You'll regret it if you don't go."

He sighed and frowned.

"Just pay attention to them—ignore the other stuff."

He offered a dark half-laugh. "Not as easy as it sounds. You're going out on Sunday, too, right?"

An odd expression crossed her face as she nodded and answered, "Yeah, Jackie is having me, Steph, and Carolyn over." Lauren put her feet up on the coffee table. She wasn't sure she wanted to spend the day at Jackie's, but at least Carolyn and Steph would be there.

"Why the face? You love spending time with your sisters."

"I do, but I don't know. Just seems strange. Jackie never does girls' night. Probably just wants to prove she's the next Martha Stewart."

Sunday dinner at the Padovano's was awkward at best. Danny and his mother barely spoke. Heather was chilly to him. Between his earlier visit to Connecticut when he and Heather had their unexpected interlude, and a few phone calls they'd had since then, he'd thought they were making some progress towards being civil. But as soon as Cole's cake was eaten and gifts were opened, Heather started to hustle the boys out, saying it would be a long drive back to the cottage.

"But I want to stay," Matty said. He dragged one sneaker toe across the floor.

"Me, too," Tommy said.

"Not tonight," Heather told them. "Go get your stuff."

The boys sighed and dragged their feet. Tommy gave his father a hug. "We miss you, Dad."

It was a knife to Danny's gut. "I know, kiddo. I miss you, too. I've got a couple days off from work soon and I'll come visit." He wished he could suggest they stay, but there would be no one to watch them during the day.

"What's going to happen when we have to come back for school?" Lucas asked. "Where are we going to live?"

Danny's answer was immediate. "At our house. That's your

home." There was no way he was making them live anywhere but the house they'd grown up in.

"Will you be there?" his oldest son asked.

Danny almost said yes, but then said, "Your Mom, and I need to figure that out." It was something he'd been thinking about but hadn't discussed with Heather yet.

All three boys turned to look at their mother.

"Your father and I need to talk about things. Now go on, say goodbye to Cole and get in the car. We have a long drive back tonight." The boys reluctantly went into the other room.

"You can stay at the house, Heather," Danny told her. "If you don't want me there, I'll figure it out."

"I'm sure that wouldn't be too difficult."

Danny ground his teeth. "Heather..."

"What? Is the detective afraid of the truth now? You're not going to sleep on your father's sofa when you've got your girlfriend to go to... I mean, clearly you've got your new, famous friends now." Heather folded her arms. "And don't play dumb, Danny. I saw that photo in the paper. *Everyone* saw the photo in the paper."

That fucking picture, Danny thought. "That's not..." Heather turned her back on him to look at Richie and Deb, and Danny bit his lip.

"I'm sorry," she said. "I shouldn't be starting a fight in your house. Thank you so much for dinner; it was really nice to see you."

"You and the boys are always welcome," Deb answered, pulling Heather in for a big hug.

Heather said goodbye to the rest of the family and followed her sons outside without a word to Danny. As the front door shut behind them, Danny muttered a curse under his breath. He couldn't let the evening end like this.

He followed her out to the driveway, calling Heather's name as he hurried down the walk. She turned around but Danny saw the tears she tried to wipe away and hide.

"Heather, hang on for a sec," said Danny as he took her arm. She tensed but didn't pull away.

Lucas glanced at them and turned back to the house. "I forgot something. Be right out." He took off before they could object.

"Boys, get in the car," Heather told the other two.

"But Mom..." Tommy whined.

"Listen to your mother," Danny said. "And no backtalk."

"Fine. C'mon, Tommy." Matty took his brother's hand.

Danny and Heather waited until they got into the car and shut the door. They walked a short distance away and stood on the sidewalk, facing each other.

"What?"

"I want us to have a civil, adult conversation," Danny said. "I'm sorry that photo upset you. There were photographers everywhere. It wasn't like I asked them to take it." His unhappiness over the picture, having his private life spilled all over the media, nagged at him.

Heather deflated. "When I saw it, I hardly recognized you. I mean, you looked like you, but at the same time... the man in that picture isn't the man I married."

And you're not the woman I married either. We've both changed, he thought, but he kept the comment to himself. "What do *you* want, Heather?"

"You know what I want," she said. "I want us to be a family again. I want us to try to figure this out, but I have to ask you a question, Danny, and I need an honest answer." She jammed her hands into the pockets of her shorts. They had little stars on the pocket trim.

He waited.

"Do you want the same thing?" she asked. "Or do you want a divorce?"

The question took the wind out of him. Although the word had been bandied about, Danny hadn't given much serious thought to a split, although he wasn't sure why. His eyes got misty as the reality of that word clawed its way into his gut. He'd thought about what life would be like if he was with Lauren and couldn't see the boys all the time, but he realized that he'd never actually thought about asking Heather for a divorce as part of that train of thought. He'd skipped over that part—or ignored it completely. The realization shook him to the core.

"Do you?" She repeated the question.

"I... No... But..." Danny stammered over his answer, utterly in turmoil, his impending failure as a husband looming larger than it ever had.

Heather reached out and took one of his hands. "Danny, I am so angry with you. But I'm still willing to try working this out." She sighed. "But it is the same as I said before: we can't if you're still seeing her. You can't be with both of us. You need to decide what you want. *Who* you want. And..." She dropped her eyes and let go of his hand.

"And?"

"And you have to decide soon. Summer's almost over and I can't keep doing this anymore."

She walked away, and the pain in Danny's heart was sharper and deeper than he expected. He almost called out to her. As the car door slammed, Lucas came running out of the house. He stopped when he reached his father.

"I'll see you soon, Lucas." Danny hugged him.

"Dad? Can I talk to you for a minute? Man to man?"

If Lucas hadn't looked so serious, Danny might have laughed. "Man to man? Of course. What's on your mind?"

"I just, well..." Lucas hesitated. "I was thinking about when I messed up Mr. Fiorino's car with my baseball. You always told me that mistakes happen, and we learn from those. And when you make one, you gotta own up to it."

"You're absolutely right. You've got to take responsibility." Danny tried to hide his discomfort. It was hard to hear one of the life lessons he'd tried teaching his son turned back on him. In fact, "hard" was a colossal understatement.

“And then you have to make it right,” Lucas said. “Fix whatever got broken, even if what you did was an accident. Even if fixing it is hard.”

His son’s expression was earnest and thoughtful, and Danny could tell he’d been thinking about this for a while. Danny glanced from his son to the car where his wife sat waiting, torn between paternal pride and eviscerating guilt.

“When did you get so grown up?” Danny asked.

“C’mon, Lucas! We gotta go!” Matty hollered from the car, shattering the moment into a thousand pieces.

“Shut up, Matty!” Lucas shouted back.

“Your mom’s waiting,” Danny said.

Lucas gave him another quick hug. “I miss you, Dad.”

“I miss you, too.”

Danny stood in the driveway, watching their taillights disappear and feeling very empty and alone. One way or another, he had to decide.

CHAPTER THIRTY-SIX

Danny had only been home for an hour and was still agonizing over what Heather—and Lucas—had said. And if the person pounding on his front door didn't stop, they were getting punched in the face. He flung the door open, ready to tear whomever it was a new one—but he bit his tongue when he saw Joey standing there. He glared and his brother stared right back, unflinching.

"You gonna invite me in? Or just make me stand on the friggin' front steps?"

"What do you want?" Danny had really had enough of family for one day, but he stepped back, letting his younger brother into the kitchen.

"Wanted to see if you were okay. Was a rough time at Ma and Dad's."

"I don't need a shrink."

"Debatable."

Joey went to the refrigerator without asking and took out two beers. He put one on the laminate kitchen table in front of Danny and opened the other for himself. Danny looked at his brother for a long time. Joey just waited, unperturbed by the silence.

"I wish Ma would stay out of it," Danny said. "She went to the studio the other day and unloaded on Lauren."

Joey swallowed his beer wrong and started coughing. "Jesus H. Christ. That explains a lot. At least she's talking to you. Do you remember when she found out that her friend Edie cheated on her husband? Ma never spoke to her again."

The word "cheated" got Danny's hackles up. "Look, if you came here to lecture me, then save it and get the hell out—"

"—That's not why I—"

"—because I've really had enough of being judged by everyone!"

"Well, if you'd shut the fuck up for a second and listen, maybe you'd know why I was here." Joey used his Army voice, and the authority in it brought Danny up short. He shut his mouth, swallowing whatever else he was going to say, and held up his free hand to show he wasn't going to interrupt.

"It's an ugly way to say it," Joey said. "But straight up, you're married, and if you're sleeping with Lauren, you're cheating on your wife. Doesn't matter if your marriage is in trouble or you're separated or whatever. And honestly, bro, I don't like what you're doing. But I want you to know that I'm not judging you one way or another. I get it, sort of. I was little, but I remember what you were like after Lauren left."

Danny looked down. He thought he'd done a better job concealing his misery back then. He'd tried to hide it, ignore it, bury it, and he'd believed it had worked. Clearly, he'd been wrong—he hadn't hidden his broken heart from everyone nearly as well as he suspected.

"I'm not you," Joey said. "So, I don't know how you feel about her, or about Heather, or about any of it. But I whatever you decide to do, I got your back."

Danny slumped in his chair, relieved by his brother's words. "That means a lot to me."

"I got you, man." After a pause, Joey said, "Can I ask you something?"

"Shoot."

"How did it happen? I mean, when did it go from thinking to doing?"

After another swallow of beer, Danny put the bottle down. There wasn't a reason to whitewash anything for Joey. "I've always thought about Lauren. Hard to stop after the band hit it big."

"Fair enough."

"But I was too messed up... I don't know. I assumed she hated me. Maybe I'd be better off if she did." Danny offered a bitter laugh. "When Cole wrote the paper, it brought up a lot of memories. Honestly? There's part of me that's always wondered if I should've gone to LA."

"Then you saw her at the Sandoval interview." Joey rested an elbow on the chair back.

"You saw it, too?"

"Don't be stupid. Anyone who's a Kingmakers fan watched that interview."

"Yeah. And I wanted to go," Danny said. "I *did* want to see her again. Figured what harm could it do? I thought we'd hug, catch up for a few. Go our separate ways." The chair creaked when he leaned back, and he drained the rest of the beer in a single gulp.

Silence gathered at the table again, and Joey took it in stride, waiting patiently for his brother to continue. Eventually he pushed the conversation along.

"And then there was the big reveal."

"That fucking disaster." Just the thought of it got Danny riled up. "I want to make this clear: last couple of years, me and Heather, we've been having problems. I don't want you—or anyone—thinking that it was all sunshine and roses before Lauren came back."

"Understood."

"Heather's always been a little jealous. But she started acting crazy after that TV spot. And I swear to you... I wasn't with Lauren, not then. I got so mad that my own wife wouldn't trust me or listen to me—I shut down."

"So, when did it start?"

Before he answered, Danny stood up and gestured. The living room would be more comfortable than the hard kitchen chairs. Joey moved to the sofa and put his feet up on the coffee table. From his recliner, Danny continued the story, sharing details like running into Lauren getting pizza and then choosing to not tell Heather. He admitted his strategy for avoiding fights hadn't worked the way he planned.

"You know," Danny said, "I finally thought, maybe it's me. Maybe I'm the one making myself crazy. If I could talk to Lauren for a while... catch up, maybe talk about how we left things back in high school. I thought I'd stop thinking about her so much. Get some *'resolution'*." He air-quoted the word. "So, I went to see her. I guess part of me wanted to see if she felt the same..."

His voice faded as he frowned, thinking about that night.

"Did you go hoping something would happen?" Joey asked.

Danny tried not to flinch at the question. "Honestly? Part of me did. Everyone already thought I was sleeping around. I'd been convicted, so I thought maybe I should do the crime, you know?"

Joey's expression stayed neutral.

"You think I'm an asshole." Danny's voice was bitter. He leaned his head back into the chair's padding, feeling very alone. He wouldn't blame Joey for thinking he was a reprehensible human being. He certainly thought he was.

"I didn't say that."

"Didn't have to."

The brothers eyed each other across the coffee table until Joey said, "I asked to hear your side of the story. I'm not going to force my opinion down your throat."

Danny appreciated that but turned his face away for a second so Joey wouldn't see the shine in his eyes.

"Did Lauren know you were coming?"

"No, I dropped in. Flashed my badge to make security call and tell her I was there. We had a great talk, and we got into a lot of stuff. And then I went to leave... and all those old feelings were still there. I couldn't stop myself—we kissed. I mean I *really* kissed her, and if she had offered to go to bed with me right then, I wouldn't have thought twice about it."

"But you stopped."

"She stopped me."

Danny went on to tell Joey about what Lauren had said that night. What it would mean for his family. For him. And how crystal clear she was about leaving when the album was done.

"Lauren's never pulled her punches," Danny said, wishing he had another beer. "Not then, not now. She was right, so I left. But it didn't make things better. We met up a few times after that, but never at her place. Always somewhere public."

"Like when I saw the two of you in the park," Joey said.

"Like the park. Damn it, I really was trying to do the right thing, Joey. To stand by my vows, but no matter what I did or what I said, it wasn't good enough for Heather. It really hurt that she didn't trust me. And then when she left and took the boys?"

He looked at his younger brother with a stricken expression. Heather leaving had gutted Danny, and he knew it was splashed across his face. "She walked out on me. Yes, I kissed Lauren. That's on me. But before Heather left, I had *not* slept with her. Maybe going to Lauren that night was my way of hurting Heather back for taking them without telling me."

"If Heather believed you right from the start, would things have been different?"

Danny sighed. "I'd like to say yes, but I don't know. Maybe if we'd talked about it more. Maybe if I'd told Heather how I was feeling. If she'd talked to me more about how she was feeling. We were having problems anyway—this just brought it all to a head." He let the observation fade away.

"I guess the question is, what now? Like you said, eventually, Lauren's going to leave."

Danny considered his answer for a long moment, thinking about Heather and his kids, the rest of the family, his career as a detective. Thinking about what Lucas had said to him earlier that day. He slumped, defeated.

"I don't know. But I have to do something."

CHAPTER THIRTY-SEVEN

While Danny endured Sunday dinner—and his heart-to-heart with Joey—the Stone sisters all met at Jackie's house. Jackie had outdone herself with the cooking, proudly wearing the mantle of domestic goddess. For Lauren's older sister, life was meant to be lived predictably and by a plan. Six months after graduating from college, she'd married her husband, Chris. Twelve months later—almost to the day—she gave birth to their oldest child, Audrey, who was followed by Kristie, Joshua, and Elijah. Her husband's role as senior vice president for a well-respected accounting firm afforded them a very nice house and cars that spoke of their upper middle-class status.

Nothing was ever out of place in Jackie's life, and it was important to her to have the traditional family that went to Mass every Sunday, played by the rules, and was well-respected in the community and the church. Anything or anyone who deviated from that plan—like Lauren—was addressed with stern disapproval.

Jackie and Lauren were about as different as two sisters could be. In fact, most of the time Lauren thought Jackie had a major stick up her ass. Even when they were kids Jackie had always been bossy, taking on the role of surrogate mother whenever she could, and telling all three of her younger sisters exactly what she thought of their behavior. Truth be told, Jackie reminded Lauren a lot of Deb Padovano.

Lauren was pleasantly surprised at how smoothly the day was going. The stunner of the afternoon had been Carolyn's announcement that she was pregnant. Beyond that immediate good news, Jackie's focus was on Audrey starting her sophomore year at the University of Oregon, vacillating between dramatic complaints that her daughter was so far away and bursting maternal pride over the major scholarship Audrey had won to study chemistry there.

The four sisters were in the kitchen, snacking on the last of the desserts, when there was a lull in the conversation. Then Jackie said, "I need to talk to you, Lauren."

Lauren pursed her lips—she knew that prim tone.

"This is supposed to be a fun afternoon, Jackie," Carolyn said. "No serious talk."

Her attempt to steer the conversation in a different direction went unheeded as Jackie looked right at Lauren with a strict matronly stare. "Lauren, what in heaven's name do you think you're doing? I mean, people are *talking*."

All the muscles in Lauren's neck and shoulders clenched. Oh, hell no. She was not going be lectured by Jackie about her moral failures. Not today, not after all the shit that had gone down with Danny's mother the night she showed up at the studio.

"Jackie. Don't." Lauren stood up straighter and pressed her palms on the island's smooth butcher block. She wondered if her fingernails would leave gouges in the pristine surface.

"I didn't want to believe the rumors I'd been hearing," Jackie said. "Then I saw that picture in the paper of you running around with Danny." She put her hands on her hips, waiting for an explanation as if Lauren was a wayward toddler to be scolded.

"I'm not 'running around' with anyone. His wife walked out on *him*." Glacial didn't even come close to describing Lauren's tone.

"They were very happy until you came back." Jackie's declaration was full of conviction, as if she had inside knowledge into the state of Danny's marriage. "Now, suddenly his wife is gone and the two of you are hot and heavy again? Steph, Carolyn, I know neither of you approve of this!"

"Don't pull us into—" Carolyn warned.

"Really, Carolyn? Don't tell me you approve of this *inappropriate* behavior?" Jackie heaved a disgusted sigh at Carolyn while Stephanie remained speechless, tears starting to brim in her eyes.

"Okay, *Jacqueline.* You want to do this? Then let's do it." If her sister wanted a fight, Lauren was happy to give her one.

"Fine! You should be *ashamed* of yourself." Jackie didn't hesitate to launch the next salvo. "He's married! Bad enough that you slept with him back in high school before you were married! What are people supposed to think?"

Lauren's eyes flashed. "People should mind their own fucking business."

"Language! You know I don't allow profanity in my house!"

"Danny and I have... a complicated relationship." Lauren gritted her teeth.

"Complicated? Please. You'll spread your legs for him at the drop of a hat."

"Excuse me?" Lauren was stunned. That was the most vulgar thing Lauren had ever heard Jackie say in their entire lives.

Jackie barreled on. "But I'm not surprised. I mean, look at you. A life of one disaster to the next, one scandal to the next. Living like a gypsy. Drinking, drugs, who knows how many sexual partners... And now sleeping with a married man. He took vows, Lauren. Sacred vows. And you're making him break them."

"I'm not *making* him do anything." Lauren's voice got louder as she got angrier. "Not everyone lives by your rules, Jackie. For Chrissakes, do you even hear yourself?" She started to turn away, tired of defending herself, a little part of her wondering if she deserved Jackie's contempt. But that moment of remorse was overwhelmed an instant later.

"You don't even care that you're going to hell, do you?"

"Oh, you nailed it," Lauren said. "That's me, the unrepentant sinner! If I'm already going to hell, what's one more sin—I mean, c'mon, if I'm going, I may as well walk in like I own the place."

The cheeky disdain made Jackie huff. "You only care about what you want—doesn't matter what happens with everyone else."

This felt like the confrontation with Danny's mother all over again. She flung her arms in the air. "Oh, that's right. It's all my fault. I mean, it isn't possible that I might actually still love him? No, no, I only want the sex—must be that broken moral compass of mine. I mean, why else would I be *fucking* Danny-goddamn-Padovano?"

Lauren deliberately used the f-word again, knowing it would push all of Jackie's buttons.

"Falling back on crassness. So typical!" Jackie raised her chin, wrapping herself in an invisible mantle of superiority.

"No, it's so typical of *you*, Jackie. You totally buy into the idea that sex is bad and something to be ashamed of. God forbid you want it before you get married. Or that it feels good and you enjoy it!"

Jackie's face turned blotchy. "I saved myself! Saved myself for my husband. You... you just threw your virginity away."

Lauren hated the way Jackie made it sound like trash. "I didn't throw anything away. I gave it to someone I loved."

Behind Jackie, stuck to the refrigerator with two big daisy magnets, was the annual St. Catherine's calendar. The school sold them every year as a fundraiser. August featured a picture of Jackie's younger daughter in her cheerleading outfit.

"Shit, I was *Kristie's* age when I gave it up to Danny," Lauren said, goading her sister even harder.

"Kristie would *never*!"

Lauren wasn't proud of it, but she took perverse pleasure in watching Jackie seethe at the thought of her sixteen-year-old daughter having sex. Knowing the daughters were a soft spot, Lauren dug in.

"You keep telling yourself that. Keep telling yourself that your girls are going to be precious little virgins when they get married. Just like you—"

"—*Enough!*—" Carolyn shouted to no avail.

"—Not like their screwed-up aunt who did it when she was sixteen and proceeded to fuck her boyfriend every chance she got after that. You know, we even did it at Mom and Dad's once, when they were out, and you were supposed to be 'in charge.'" Lauren made quote marks with her fingers. "And you never even knew."

"Shut your mouth! Just shut your mouth, you... you *slut*!"

Lauren's face jerked to the side as Jackie's hand cracked against her cheek. For a split second, the only sound in the room was stunned silence. When did Jackie grow a big enough pair of brass ones to slap her? Lauren put her own hand up and gently touched the stinging red welt on her cheek. That broke the spell.

"You *bitch*!" She lunged forward and grabbed Jackie by the front of her shirt. Lauren forced Jackie to back up while her sister flailed, unable to break away. It had been a long time since Lauren had been in a bar fight, but she knew how to hold her own. Only her surprise at the entire altercation, and the fact Jackie was her sister, kept Lauren from punching her as hard as she could. Repeatedly.

"STOP IT! Both of you, stop it!" Stephanie hollered at the top of her lungs. The anguish in her voice broke through the red haze, and Lauren let go of Jackie's shirt. She stepped back, vibrating from the anger and adrenaline coursing through her. All four women looked at each other.

"Get out of my house," Jackie said.

Lauren grabbed her purse and keys from the kitchen island. "Fine."

An hour later, Lauren was back in her apartment, pacing and infuriated. She resisted the urge to call Danny. She wasn't about to interfere with Cole's birthday party—or his time with his boys—with her sibling drama.

Her cell phone buzzed, and she let it go to voice mail. It buzzed a second time. She ignored it again. By the fourth time, she realized whoever was calling wasn't going to quit, and she looked down to see Carolyn's picture on the screen. Lauren put the phone to her ear. She didn't even say hello.

"I know you can hear me."

"What do you want?"

"I'm downstairs. And I'll keep calling until you let me up."

"Fine."

When Lauren answered the door, she knew she looked like hell based on the way Carolyn's face softened with concern. She fiddled with the hem of the old Pearl Jam t-shirt she was wearing and invited her sister in.

"Looking good," said Carolyn, eyeing the large rip in Lauren's yoga pants.

"Not in the mood."

Carolyn put her hands up, acknowledging she wasn't there to pick a fight, and Lauren exhaled.

"C'mon, let's sit outside," Lauren said. She walked out onto the patio without waiting for her sister's answer.

It was a beautiful evening and there was a nice breeze on the patio. The sounds of the city seemed very far away. Carolyn made herself comfortable in one of the chairs while Lauren rummaged through the bar fridge and pulled out a ginger ale for Carolyn. She cracked the can open, the soda fizz popping. Lauren poured herself a Coke and added a healthy shot of rum. She sat down in the soft chair next to her sister.

"Jackie was out of line," Carolyn said.

"You think?" There was a bitter edge to Lauren's comment. "Gotta admit though, never would have thought she'd have the balls to actually hit me." Lauren swallowed half her drink in one gulp. "I mean, who the hell is she to judge me?"

"She thinks her shit doesn't stink." Carolyn's statement was matter-of-fact truth and elicited the smallest chuckle from Lauren.

"She thinks it smells like roses, probably. She's had her little perfect life. She got out of high school, went to college, met Chris there. And you know she had a fucking chastity belt on until their wedding night. No way she was putting out before she got that ring."

"I'm surprised she put out enough to have that many kids," Carolyn said.

Lauren tried not to smile but failed.

"But there's something you need to remember about Jackie—"

"You're defending her?"

"No. I'm trying to explain her." Carolyn pulled both her feet up and tucked her legs under her. She reminded Lauren of a meat-loafed cat. "Remember, you're everything she's afraid of. She tries to control her life because if it's impeccable on the surface, then everything's okay. But you put it all out there. You take risks—big risks—and if you get banged up and bloody, you come back stronger. She doesn't understand that, and it scares her to death."

Lauren thought about that. It didn't make her any less angry, but it did make sense. She swirled her glass, watching the liquid shift and slide.

Out of the blue, she asked, "Do you think I'm a slut?"

Carolyn choked on her soda. "What?"

"Do you think I'm a slut?" Lauren was almost afraid of the answer, afraid that Carolyn saw her the same way that Jackie did.

"No! Absolutely not. This situation with Danny is, well, it's a little messed up. You've always cared about him—maybe too much. But I know you, and you're not just doing this for some good sex—"

Relief washed through Lauren.

"—But you know, if you were having outrageous three-ways each night with hot young groupies? Then I might have to think you're maybe a teeny bit slutty."

"I can honestly tell you; I have never had a three-way with any hot young groupies." Lauren laughed and felt the remaining knot of anger coiled in her chest loosen and drop away. "As for the rest of the band's choices?" She offered a shrug and a smirk.

"No! *Who*?" Carolyn was beside herself. "Seriously? You can't leave me hanging like that! Stevie? —no, he's not the type. Is he? Ox's too straight-and-narrow. Wait, was it DJ? I could see DJ—" She gasped. "Oh my *God*! *Augie*?"

Lauren laughed but didn't answer the question. All five of The Kingmakers had a long list of escapades that would, someday, make an epic band memoir—but until then, there were secrets that stayed with the band. And who she, or anyone else in the band, may or may not have had a threesome with was one of them.

"Can I ask you something else?" Carolyn asked after they stopped laughing.

"Sure."

"How's the sex with Danny?"

"Carolyn!"

"What? I'm pregnant, my hormones are off the chart—I can say whatever I want. So 'fess up. Is it better than you remembered? Worse? What?"

"Better," Lauren said, feeling a blush creep up her neck. She drained the rest of the rum and Coke as her thoughts churned.

"If things are so good, why do you look so sad?" Carolyn asked.

"I don't... Shit, I don't know." Lauren did know, though. It didn't take a psychic to know this was all going to end. She went back to the patio fridge and reached for the rum. As her hand grasped the cool neck of the bottle, she changed her mind. Drinking wasn't going to solve anything. She pinched the bridge of her nose.

"Have you guys talked about what's going on here?" Carolyn asked as her sister sat down again, a can of soda in her hand.

"Not as much as we should," Lauren said, the admission rankling her. "We skirt around it, but it's the elephant in the room. And it's getting bigger. If I ever get my head out of my ass and write some good songs, the album will be finished. Then I'm gone. Something's got to give before the tour starts."

"What do you think's going to happen?"

Lauren gulped her drink and felt the sadness drape over her. "I think I'm going to go down with the ship. One way or another, I'm going to lose him. Again."

Even as she said it, a little voice in the back of Lauren's head laughed at her pain. That little voice that had been cropping up more and more. The one she thought she'd left behind a decade ago.

CHAPTER THIRTY-EIGHT

Danny's head was splitting. After dinner at his father's house the previous week, he'd only seen Lauren briefly. She'd obviously had an awful time at her sister's, but all she would say was that she was never speaking to Jackie again. After that, she'd disappeared into the studio, and he'd been sucked into a kidnapping case that had dominated his thoughts and his time.

Because of the case, Danny hadn't been home for close to 24 hours. It was early afternoon, and his lieutenant had sent him and Matsui home to get some rest. He walked into his house and threw his wallet and keys on the counter. He'd felt the pain of the kidnapped boy's parents to his very core, and all he wanted right now was to hug his sons. Every day he missed them more, but tonight? The ache bordered on unbearable.

After throwing on old shorts and a t-shirt, he stared into the refrigerator. His choices were pitiful. He grabbed a container of left-over Chinese takeout, gave it a sniff, and judged it edible. He flopped down in his recliner and reached for the remote. Next to it was a picture of his family. He picked it up—it was from a trip to the beach last summer. The whole family was smiling and happy.

We looked happy back then, but were we? How can you go from happily married to living separate lives and wanting something more? Were we ever happily married? Can I fix this? Should I?

Despite how tired he was, Danny got up, grabbed his keys, and headed out. He drove to St. Catherine's but then idled in front of the church. Gunning the engine, he pulled away. Twenty-five minutes later he found himself on the other side of the Verrazzano-Narrows Bridge and on Staten Island—and in the parking lot of St. Sylvester's.

At the door of the church he paused, dipping his fingers in the holy water, and making the sign of the cross. His feet felt rooted, but he squared his shoulders and walked with purpose to the confessional. Sitting in silence, he almost bolted, but soon there was a rustle of cassocks and a soft thump as the priest sat down. Danny bowed his head.

"Forgive me, Father, for I have sinned..."

In the city, Lauren was brooding. She hadn't seen Danny in three days and on the phone, he'd been distant. She'd seen the headlines about the kidnapping and tried to chalk it up to that. Nevertheless, a nagging feeling something else was going on, that something was wrong, ate away at her.

She took her ever-present notebook and went out. In the park, she found a bench and started to people-watch. Jotting down notes about things she noticed, she created tiny stories. It was a trick she'd used before to jumpstart her writing. The sticky, late August heat and humidity clung to her and didn't improve her mood. Lauren soon retreated to the cool of her apartment to shower the stickiness away. It was close to six o'clock when she stepped out onto the bath-mat, wrapping herself and her hair in plush towels.

When Danny called later to tell her he was pulling up to the building, hearing. his voice softened her whole disposition. She hung up the phone and sighed, relieved that she'd be able to see him.

Whenever she was out of sorts with the band, all the crap and frustration seemed to fade and disappear when Danny was around.

She puttered in the kitchen until she heard the door open. He was wearing faded jeans and an olive-green t-shirt that said ARMY across the front. She liked how he looked in jeans. He might have to wear suits for work, but Lauren far preferred him in casual dress.

"I missed you." Lauren gave him a kiss, but the one he returned was distant. In an instant, she was wary and on edge. He took her hand and led her to the living room.

"Everything okay?" she asked as she sat next to him and put a hand on his leg. She told herself the serious demeanor could mean anything and hoped no one was sick.

"Lauren... I've been doing a lot of thinking."

"Oh." Lauren drew her hand back. His somber tone sent tendrils of unease through her body. This wasn't about anyone being sick. This was about her.

"School's starting soon." He cleared his throat and stared straight ahead. Lauren closed her eyes and felt a part of herself crumble. She knew exactly what was coming. Danny took her hand, but she wouldn't look at him.

"You know I love you... But they're my family. Those boys are my life. For their sake, I have to try to work things out with Heather. So, when they come back, they'll be at the house and so will I."

"I see." Lauren's stomach turned over. She knew Danny loved his boys and would do anything for them. Even let her go. She looked up and made eye contact—and it was Danny's turn to drop his gaze.

"And that means we have to stop." His voice got thick. "I have to stop coming here, seeing you."

"Danny..." Lauren hated the note of desperation in her voice, the fear. She'd known all along that this was coming. Even known, deep down, that it was the right decision—and despised herself for not being able to make it herself. But hearing him say it out loud ripped a ragged, gaping hole right through her. Then the tears came.

Danny pulled Lauren into his arms and rocked her. "I'm so sorry," he whispered through his own tears.

They sat together for a long time. Lauren knew there was no other choice for them: Danny would be miserable on the road, away from his family, constantly dealing with the drama and intrusions that were stitched into the fabric of her existence. And Lauren wouldn't—couldn't—give up The Kingmakers. The music was everything to her. She couldn't be like Carolyn or Jackie. They were married, had families—the lives they had were exactly right for them, but not for her. And she couldn't be like Steph with her numbers, formulas and spreadsheets. Finally, Lauren pulled away and went to look out the window. He got up to follow her, but she held her hand out, stopping him.

"You need to go."

"Lauren..."

"No, you're right," she said. "I knew this was coming. I should have broken up with you myself, but I didn't have the guts—or the good sense to do it." She turned away, struggling to keep her voice steady and the tears at bay.

The floor creaked behind her. She could feel him come closer, but he didn't touch her. "Lauren. I, I'm sorry... I never..."

"I know you didn't." She turned around, wishing she could hide the anguish she knew was painted across her face. "Just go. Now."

Unable to bear seeing the pain in his face that reflected her own, she turned back to the window again and stared out at the sky. He stood behind her for what felt like an eternity before she heard him step back. His footsteps faded, then the squeak of the doorknob.

She heard one final, soft "I'm sorry," before the door closed.

After Danny left, Lauren wept until there were no more tears. She tormented herself trying to think of something she could have said or done differently, something that would have changed things. Berated herself for not being brave enough to end the relationship after that first night. Tortured herself with recrimination and self-doubt.

The cavernous apartment felt huge, cold, and empty. On the balcony, she stared out at the city as the empty hole in her heart consumed her. She clutched the railing as the sorrow turned into anger. She spun abruptly, kicking one of the chairs so hard it flipped over backward, knocking a vase of flowers off the table. It smashed on the balcony tile. A million jagged little shards. Just like her life.

Lauren dropped to her knees, a sliver of glass digging into her knee. The slice of pain brought her back to her childhood, a day when Stephanie had fallen and scraped her knees. All her baby sister had wanted was ice to numb away the pain. Lauren had held an ice bag on Steph's knee until she stopped crying.

But Lauren hated that dull, numb feeling.

When she was in pain, she wanted to run, to fly. To move so fast the anguish peeled away from her and tumbled into oblivion, unable to keep up. And there was only one way she knew to make that happen. Only one thing in the world that could let her outrun her ache: getting back on that white horse.

Over the years since rehab, she'd been tempted to go back to the coke, but never like this. Lauren fished her iPhone out of her pocket and started to scroll through her contacts. She reached one name and stared at the initials: DFG. He wasn't a dealer, but he knew all the right people. She reached out a finger to tap the number and then threw the phone down.

No, she told herself. *You can't go there. You can't.*

But God, she wanted to.

More than she had in a very, very long time.

Lauren grabbed the phone again, and she hit the delete button, erasing DFG from her phone. Then she went to a different, very specific number. Her hand was shaking as she put the phone to her ear.

The phone's ring pulled Augie out of his sleep. Aggravated, he fumbled in the dark to find it. Who the hell was calling him at this ungodly hour? He didn't even look at the screen when he answered.

"Hmm?" His voice was thick and slow.

"Augie?" On the other end of the phone, Lauren's voice was almost inaudible.

His sleepy brain-fog vanished. "Lauren? Lauren, what's wrong?" Augie sat up in the bed and flung the covers away.

"He ended it, Augie. Danny left."

That rat-bastard, he thought.

"I'd forgotten how much it could hurt. I mean, my brain remembered but my heart didn't. I just want to stop feeling the hurt..."

"Lauren, I'm coming over. Stay there. Okay? *Don't* go anywhere."

There was silence on the other end of the phone.

"Lauren?" Augie had his phone pinned by his shoulder and was trying to drag on his jeans. "Promise me you'll be there."

"I'll be here."

"I'm leaving now.'

"Whatever." She disconnected the call.

Augie scrounged up a t-shirt and didn't even bother with socks before he jammed his feet into his sneakers. In the hall, he kept pressing the elevator down button over and over, as if that would make the doors open faster.

Outside, he hailed a cab and jumped in the back. Traffic was light but the trip still felt like it took forever. When they arrived, Augie literally threw the fare at the driver as he leaped out of the cab. He ignored the obscenity the cabbie hurled at his back and raced to the desk. Carlos, the night concierge, looked up in concerned surprise.

"Mr. Stone?"

"Lauren called me," Augie said as he went right to the elevator. "She knows I'm coming."

"Is everything alright?" Carlos asked.

Augie hesitated, not wanting to reveal too much, but not wanting to lie to the man outright. "Ah, guy trouble," he finally said.

The gilded doors crawled closed, and the elevator made its leisurely ascent to the top floor. Augie paced back and forth and squeezed through the doors before they opened fully. Lauren's apartment door was locked when he tried the knob.

"Lauren? Lauren!" He banged it with the flat of his hand. "Open up. It's me!"

The lock clicked. With her red eyes and blotchy cheeks, Lauren looked like hell. For a moment her expression was blank, and then she threw herself into Augie's arms. Tears gushed. Augie hugged her and ground his teeth. This was exactly what he'd been afraid of when he realized that Danny was back in her life.

"Okay. Let's go inside." He managed to untangle himself from Lauren. She headed back into the apartment, and he followed. Lauren went to the sofa and curled up in a corner, hugging a pillow close to her, a fistful of tissues in her free hand. For the next hour he let her cry and talk and yell—whatever she needed. After a time, the tears lessened.

"I love him so much," she said. "And I've loved him for so long."

"I know." It felt like a meaningless platitude, but there was nothing else he could say.

She jerked her head up and looked at him. "What's wrong with me?"

"There's nothing wrong with you."

"Of course, there is." The tears started again, and her gaze wandered to the window. "There must be. Twice I've lost him. What about me isn't enough?"

"You got it all wrong," Augie said. "It isn't that you're not enough; you're too much for him. You always have been. I know you love him, but you have to think about it."

"I am thinking about it."

He didn't believe her.

"Sharing you with your fans the way he'd have to would blow his mind," Augie said. "I know you don't want to hear this. But one way or another, this relationship was going to end."

Her face twisted, and she curled up tighter. He hated saying it while she was hurting so much, but it was the truth. It killed Augie to see her like that. Breaking up with Danny all those years ago had torn open a part of her heart and soul. Now Danny had ripped it open all over again, as raw and painful as it ever was before.

Augie wanted to beat him senseless.

A morose sigh slid out of Lauren. "I'm an idiot, Augie. A goddamn idiot. What made me think he would ever love me enough to come with me?"

Augie wanted to shake her and repeat what he'd said. Remind her that *Danny* was the one who was lacking. That *he* was the one who wasn't enough for *her*. But she would have to come to that conclusion herself. He couldn't force her to see it.

The circuitous conversation continued, with Lauren careening from self-loathing and crushed self-esteem to anger to clarity and back again—and Augie went on the ride with her, patiently waiting and listening until she exhausted herself.

Finally, when she was wrung out, Augie was able to persuade her to go to bed. Lauren found him in the morning folded into the recliner, the TV still on. She ordered him to go home because she wanted to be alone. They argued briefly, but eventually Augie relented.

When he got off the elevator, Augie went to the desk—Carlos was just leaving and George was starting his shift.

"Is Miss Stone feeling better?" Carlos asked.

Augie didn't answer the question. Instead, he said, "If Danny Padovano shows up to see her, do *not* let him up there. In fact, tell him to fuck off."

CHAPTER THIRTY-NINE

While Augie complied with Lauren's order to go home, he didn't leave her alone. He called and texted his cousin several times. Lauren answered a few but ignored most. In the afternoon, he showed up unannounced to find her aimless and in tears, just as shattered as she had been the night before. This wasn't the first time her heart had been broken, and Augie knew it wouldn't be the last. But since she was connected to Danny on such a deep level, he knew this hurt was far graver than anyone understood.

He called the rest of the band so they weren't blindsided on Monday. DJ took it the hardest, cursing Danny's name so furiously, Augie felt compelled to warn the keyboardist not to do something stupid. Stevie was concerned and Ox didn't say much, but that was typical Ox.

When Augie arrived at the studio on Monday, he said good morning to Tisha and headed into Studio A. The others looked up, clearly expecting Lauren to be with him.

"Where is she?" Ox asked.

"On her way," Augie said.

"How's she doing?" DJ asked.

"She was a wreck when she called me Friday night. She thinks she's a fool, and that there's something wrong with her..."

"Nothing wrong with her," DJ muttered under his breath. "She deserves so much better than Jackass."

Lauren arrived a few minutes later, and all of DJ's bluster and fight vanished when he saw the forlorn expression on her face. All he really wanted to do was hug her and tell Lauren that he'd make sure everything was okay. But he held back as she brushed off any comments and said she wanted to get right to work.

And work they did until it was time a bit of sustenance. Lauren picked at her lunch, using a big breakfast as an excuse for her lack of appetite. DJ didn't believe her—and could tell Augie didn't either.

As lunch wrapped up, Lauren wandered into one of the other studios. DJ followed her. She sat down at the keyboard and ran her fingers back and forth over the keys, random notes spilling out as she did.

"Push over," DJ said. "You're hogging the whole bench."

Lauren obliged, and he sat down. With the two of them on the bench, there wasn't much room. He glanced over at her and saw tears sliding down her cheek.

"I know I've always given you shit about your boyfriends, but I really am sorry."

"No, you're not," she said, her voice catching. "You can't stand him."

DJ wasn't going to lie to her. "I don't like him. But I am sorry." He paused. "He's still a dick. I can go rough him up in a parking lot if you want. That make you feel better?" The thought of clocking Danny right in the head gave DJ a warm fuzzy feeling.

"No. I'd prefer that you not get shot by his partner." The smile that cracked her face was fleeting.

"Would be totally worth it."

Her mumbled response made it very clear, even though he couldn't make out the exact words, that she didn't believe him.

"Look at me," DJ said.

Lauren looked away.

"Lauren. Please look at me." He reached out and gently turned her face back. Her dark eyes held nothing but sorrow and self-loathing, and DJ felt a knife go straight through his own heart. "You deserve so much better. Someone who gives you their whole heart. Who loves *you* and loves you for who you are *now*—all of you, all the light and all the dark—not who you were twenty years ago."

"Wouldn't that be something?"

DJ put his arm around her shoulder and kissed the top of Lauren's head. "Yeah," he said, his voice almost lost in her hair. "It would be, wouldn't it?"

Lauren reached forward and picked out three notes on the keyboard. DJ followed suit and mimicked them. She played a few more and he repeated those. Lauren's next set was more complicated and faster. He matched it perfectly, and another tiny smile cracked her downcast expression. A moment later they were furiously playing simultaneous versions of "Chopsticks," increasing the tempo until they couldn't go faster, and both dissolved into laughter.

After, Lauren rested her head on DJ's shoulder. "Thanks, man."

"I've always got your back, Lauren. You're my girl."

He meant every word.

While DJ and Lauren dueled at the piano, Danny sat glumly at his kitchen table, exhausted and defeated. He'd hardly slept after breaking off his relationship with Lauren, and it had taken all his willpower to resist calling her. He'd dozed a few times, but the sleep was always fitful. On Sunday, Joey and Maggie had both called to check on him when he didn't show up for church or dinner. He'd lied and told them he was sick, then used the same excuse that morning when he called his lieutenant.

Ending things was the right call. At least, that's what he told himself. When he'd gone to Lauren, he thought that knowledge would somehow spare him some suffering. He was a fool to think that. The memory of her hurt, haunted face was all he could see when he closed his eyes.

When Lauren left him behind all those years ago, he'd wondered how she could just go so easily. Care so little that she could leave and not look back. Now that he was the one leaving, he realized it might not have been so easy after all. Back then he'd thought he was so grown up, but he was only an immature boy. That small epiphany didn't help, though. All it did was carve the canyons of his sorrow a little deeper.

He wanted to apologize, tell Lauren he was sorry. He picked up his phone to call her and put it down. What was he doing? Lauren wasn't the woman he should be calling. He pushed another number.

Heather didn't even say hello. "What do you want?"

He almost snapped at her but stopped. He'd earned that.

"Can we talk for a minute?"

"I suppose."

That short reply was heavy with weariness and suspicion. She was bracing for the worst, expecting him to say he was leaving her for good.

"I... I think... We..." He sighed and looked down. There was a round stain on the table from a coffee cup. It was the kind of thing that made Heather crazy.

"Say what you have to say."

"I ended things with Lauren."

There was a sharp intake of breath and then silence on the other end of the phone.

"I told her I had to try making our marriage work," Danny said. "That I had to put my family—our family—first." He knew he'd done the right thing, but Danny felt like a shell of a man. Hollow, empty, aching.

"You still want to be married to me?"

"Yes."

There was more silence and his chest got tight. Shouldn't she be happier about this? It was what she wanted—at least what she said she wanted.

"Heather?"

"Why?"

"Why? Why what?"

"Why do you want to stay married to me?" she asked.

Oh, for the love of Christ. "You're my wife."

"That's not a reason. And after this summer, being 'your wife' doesn't mean much."

Danny could feel anger starting to roil in his gut. He was trying to do the right thing. Taking the first step at making amends. But he checked himself. It would take more than a phone call for Heather to believe him.

"I still love you," he said.

"I see." There was a softening in her voice, so slight it was nearly imperceptible, but it was there.

"And I want things to work between us," Danny said. "When are you and the boys coming home?" He fought to keep all his tangled emotions from coming out in his voice.

"Saturday. The boys have made friends here, and there's a big neighborhood beach party on Friday."

"I understand. I don't want to disappoint them."

"I'll have them call you tonight after supper," Heather said. "Maybe we can talk a little more then."

They said their goodbyes, and the line went silent. Danny put the phone down. He wondered why he didn't feel happier.

The days dragged for the next week. Danny was little more than a robot at work, and when he wasn't there, he was holed up at his house nursing his broken heart over Lauren and agonizing over how to fix things with Heather. He did his best to scrub the house so that it wasn't a complete disaster, and when he was done, he assessed his work and deemed it passable. But it certainly wasn't the way Heather would have done it.

The headache he'd been enduring felt like someone was beating the inside of his skull with a hammer. He cupped some water in his hand and used it to wash down a couple of ibuprofen tablets. He'd slept poorly all week, his restless mind racing as he thought about how he'd left things with Lauren the week before. Remembering the look on her face when he left. He wondered if she hated him. He hated himself, that was for sure.

On Saturday, Heather and the boys arrived around noon. Danny helped get the bags out of the car, and they all shared lunch. The boys filled the house with happy, almost ceaseless chatter, which brought Danny an inordinate amount of joy. And, for a time, it kept the awkwardness at bay. In the afternoon, they went outside to see their friends from down the street, excited to tell them about their summer at the beach.

Heather glanced at him as she closed the laundry room door. Danny had caught her surreptitiously watching him a few times. He knew he looked like crap—his warring emotions were taking their toll.

When she came into the kitchen, Danny said, "Heather. This whole summer… I just… we just…" He ran a hand through his hair, frustrated by his inability to articulate what he was thinking.

"We stopped trying," she said. "We both did, long before this summer. When there was too much going on, it was too easy to sacrifice each other. I'm glad you want to try, Danny." Shaking, she put her arms around him.

He realized she was trying not to cry, and he felt his own emotions well up in his throat. After a deep breath, he collected himself and they stepped back, both retreating to a safe distance from each other.

"What do we do now?" he asked.

"I want us to see a marriage counselor," she said. "And I want us to talk with Father Rob."

Inside, Danny recoiled. He wasn't crazy about the idea of talking to Father Rob about all of this; he'd gone to confession at St. Sylvester's expressly because he didn't want to do it with Father Rob. And he especially didn't want to be confessing his mistakes to some shrink. But he'd told himself that he would do whatever Heather wanted to try repairing their marriage.

She was watching him. Waiting for his answer. And she knew how he felt about therapists.

"Okay," he said, trying to keep the reluctance out of his voice. "We'll try it."

"Thank you, Danny." Heather smiled, and it was the first genuine smile she'd offered him in a long time.

CHAPTER FORTY

The "Chopsticks" moment with DJ was the last happy thing that happened to Lauren—or The Kingmakers—for the next three weeks. As August drifted into September, and September's days began to slip away, Lauren continued her slow spiral downward, dragging the band in her wake. Work on the new album had been difficult before her affair with Danny crashed and burned. Now it was close to disastrous.

Lauren's frustration and anxiety grew, as did her depression. The band was churning over songs for the album, and she blamed herself. They disagreed about the musicality, the tempo, and the thousand other details that went into a song. And Lauren knew her inability to string together a set of lyrics worth a damn was just gas on the fire. She'd brought several half-finished songs to the studio and didn't like any of them, but with her inability to break free of the darkness consuming her, she just kept trying to fix the unfixable.

Feedback from the band wasn't helping. They couldn't seem to reconcile her lyrics with music and vice versa. Fitz was doing his best to coach her and steer the band through this conflagration. Lauren could tell he was growing more frustrated by the day—and they were all keenly aware of looming production deadlines. She wasn't sure if she wanted to scream or cry... or just stop caring.

"That's not the right tempo for this," DJ said to no one in particular.

Stevie shot him a look. "It's what's working for me. Don't like it, come over here and bloody well play it yourself."

"Dude!" Even Augie's tone was terse. "Not helpful."

"Neither is the drumbeat. We're all over the place; this is noise not music," DJ said.

"Asshole," Augie shot back.

"Are you hearing anything, *chica*? Might be nice to at least know what kind of song you're tinkering with." Ox made no effort to hide his frustration. Then, under his breath, he said, "Prince writes a song a day."

"Back the fuck off." Lauren threw her pen across the room. Where were her lyrics? She was utterly dry, out of ideas. The pain of her breakup and fear of a failed album consumed her. That awful voice in her mind that fed her despair and self-loathing was cranking up the volume. *I can help you,* it whispered. And every time it did, Lauren disintegrated a little more, like bits of sand disappearing in an hourglass.

"We've been backing off." Ox thumped down in a chair. "That's our whole problem. Our production schedule's spinning outta control. We're getting nothing done. Anyone remember what changed about a month ago?"

"Not relevant." Lauren forced the words out through a clenched jaw.

"Not relevant my ass," Ox said, glaring at her.

Lauren launched herself out of her own seat. "You got something to say to me? Any of you? Then say it. If not, stop being a bunch of little bitches! After your second divorce, Ox, did I bail on you? Have I bailed on any of you? No. We worked through it no matter what kind of shit we had going on."

"No, you didn't," Stevie said. "And we supported you while you got your shite together in rehab."

"And I appreciate that. So maybe you could all cut me a little fucking slack. Problems don't just disappear; they stick with you for a while." She found another pen and went back to scribbling in her notebook.

The tension between Lauren and Ox continued to simmer. It lurked in the shadows and followed them back to Velocity the next day. Everything came to a head when Lauren tore into Ox over a minor disagreement, and he laid into her just as hard in response. Augie walked out of the studio and into the control room to get a little space. Behind him, a string of expletives erupted, followed by a loud crash and more curse words as a stool went flying backwards.

Ox stalked out, shoulders tight, his mouth compressed in a thin line. Augie glanced through the open door in time to see Lauren tear up several papers and fling them around the room.

"Calling her a 'crazy-ass, control-freak bitch' didn't exactly improve her attitude, Ox," Stevie said, following the bass player out.

"*Púdrete!* That's exactly what she is," Ox, who was normally as patient as he was stubborn, sounded furious. "I get she's hurting, and I'm sorry, but I'm not her punching bag. I ain't putting up with that shit."

Augie sighed and looked back at his cousin. Inside—and out of breath from her outburst—Lauren's hands were clenched into fists. Her unruly hair was pulled back, and with it away from her face, the dark circles under her eyes were pronounced. She looked thin, and it wasn't a healthy thin. Augie's anxiety welled up.

Fists still clenched, Lauren stalked out of the booth. "I'm going home."

"Good. Go," Ox said. "At least when Taylor gets dumped, she gets some goddamn mileage out of it."

"*You are such an asshole*!" She stormed out.

"Nice fucking job," Augie said.

"Ox's got a point," DJ said, his worried eyes on the doorway where Lauren had vanished. "It's never, *never*, taken us this long to do an album. We don't even have something that resembles a hit—we're exceling at mediocrity and she's completely around the bend."

"I'm not arguing that point, mate," Stevie said. "But we're not helping by talking to her like she's washed up. What else can we do?"

"Only thing we can do. We wait," Augie said.

"Come off it, Augie!" At this point Ox was yelling at everyone. "Stop covering for her. She's not the only one in the band. We've been waiting and it hasn't gotten us shit."

Augie got right in Ox's face. "Then what do you recommend we do? Come on, dude, I'm waiting. Lay it on us."

Fitz shouldered between them. "Enough," he said in a voice laden with disgust. "All of you get tha hell out."

Augie backed up a step. "Fine. Let's regroup Monday afternoon. That gives us five days to calm the fuck down. We'll see how everyone's doing Monday and do a full day Tuesday."

"If you don't buckle down after this break, our timeline is bloody well blown," Fitz warned. "And I've never not delivered an album. Ever."

"We'll get it done. We always do," Augie promised.

"Who's going to tell—" Ox started to say.

"I'll do it," Augie interrupted. "For the next few days, you just keep your mouth shut."

Ox grunted at him and stomped off.

When she left the studio, Lauren didn't go home. She went into the city and wandered. Stuck in her own head, she didn't pay attention to the people around her or even where she was going.

Her phone vibrated, and she glanced at it. A text from Augie said that the band was putting things on hold until Monday afternoon. She felt her lip quiver—she was screwing everything up. All the band's problems were because of her. She didn't respond to her cousin.

Several hours later, she found herself on the far side of Central Park. One of the wood benches with wrought iron arms was open, and she sat in the dead center, hoping that might discourage anyone from trying to join her. Pigeons and sparrows gathered around, hoping for crumbs. From behind her sunglasses, she watched people come and go. It didn't take long for her to notice the young man several benches down who had a stack of newspapers next to him. He didn't seem to be pushing the material on anyone but was more than happy to exchange one for money when someone sat down. All under the watchful eye of two of his friends who loitered nearby.

A stressed-out Wall Street type in a suit sat down and talked to the man for a minute. After he paid, Lauren caught the smallest flash of a plastic packet being tucked between the pages before it was handed over. She wasn't surprised. She'd played that game plenty of times back in LA. Find your dealer, pay your money, and have your personal choice of poison slipped into your pocket or tucked in a newspaper. Then off you went. Or, once you got rich enough, the dealer would deliver right to your door.

A taste of that would solve your problems. The little voice in her head was a whisper. She closed her eyes and pretended not to hear it, but the voice pushed. *All that pain, all that hurt? You never felt it before. A little up your nose and the whole world changes. Gets faster, brighter, better. You know it does.*

Lauren ground her teeth. She knew the voice lied, that using would make everything worse. But she had to admit, she'd been thinking about it: the haze of energy and excitement that came with a cocaine high. A euphoria that blocked all the bad shit out. Didn't have to think about the things she didn't want to think about. Or feel things she didn't want to feel. She could outrun all of it. Things like her writer's block. Things like Danny.

A physical pain twisted her up and turned her inside out.

Danny...

At night, she couldn't sleep. She would stare out the window, missing feeling him beside her and hating the idea that he was sleeping with Heather. Then she would berate herself for those thoughts—she couldn't fault him for that. Heather was, after all, *his wife*. And she was, well, nothing.

You don't have to feel like nothing anymore...

Lauren looked over at the man on the bench.

Danny was gone. Her writing talent was gone, and that meant her career was gone. After the fight today, it was entirely possible the band was gone. Why on earth would they let her keep dragging them down? They were better off without her. She had nothing left and nothing to lose.

Ten minutes later, she was walking home, her fist clenched inside her pocket around a small bag of cocaine.

CHAPTER
FORTY-ONE

Being required to talk about his feelings twice in one day was a piss-poor way to end the week. An hour earlier, Danny had finished a session with Father Rob. He believed in God, he had faith, but he was profoundly uncomfortable talking to Father Rob about the state of his marriage—and what he had done with Lauren. Adultery was a mortal sin, but to be absolved, he had to be truly sorry.

And he wasn't.

Not if he was being honest with himself.

Now he was sitting in the parking lot of a dull office building covered in faded brick, waiting to meet Heather for their first session with the "real" marriage counselor. He glanced at his watch. The boys hadn't been in school long, but they already had numerous after-school activities—Heather was bringing them to his parents' house before she met him.

Danny sat in his car with his eyes closed, his head leaned back against the headrest. He was sorry, just not in the way that Father Rob wanted him to be. He saw the distrust and hurt in Heather's eyes every day, and he regretted that deeply. He regretted the uncertainty his sons had experienced during the summer. But he couldn't truly be sorry for the time he'd spent with Lauren. She mattered to him and always would. And the more he was pushed to talk about it, to make a public demonstration of his remorse, the more resentful he became.

Heather's dark silver sedan pulled into the parking lot. Danny gave the car a critical once-over. It was getting old. They'd have to figure out how to fit a car payment into the budget soon. He got out of his Jeep and waved to her as she parked.

"Hi," she said, offering her cheek for a kiss. "Have a good day?"

"It was okay. Lot of paperwork." Danny stuffed his hands in his pockets as they looked anywhere but at each other.

"Well," Heather said. "We should go in."

Danny nodded, but inside, he cringed.

In the office, they settled into opposite corners of the sofa. The doctor sat across from them in a plush leather chair. He introduced himself and asked them both what they wanted to get out of therapy. Heather said she wanted to figure out where they'd started to go off the rails and get back to where they were before. She also wanted to find out if she could trust Danny again. Danny told him that his main goal was to rebuild his relationship with Heather. What he didn't say was that he hoped the doctor could tell him how to stop caring about Lauren.

"And what's been the biggest source of mistrust?" the doctor asked.

Heather looked at him, and Danny set his jaw. This seemed to be part of the penance Heather had constructed for him: confessing his sins out loud.

"I had an affair with an ex-girlfriend."

"And he lied to me." Heather laced her fingers and kept her hands in her lap. She didn't look at Danny while she spoke.

"I see," was all the doctor said.

Danny looked out the window and wondered how Lauren was doing, but then refocused on the doctor, chagrined he'd let thoughts of her distract him. *I'm sure she's fine—she probably doesn't even think about me.* But even as he thought it, in his heart he knew it wasn't true.

CHAPTER FORTY-TWO

Except for the little, crumpled plastic bag full of powder, the coffee table was empty. Lauren paced back and forth like a caged panther, warring with herself. All the way home, she'd tried to cling to her sobriety while the slithering little voice kept attacking.

Why try? You've lost everything. You'll feel so much better. You know you will. It won't matter what anyone else says, you won't feel any of it. It will all be dust in your rearview mirror. No more pain, no more doubt.

She flung herself onto the sofa and folded herself into the middle cushion. But her eyes remained riveted to the bag—and the powdery contents inside. It felt like the coke had a hook inside her chest and she was being dragged closer to it with every passing moment.

I don't need it. I don't, she told herself.

Liar.

Lauren's throat tightened. She picked up a framed picture that was lying on the cushion next to her. She'd been looking at it the night before and had tossed it aside when she tried to go to bed. Protected under the glass was a singular moment of joy: the minute she'd left Bruno's party with Danny. Happy, laughing. A captured instant when she was living the life she'd always dreamed of: the music, the success, the fame—and Danny with her to share all of it. A moment she would never have again. One moment to show her so very clearly that she had nothing now.

Lauren hugged the picture to her chest and tried not to cry. She was so tired of crying. So tired of feeling hollow. She let her gaze drop to the scene again and ran her fingers over the frame's glass front. *I don't deserve to be happy...*

The voice whispered again, *You don't have to feel like this.*

I'm not... I can't... Lauren didn't even finish her thought. She was exhausted. She didn't have any energy left to argue with the voice. Why should she bother? She set the picture up on the table and picked up the bag of coke.

That's right! Just a little stardust and you can fly again. All the pain, all the sadness—it won't ever be able to catch you again. The voice rejoiced, sensing victory. *You'll be able to write again. You'll be invincible.*

Lauren's hands started shaking and she flinched like she was coming out of a trance. She wouldn't be invincible, she'd be dead. Then a darker thought crossed her mind: *Maybe that's the answer. They'd all probably be better off without me. Augie could finally play his song—*

Horrified by the dark turn of her thoughts, Lauren leaped up. She raced into the bathroom and tore the bag open. Dumping all the white powder into the toilet, she flushed it and threw the plastic in as well. She watched it swirl around in the water and lurched forward onto her knees, bile burning up her esophagus. As the last of the white and the plastic disappeared, a keening cry slipped out of her throat.

As she raised her hands, intending to cover her face while she sobbed, Lauren realized that a dusting of the cocaine had clung to her fingertips. She scrambled to her feet. It took two tries to force her shaking hands to open the faucet. Pumping out a ludicrous amount of soap from the dispenser, Lauren scrubbed her hands under the scalding water until they were red and raw.

She almost didn't recognize the woman looking back at her from the mirror. Hollow cheeks gave her a haunted, lost look. Dark circles shadowed her eyes. In each line in her face, she saw every mistake she'd ever made in her life. To the outside world, she was a resounding success, but all she saw in the mirror was a miserable, abject failure. The pain flared anew, ripping through her, fanning her smoldering insecurities and fears.

I should have snorted it all and ended this farce.

Lauren sagged down to the cold tile floor and wept.

At Mass that weekend, Danny sat and stood when required, but he didn't hear anything Father Rob was saying. He was lost in his own head, and—despite his best efforts—found himself thinking about Lauren again. It had been weeks since he'd seen or talked to her. The first couples' therapy session with his wife had been hellish. He knew what he'd done, but listening to Heather talk about how he'd screwed around with another woman and lied to her was hard. Hard didn't even come close, actually.

But he'd had plenty to say as well. As much as he wanted his private life to stay private, he didn't have that luxury. He knew it had been hard for Heather to hear how he'd hidden away his feelings for Lauren all these years. And how his feelings for her wouldn't go away overnight. He wondered if they would ever go away at all. Every time he thought about Lauren, his heart died a little all over again.

He knelt with everyone else and folded his hands. *Holy Father? You're probably pretty pissed off at me, but I need you to do something. I need you to watch out for Lauren. Keep her safe. She doesn't deserve the pain I gave her. If you could take it away from her and give it to me, I'd shoulder it. I'll take whatever punishment I get, whatever penance I need to do. But please don't let her be miserable anymore because of me.*

The Kingmakers regrouped at Fitz's studio on Monday afternoon. Augie was the last to arrive and was staring at his phone's screen as he walked in. He was a little worried; Lauren had been incommunicado for the entire break. The background chatter and noise ceased immediately as the door closed behind him. When he looked up, it was clear the rest of the band was already pissed off.

"Where is she?" Stevie asked.

"She's not here?" Augie's stomach turned into a knot.

"Obviously not," Ox said.

Augie skewered him with a nasty glare. "Who was the last one to talk to her?"

"I sent her a text after I left here the other day," DJ said. "I got one little emoji back, but that's it."

"I haven't," Steve said. "Not since all the shit hit the fan last week. I went away with Gabby and Maya."

Augie looked over at Ox. The stocky bass player shrugged, but there was an undercurrent of worry in his voice. "I was the last person she wanted to talk to, so I didn't call her at all."

"She always talks to you, Aug," DJ said. "Even when she isn't talking to the rest of us, she *always* talks to you. She hasn't called? Not at all?" He fished his car keys out of his pocket.

Augie grimaced, his worry increasing exponentially with every passing moment. "No calls, no texts. Nothing. I thought she might have taken off for the weekend – you know, go to the mountains or something. Remember when she vanished for three days to Tahoe? I was freaking out back then, but she showed up on time to get back to the studio."

"Jackass hadn't crushed her heart that time." DJ pulled out his phone and pushed the speed dial for Lauren's cell. It rang and went to voice mail. Stevie followed suit, sending a text, and then calling her number. The text disappeared into the ether, and his call also went to voice mail.

"Shite. Voice mail for me, too." Stevie stuffed his phone in his back pocket.

Oh, dear God, please let her be okay. Augie locked his hands behind his head and took a deep breath. It was a vain attempt to calm his racing heart. "Come on, we have to find her."

"I have the SUV today. I'll drive," DJ said. He was out the door before he even finished talking.

As the rest followed, Stevie caught Augie by the elbow. "Augie, mate, what if she's..."

"*Don't* go there." Augie didn't know if Stevie was going to ask if she'd gone back to the coke, or if she was dead, or maybe both. But Augie didn't want to even entertain either thought.

At least twice, DJ blew through yellow lights that were on the verge of red, and once Ox got into a shouting match with the car next to them when the driver took exception to DJ's driving. They were lucky they didn't cause an accident as they weaved in and out of traffic. At the Somerset, DJ ended up half on the sidewalk, scattering the pedestrians.

George looked up, alarmed, as they all rushed to the desk. He started to get up. "Mr. Stone? Is something wrong?"

"Hopefully not," Augie said. "None of us have heard from Lauren. Have you seen her?"

"I was off for the weekend. The last time I saw Miss Stone was when she came back on Thursday evening. It was just before I went home. She did seem distracted. Let me check the book." He opened a small, leather-bound notebook. Everyone who worked the private front desk made a note of who came and went from the hotel.

"No," he finally said, frowning. "There's no record that Miss Stone has been out since then. No one has come to see her either—"

"Fine, yes. Let's get a fucking move on," DJ said. "C'mon, c'mon, c'mon!"

Inside the crowded elevator, George swiped his card and pressed the penthouse button for them. The doors slid closed, and the guys rode up in silence, listening to delicate classical music as it piped through the speakers. It was the longest elevator ride any of them had ever taken.

CHAPTER FORTY-THREE

Lauren screamed as her apartment door burst open, nearly dropping the bottle of juice in her hand. A large splash of liquid landed directly on her grungy yoga pants. All four of her bandmates stood in the foyer, staring at her as if she was completely bonkers.

The first thing out of Augie's mouth was, "Oh, thank God."

DJ let out a long low whistle. "What happened?"

She followed their gazes and blinked, everything around her coming into a sharper focus. The apartment was filthy. Clothes were strewn over chairs and on the floor. Dirty glasses and dishes filled the sink. The counters had stains on them. An empty bottle of high-test rum lay on its side on the island with a half full bottle of tequila next to it. And hundreds of sheets of paper—most crumpled—were scattered everywhere.

Lauren's surprise at her band's arrival transformed into annoyance, and she scowled at them. "Why are you here? We're taking the weekend off—giving ourselves some time to chill out or calm down or whatever-the-fuck you guys wanted to do."

"The weekend?" DJ looked shocked. "Lauren, it's Monday afternoon. We were all supposed to be at the studio an hour ago."

"What do you mean 'already Monday'?" Perplexed, Lauren looked around again. "Must have gotten distracted. I've been writing, or at least trying to write. But it's just more crap." She gestured at the morass of loose sheets scattered across the living room, covering the coffee table, and littering the floor.

Lauren suddenly felt like she was roasting in a sauna and pulled off the zip-up sweatshirt she was wearing. She tossed it on a chair. It didn't catch and slid, limp, to the floor.

"Jesus, Lauren. How much weight have you lost?" DJ asked. "You haven't looked like this since before you checked into rehab."

Lauren glanced away, tears stinging her eyes, and shrugged. "I haven't been very hungry..." She yelped in surprise as Augie grabbed her by the arms and spun her to face him.

"Lauren! Look at me!" he said. She tried to jerk away, avoid his worried eyes—she knew exactly what her cousin was searching for: the wild look that said she'd been flying high and was crashing down.

"Augie, I—"

He didn't let her finish. "Tell me right now, Lauren. The truth. Are you using again?"

She'd been clean for ten years, but that didn't mean a damn thing—everything could unravel in a heartbeat. It almost had. She looked at the floor, ashamed of what she'd almost done.

"Lauren?" She could hear the fear in Augie's voice.

"I haven't used. I haven't. But... I bought some. Enough to finish everything."

She looked at them all, but the stricken look on Augie's face as he tangled his fingers in his hair crushed her.

"After the blow-out at the studio, I wanted to stop feeling so empty," she said. "Forget what a fucking failure I am." She started to shake and crossed her arms to hug herself as if she could force the trembling to stop.

"Where is it?" Augie demanded, but Lauren just kept talking.

"I didn't use it, Augie. *I didn't.* But God, I wanted to."

"You didn't answer his question," DJ said. His voice was soft, gentle, speaking to her as if she was a wounded animal.

"I flushed it. I swear to all of you, I got rid of it. You have to believe me. Please..." Lauren looked at them all, one at a time. Ox glanced away, unable to look at her. Their distress, their disappointment, devastated her, and for a moment she regretted not going through with it. Maybe it would have been easier to just let the darkness consume her.

She reached out and grabbed Augie's arm, unable to bear the sorrow she saw in her cousin's eyes. "Augie, I swear I didn't." Her voice cracked. "I... I swear on Carolyn's unborn baby."

That was about as serious an oath as Lauren could make, and the expression in his eyes changed when she said it.

"I believe you," Augie replied.

Lauren looked at the floor, too humiliated to trust him.

"Lauren," DJ said. "I believe you, too. I *trust* you." She dragged her eyes up to meet his. They were so blue it would be easy to get lost in them.

A moment later, Ox and Stevie echoed what the other two said. She didn't deserve their trust, or their faith.

Finally, she asked, "Why are you all even here?"

"We were worried when you didn't show up today," DJ said. "Then you didn't answer when we called."

"You called?" Lauren furrowed her brow. She didn't remember anyone calling. "Oh. My cell. Right. After I flushed the coke, I spiraled. I started looking through my contacts. Looking for someone—anyone—who could bring a little taste over to hook me up... I put the phone in my lock box. And then I flushed the key."

Her laugh was weak. "Ridiculous, I know. But I guess it worked. After that, I had to do something with the pain. Put it somewhere that wasn't up my nose. I started writing. It's probably a steaming pile of shit like everything else I've been writing lately." She waved absently at the room again

Ox picked up a few of the crumpled balls of paper from the floor and unfolded them.

"Don't waste your time." Lauren couldn't bear being the brunt of his criticism again.

"You never know," he answered.

"I do know. You'll hate it. Everything I've written for this album is shit. I'm finished."

She grabbed at the paper, but Ox held it out of her reach. She tried once more, and he still played keep-away. Lauren stopped, uncertain if she wanted to scream at him or cry. She heard more rustling. The others were grabbing crumpled papers, too. She tried, in vain, to crush the big, wracking sob that erupted out of her.

"I've lost it. The album's a disaster and it's my fucking fault! Don't waste your time looking at that crap." She wiped her eyes with the hem of her shirt.

"*Cállate,*" Ox said, his eyes skimming the paper.

Lauren flinched like she'd been slapped. Had he really just told her to shut up?

"Just *chitón*... shush. Be quiet for one second." He scanned one page and then another. When he looked up, he was smiling. "Lauren, this shit's good. I mean, it's *really good*."

"Whatever." Lauren didn't believe him. He was probably just saying what she wanted to hear.

"These are some of the best ideas you've come up with. Ever," DJ said.

"Dude, give it here." Augie waved his fingers, and DJ handed him a few sheets of paper.

Lauren felt her insides crumble. They'd all had front-row seats to her songwriting disintegration. The dross littered across her floor would hammer that last nail into the coffin.

Then a smile cracked the serious expression on Augie's face. It grew wider, brighter, and when he looked over at her, she could see his dimples. "This is amazing!"

She so desperately wanted to believe them, to hope, but the fear that they were bullshitting her was a step away from paralyzing. "Maybe we should go through a few? Just be sure?" Her questions were tentative.

"Hell, yes. But first, you're taking a shower," Augie said.

"A shower?"

Her cousin arched an eyebrow. "Seriously, Lauren? Those clothes are nasty and you're pretty rank—have you showered since last week?"

"Excuse me?"

As he opened the patio slider, DJ said, "He's saying you smell."

"I do not!"

"Trust me—you do," Augie told her. "And if you don't smell like soap and shampoo when you come out, I'll drag you back in there and scrub you myself."

"The hell you will." For a split second, Lauren protested but then relented and let Augie steer her towards the bathroom. At the doorway, Lauren planted her feet again and started to argue, her innate dislike of being told what to do bursting out. But Augie just pointed at the bathroom. She relented, too tired to quarrel.

Shutting the door behind her, she pulled her hair out of the messy knot at the back of her head. It hung down, lank, tangled, and dull. She peeled off the yoga pants and kicked them away. Yanking the tank top over her head, she held it for a moment and inspected it. It really was disgusting, discolored with sweat stains and some other blemishes she couldn't identify. She gave it a sniff and recoiled. The shirt found a new home in the waste basket.

Lauren cranked up the hot water and climbed into the shower, and stood—rigid—under the spray, trying to keep everything inside. Then all at once, her shoulders dropped, and more tears came. She didn't try to stop it this time or control it. She nearly fell to her knees as she cried. She wept for her own broken heart. And for Danny's broken heart. For what they'd had in the past, and for what could never be. As she cried, the tears dulled the razor-edged, shattered pieces inside her and washed away the debris she'd been drowning in.

When the worst of the tears abated, Lauren washed and rinsed her hair twice before working a dab of conditioner through it. She thought about the four men out in her apartment... Her four brothers-in-arms—her second family. They'd come looking for her because they were worried. Because they cared.

They didn't give up, even when I almost gave up on myself, she thought. *They've been there for me no matter what, for twenty years now. How could I ever think I have nothing when I have the four of them?*

CHAPTER FORTY-FOUR

The band spent the next two days camped out at Lauren's. They organized her notes and sifted through the ideas, prioritizing the ones they all liked best, and toyed with arrangements. Standing in the kitchen, a warm cup of tea in her hands, Lauren watched them work. Ox and Augie were tinkering on the percussion for one idea while DJ listened with his eyes closed. Stevie waited, keeping time with his foot, and then started picking out a few chords on the guitar.

She smiled. The past few days had been brighter. Getting out of bed was easier. She was still mourning her break-up with Danny, but the despair that had clung so tightly was now gray, not an inky abyss. She'd spent a week scraping along rock bottom, and she was so grateful that the words had finally rushed out—and the band hadn't abandoned her. She was bruised. Battered. But she'd survive.

Lady Gaga's "meat dress" graced the front of the newspaper that half-covered Augie's vibrating cell. He pushed the paper aside and tapped the green answer button. "Hey, Fitz. No, I wasn't kidding. Ditch all the other stuff. Yes, *all* of it. We get serious when we come in tomorrow." He put a finger in his ear to block out the background noise. "No, I'm not fucking around with you."

He looked up with his big, dimpled smile. "According to Fitz, we're 'going to give him a bloody fekking heart attack' and 'if we don't bloody buckle down tomorrow' he's going to 'feed us to the fekking crows.'" Augie's imitation was dead on, and they all laughed.

They didn't let him down. Lauren got to the studio before anyone and was working on a song when Fitz arrived. She acknowledged him with a nod, and he sat down in the control room and listened. The longer he listened, the bigger his smile got. Lauren's voice was soft and the notes were a little hurried, but there was heart in her song. And that was how the great ones started.

For the next two weeks straight, The Kingmakers put in a series of eighteen-hour days. By the end, they were exhausted, but they'd brought four of the ideas from scribbles on paper to nearly finished tracks, and another ten were well on their way. The excitement and enthusiasm the band felt was contagious. They started talking about tour ideas and concepts for some of the videos that would be produced with the singles. And the idea of turning the project into a double-CD was floated more than once. They still had disagreements, and there were a few temperamental moments, but they were easily resolved.

"Easily resolved" wasn't a term that applied to Danny and Heather's counseling. While they'd made progress, they were still running into surprises and roadblocks that made Danny feel like he didn't know what the rules were. The therapist assured him that the pendulum between progress and setbacks wasn't uncommon.

Their most recent session was unequivocally a setback. On the drive to the doctor's office, a Kingmakers song came on the radio. When Danny didn't instantly change the station, Heather unloaded on him. They continued the fight from the car, through the parking lot, into the doctor's waiting room, and into the office itself.

"Why did the song make you so angry?" the doctor asked. The doctor's voice was devoid of emotion, and it pissed Danny off.

"I don't want to hear her music. He shouldn't want to hear her music." Heather's shoulders were rigid, her arms strapped across her chest. "How can she be out of our lives when she's *everywhere?*"

"What do you think of this, Danny?" The doctor's bland monotone was a pebble in Danny's shoe.

"I don't think you get to dictate what I want." Danny didn't look at Heather even though his answer was directed at her. "It's a song. Maybe it has something to do with me, maybe it doesn't. I'm not going to go around blasting The Kingmakers' music at the house. But you can't blame me every time a radio station plays one of their songs. It isn't like I asked them to."

He worked his jaw. There was something he wanted to tell Heather. He wasn't sure if it was a good idea now, based on this whole discussion. But avoiding it wasn't going to make it easier or better.

"There is something I wanted to mention to you, Heather. May as well do it now."

"What?"

Danny watched the color drain from his wife's face. She set her jaw, undoubtedly expecting a devastating revelation.

"I *do* think about Lauren and her music," he said. "After we broke up in high school, I didn't know how to deal with it. I'd never had a broken heart before. I buried everything as deep as I could and ignored it. Hoped it would go away. And I tried to ignore her music, thinking all I was going to hear was how much she hated me."

He sighed and looked at his wife, who was at the far opposite side of the sofa. The chasm between them looked infinite.

"Clearly she got over it." Heather's voice was sour.

Danny gave her a hard stare before he continued. "No, she didn't. And she didn't hate me either. It turns out that neither one of us got over it. Yes, I had an affair with Lauren. It was my decision, and I'll own that. And I *am* sorry for how much that hurt you." He at least got a huff of acknowledgment from his wife for the apology.

"But the truth—and you wanted the truth—is that before I met you, she was the love of my life," he said. "I didn't understand it before, but I'm still getting over that broken heart from all those years ago. And I need time to work through it."

Heather flushed a bright, furious red. "You're still getting over it? You need *time*?"

Their therapist interrupted. "Heather. I know it hurt to hear that. But one of the things you said you wanted from these sessions was the truth—genuine candor. That's what Danny's giving you right now. It's okay to feel the emotions you're feeling, but you shouldn't punish him for doing what you asked."

Heather squirmed in her seat. Tears flowed down her cheeks. "I know. But I don't have to like it."

"I'm not asking you to like it," Danny said. "I'm asking you to try understanding it."

"I do appreciate the honesty, I do," Heather conceded. "But whenever I hear her music, all I can think about is that you still feel something for her. And that cuts. Deep. I'd be perfectly happy if I never heard another of her songs again. Ever."

"I understand," Danny said.

"Is there anything else you want to share, Danny?" The doctor asked.

"When The Kingmakers start their tour, I'm going to go see the show."

Heather exploded. "Are you *fucking kidding* me?"

Danny wasn't surprised by her response. He'd known she would blow a gasket over it, but it had been on his mind for a long time.

"No, I'm not kidding." He kept his voice quiet and level and resisted the urge to plunge into the fight.

"How can you even say that to me? After everything you did with her?" Heather reached out for the glass of water on the table. Her hand shook as she lifted it. For a second, Danny thought she was going to fling it at him.

"And frankly, I'm telling you. I'm not asking for permission." Danny heard her sharp, shocked intake of breath. "I wanted you to know up front so you don't think I'm sneaking behind your back. I'll even take someone with me. Joey. Maggie. Maybe even Cole. I'll even take you if you want—"

"—Absolutely not! —"

"—But I *am* going to go. What I will promise you is that I won't go alone."

The rest of the therapy session was unproductive, and Heather refused to talk to Danny on the way home. He didn't care. He'd made his mistakes, and so far, he'd done everything his wife asked since they got back together. The therapy, the discussions with Father Rob. All of it. He needed to—and the triteness of the pun made him cringe —face the music, and he wasn't going to back down on his plan.

The next day was a gorgeous—a warm October reminder of the receding summer—and rather than the traditional Sunday afternoon dinner, the Padovano clan opted for a final backyard cookout. Richie, doing a respectable impression of Patton marshaling the troops, manned the grill. Across the yard, Joey was tossing a football with Lucas and Matty. Danny came out of the house and put a bowl of garden salad on the long table, then went to stand by his father.

"How are things going?" Richie asked.

Danny knew what he was referring to. "We had a rough session Friday. Real rough."

Richie nodded. "Have you seen Lauren?"

The question caught Danny off-guard. "No, I told Heather I wouldn't, and I haven't..." His voice faded and his eyes unfocused.

"And it's tearing you up, isn't it?"

Danny's sigh weighed a thousand pounds. "If you'd told me when I got married that I could be in love with two people at the same time, I would have told you that you were full of it. But now? I've lived it, and no matter what I do, someone still gets hurt."

His father turned pensive for a moment. He flipped the burgers and said, "Of all three of you kids, you're the most stubborn. Maggie's a close second. But I learned a long time ago that telling you what to do or think is the fastest way to get you to do the exact opposite. It's a lesson I wish your mother would learn sometimes."

"Tell me about it."

"You're between that rock and a hard place, Danny. And you're right—whatever you decide, someone you care about gets hurt. You get hurt. You've had to make hard decisions about what you're willing to give up and what you can't live without."

What I can't live without...In an instant, Danny thought of his boys: helping Lucas get ready to talk to the girl he really liked... coaching Matty in basketball... playing knights and dragons with Tommy. He swallowed hard.

"For what it's worth," his father said, "I think you're back on the right course, Danny. You need your family, and they need you."

"But what about Lauren? What does she need?"

Maggie and Cole—along with Deb—overheard Richie's comment and Danny's question as they came out of the house. Without hesitation, Deb weighed in with her own answer. "That woman needs to mind her own business. After all the trouble she's caused..."

"Stop!" Cole's voice was surprisingly forceful. "Didn't you hear anything that Father Rob said at church today? He talked about how even good people sin, and about how they deserve our prayers and compassion, not our condemnation. You know, casting the first stone and all that? Don't judge lest you be judged?"

"Cole! I'm not the one you should be angry with." Her grandmother sounded prim and snippy.

"Yes, you are! I am mad at you. I'm mad at Uncle Danny and Aunt Heather. And I'm mad at Lauren, too. All I ever hear is how I'm supposed to act like a grown-up, but you act like the mean girls I go to school with. What ever happened to talking to each other? Not making assumptions? Taking responsibility for your mistakes—because we all make them!"

Danny was stunned. Cole had never spoken to any of them like this—and she sounded like an angry adult, not a child.

"You're too young to understand—" Deb started to say.

"—Maybe I am," Cole interrupted. "I don't know how I feel about what Lauren and Uncle Danny did. But it seems to me that you're happy to spread a whole lot of blame around and not a whole lot of forgiveness."

Deb was gripping the gold crucifix she always wore on a chain around her neck. She was about to say something, but Cole looked directly at her and said, "I bet you've never said a prayer for Lauren, have you, Nanny?"

For once in her life, Deb was at a loss for words. She turned on her heels and disappeared into the house.

CHAPTER FORTY-FIVE

Tisha summoned Lauren to Velocity's main reception area, telling her she had a visitor in the lobby. Lauren was puzzled. She wasn't expecting anyone, and a small part of her twisted inside, remembering echoes of the last unpleasant surprise visitor. And when Lauren saw Cole standing by the reception desk, dressed in her St. Catherine's school uniform with her book bag slung over her shoulder, all she could think was, *Oh shit.*

"Hi, Lauren," Cole said.

"Hi." Lauren hesitated. "What are you doing here, Cole?"

Cole's face fell. "I'm sorry. I didn't mean to just show up. I've wanted to take you up on your offer. Come and watch a session, but..." She bit her lip.

"But your mother said no," Lauren said.

"Kinda."

"And you showed up anyway." A little part of Lauren totally respected Cole's power move. It was something she might have done as a teen. But she also knew, given the circumstances, all hell would break loose if it looked like she put Cole up to this.

"Seize the day?" Cole asked with a hesitant smile.

Despite her best efforts, a grin broke through and twisted the corner of Lauren's mouth. "How did you get here?"

"I told my mother that I was going to the library."

"Oh, Christ. You lied to your mother?"

Cole managed to look embarrassed, and then everything tumbled out. "Pretty much. I got a taxi from the library to here. Figured I'd text my mom later and let her know I needed to be picked up somewhere else. I'm sorry to just show up. I've been asking to come since you invited me, and I always get the runaround. There's always a reason not to, but I know it's just because they're uncomfortable. So, I figured I'd just handle it myself. I hope you're not upset. It's just that getting to see The Kingmakers record? It's a once-in-a-lifetime chance. I couldn't not come... You're upset, aren't you?"

Cole finally ran out of breath and paused.

Lauren blew out a sharp breath. "No... but you shouldn't be sneaking behind your mother's back, Cole. Not cool." A little part of her couldn't believe those words had come out of her mouth.

"But—"

Lauren held up her hand, silencing Cole. "Don't you 'but Lauren' me. Here's what we're going to do: Tisha is going to call your mom's office and let her know where you are. For as long as it takes for her to get here, you can stay and listen. And you had better make it crystal clear to her that this was *your* idea, not mine. Understand?"

Cole nodded. "I understand."

Lauren turned back towards the door, and Cole started to get her bag and follow her. "No."

"But you said—"

"—Yes, but I don't think it's on Tisha to tell your mother what's going on. She should hear it right from you. *After* you talk to her, then Tisha will bring you to the studio."

Lauren wished she had a camera to capture Cole's hangdog expression. As she walked down the hall, she heard Tisha say, "Miss Padovano-Shea? Hello, my name's Tisha and I work for Velocity Studios. Your daughter is here and would like to speak to you..."

"What's going on?" Augie asked when Lauren returned. "Who's here?"

"Cole."

His face was blank for a second, and then he did a double take. "Wait, Cole? As in: Maggie's kid? That Cole?"

"One and the same. And she didn't tell her mother she was coming here."

Augie howled with laughter. "Maggie's going to be *pissed*."

"No shit. She's out with Tisha now, calling her mother so Maggie knows where she is—and that I had nothing to do with this bright idea." Lauren shook her head one more time and looked towards the control room. "Fitz, I told her she could sit and watch until her mother arrived."

"I'll make it work," the producer said over the speaker.

"Okay, before Hurricane Maggie lands, let's get back to this." Lauren gave Stevie a nod, and he started to pick at the strings on his guitar. Everyone refocused on the song they were working on. Lauren stopped them twice to talk about where Ox's bass line was hitting, and DJ added an extra melody on the keyboard that Fitz suggested. As they were finishing, the door behind Fitz opened, and Tisha escorted Cole in.

"Tha' twas great," Fitz crowed. "I'm so pleased with you all. Take a few, and we'll try another run through. We're close, but I want ta try tweaking the intro a wee bit more."

Lauren gave him a thumbs-up, but then there was an odd silence as Fitz muted the intercom. She saw him swivel in his chair to face Cole. Lauren couldn't tell what they were saying but based on Cole's large eyes and frequent head nods, she guessed Fitz was putting the fear of God into her, and that she had best sit quietly and watch or he'd kick her out.

The intercom crackled as it came back to life. "Alrighty then, I have ta speak with Tisha for a moment. I'll be back in a jiff." When Fitz left, Lauren caught Cole's eye and waved her in.

"Gentlemen, this is Cole. Cole, this is Augie, DJ, Stevie, and Ox."

"Hi! Oh man, this is so... I'm a huge fan!" Cole tried—unsuccessfully—to not gush.

Lauren and the band spent the next twenty minutes answering questions about recording and touring and showing Cole a few things about the different instruments. Augie let her play the drums, and DJ invited her to mess around on his keyboards for a minute. Lauren elbowed Augie, and they shared a laugh as Cole watched DJ with big eyes, her crush on him getting clearer, and worse, by the moment. Lauren also wrangled them all for a group photo with Cole.

When Fitz came back, Tisha followed on his heels with some water for the band.

"Time to get crackin'," Fitz announced. "Cole, there's a chair for you out here with me, but remember, you need ta stay quiet while we work. Or...?"

"Or I have to sit 'my wee skinny arse' in the waiting room with Tisha."

"Good lass." He chuckled.

Lauren put her headphones on and got up from the padded stool. She preferred to stand when she recorded. She adjusted her microphone and waited for the cue from Fitz. He ran the band through three songs. Two were high-tempo rock songs, and Lauren could see Cole nodding her head in time with the beat. The third was a gentle, slow ballad about living with memories that haunt you. She nearly lost her place in the lyrics when she looked up and glanced into the control room. Fitz was absently handing a box of tissues to Cole.

They ran through one more song when Fitz flipped on the intercom and said, "GREAT! That's tha sweet spot, darlin'. You take a quick break, have some more water. DJ—I want to work for a bit on tha intro before we do more vocals."

Lauren was surprised Fitz had called a break so soon and was about to say she could keep going when she caught sight of Maggie.

And based on Cole's sheepish expression, Maggie was clearly letting her daughter know exactly how much hot water she was in. Lauren pulled off her headphones and went to the door.

"Can't we stay for a few more minutes, please?" Cole said.

"You're going to try negotiating after you lied to me?" There was no masking the incredulity in her voice, and Maggie planted both hands firmly on her hips.

"Maggie. Hey," Lauren said as she shut the studio door behind her.

"Thanks for letting me know about this one," Maggie said. "I'm sorry she bothered you. I hope she wasn't too disruptive."

Cole looked at the floor.

"No, it was fine," Lauren said. "I'm just glad we were here. Some days we work at my apartment or Augie's loft."

"Lauren..." Cole bit her bottom lip.

"Spit it out, whatever it is," Lauren said when Cole didn't continue.

"About you and my Uncle Danny—"

"Cole!" Maggie sounded mortified.

"No, it's okay, Maggie." Lauren could hear the tightness in her own voice.

"I just, well, I mean..." Cole struggled to get her words out.

Lauren assessed the expression on Cole's face: the furrowed brow, the pinched lips, and she took a stab in the dark. "You're angry with me. I've disappointed you."

Cole still looked conflicted. "A little. But I'm kinda mad at Uncle Danny, too. Maybe I'm too young to understand how you feel, but I am old enough to know that people aren't perfect. And sometimes love makes you do dumb stuff."

Lauren exhaled hard. *Love makes you do dumb stuff.* That was a colossal understatement if she'd ever heard one, but it was the complete unvarnished truth as well.

"Yeah. Yeah, it really does," she said. "You make decisions in the moment that—under any other circumstance—would never cross your mind." She paused, looked at Cole, and remembered how starstruck the teen had looked when they first met. "I'm sorry if I disappointed you."

Cole pursed her lips and looked thoughtful. "Everyone makes mistakes. Father Rob says it's all about forgiveness."

"Father Rob seems like he's a smart guy." After a moment's silence, Lauren screwed up the courage to ask, "Maggie, I know I probably don't have any right to ask, but how's Danny?"

"He's getting by, but he's hurting. He and Heather are having their ups and downs."

"You might not believe me, but I do want him to be happy."

"I know you do. He wants the same for you."

"Dude," Augie said from behind her. "We need to get back to it. Hey, Mags. Looking good!"

"Hi, Augie. Nice to see you."

"I do have to go." Lauren gestured back towards the recording room.

"Us, too," Maggie said. She looked at Cole. "And we need to have a mother-daughter discussion. Privately."

"I know."

Lauren admired that there was no regret in Cole's voice.

CHAPTER FORTY-SIX

The Kingmakers continued making significant progress on Lauren's songs, and she pumped out new ideas at an unrelenting pace. The successful work kept Lauren more focused, but it was hard for her to come back to the apartment at night, alone. Although the worst of her depression had lifted, the emptiness and solitude still gave her ample time to brood about Danny.

Tonight, it was harder than usual. It was already well after eight o'clock. The studio session had gone later than expected, and Lauren was excited about the progress they'd made. She was feeling more and more optimistic about the album. What frustrated her was that she had no one to share her excitement with. Earlier in the week, she'd nearly talked both Steph and Carolyn's ears off and didn't want to subject them to that again. The same for her parents. And she still wasn't speaking to Jackie.

She considered going out, but clubbing wasn't going to help. She'd end up having a drink, which opened the door to too many stupid choices. Despite her confession to Augie and the rest of the band, none of them truly understood how close she'd been to relapsing that awful night.

The staccato vibration of her phone distracted her, sending Lauren on a short chase until she found it on the kitchen counter.

The message was a text from Danny: *<Need to talk to you. Can we meet?>*

Lauren pulled her hand away from the phone as if it would burn her. She and Danny hadn't spoken since the night he ended their affair. Had something happened?

She picked up her phone and replied: *<I'll be @ Red Parrot @10>*. She hit send before her better judgment—which was screaming at her, sounding distinctly like Augie—could do anything about it. The "swoosh" told her the text was loose in the wild. Meeting up with Danny was probably a worse idea than going out clubbing, but at least this addiction wouldn't kill her.

Lauren got to the café a few minutes before ten. She went to the counter and browsed the menu. One of the baristas recognized her and asked for an autograph. Lauren was happy to oblige. She pondered her choices and finally ordered a decaf coffee and a cinnamon roll. When the server brought it over to her, Lauren laughed. The cinnamon roll was the size of a dinner plate and looked as if it had a full pound of icing on it. It was sticky, sweet, and utterly delicious.

She cleaned off her hands, took a photo of herself and the half-eaten bun with her phone, and texted it off to Augie with a note that said, *<See? I'm eating! Satisfied?>* She knew he'd be happy she'd eaten something that decadent.

A minute later his first response arrived: *<Good.>* Quickly followed by *<Jesus, UB up half the night on a sugar high. Have a cheeseburger.>*

<Had chicken earlier, MOM.>

She didn't blame Augie for nagging her. She'd lost too much weight over the summer and had to get into better shape. The album launch—and the supporting tour—weren't that far away.

Ox and Stevie were lobbying hard for a minimalist tour. Good lights, plenty of video screens for fans in the nosebleed seats, but no fireworks or complicated set design. They wanted this show to be about the music itself, and Lauren was warming to that idea. Originally, she wanted to go bigger—much bigger—and use the tour to stick it to the critics who said The Kingmakers were through. But the more she thought about it, the more she realized Ox and Stevie were right. The music had to speak for them, not the spectacle. But minimalist or not, a tour was a tour, and she had to be ready for the grueling schedule.

A glance at the art deco clock on the wall told Lauren it was after ten. She tapped her foot restlessly. After two more bites of the pastry, Lauren felt stuffed and had to take a break. She dipped her napkin into her water glass to get the frosting off her fingers. The clock on the wall relentlessly ticked towards ten-thirty. She wasn't going to sit around waiting any longer. Flagging the waitress down, she had the remnants of the cinnamon bun wrapped up in a to-go container.

Outside the shop, Lauren flipped up her jacket collar. The fall wind was brisk, and she shivered a little. A random piece of paper skipped along the sidewalk, and the same gust blew her hair into her face. As she turned the corner to head back to the Somerset, she heard his voice. Her heart turned over in her chest.

"Hey."

"Started to think you weren't coming."

"I almost didn't."

Lauren didn't bother asking why. She tipped her head towards the café and pulled up her jacket collar to block out the wind. "Want to go back?"

"No. But I'll walk you to the hotel."

As they fell into step together, it was all Lauren could do not to reach out to take Danny's hand. She stuffed her own hands in her pockets. They talked a little, but it was a superficial, fluffy conversation. Deep down she knew ending their relationship was the right decision, but she couldn't just turn her feelings off. And the exhilaration that seeing him brought was tempered by a healthy dose of self-reproach. What was she thinking, agreeing to meet him? If he was seriously trying to repair his marriage, this wasn't going to help.

"Matty announced at dinner the other day that he wants to be a soldier like his uncle for Halloween," Danny said.

"That's sweet."

They lapsed into silence after that. Lauren wanted to say something, anything, but she wasn't sure exactly what she was supposed to say. The uncertainty hurt.

Soon, they reached the hotel, and Danny walked her into the lobby. Near her elevators, Lauren stopped. She didn't want to say good night. She wanted to stay up half the night telling Danny about how well things were going in the studio. She wanted to share previews of the songs. And she wanted to tell him how much she missed him.

What she did *not* want to tell him was how much pain she was in and how she had walked right up to the edge of relapsing. She knew they weren't going to end up together... because as much as she wanted Danny, he wasn't who she really needed. That had become clear to her in the aftermath of their affair. But before she could articulate any of what she wanted to say, an abrupt movement caught her eye. Across the lobby, a tall, lanky man leaped to his feet. He wore a green canvas vest and had a stocking cap stuck to the top of his head.

For a split-second, Lauren's heart froze—he was dressed like one of the local paparazzi she'd become familiar with—but then the stranger waved to another man, and they clapped each other on the back as if they were old friends.

"Lauren?"

"Sorry, I thought I saw someone I knew. What did you say?"

"I asked if I could come up for a minute."

"I don't think that's a good idea." She waffled. It was a terrible idea. Out of the corner of her eye, she saw the green canvas vest again. But talking here, where so many eyes could see them, wasn't going to work.

Lauren thought about what Cole said, about how love can make you do stupid things. She sighed and added one more to her own personal dumb decision list. "Okay, come on up. At least we'll have some privacy. The last thing you need right now is a photo of us showing up in the paper." A dash of bitterness flavored her words.

In the confines of the elevator, they stood on opposite sides, but the tension between them increased with each passing floor. Lauren studied Danny's reflection in the shiny interior panels. He looked defeated, an expression she'd never seen on him before. The doors slid open, and the silence from the elevator escorted them to her door, thick and oppressive.

"You said you wanted to talk to me."

"I'm sorry," Danny said. "About hurting you. About everything."

"I know. We made a mess of things." She opened the door and invited him in with a sweep of her hand.

"I've been worried about you. Are you okay? For real?"

Well, that's the million-dollar question, isn't it? she thought. "Not really. I almost torpedoed our new album—and the band nearly imploded. I've been consumed by what ifs. Thinking about you and if —somehow—things could have been different. I almost—" She bit her tongue to stop herself from blurting out that she'd almost started using again.

"You almost what?"

"I almost lost everything that ever mattered to me because I was chasing a ghost." When he looked away, Lauren knew she'd hurt him with that. "And what about you? How are you, Danny?"

"I'm so confused. I love Heather. I mean, she's my wife, the mother of my children. She's kind. Generous. Forgiving. She makes a dynamite lasagna." His chuckle was soft. "But I love you, too. And I don't know how I can do both."

It was Lauren's turn to glance away as he continued.

"You're everything I'm not, Lauren. You're free. You're open. Everything about you is an adventure. We have this connection—we always have. And you know me better than anyone else. We're soulmates, I guess, even though that sounds like weird New Age crap. But our lives are so different... you'd have been better off never having known me."

"That's not true," she said, resting a gentle hand on his cheek. "You helped make me who I am."

He took her hand and kissed her palm. Lauren's heart stuttered and her resolve faltered as Danny laced his fingers through hers.

"Kiss me," he whispered.

"Danny..."

"Please."

She couldn't say no. Lauren gave him a soft, lingering kiss and felt Danny respond. Passionately. Desperately. The emotions surged through her blood. Lauren knew they didn't have a future together, but they could have one last night.

The sex was powerful and carnal, but it was tender and sad as well. After, as they lay in Lauren's bed, exhausted, she knew that it was the last time. She looked at his face, taking in the details and burning them into her memory.

"Part of me will always love you," he said. "You know that, right?"

"I know," she answered. "This—thing—between us. A little piece of it will always be there. But it can't ever be what it was."

"Lauren—"

"—Work it out with Heather," she said.

"What?" Danny tensed beneath her hand.

"You fell in love with her once. Do it again."

Danny didn't answer. Instead, he rolled up on his elbow and looked down at her. He shook his head. "I don't know."

"Don't know what?" Lauren asked. The way he looked at her gave her pause.

He didn't answer. Instead, he toyed with some of her dark hair where it spilled across the pillow. Then he glanced at the clock.

"I'm sorry I screwed everything up for you," Lauren said.

"No, I'm the one who screwed it up. It's on me to fix it, or at least try to."

Lauren didn't say much as she helped him gather his things. They walked to the door, and Lauren gave him a once-over. He didn't look too rumpled and out of sorts. She looked into his eyes, trying to read his thoughts. He leaned in and kissed her.

"I'll see you soon," he said.

Lauren knew that wasn't going to happen. In fact, there was a good chance that she would never see Danny again. But she couldn't bring herself to say it. It seemed too callous.

"Bye, Danny."

She opened the door for him and watched until he reached the elevator. Looking back at her, he gave her a smile that never reached his eyes. After the doors slid shut, Lauren closed the apartment door. With an unhappy sigh, she turned the lock. It sounded very loud—and extraordinarily final—as it clicked into place.

CHAPTER FORTY-SEVEN

Lauren was lying on the floor in Studio B like a little kid, chin propped in one hand as she looked down at her ever-present notebook. She chewed on the end of the pen. The previous week had been spent on shoots for the music videos that would be released along with the singles. It was exhausting and she'd slept like she was dead the night before.

Augie knocked on the doorframe. "We're going to do a final listen to 'Sinners & Saints' before we call it a wrap. Gonna join us?"

"Sure." She pushed herself up from the floor but never took her eyes off the paper.

"What are you working on?"

"New idea," she answered. "Not for this album. It's not ready yet."

"Want to share? You've been a little close to the vest lately."

Lauren knew he meant she was withdrawing, like she had when her affair with Danny ended. He wasn't wrong. After that last night, Lauren had pulled back from the band a little. But it wasn't the dark morass of pain it had been before. It was a mixture of guilt and sadness, and of finality. She'd felt the band's attention, but they gave her space.

She only answered Augie's overt question. "It needs work, but this is what I'm messing with: I wander the halls of this broken old house, looking for a ghost I have to set free. Cold winds blow and sweep clean my heart as the love we shared falls, leaves to the ground. One last time, I had to know, I said I loved you years ago, but now it slips away." She stopped, made a face, and passed judgment. "There's something there, but I haven't quite caught it yet. What do you think?"

"Good start. I like the concept," Augie said. "So did you?"

"Did I what?"

"Set the ghost free?"

Lauren stopped, her words catching in her throat. She swallowed hard. "I did. I had to say one final goodbye, but I did."

That was as close as Lauren was going to come to confessing her sins to Augie. What she and Danny had done that summer—and that last night in October—were her memories and her regrets. No one else could carry them for her.

"You okay with that?" He leaned against the doorframe, thumbs hooked in the pockets of his jeans.

Lauren searched her cousin's face. She saw nothing but care and concern. "I am. Once upon a time it worked, and I'll always have that. It's part of who I am, and I'm grateful for that. But I need to write a different happy ending for myself. And it's not with Danny." She gave Augie's shoulder a squeeze as she slipped past him.

The next day was another busy day for the band. Lauren excused herself from the studio to take a call, and when she came back, DJ was at the piano. Fitz was recording whatever it was, so she hung back, closed her eyes, and just listened. DJ leaned into a distinct, melancholic instrumental melody and then began to sing. His soft, warm voice had a full timbre, and his lyrics gave her chills. He sang about saying things he regretted, about leaving when he should have stayed.

"... with all we've been through, I just think of how empty my life would be without you..."

When he got to the end of the first chorus, Ox let out a low whistle. Next to him, Augie was nodding in agreement—he also knew great when he heard it.

"Well? What do you think?" DJ grabbed a bottle of water, cracked the cap, and took a drink. He wiped his mouth with the back of his hand.

"Amazing," Lauren said. "When did you come up with that?"

"Not long after the day we all showed up at your place," he answered.

"Ah. Well, it needs to be on the album."

DJ looked genuinely surprised as the others echoed Lauren's comments.

Fitz grinned. "Tha lot of you are killin' me. First you get shite done for months and almost give me a bloody coronary. Now? There's no end in sight. Not tha I'm complainin', mind you. But tha record company is screaming for tha masters. Tha production house is screaming for tha masters. We'll get the digital files done, but at this rate, the CDs won't ship before the holiday. Now you want to add this one?"

"Can we make it happen?" Augie asked.

Fitz answered with a nod and a hearty, humor-filled laugh. "It's a damn good song, and with DJ singing? Tha's a bonus. But no more. We're out o' time—and out o' room on the album. And I need you ta get this one recorded right when we get back from Thanksgiving. Otherwise, we won't make tha deadline, and I've already pushed it out twice. Do no' make a liar out of me!"

They spent the rest of the day finishing up two of the other songs, and by the time dinner rolled around, Fitz was able to check them both off as complete. Lauren glanced at the wall as they gathered up their things. It was where Fitz had stuck the article about the band being washed up. Lauren had put a second one up, one that also claimed The Kingmakers were finished and out of original ideas. For a while, both had made her feel defeated and sad. Lately, they just made her angry, and she made a silent promise to herself that they'd eat their words.

But there was still a lot of work to do before they could deliver the album, and not much time left to do it. They were starting the tour in the middle of January with a sold-out show at Madison Square Garden. Then it would be off to Boston and then to California. The rest of the U.S. and Canada would follow, and then they'd hit Europe, Asia, and South America.

"And you." Fitz pointed at Lauren. "Brilliant bloody work, but any new ideas go on tha next album. You've got ta promise me that. Goes for you, too, DJ. Great surprise today but save any others for tha next act. Now, go enjoy your holiday."

Lauren dawdled while the others left. DJ and Ox had planes to catch, and Stevie was headed to meet up with Gabby's family in Maryland. Out in the Velocity parking lot, Augie was fussing with his car, and she knew he was waiting for her.

"Haven't changed your mind?" he asked.

"No."

He sighed. "It's Thanksgiving, Lauren. When was the last time either of us was able to be home with our families for this?"

Every year, both sides of the Stone family crammed into one house for Thanksgiving. Hosting duties alternated, and this year the responsibility belonged to Augie's parents. It was an overwhelming number of people, but it was a family tradition. Most of the time,

Augie and Lauren could never make it—they'd end up calling from some crazy venue where they were doing a show.

"I know." She ground her teeth. "But I'm not dealing with Jackie."

"Don't let her be the reason you miss seeing the rest of your family. Or mine."

The thought of not seeing her other sisters—or Augie's brothers—hurt. But she shook her head. "I don't think Jackie will keep her mouth shut. And if she starts it, you *know* I'll finish it."

"Seriously, dude. Think about it. Once we leave on tour, it will be at least a year, maybe two, before we can spend *any* time with them at all. Don't waste this chance."

Lauren stuffed her hands into her jacket and leaned against the car. "You and your damn logic." She scowled. Sometimes she really hated it when Augie was right. Two years was a long time, and a lot could happen. She'd seen first-hand what touring without resolving a family issue could do. It was what had ended Ox's first marriage, and the damage had been so bad, he hadn't seen his children for three years.

"Fine." Lauren pulled out her phone and dialed her father's cell. She put it on speaker. After some pleasantries, she got to the point. "So, I know I put Mom in a tailspin about Thanksgiving when I said I wasn't coming. Can I change my mind?"

"Of course! You're always welcome, you know that."

She smiled. "Thanks, Dad. I'll see you at Aunt Viv and Uncle Bobby's, but I need you to do something for me. I need you to tell Mom and Jackie—especially Jackie—that I don't want to hear a peep about what went on between me and Danny. Not a word."

"I'll tell them both, I promise."

"Thank you. See you soon. Love you."

"Love you, too, sweetie."

"Satisfied?" Lauren asked Augie when she hung up.

"I'll drive us both," Augie said. "Pick you up at eleven? That should get us there in plenty of time to hang out before we eat." He got into the Mustang and put the window down.

"Sounds like you don't trust me to show up on my own."

"I have no idea what you're talking about." Augie's answer was almost drowned out by the growl of the Mustang's engine.

CHAPTER FORTY-EIGHT

Thanksgiving morning, the grass and leaves were coated with frost. But the morning sun melted it away. Danny didn't get roped into working the holiday shift, so the Padovano Thanksgiving was in the early afternoon. The kitchen was crowded, and Joey was in the back yard roughhousing with his nephews. Inside—while Deb held court in the kitchen—Richie asked Danny to take a couple boxes upstairs and put them in his old bedroom. Danny managed to scoop up four of them, and Cole grabbed the last one.

He thanked Cole for, and she hustled back down to help set the table. One box didn't have a lid. Inside was a pile of old photos. He sat on the edge of the bed and pulled a handful out. There was one of his father shoveling the walk after a winter storm, all the kids playing in the drifts behind him. Another was of Maggie holding Joey when he was just a baby. And another was of him and Joey in that very room. And there was one of his Uncle Larry in his police dress blues, with a five-year-old Danny looking up in admiration as he saluted his hero.

He flipped through a few more and then stopped. The picture that caught his eye was of a family vacation when he was about seven years old. He was sharing an ice cream with his grandfather at a small wooden table. Holidays always made him miss his grandfather—he'd died a few years after that vacation. They should have had a lot more time together.

He put the photos back in the box and slid all of them inside the closet before shutting the door. He sat back down on the bed again, remembering when he was a kid and he, Maggie, and Joey would play together on rainy days.

Across from him was a small bookcase. Years ago, the shelves were filled with kids' books, baseball cards, and model cars. Now they held a mix of books, pictures, and a few other things, including what looked like an old t-shirt. He pulled one book off the shelf: his yearbook. *Dad must have put this up here after Cole did her report.*

He flipped through the pages of candid photos, the simple act of flipping the pages reminding him how hard he and Lauren had laughed the first night he went to her place. There were five pictures of the two of them. In one, he had his arms wrapped around her. Another was from the prom. The third was a random shot in a classroom with Lauren making a goofy face behind him. The other two were of them with friends, cheering at a football game. In one, he had Lauren on his shoulders. He thought about that last night with her and felt worn out.

He heard Joey's footsteps coming up the stairs. "C'mon, bro," his brother said. "Dad says the turkey's ready."

"Yeah, okay. I'll be right down." Danny didn't turn around.

"What you looking at?"

Danny held up his yearbook. It was open to the picture of Lauren. The unexpected rendezvous with her had lingered in his memory. More than once during the interminable sessions with the therapist and Father Rob, Danny had questioned all his decisions. But then his guilt had brought him back into line, re-orienting his focus on his sons. Danny touched the photo with his fingers and then shut the book.

"I fucked up. End of October, I went to see Lauren." Danny hadn't told anyone about that night. Joey remained silent, and Danny wished he'd say something. Anything. And he heard Joey's unspoken question in the quiet.

"Go ahead. Ask," Danny said.

"Did you sleep with her?"

Danny's sigh was deep, but he looked his brother in the eye. "I did."

If Joey was surprised by the honesty, his face didn't show it. "Does Heather know?"

"No." Danny's voice was resigned. "But something changed. Deep down, you could just feel it. Lauren's done with me." He frowned. It still hurt to think that he wouldn't be with her anymore, and to know she was leaving for her tour. The hurt was duller now, more an ache than the lancing pain it had been at first, but it never seemed to go away.

"Go ahead, tell me what an asshole I am." The words were bitter in Danny's mouth.

"You're doing a pretty good job of that all by yourself. Don't need my help." Joey squeezed his shoulder and let go. "I don't know, man. I can't tell you if you should or shouldn't have seen her. You gotta work that out for yourself."

Danny glanced over at his brother. Joey was just like their father: circumspect, thoughtful, fair. He looked down at the yearbook that was still in his lap and put one hand on the cover. "It meant a lot to me when you said you'd back me no matter what I decided."

Joey clapped him on the shoulder again, harder this time. "C'mon. Sitting up here staring at that old yearbook isn't going to change anything. Let's go eat and watch a little football."

Several miles away, the engine of Augie's Mustang rumbled as he pulled over and parked in front of the house where he grew up. It was a half-mile from Lauren's parents' place. He smiled as he turned off the engine and ran his hands over the steering wheel.

"You are way too in love with this car," Lauren said, easing up from the passenger seat.

"Whatever. I know every time you're out in the little Lexus you're leasing, you're doing the exact same thing. Besides, what's the point of being a rock star if you can't have the stupidly fun cars that go with it?"

"Point taken," she said with a laugh.

Augie opened his door. "Ready?"

"No, but I can't change my mind now." Lauren had barely made it three steps up the walk before Carolyn's twins flew out the front door. They mobbed Lauren and then turned their attention to Augie, who managed to pick both boys up at the same time and hang them upside-down until they were shrieking with laughter. The twins were followed by two of Jackie's brood, Joshua and Kristie. They tried very hard to remain cool and grown-up as they said hello, especially Kristie, who had turned sixteen over the summer.

As soon as Augie put them down, the twins pounced on Lauren again, pulling her inside and announcing to the world that they'd found Aunt Lauren wandering around outside. She was immediately wrapped up in a hug from Augie's parents—her Uncle Bobby and Aunt Vivian. Carolyn shouted a hello from the other room. Steph gave Lauren a smile, but with her arms full of plates, couldn't stop.

As she turned into the living room, Lauren squeezed between bodies—with both families, there were nearly thirty people stuffed into the house and yard. If she didn't spend half her life surrounded by fans, roadies, and the press, Lauren would have found the chaos in the house utterly overwhelming. But she just settled in and let it move around her. Augie's four brothers were in the back yard, but Lauren figured she'd wait for him to fight his way through the kitchen crowd so they could meet up with them together. It took

Augie ten minutes to run the gauntlet from Stephanie to Carolyn to Jackie before he reached Lauren.

"Groupies got nothing on family," Lauren said.

"You aren't kidding! Come on, let's go see my bros."

A chorus of hellos greeted them when they walked outside. Augie's brothers—Marty, Nate, Johnny, and Ryan—were all there. Marty and Nate's wives were watching some of the younger kids play and waved at the two new arrivals. The conversation soon centered on the absence of Johnny's longtime girlfriend and the fact that, after ten years, he still hadn't proposed to her. It wouldn't be a Stone family event if they didn't give Johnny a hard time about not being married yet.

A piercing squeal interrupted the conversation as Nate's daughter, Kate, came running toward them, her mother hot on her heels. Augie squatted down and held out his arms as she ran towards him.

"There's my beautiful princess!" he said as he scooped her up. The three-year-old shrieked again, thrilled to be the center of attention. While Augie played with his niece, Lauren fielded questions from all four of her cousins, doing a fair job of keeping everything straight. If they knew about Danny, they didn't say anything, although Marty and Nate's wives pumped her for information about what Jon Bon Jovi and Dario D'Scala were really like.

Dinner was a loud, happy, boisterous affair that filled tables in two separate rooms. Lauren made sure she sat as far from Jackie as possible. As they worked their way through a mountain of food, the family asked Lauren and Augie about the new music and the tour. They promised everyone that for opening night at Madison Square Garden, there would be a suite and tickets for the whole family.

Dessert was served buffet-style in the kitchen, and Lauren jockeyed for a good spot in line, jokingly trying to shoulder out her niece, Kristie. She caught Augie's arm as he walked by with a plate of pie.

"How'd you get to be first in line?"

"I've been lying in wait by the pantry for the past twenty

minutes. No way I was missing your mom's pumpkin pie. Only real reason I came here today." He stuffed a bite in his mouth.

"Thanks for talking me into coming today, Augie. I'm glad I did."

"*De nada*. Now if you'd just listen to me all the time."

"*Not* going to happen. Go eat your pie."

The dessert table almost had too much to choose from, and despite being full, Lauren finally settled on Aunt Viv's cherry cobbler. The pumpkin pie was a temptation, but she figured she could always go back for more of that later. While she nibbled, she talked more with her cousins and caught up on the family gossip she'd missed during the meal. After dessert, Lauren grabbed her coat.

"I'm going to get some fresh air for a minute and play with the rug rats. Save me a good seat for the game," she said to her father.

"You bet, sweetie."

Out in the backyard, the younger cousins were kicking a soccer ball around, creating some sort of keep-away game with rules that seemed to change every few minutes. The kids, however, were doing a good job of working things out. Lauren only had to warn them once to behave.

"We never played that nicely," Carolyn said as she strolled up.

Lauren shook her head. "Jackie always tried to boss us around since I'd never play the way she wanted."

"You still don't."

Lauren laughed. "No. No, I don't. But at least I've only gotten the stink-eye from her a few times today."

Carolyn rubbed the swell of her belly. About six months pregnant, she was definitely showing.

"How are you feeling?"

"Fine. No more morning sickness. But I'll tell you, that's the last time I go clubbing with you." When Lauren didn't respond, Carolyn deliberately rubbed her pregnant belly again and added, "Do the math."

Lauren let out a little gasp. "Ohmygod. You got pregnant the night we went to Blue Ruby!"

"You did promise Greg you'd bring me home drunk and silly!" Carolyn's laugh was infectious.

"I guess I did, didn't I?"

They continued watching all the kids play with exuberant abandon until Carolyn's twins laid hands on a yard rake with metal tines, and she yelled, "*I don't think so!*"

They dropped it immediately.

"Respect," Lauren said. "Major Mom voice. I'm impressed." She fist-bumped her sister.

"I love them, but they're completely feral," Carolyn said.

"So were we."

One of the twins ran over and presented Lauren with a white rock from the flower garden. She barely had time to say thank you for the surprise gift before he dashed away to chase his brother.

"Me and Steph are worried about you," Carolyn said. "You're looking thin. Are you doing okay with the whole Danny thing?"

Carolyn was probably the only one who could have asked her about Danny without it sounding like a judgment or accusation. She'd let Carolyn and Steph know about her breakup and although she knew they meant well, Lauren had kept them at arm's length for a while.

"We *are* worried," echoed Stephanie, who'd just come over to join them.

"I know you are. Believe it or not, I've put weight on. Augie makes sure I eat. Am I okay? Mostly. Some days are better than others, you know?"

"I'm sorry," Carolyn said. "I know how much you care about Danny. I guess, at least now you won't always wonder 'what if' when you think about him."

"She's right," Steph said. "I think it was better than not trying."

Lauren looked at them both for what felt like a long time. "You've always had my back, even when I've done some damn stupid things. You do know how much that means to me, right?"

Carolyn smiled again. "You're our sister, Lauren. We love you."

Stephanie surprised her with a hug. "You live a big, bold life, Lauren. You see what you want, and you go after it even if it means a huge fall if you fail. If Jackie has an issue about how you live your life and what you do, well, she can... she can..."

"She can piss off," Carolyn finished.

CHAPTER
FORTY-NINE

After Thanksgiving, everything became even more intense for The Kingmakers. Tony, the owner of Red Ridge Entertainment had been so anxious to keep the band as a client after the debacle with Roberta, he promised them he would handle their account personally. And he hadn't disappointed. Tony had designed an extensive publicity plan, including several stops at radio stations throughout the U.S. to talk up their new double album—officially titled *Stone Heart*—and the first single. They started in New York on Z83 and Jamie Dolan's Rock and Roll Morning Show and then WXVV with Conrad Kane during the drive home. From there, they shuttled up to New England. The following day they hit the morning show on Providence's rock station, then went on to an extensive discussion with one of the top stations in Boston.

"Leaving," the first single from *Stone Heart*, made its debut at Number 10 on the Billboard charts and went straight up from there. For the next two weeks, the band bounced from rehearsals to interviews at other major markets throughout the country and back again. They even squeezed in time for a photo shoot and sit-down interview with *Rolling Stone* magazine.

The band's rising success made December a difficult month for Danny. Between *Stone Heart*'s debut, a spike in Heather's jealousy, and his stubborn insistence on going to the concert, any progress they made towards repairing their marriage faltered. After one particularly bad row, Danny spent a few nights sleeping at his parents'. He found himself questioning his decisions at every turn.

He and Joey had been trying to make time to hang out and watch a football game together, but Danny's schedule had made it difficult. Finally, the universe had seen fit to give them both a quiet Monday night, and a playoff berth was hanging in the balance.

"Do you have any idea what Ma would say about this place?" Danny surveyed the mess in Joey's apartment.

"Exactly why I haven't had her over. Get that pizza in here, I'm starving."

After he rummaged in the refrigerator and grabbed a couple beers, Joey pulled some random shirts off the sofa and tossed them to the side. He turned the TV on and clicked to the sports channel. The game was about to start, so the commentators were nattering to fill the time, but Joey hit mute.

"Thought you might want to take a look at this before we get into the game." Joey tossed a copy of the newest *Rolling Stone* onto the table. On the cover was a picture of The Kingmakers. Standing clustered together, each one had their arms folded, and they stared at the camera with knowing, satisfied smiles. The headline blared "Return of the Kings." Danny couldn't blame any of them for looking smug over that.

"This new double CD of theirs is already putting up huge numbers," Joey said. "It's going to be a *monster*."

Danny flipped to the cover story. There were several photos of the band, and the article was a combination of essay and interview. He skimmed the essay part since it mostly talked about the band's history and how the establishment had written them off. He knew that story. He was more interested in what the band had to say.

RS: A lot of people dismissed you when the Stone Heart project got delayed. What's your secret for staying relevant after all this time?

DJ: No magic formula. Be nice if there was one. The magic's a crapload of work, sweat, and tears.

Lauren: Well, that's true—the hard work part—and I think it shows that if you write a song people connect with, that's meaningful to them on some level, then you're always relevant.

Stevie: Right. If it punches you in the gut or in the heart and makes you feel something, anything, then you've got something there. And I think the level of connection throughout the Stone Heart album is amazing. I know every a new song came into the studio, I felt it.

Augie: Lauren did an epic job writing this time around. We all contributed, but she took it to a whole different level. A song has to come out of your head and your heart.

RS: The head and the heart, huh? What inspired you then, Lauren? There are some powerful songs here.

Lauren: Honestly? I went through some hard personal stuff during the middle of production, and I went down some dark roads for a little while. But instead of turning completely self-destructive—which we all know I've done before—I threw everything I was feeling into my lyrics. There are also plenty of fun songs, too, so don't think the whole thing is one long litany of heartbreak.

RS: So that's how it got its name, Lauren? As an autobiography of your heart?

Augie: Hey, I'm a Stone too!

Lauren: Actually, it came up organically. We were all taking one day, and someone said life would be easier if you just had a heart made of stone because then you don't have to feel the hurt.

Ox: Right. But the key is that, yeah, if you're made of stone, you don't feel anything bad. But you don't feel anything good either. And the more we talked, it just felt right.

DJ: And Fitz is encouraging us to do a DVD along with the tour. He said it was a great opportunity to talk about the why behind the songs, the stories behind them. So we tossed it around and thought a semi-unplugged storyteller format would work great.

Stevie: Not sure when we'll fit that in with the tour starting in January.

Lauren: We'll find a way to get it done. I think it is a great idea. Gives people more insight into our own thinking and the things that matter to us. I really like the idea of an intimate setting. I think it is a way for me, personally, to feel very close to our fans.

RS: Okay, one last question. What are you all like on tour? What is it like to spend a year on the road with The Kingmakers?

Stevie: Be ready for a wild ride!

DJ: He's not kidding, but when we're out on tour, I'm a dream—Lauren's mental, though.

Lauren: A big pain in the ass is what you are. But I'll admit, I can be a head case.

Augie: That's because you're a perfectionist. You want every show to be flawless for our fans. We all do, but you get a little, well, intense.

Lauren: It's so important to do a good show. I've said it before—people are paying their hard-earned money to buy our music and see us in concert. When they walk out of that arena, I want them to think, "damn, that show was worth every penny I paid!"

Ox: And you never let us forget that. It's easy to get caught up in everything else. But for the question? If you were on the road with us for a year, you'd see that we're a family. Most days we love each other, some days we hate each other. At times we fight like cats and dogs. But we've never had a fight so bad that we haven't been able to get past it.

RS: Thanks for sitting with us today, you guys. Congrats on the new album and good luck on your tour!

On the last page of the article, there was a large call-out about Lauren. Titled "Long Live the Queen," the photo showed her on stage, lifting her guitar beneath the glare of a spotlight. All Danny could think when he looked at it was that was where Lauren was supposed to be: on a stage. The profile itself didn't tell him anything he didn't already know, but it was still interesting to read the brief chronicle of her rise, fall, and re-emergence onto the rock-and-roll scene.

Danny closed the magazine and glanced at the TV. Joey had paused the game so Danny hadn't missed any of the action.

"Hey, thanks for saving me this."

"I wanted to read it myself," Joey said, his words garbled around the piece of crust he was chewing. "Figured you wouldn't be able to get a look at it in your house."

Danny grabbed a slice for himself. "I saw it when I was at the store with Heather the other day and tried to not even look at the magazine shelf. Wasn't worth the fight. We've already had too many over the past month."

"You still want to go to the show? Tickets go on sale Friday. It's going to be tough to get them."

"I want to go. That's one of the things Heather and I are fighting about. But I've done everything she's asked: the therapist, talking to Father Rob, all of it. I need to do this, so I'm not giving in on it. You still want to go with me?"

"Hell, yes," Joey said.

CHAPTER FIFTY

The weeks leading up to the tour launch were a whirlwind of preparation and rehearsal until everything came to a brief, screeching halt for Christmas. Lauren didn't mind; she welcomed the break—not only did she get a chance to spend it with her family, which was a gift in and of itself, but she also got to be part of a mini family baby shower for Carolyn.

After the holiday, rehearsals resumed. They went well except for a few notable exceptions. The most glaring was the day the lighting guru, Mario, couldn't hit his marks or his timing to save his own life. It was so bad that Augie called him out and told him to either pull his shit together or to get out. It seemed to do the trick because the next day, everything went off without a hitch, and the band wrapped up the rehearsal tired and happy. After, they went to a nearby Chinese restaurant and powered through the buffet for dinner.

"You guys set with the family suites?" Ox asked. During every tour, in each band member's hometown, part of the tour contract included a complimentary VIP suite for family and friends.

"I know I am," said Augie as he looked over at Lauren.

"I made sure that we got adjoining suites for your family and mine," she told him. "I confirmed them yesterday."

"I bet your sister's going to be mad she missed the show," DJ said.

"Miss it?" Lauren started to laugh.

"Dude, you clearly don't know Carolyn," Augie said.

"Isn't she due to have that baby any day now?" DJ asked.

"She sure looks it," Lauren said. "But she's not due until early February... And if you think she's going to miss this just because she might give birth at the Garden, you'd be mistaken. You should have seen it when Greg hinted that maybe she should skip the show. I thought she was going to have the baby right then and there."

"So obviously you're not the only one in the family who can throw a tantrum." Ox leaned to the side to avoid the piece of ice Lauren dug out of her drink and flung at him.

"What's up with the other seats?" Stevie asked Lauren. "I heard Tony say you bought out a second suite and like fifty seats in one of the good sections."

"I did." Lauren's answer was simple and short. Too short.

"For who?" Stevie asked.

In the few beats of silence that followed Stevie's question, every head at the table turned to focus on Lauren.

"I'm giving the suite to the Padovano family."

Ox's mouth dropped open. *"¡No mames!"*

She took another bite of food while the rest of the band continued staring at her. Once she finished chewing, Lauren said, "Tony's delivering the tickets today. I told him to give the tickets to the family. Whether or not they come to the show is up to them." She took another deliberate bite of food, drank some water, and didn't say another word about it.

Under his breath, DJ whispered, "I'll kick his ass if I see him."

Next to him, Augie whispered back, "You and me both, brother." They bumped fists under the table.

"Then what's up with the other fifty tickets?" Ox asked.

"I'm donating those. I sent a note along with the package asking Joey to figure out a way to share them with some veterans."

Danny rapped his knuckles on his parents' kitchen door before letting himself in. His father had left him a voice mail earlier, asking him to stop by on the way home, but he hadn't elaborated. At first Danny had been worried something had happened at one of his father's jewelry stores, but no reports had come in. And if there had been a robbery or anything like that, Joey or his dad would have called him. At least, he *assumed* they would.

"Dad?"

"In the living room," Richie answered.

Richie marked a page in the book he was reading and slid it onto the coffee table. Danny sat in the chair across from him. His father pushed his reading glasses on top of his head.

"Everything okay?" Danny asked. "Your voice mail was a little cryptic."

"Things are fine," Richie said. "I wanted to tell you about what happened at work today."

"You didn't get robbed, did you?" Danny nearly jumped out of his chair.

"No! Nothing like that," Richie said. "But I did get a visit from a man named Tony Vaughn. He owns the entertainment firm that represents The Kingmakers."

"I know the name." Danny's palms started to sweat. What would Lauren's publicist want with his father? The last publicist that got in touch with his family pretty much threw a grenade into his life.

"Lauren sent tickets and backstage passes for the opening night of her tour. One set was for Joey, and she asked him to share them with other veterans. The rest are for us—to do whatever we want with them."

Danny's face fell. She'd sent tickets—but to his father? To Joey?

He leaned forward and put his elbows on his knees, holding the sides of his head in confusion.

"She also sent me a note, and a picture, with the tickets."

Richie held out a sheet of paper and a four-by-six color print. Danny took it, immediately recognizing Lauren's neat script. The photo was a candid shot of him and Lauren from the past summer. They were sitting together, talking, and smiling, unaware they were having their picture taken. They looked happy. He vaguely remembered seeing it at Lauren's place—Stevie had taken it. Or maybe Augie.

Danny scanned the letter:

Dear Mr. P.,

I hope you've been well. I'd like to invite you and your family to the first night of our new world tour at Madison Square Garden. Enclosed, you'll find 20 tickets and 20 passes to the after party.

After everything that went on this past year, I might be the last person you want to hear from. And going to the show may be the last thing any of you want to do. I'd understand that. But it was important to me, though, to invite you all. If you don't want them, please donate them somewhere or use them to raise money for a charity.

I hope you know that I never meant to hurt your family or disrupt your lives. When I came back to New York, I really didn't have plans to see Danny. But you know what they say about good intentions. I want you to know that anything that happened with Danny started because I've always loved him. From the very first day I met him when we were kids.

I'd like to tell you this in person, but I think I'm too scared. It seems funny to say that. My sister says I'm brave, and maybe in most cases, she's right. I've never cared much about what most people think of me. You are one of the few whose opinion DOES matter. You were always so encouraging and supportive when I was a kid. I've never forgotten that, and I think I am too scared to face you now because I'm afraid I'll see disappointment on your face.

Despite everything, I hope you'll all come and enjoy the show.

All the best,

Lauren

Danny put the letter down. His emotions churned. He'd been trying—really trying—with Heather and had kept his focus there. But ever since that unexpected interlude with Lauren, he'd been wondering if he made the right choice. He'd convinced himself he had. But now? Now he felt like the ground under him was soft, unstable, and he was off balance.

"What do you want to do?" Richie asked.

"Do?"

"About the tickets. Do you want to go to the show? Give them away? Throw them away?"

Danny's head jerked back. *Throw them away? No way in hell.* "I do want to go to the show. Joey and I have been trying to get tickets. During one of our therapy sessions, I told Heather I was going. She got pissed."

"I can imagine."

"I'll take two for me and Joey, and I'll take two to give to my partner Jason and his wife. But other than that, I'd say take what you want and tell Maggie she can have the rest for her, Cole, and Cole's friends."

"I'll take one for me. I don't think your mother will want to go."

"I think Ma would rather talk directly to the Devil himself," Danny said.

"What about Heather and the boys?" Richie asked.

"No. I know Heather won't go. Tommy and Matty are too young." He pressed his lips into a thin line. Lucas would be mad, but he couldn't take one son and not the others. And he didn't want to put Lucas in the position of choosing between him and Heather.

"Fair enough." Richie took four tickets out and handed them to his son.

Danny stared down at them. "Why did she send them to you?" His father stayed silent, and the answer became clear to Danny in a flash. "Because she didn't want to make things hard for me. If she'd sent them to me, she would have put me in an impossible spot."

He was very aware he'd been in that impossible spot for months, and he'd put himself there.

CHAPTER FIFTY-ONE

The night of the concert, Danny was outside Joey's apartment at six-thirty, leaning on the horn. Someone behind him honked and gestured rudely as he passed. Danny yelled back. Joey and Vinny came out the front door, and Danny rolled the window down. A bracing rush of January cold flooded the car.

"Put some speed on it, Grandma!"

"Keep your shorts on," Joey said as he jumped in the Jeep and Vinny climbed into the back.

"Atomic Alcatraz is pretty good," Vinny said. "Couple songs aren't half bad."

"How'd things go when you left?" Joey asked his brother.

Danny waited to answer until he'd pulled out into traffic. "Not so good. This whole week hasn't been so good. And tonight was, well..." His face was grim.

"Sorry, man."

"Not your fault. But I don't want to talk about that." Danny wished Heather could understand how important this was to him, but his wife had made it excruciatingly clear before he left that she could not. And that there would be consequences for his actions. He'd left the house pissed off and questioning all of his choices.

It was a sold-out show, and the area around Madison Square Garden was packed. Most of the family was at the suite when they arrived. Cole and her friends were crowded at the front, a swirling knot of teenage excitement. Danny roamed around the suite, restless, until—finally—the opening act came on.

Danny listened for a bit. He didn't want to like them but caught himself tapping a toe. An hour later, Atomic Alcatraz wrapped, and the lights came up. Roadies swarmed the stage, an army of black t-shirts and jeans, swapping out equipment and bringing The Kingmakers' instruments onto the stage.

Not interested in the logistics, Danny wandered out into the hall. There was plenty of food and drink in the suite, so he didn't have to worry about buying anything. He lingered on the fringes of a merchandise table. There were multiple styles of t-shirts emblazoned with The Kingmakers' logo and tour name. The vendor was doing a brisk business, and Danny was tempted to get shirts for the boys because he knew they'd love them—but it would be a slap to Heather, and he wasn't going to do that.

On his way back, he bumped into Lauren's father. "Danny!" Jack Stone said jovially. "How the heck are you?"

"Good, Jack. Appreciate you asking."

"You looking forward to the show?" Jack gestured out towards the stage.

"I am. Although probably not as much as my niece and her friends."

Jack chuckled. "I understand. We have the same thing going on in our suite. Except I think Carolyn is more into it than the kids are!"

As if on cue, Cole and her friends—along with Lauren's niece and nephew—swept by, gossiping and comparing swag they'd purchased from the vendor tables. Cole paused long enough to wave her concert shirt at Danny and yell, "This is the best night EVER!"

After, Jack said, "You know I've seen every show she's done in this city? From that very first tour. I'm awfully proud of Lauren."

"I know she always appreciated how supportive you've been," Danny said.

"I just want to see her get out there on stage and see that smile."

"That smile?"

"Oh, you've seen it," Jack said. "You'll see it tonight. She'll get lost in the music and get this look on her face. It says she's right where she wants to be. Where she needs to be. That the music is her world, and she doesn't need anything beyond that. I love seeing that smile on her."

She doesn't need anything beyond that... Danny wasn't expecting the sharp stab of pain that came with Jack's observation. He said goodbye and slipped into the suite.

A moment later, the lights went down, and the crowd went wild in anticipation of The Kingmakers taking the stage. Shadows drifted out, finding positions at the different instruments, and the noise from the crowd ratcheted up. Cole and her friends started to clap, shout, and whistle. Danny found his seat and peered at the figures on the stage before looking up at the giant video monitors.

A few notes from DJ's keyboard drifted over the thunderous crowd, and a single spotlight illuminated his part of the stage. Another light slowly came up over the riser in the back. Augie's drumbeat picked up and was joined by Ox's bass and Stevie's guitar. Then a final spotlight illuminated, revealing Lauren at center stage, guitar hanging behind her, arms spread wide, and her head tilted back. Her eyes were shut, and as the audience's roar peaked and washed over her, she pulled the guitar around. Her fingers flew over the frets, and she launched into the first verse of "Sinners & Saints," one of the songs from *Stone Heart.*

Twenty thousand fans went crazy.

Danny stared at the larger-than-life image of Lauren projected on the huge monitor. She wore a fitted leather vest that laced up the front. It clung to her figure and offered a tantalizing hint of breast.

Her jeans had insets filled with black and silver-blue metallic print. She was, of course, wearing boots, and they were covered with silver and crystal straps that glinted as she moved.

The next song was a fun anthem to rock and roll, but the third was the new single, "Leaving." Danny knew this one—he'd heard it on the radio several times—and he took a deep breath. The song was about heartbreak and walking away.

"There wasn't a choice, I couldn't stay. I saw all my dreams start to fade away. As the space in between us stretches for miles, every mistake makes my heart break just a little more..."

Lauren's voice filled the arena and left a deep, abiding ache in Danny's chest that fed the doubt he'd been feeling that day.

After the soft anguish of "Leaving," the band cranked the tempo back up. In this song, Lauren had a substantial guitar solo. As she stood on one of the platforms, she started to smile. Danny immediately knew it was "that smile." The one her father talked about. The smile that said standing there on stage was, really, her one true love.

And in that moment, Danny knew that he couldn't have asked her to stay back in high school. He had no doubt that Lauren loved him, but he couldn't compete with the stage and the spotlight. She would wither without it.

I can't compete with it. But could I be part of it? He thought about Bruno's party, the press, the fans. It made his stomach clench. *She said that I'd hate living in her world. But what if she's wrong? There are plenty of celebrities who make relationships work. Why couldn't we?*

A not-so gentle elbow jostled Danny out of his thought. "You okay?" his brother asked.

"Fine."

"You going to go to the after party? I don't care either way, but me and Vinny will need to get a ride share home if you leave."

"I don't know. Maybe. I want to, but I'm not sure it's the best idea." The screaming fight he'd had with Heather before he left the house was still sharp in his mind. He was glad the boys had been out with friends and hadn't seen it.

On stage, Lauren was in the zone. She felt like she could accomplish anything as the music flowed and the crowd responded. She grabbed her microphone and let her eyes rove over the floor and up to the higher balcony seats.

"We've got a special song for you right now," she said. "This one was a late addition to *Stone Heart*. Here's "Empty Chair"—written and performed by our very own DJ Scott!" With a flourish, she pointed to where DJ sat at his keyboards. He started playing the song he'd written, and Lauren brought her microphone back closer to Augie.

Out in the crowd, people started holding up glowing cell phones, but Lauren did see a few of the old guard out there with their lighters aloft. In moments, the whole stadium was filled with soft glowing light that swayed to the tempo of DJ's song. As he reached the end of the last repeat of the chorus, and the crowd's enthusiasm swelled, Lauren looked up to find DJ looking at her as he sang, "...with all we've been through, I just think of how empty my life would be without you..."

DJ gave her a wink, and she smiled.

Seeing the interaction on the monitors, the crowd roared even louder.

The Kingmakers had played for close to two hours by the time they closed the main set. They were all exhausted but soaring on adrenaline when they bowed and waved to the crowd. Backstage, they laughed and hugged and high-fived. The crowd's applause, chants, and stomping shook the building. Then the lights went down, and each one of them could feel the throng's energy level surge again as the band returned for the encore. Lauren went up to her microphone and put her hands on her hips.

"Well, clearly you guys still want to rock," she said. "You don't need to ask us twice! One... two... three... four...!"

The band ripped through the first two songs, and when they got into the third—and final—song, they improvised a longer musical section. The volume dropped slightly when Lauren grabbed her microphone and sauntered along the edge of the stage, her steps fluid and cat-like.

"We've had a great time tonight. Are you having a good time?" she asked as she paced. The crowd bellowed back at her enthusiastically. "Awesome! What would you think if we added some friends to the mix?"

The crowd thundered again. And as Lauren dove into the next verse, another guitarist joined them on stage. He wore nothing but black leather pants, giving the audience ample opportunity to check out the dozens of tattoos that adorned his arms, shoulders, chest and back.

"That's Raphael Zima!" Cole shouted.

"Who?" Maggie asked.

"He's the guitarist from Psychic Soul," Danny said. "You didn't know that? You're showing your age, Mags."

Maggie made sure Cole wasn't looking before she flipped Danny off.

On stage, Raphael jammed with Stevie and moved close to Lauren to sing before moving to one side of the stage to play for the crowd. A minute later, Lauren reached another pause in the song. She smiled and looked to the side of the stage opposite where Raphael had come from. From behind one of the stage levels came two more people. One was wearing a long coat and playing guitar. The other wore a simple black t-shirt with jeans and held a microphone in one hand. The singer high-fived Lauren, and both were laughing as they started to sing together.

Next to him, Cole's friend Lola grabbed Cole's arm and yelled, "Oh. My. GOD!" That's Dario D'Scala and Luke Mayweather from Big

Mac Daddy! I *love* Dario! Is he going to be at the thing after the show?"

"I hope so," sighed their other friend, Rebecca.

Danny didn't like the way Dario was looking at Lauren and had to remind himself that he had no right to be jealous. He shoved the emotion aside—these were the last few minutes of the show, and he didn't want to miss any of it.

After tonight, she'd be gone.

Even after everything, that knowledge hurt worse than he could have imagined.

On the stage, Lauren, Ox and Stevie gathered at the central microphone. Their musical guests closed in around them, and they finished the song with a crescendo. As DJ and Augie came down to join the rest of the band, Lauren encouraged the crowd to cheer for their guests. Raphael, Dario, and Luke waved before disappearing backstage.

"Thank you all so much for coming out tonight," Lauren said to the audience. "If it wasn't for all of you, we couldn't do this. We had so much fun playing for you, and we appreciate you supporting us all these years. You're the best fans in the world."

Her statement was greeted with another roar of approval. The Kingmakers gave the audience one final wave.

"We love you, New York! Thank you—and good night!"

The stage went dark, and Danny felt an unseen door slam shut.

CHAPTER
FIFTY-TWO

Lauren arrived at the after party still wired from the show. Opening night had been everything she'd hoped it would be, and the audience's enthusiastic embrace of the band and their new album washed away any lingering doubts lurking in the corners of her mind. Now it was time to celebrate.

She grabbed the door handle and pulled. Inside, the room teemed with guests, all laughing, eating, and drinking. She could see members of her family, and of Augie's, mixing with the others. Steph was in an animated conversation with Tisha. Nearby, the members of Atomic Alcatraz and their entourage of friends and groupies were raising their own ruckus to one side of the room.

She loved this. Every last bit of it.

Lauren made her entrance quietly, but it didn't take long before Carolyn's excited squeal alerted everyone to her presence. Drained from doing her best to dance during the concert, Lauren's sister was in a chair rubbing her belly. Lauren sat down next to her to talk, but before long, she was shooed away and ordered to get something to eat. Starving, Lauren didn't have to be told twice.

As she dusted crumbs off her hands, she spotted Richie and Joey.

Danny wasn't with them, and she wondered if he'd come to the show. Part of her hoped he had, but another part was relieved not to see him.

"How long will the tour be?" Joey asked.

"At least eighteen months. If *Stone Heart* does well, we may extend our dates." Lauren was smiling as she talked about being out on the road.

"I don't think you have to worry about 'if'," Richie said. A vague call of "Grampy!" distracted him, and he excused himself from the conversation.

"He saw the whole show," Joey said without any preamble. "He thought you sounded great. But I think a couple of the songs hit too close to home."

Lauren didn't try to hide her sadness. She'd poured all of it into those songs—every bit of love and pain, joy and heartbreak. And she knew some of them would have hit Danny right in the bruised, broken part of his heart, too. For a moment she was disappointed he wasn't there, wishing she could hear right from him what he thought of the songs.

But her melancholy train of thought derailed when the rest of The Kingmakers joined them. Joey let his inner fanboy shine through as he shook hands with all of them. They toasted the band's successful show, and Joey gave them a glowing critique of the "Leaving" video.

"Incoming," Ox said.

Maggie was walking towards them, surrounded by a cyclone of teenage girls.

"Dude, that's terrifying," Augie said.

"That's Jacka—I mean, Danny's sister, right?" DJ asked.

Lauren stuck her fingernail in his ribs. She knew he didn't like Danny, and she was well aware DJ referred to him most of the time as "Jackass." But if he said it in front of Joey, she was going to kick DJ's ass. If Joey didn't do it first.

"That's Maggie," she said. "And Cole. And—I'm guessing—Cole's entourage."

"Doesn't look like the kid who came to the studio." Stevie said it, but Lauren was thinking the same thing. Gone was the conservative school uniform Cole had worn when she dropped in at Velocity. Tonight, Danny's niece was decked out in black jeans and a ruby shirt with cut-outs that exposed her shoulders. She wore chunky earrings and had several bangle bracelets on one arm. And with makeup on, she looked several years older than seventeen.

"Hi, Cole," Lauren said.

"Hi, Lauren! It was a great show, *great*. I had such a good time. We all did. These are my friends, Anne, Lola, and Rebecca." The chorus of impressed hellos overlapped each other as Cole continued. "You sounded so good. Seriously, just..." She offered a dramatic chef's-kiss gesture. "... Perfection!"

"And I loved Augie's drum solo," Lola said, batting her eyelashes. Lauren could see him struggling not to laugh at Maggie's eyeroll over Lola's moon-eyed crush.

"It was! And when DJ did 'Empty Chair?' O-M-G." Anne turned six shades of red when DJ smiled at her.

The girls continued with their effusive praise while they got pictures with the band. As Augie autographed Lola and Anne's arms with a marker, Rebecca told Stevie that his guitar playing was far superior to Dario's, even though she thought Dario was totally hot. Stevie promised to keep it between them so as not to hurt Dario's feelings. At the mention of Dario, the girls headed off as a herd to try to find him and Raphael.

Nearby, Atomic Alcatraz's raucous laughter carried across the room. They were sharing beer and champagne with several young women dressed in short skirts and very high heels. One pressed herself up against the lead singer and let out a squealing laugh when he grabbed her ass.

Joey scowled. "Any of them put a hand on Cole's behind like that and I'll bury 'em in the park."

"You must get a lot of that," Maggie said to the group.

Lauren didn't hear who answered Maggie. There were fans—and groupies—in every city, and she'd encountered her share of both. And while she wasn't one of these singers with multiple partners in every city, she wasn't a saint either.

Augie's voice interrupted her thoughts, and she came in partway through what he was saying to Joey: "... you know? You can have a whole lot of fun, but you learn quick that girls like those over there? Most are interested in *what* you are, not in *who* you are."

"It can be fun for a night," DJ said. "But that's why when you find a good *woman*, you need to hold onto her. Or at least you try to." He caught Lauren's eye, and she was about to respond when her father waved to get her attention.

"Sweetie, Carolyn's getting ready to go. I thought you'd want to say good night."

Lauren quickly excused herself from the conversation, and Augie followed her. As she threaded her way through a knot of people, Lauren abruptly found herself face-to-face with Jackie.

She was confounded. Jackie had never come to a show before, and after the incident at the sisters' "girls' day", Lauren assumed she'd refuse. They exchanged polite hellos, and Jackie offered a few kind words about the concert.

There was another long, self-conscious pause as both struggled with what they wanted to say, what they should say, and what neither was willing to say. Finally, Jackie broke the silence. "Well, I've got to find the kids."

Lauren turned as her sister brushed by. "Jackie, wait."

"What?"

"I'm glad you came tonight."

A smile ghosted Jackie's face. "I'm sorry," she said. "About before."

"Me, too," Lauren said. "I could have handled things differently. Better."

"Take care of yourself on tour. You might be a big star, but you're still my baby sister."

Before Lauren could say anything else, Jackie gave her a small, awkward wave and hurried away. And she knew that was about as much vulnerability as Jackie was going to offer anyone.

When Lauren found her, Carolyn was struggling with her jacket. Her husband tried to help, only to be tartly told she was perfectly capable of dressing herself. After flailing her arm again in her third unsuccessful attempt to untangle the sleeve, she relented and let him adjust the coat.

"Carolyn! Thank you for coming tonight." Lauren threw her arms around her sister. She was going to miss everyone in her family, but she was really going to miss Carolyn.

"I wouldn't have missed it," Carolyn said. "You were as amazing as ever. Promise you'll call?" She wiped a few tears away. "Damn pregnancy hormones."

"Of course! And you'll call as soon as you have the baby, right? I don't care what time of day or night it is."

"I'll even pinky swear!" Carolyn held up her hand, and the two sisters locked their little fingers.

Carolyn tucked her arm through Greg's. Lauren watched them go, but any sadness she felt was melting away like spring snow in the face of her excitement to be back out on the road.

Augie appeared next to her. "Dude, I swear to God, I was afraid she was getting carted out of here in an ambulance tonight because she went into labor."

Lauren scoffed. "Ambulance? No way. She'd have delivered that kid right in the suite. Then held the baby up like she was presenting the Lion King."

"I'm totally calling Carolyn 'Rafiki' from now on," Augie said when he finally stopped laughing long enough to breathe again. Egged on by his hysterics, Lauren was laughing almost as hard as he was.

"Pull your shit together, Giggles," Lauren said. "Let's go make the rounds. We gotta get on the road."

Behind her, Augie sang "Ah-seh-kenya."

It took them thirty minutes to say their farewells and thank everyone for coming. Both of their mothers cried. Both fathers pretended not to. Lauren managed to say goodbye to Cole and her family. When she got to Joey and Vinny, she told Joey to get a picture as she put her arm around Vinny. Then she planted a kiss right on Vinny's lips. He turned a shade of scarlet she didn't realize was possible. A few more hugs and handshakes later, the room only had a handful of stragglers left.

"You ready?" she said to Augie. "Boston's waiting."

"The world's waiting. Let's do this." His bright smile, full of anticipation, vanished. "Oh, fuck me."

"Augie?" Lauren turned to see what the problem was.

Danny stood in the doorway.

CHAPTER FIFTY-THREE

Everything around Lauren clicked into slow motion. During that last night together, she'd made her peace with their relationship ending. Now, as she saw the look in his eyes, she wasn't convinced Danny had done the same. He came straight to her.

"Lauren..."

His voice was full of hope. *Not again,* Lauren thought. *We've been down this road.*

An uncomfortable silence followed until Lauren looked at Augie. "Give us a minute?"

"The bus is waiting."

"I'll be right there," Lauren assured him.

"The bus?" Danny asked as Augie reluctantly walked away.

"We're doing part of the tour old-school—with actual tour buses," she said, pushing some hair behind her ear. "Probably a dumb-ass decision for the Northeast in January. We'll mostly use them down south and in Cali. Although I have to say, these tour buses are a lot cushier than the first ones we ever got to use. Our manager's made a whole promotion out of it." She knew she was talking too much, but it was better than the uncomfortable conversation that was barreling towards her.

"Hey! Lauren! Sorry to interrupt..." Still shirtless, Dario D'Scala barged in. He gave Danny an unconcerned glance that said he wasn't sorry at all. Planting a kiss on her cheek, he slid an arm around Lauren's waist.

"Dario, this is Danny."

"Oh. *Danny*." Dario's eyes lit in a way that said someone had told him exactly who Danny was. "Anyway. Lauren. Baby doll. Great show tonight. Our tours are going to overlap in a few places. You game for a guest shot like we did tonight? Maybe in Chicago?"

"Of course! Have your manager call Tony and we'll figure it all out."

"Stupendous." Dario gave her another kiss, Danny another dismissive once-over, and sauntered away with enough rock-star swagger to stop a train. Danny was too busy glowering at Dario's back to hear Lauren's question.

"Hey! I'm talking to you." She snapped her fingers in front of his face, and he reddened. "I asked what you thought of the show."

"Absolutely amazing," he said.

The praise pleased Lauren more than she was willing to admit. "I'm glad you came, but I didn't think it would be..." She almost said "allowed" but swallowed the word, not quite sure how to say it.

"I almost didn't come, but I knew it was my last chance."

Last chance? Oh, shit, Lauren thought. She took a step back. They'd already been through this. She didn't want to do it again. The answer was going to be the same.

"Lauren, shake a leg," DJ said as he and Ox came up to them. "We've got to get rolling if we're going to be on time for Boston."

"I'll be there in a second," she assured both. She lifted her shoulders and let them drop, trying to relax a little. Augie and Stevie were waiting by the exit on the opposite side of the room, and her cousin was looking anywhere but at her.

DJ looked Danny up and down. "Everything okay here?"

The question was for Lauren, but DJ's eyes remained on Danny. Although his voice was soft, his body language told a different story. He squared up, folding his arms across his chest.

Danny's answer was curt. "Everything's fine."

"I'm not talking to *you*."

"Hey!" Lauren's sharp voice was a slap to both. "Put your dicks away. Both of you. You—" She put a hand on DJ's chest and gave him a gentle shove. "—You go on, I'll be at the bus in a minute. And you —" She pointed a finger at Danny. "Just—enough."

Danny started to open his mouth.

"Do *not* say anything stupid," she warned.

DJ mumbled an apology to her—not to Danny—and walked away with Ox. They loitered at the exit with Augie and Stevie until they realized she was going to stare at them until they left. Lauren knew they meant well, but this discussion was none of their business.

"They're waiting for me," she told Danny, and then she sighed. The day she first left for California floated through her memory. "This feels way too familiar."

"I'm sorry, Lauren. I never meant..." His voice faded away.

"I know you didn't. I didn't either." All the drama, all the turmoil. None of it had been Lauren's intent. The lingering silence crept back and threatened to swallow them both.

"There's a certain peace in it. Being done," Lauren said. "To finally come to terms with the fact that something you wanted so much can't happen. Maybe I needed to know that we tried, even with the deck stacked against us."

Danny shook his head. "What if we're not done? What if we—"

"What we had when we were kids was special," she said. "Wild. Beautiful. Wonderful. Sad. But we're not who we were back then. We are who we are now—and this version of Danny and Lauren? It wasn't meant to be." She hated saying it, but it was the truth.

"You don't know that."

"Yes. I do."

He opened his mouth to argue, but Lauren raised a hand to stop the argument before it mushroomed.

"We ended a long time ago, Danny." It was a stark truth, but Lauren wasn't cruel about it. "I held on to you all these years because I believed you were the only one who'd ever loved me for who I am. But the person I am now is *so* different from the one I was back then."

Danny reached out and tried to take her hand. She hesitated for a split second, warring between wanting to lace her fingers with his and knowing it was a mistake. She pulled her hand back and pressed it to her forehead. This was insanity.

"What about working things out with Heather?" she asked.

"We might be too broken to fix." The flat, resigned acceptance in Danny's voice startled her. Lauren turned her face away, the unspoken implications of his statement cutting her to the bone.

"Don't look like that," he said. "Me and Heather, we were broken before you came back. I just don't think we knew it."

"That doesn't mean we—"

Danny interrupted her. "I've spent years wondering if I could live this life, be with you. I love you, Lauren. I do. We could make this work—"

"No, Danny. No, we can't." This time, Lauren wasn't as gentle. There was bite behind her words, and willpower. His head jerked back in surprise.

"You'd hate this life," she said. "The unpredictability, the chaos. The publicity. And this vision you have, our life together? What does it look like?"

"I don't know. We'll figure it out as we go."

Figure it out as we go? Lauren managed not to laugh. Life-by-the-seat-of-your-pants wasn't Danny's way of moving through the world. He was, she realized, a lot like Ox in some ways: predictable, solid, steady. And she admired those qualities, but that didn't change anything.

"There's nothing to figure out," she said. "You'd come on the road with me, live out of a suitcase, never the same bed twice. You'd never see Lucas, Matty or Tommy—or your family."

"No, I'd—"

She cut him off before he could continue. "Or you'd stay home while I toured, stuck in an empty house on the West Coast. Alone. Still without your family. Your friends. Your sons."

The skin around Danny's eyes wrinkled as her words sank in, the spark of hope he'd brought with him obscured by a cloud of doubt. It didn't make her feel good.

"You assumed we'd live here—in New York—didn't you? My home's in California." As she looked at Danny, Lauren realized she felt more fondness than pain. The hurt was still there—might always be there—but it was softer now, the edges blunted.

"Danny, my life would grind you up and spit you out. And you'd eventually *hate* me for it."

He faltered in the face of her resolve.

She took his face in her hands and kissed him. When it ended, he asked, "What was that for?"

"That's the goodbye kiss you could never give me." Lauren took a step back, putting more distance between them, and started to turn away.

"Lauren..." Danny swallowed hard.

"I have to go. They're waiting for me."

She didn't look back.

EPILOGUE

A year into the *Stone Heart* World Tour, The Kingmakers made a quick stop in Los Angeles for the Grammy Awards. After sweeping the Rock Category, they did a group performance with several other artists, joined onstage by several rock luminaries including Steven Tyler and Dario D'Scala. The eclectic group got a standing ovation from the star-studded crowd.

When it came down to Album of the Year, The Kingmakers faced some stiff competition, and they looked legitimately stunned when their name was called. The band whooped as they clambered out of their seats and high-fived each other all the way to the stage. Lauren hung back and let the guys have the spotlight to thank everyone who'd helped make *Stone Heart* such a success.

As they shared their appreciation and gratitude, Lauren thought about everything that happened during the album's creation. Her affair with Danny nearly destroyed her, nearly wrecked the band. But at the same time, he'd helped make *Stone Heart* the success it was. She owed him for that, and—for a moment—Lauren considered thanking him.

She decided against it. She'd heard through the grapevine that

Danny and Heather had separated—temporarily—for several months before attempting to reconcile again. Beyond that, Lauren wasn't sure if they had worked things out or not. She'd explicitly told Carolyn that she didn't want to know.

Just before the outro music started to pipe them off, Lauren—with a helpful shove from Augie—stepped up to the microphone. She looked at the gold gramophone award in her hands. When she looked up, her eyes were shiny.

"I have to thank my family for all of their support—Mom, Dad, Carolyn, Steph, Jackie," Lauren said, biting her lower lip before she continued. "I think the guys have covered thanking pretty much everyone else—Fitz, Tisha, you're at the top of the list."

She paused and looked over at her grinning bandmates. As she caught DJ's eye, the impudent smile that crossed her face matched his. She looked down at the award once more and then out at the gathered crowd. She held the gramophone up in the air.

"Over the hill, my ass!"

The audience went wild.

AUTHOR'S NOTE

As always, if you've read this far—thank you!

This novel has been a long time coming for me. The idea for this story took root several years ago, but I wasn't ready to write it then. I thought about it from time to time, but it always came back to me thinking, *I like it, but not yet.*

Guess the right time finally arrived.

Some people have commented on me taking on a hot-button topic like infidelity. But for me, that isn't the central theme (although it certainly plays a role). What I hope is that people will relate to Lauren, Danny, and even Heather because they are all human. None of them are bad people, at least not in a black-and-white, good-and-evil kind of way—but they are human people. They're flawed. They have regrets. They're insecure. They doubt themselves. They make good decisions. And bad ones.

Just like all of us.

We've all made our own share of dumb decisions, have our own lists of regrets and what-ifs. And that's what I hope people will see in these characters. I hope you'll care about them. Get frustrated with them, angry even, but in the long run understand why they all made the choices they did (even if you don't agree with them).

I do have a favor I'd like to ask: if you enjoyed this book, please review it on Amazon!

Reviews, especially written ones, are so important for authors. Often, how successful a book is depends on reviews from readers just like you. It doesn't have to be long, only a few sentences about what you thought (and be honest). I'd really appreciate it.

Until the next time, take care and may your days be filled with many excellent books!

ACKNOWLEDGMENTS

I'd be remiss if I didn't call out a few people who helped take *Stone Heart* from an idea to where it is now.

My parents, family, and friends for always supporting my endeavors.

Jeff for being part of this crazy ride from the start. I couldn't have done any of it without you. And for making me soup when I don't feel well.

Hannah for telling every librarian she has ever met that her aunt writes books.

Toby, Jenn, Maureen, and Kirsten for listening to me pout when I hit roadblocks, patting me on the head when I was frustrated, and not cutting me any slack when I needed a little tough editorial love.

Cari and Gino, my beta readers. Having perspectives on the story from both a woman and man was supremely helpful.

John Robin and Brenda Clotildes for the last-minute proof review. The book is better for your efforts.

The entire Writing Bloc family for being the awesome people you are.

Thank you all, so very much.

About the Author

Susan K. Hamilton is the award-winning author of *Shadow King, Darkstar Rising, The Devil Inside,* and *Stone Heart*. Her short stories have been featured in several anthologies from Writing Bloc (ESCAPE! DECEPTION!, Family, and Passageways).

Horse-crazy since she was a little girl, she pretty much adores every furry creature on the planet (except spiders). She also loves comfy jeans, pizza, and great stand-up comedy. Susan lives near Boston with her husband and also shares her life with a lovely bay mare, affectionately known as La Diosa.

You can connect with Susan on Facebook at *facebook.com/hamiltonsusank* or on Twitter *@RealSKHamilton* (she's also on Instagram *@RealSKHamilton* but fully admits to doing a terrible job of keeping up on that platform). You can also visit her website at www.susankhamilton.com to sign up for her e-newsletter where you can keep up to date about new releases and other things that she's up to.

ABOUT THE AUTHOR

CPSIA information can be obtained
at www.ICGtesting.com
Printed in the USA
BVHW032215050922
646294BV00013B/415